Star

Star. Marie Friend. First edition 2009

Grateful acknowledgements.
Excerpt from *Indian Fancy* by William Hamilton Hayne;
Where Or When by Rogers & Hart 1957. Chappell & Co.Inc. NY

Je Reviens Publication ©
Woodburn, OR
starmfriend@yahoo.com
Printed in United States of America

*Dedicated to my late-husband Bill, who looked over
my shoulder as this book was being written.
And, to my late-friend Ralph who remains
a support to me in my writing.*

Namaste

Contents

INTRODUCTION

Dear Reader,

Before you settle down to enjoy this book I have a couple of questions for you. Question one: Do you ever wonder as to the amount of time (as we know it) that mankind has been searching for the truth to his/her existence?

The reality is that nobody really knows the truth as to where we came from except maybe, just maybe people who have 'died.' Try to imagine if you will the millions of years that our world has been in existence, and the eons that Man has walked on Earth. Did Neanderthal man wonder why he was here and where he was going? Can anyone remember that far back?

Although I was raised in the protestant system of the Church of England I'm one of those people who firmly believe in reincarnation of the Soul. Reincarnation is the theme of my story.

But – I'm getting ahead of myself. I still have the second question for you to contemplate. Off hand, how many wars can you think of that have been waged in the name of so-called 'Religious Truth'?

I don't want to sound as if I'm getting on a "Soap Box" but we all know that the inevitable politics surrounding religion has continued for time immemorial. And, I'm sure you'll agree that everyone feels that his or her religious belief is the truth. Yet when we get down to the real nitty-gritty of our existence - does it really matter? The only important question we inevitably ask at the end of our life is, what happens to me now? The 'after life' is still a mystery, regardless of individual beliefs.

Only one thing is certain. You and I are living now. And, how we conduct ourselves in this life is really the only important fact whether you believe in reincarnation or not.

Having said all that I'll share with you my own personal beliefs on reincarnation because this story is based on those convictions. I'm convinced that we return to this planet time and time again in order to learn from each other and to *re-member* who we really are. We are Spirit having a Human experience, not the other way around.

To me, life is like a shining star that constantly sends out its brilliant light. That star is *you* and its brilliance is one facet of your beautiful soul. Each facet of you is unique in all its glory and downright magic!

And so, this book is all about people like you.

Star tells a story of the effects of karma on one ordinary group of humans/spirits. It follows the universal law that is as natural as breathing, what goes around comes around or, what you sow you reap. The popular term used in today's modern society is Cause and Effect.

Although the main characters are fictional, the people who have shaped our history are very much fact. As these 'players' create their own destiny they inevitably help to form the destinies of their respective countries.

My characters reincarnate in three entirely different countries and periods in history. Nevertheless, each country and time-line share a common thread of religious morals and political dogmas.

Who can deny that religion and politics have inevitably shaped nations and impacted our world? For better or worse we are a product of our personal moral upbringing and our history.

From Akhenaton's ancient Egypt and this pharaoh's radical religious reforms, to the despotic political shenanigans of Henry VIII in sixteenth century England, *Star* follows the characters whose lives are woven together by 'fate' – or karma. Their destinies eventually fall into place (at least for my hero and heroine) - in New York City of 2001. Inadvertently the tragedy of 911 that we all lived through has a happy resolution for my story's 'players.'

Over three separate periods in history the same souls return to continue their lessons of life and play out their 'roles.' As a result of the shocking events of 911, my hero and heroine finally come to terms with their immortal souls, just as the reality of 911 shocked all of us into a heightened awareness of our own Spirituality.

Against a background of intrigue and moral standards of the countries involved, each century sees our stars acting out the parts they have chosen to play. They are born again and again in order to perfect their souls through human mistakes and heroic selflessness.

Do you know that reincarnation is like attending school? Oh yes. It's a guarantee that when you don't get the answer right the first time you have to come back and work out the problem again until you do. There's no cheating. Life doesn't allow you to cheat. If you try, it will throw the experience right back at you like a boomerang!

As written in Part One: *Elegy To Dead Lovers*, it is fact that Akhenaton made dramatic changes to Egypt's religious beliefs that caused upheavals in the land, especially among his priests. After centuries of praying to the same gods and goddess's, Egypt was forced to honor only one god of Akhenaton's choosing,

Aten-Ra. He did have six daughters with his Queen Nefertiti and according to ancient history one of them was betrothed to the Hittite royal house. It is also believed that one of his daughters may have died of smallpox.

Most people know that Britain's Henry VIII, (bless his egotistical heart)- had six wives and inadvertently planted the seeds of change to England's official catholic religion. Because the Pope refused to sanction a divorce from his first wife, (in order to clear the way for him to marry Anne Boleyn) - he broke away from Rome's papacy and declared himself the head of the English church. After much horrific blood shed the establishment of Protestantism in England was finally recognized as the official religion. To this day, the Church of England is still the religious head of this country.

At the time that my characters enter the 'stage' Henry is about to marry Anne of Cleves (his fourth wife). Unlike Anne Boleyn and his fifth spouse Catherine Howard, this one was fortunate to keep kept her head and got away with a divorce instead. Set against the political and moral standards of the day, *Kate* (Part Two) – continues to weave its intricate pattern that began in ancient Egypt.

We all experienced the trauma of 911 and its inevitable rippling effect on nations. Once again, *Star* reunites its characters and finally, their karma created over three thousand years past is resolved.

It's a tragic fact that the Twin Towers catastrophe still impacts the whole world with its inevitable effect on individuals and countries. But, it's the catalyst that finally teaches Life's lessons for my fictional people. *Where or When* (Book Three) embodies the old adage - "Good Cometh Out of Evil."

All my life spiritual 'lessons' have been there when I was ready to learn and like you, I chose to learn via both painful and joyful experiences. I had the advantage of being born into a family that considered the paranormal to be normal. And so, because of my metaphysical upbringing the germination of *Star* began.

This book's main characters may be fiction but the facts of history are not. *Star* is based on people and experiences that I have encountered throughout my life. In other words dear reader, they are Mr. and Mrs. Everyone. They are you.

Marie Friend
2009

PROLOGUE

In The Beginning......

Pure leagues of stars from garish light withdrawn
Behind celestial lace-work pale as foam, -
I think between the midnight and the dawn
Souls pass through you to their mysterious home.
From: Indian Fancy by William Hamilton Hayne

Clouds drifted aimlessly throughout infinity, gathering dust particles and gases in their wake. Millennium came and went as this mixture of dust and gases mingled to form star clusters that blasted across this nocturnal void. Billions upon billions of these stars spread endlessly across the universe. Blazing with power they generated unimaginable light, stretching on and on to bring life to this never-ending vastness.

Galaxies of constellations came into being, illuminating the universe with brilliance. This chaotic grandeur burst into life before dying a thousand deaths - only to be reborn in far greater intensity.

Shooting stars sped through space complimenting this magnificence with their own particular majesty. Again and again as wondrous galaxies exploded into myriad pieces, they reformed as if by magic into far greater glory.

Somewhere, somehow, a Force far greater than a puny, human mind could possibly comprehend designed and controlled all this wonder. As an artist controls a brush that sweeps across a canvass, this Cosmic Consciousness created the Masterpiece of all masterpieces.

If any human had been around to observe Creation, their brain would have exploded into tiny atoms in an attempt to absorb this omnipotence.

A tapestry of colors and gossamer threads within this Great Nebula fluctuated and changed over timeless eons. A dawning light of Awareness began to arouse the mindless universe.

The Artist looked on His/Her Creation and thought it good. All was well.

Consciousness began to bring new planets alive with loving perfection, enhancing their beauty with subtle shades of color. Variegating patterns and tones of color appeared. Greens, blues, deep purples - magentas - vibrant yellows - crimsons - - adding and subtracting as 'time' progressed.

With a sigh of satisfaction, Infinite Intelligence continued to form more and more galaxies with awesome strokes of Unconditional Love, traversing across this no-thing-ness.

Yet again, another star cluster came into existence. Only a million years old, this newest cluster seemed to bring with it a sense of its own destiny. How young and unspoiled it was!

Eventually, the Creator gave the painting more depth and meaning by adding a nuance of His/Her own Spirit. Spirit's breath touched the youngest cluster of stars so that they mirrored their Maker. The stars had been given the Light of Consciousness. A communion of new energy waves spread and mingled.

Spiritual Awareness was born.

This Artist continued to perfect his painting, improving and changing – adding and subtracting as millennium came and went. The stars continued to grow in this state of Bliss and thought waves began to mingle.

Why not explore one of those enticing planets that depended so much on them for their light? Was it possible to experience Life on these worlds? These planets certainly needed the stars to eliminate the darkness. Could not the stars improve on this fact? Could they not take their Spiritual Light to them? Why not allow these worlds to experience the Creator's Light instead of just its reflection? The Artist had given the stars – Soul.

And so, clusters of souls entered a planet and Mankind was born. They called their new home - Earth.

Man gave names to this blessed Artist's work. Sirius - Centauries - Andromeda – Pleiades, millions of constellations and planets. It was just one small galaxy amidst uncountable galaxies. Mythological tales, gods, goddesses - countless religions sprang up on Earth to try and put a name to their Creator.

Little did the star clusters know that with this knew found knowledge to explore and experience this dimension called Humanity, came a different kind of energy. It was called Responsibility. The Artist had created humans for Spirit to explore, but along with their humanness they had also been given the gift of Free Will.

The stars hadn't known that by choosing to experience human form, they had chosen darkness as well as light, pain as well as ecstasy - good as well as evil. They had chosen Free Will over Divine Will.

And so, in order to return to their original state of Bliss they would have to return to a state of Humankind again and again to *re-member* their origins. They would have to experience birth and death again and again. Mankind gave this state a name. They called it Reincarnation. The star clusters were no longer innocent.

Elegy To Dead Lovers

EGYPT: 1342 BC
AKHETATON (TEL-EL-AMARNA)

A canopy of scarlet spread across the sky as the setting sun reluctantly disappeared below the horizon. Daring the approaching night to quench its energy, its blazing reflection swept across the landscape, transforming the land's black silt into a shade as rich as dark wine.

Standing a few yards away from the Nile, the girl watched its demise and sent a silent prayer to the sun god. *Oh great and glorious Aten, exulted Lord of all Egypt, I beseech you to hear my supplications. Protect my love as he travels on his journeys. Return him safely home to me.*

Meryhken's gaze followed the course of the river as it slithered like a reptile through the desert landscape. The young face showed her vulnerability and the dying sunlight picked out strange flecks of green in the brown eyes..

Once again, the girl's gaze came to rest at the dock side from whence his ship had sailed many weeks past. She scanned the moored vessels, as if by sheer willpower she could force Oedimus' ship to suddenly appear.

Giving an impatient sigh, Meryhken returned her attention to the river that was carrying him home, following its course until it disappeared over the horizon. She noticed how the setting sun was turning its meandering waters to a burgundy hue. Somehow it made her think of a gaping wound, oozing blood. An involuntary shudder passed through her and without thinking she pulled the lightweight cloak around her slim body – as if in protection.

The pressure of a hand on her shoulder interrupted Meryhken's thoughts and she turned to the Nubian boy standing close behind. Psarta's concerned voice brought her back to reality.

"The night is approaching mistress. We cannot linger any longer."

Nodding her head, she reached up and gave his hand a gentle squeeze. "You're right Psarta," she sighed. "Meteh will likely be searching for us if we don't arrive home before dark."

Reluctantly, she turned her back on the view and began the return journey towards town with Psarta following close behind. Brushing aside her melancholy thoughts, Meryhken retraced the steps that they'd taken earlier. As she walked, her mind began to dwell on her favorite image - that fateful, fifteenth birthday. *Has it been almost a year?* It was a birthday she'd never forget…

She enjoyed her times spent with the pharaoh, the man who until Oedimus had been the center of her world. As always during their time together, Akhenaton recited to his daughter. Meryhken was an eager audience and the impressionable girl flattered the ruler's ego. On this special day he read to her his latest writings of praise. Naturally, they were in honor of the sun god and his perfection of words filled her with child-like awe. He called it his 'Hymn to the Great Spirit of Aten.'

*"Thou appearest in beauty on
the horizon of heaven.
O living Aten, the beginning of life!
When thou risest on the eastern horizon
Thou fillest the earth with thy beauty......"*

The communion between father and daughter was a bonding of spirits that neither spoke of but honored. Even though Akhenaton had many harem offspring, Meryhken was the favorite. She was also the child of his coupling with Meteh – his first concubine.

Eventually she arose to leave but Akhenaton stayed her with a hand. "One moment daughter." Beckoning for his serving maid to approach, the woman handed him a package wrapped in papyrus. He placed the parcel into Meryhken's hands. "This is for you."

At his bidding she opened it and gasped with delight at sight of an ornate gold bangle meant to join the others that adorned her arms...

Meryhken slowed her steps and turned her attention to her serpent bangle that she always wore. It was her favorite piece of jewelry with its ingeniously carved shape of a cobra, designed to curl around her slender arm. The eyes of the serpent were two exquisite emeralds that flashed sparks of red in the evening light ...

She walked along the path, still admiring her gift as she made her way back to her harem apartments. Meryhken had dismissed Psarta, as she'd wanted to be alone. Instead of taking the shorter route that was used by palanquins, she's taken the less popular walkway that meandered through the royal gardens, preferring the solitude of this little-used path with its shading Palm trees. Multi-colored flowers caressed her with heady perfume and the peaceful gardens lulled her senses.

Still intent on admiring the birthday gift, Meryhken was oblivious to anything except the flashing of the serpent's eyes. Absorbed as she was in admiring it she was unaware of the man approaching from the opposite direction…

Psarta interrupted her daydreaming as he drew alongside and took her arm. They had reached the busy esplanade at the outskirts of Amarna. Protectively, he held her by an elbow as they climbed the stone terraced steps, leading to the congested promenade. The girl was only half-conscious of the subtle changes in the atmosphere and smells of the approaching city. The freshness of the fields gave way to odors of tantalizing produce and spices that drifted from the nearby busy marketplace. Sweet ripe smells of various fruits reminded her that the harem would be preparing for the evening meal.

They entered the main thoroughfare and mingled with the bustling crowds that were going about their own business. Of course, they could have taken a detour around the perimeter of the city and avoided the marketplace. This they had done earlier on their walk to the Nile but Meryhken now needed to reach the palace before her mother became aware of her absence. Traveling through the town's center was a faster route, even if they did have to come into more contact with commoners.

Brief glances followed them as they passed through the dusty streets. They made an odd pair, the tall girl with an air of breeding and the well-dressed boy who looked around warily.

She was nervous. *I'm glad I had the foresight to bring a cloak to cover myself.* Yet, even with her head bowed and face partially hidden in its folds, her carriage gave away the fact that she wasn't a peasant girl. Meryhken walked like a queen. The hands that clutched at the robe were delicate and smooth, unlike the rough textured hands of a working girl. Sandaled feet showing beneath the hem of her cape, were dusty but without calluses.

The narrow passageways between the stalls weren't easy to maneuver and scruffy looking boys jostled them as they hurried through the busy throng. Women carrying baskets of wares on their heads eyed the pair as they passed but were too intent on their own affairs to give them more than a perfunctory glance.

Even so, Psarta continued to watch guardedly, his eyes searching the crowds around them. He felt uncomfortable, knowing that his own fine loincloth looked out of place among these half-naked peasants. Regardless, his fears were unnecessary. Shoppers were too tired after haggling for bargains all day to take notice of two strangers, while the merchants were busy closing up their stalls for the night. Weary after a long day that had started at sunrise, the venders hardly glanced at them before returning to their tasks.

The aroma of spices gave way to less pleasant odors from refuse in the streets. Psarta wrinkled his nose in disgust and sidestepped the rotting, mushy vegetables that had spilled from a stall. Brightly colored awnings that had shaded stalls were being dismantled, while young assistants were beginning to clean away the refuse.

Dust arose around Meryhken's ankles and glancing down at the dirt clinging to the hem of her dress, she lifted her skirt in protection.

The air was stupefying. It clung to the crowded streets in a heavy pall as if reluctant to let go to the evening's cooling breezes. Psarta wiped moisture from his brow, thankful that they were finally approaching the less populated edges of town. The crammed buildings and market place gradually gave way to government offices and scattered homes of officials. Here, there were fewer people on the streets as most of the upper-class citizens had already retired to their dwellings.

Luckily they passed no one that might know them and they finally came to the road leading to the palace enclaves. The familiar gates to the royal enclosure came into sight. *At last!* Psarta breathed a sigh of relief as they reached the safety of the royal grounds. But his relief was short-lived. As they hurried across the courtyard and entered the building that Meryhken shared with her mother, he saw Meteh waiting in the main hallway.

Now I'm in trouble! I should have insisted that she not go so far afield without permission. Anxiety brought a red flush to Psarta's chestnut complexion. He could see by the parent's rigid stance that she was not in a good mood.

Meryhken's reactions were swift. Even as Meteh started to scold them the girl moved forward and wrapping her arms around her, hugged the woman close. "Forgive me mother for being so late, but the evening was so beautiful and I lost track of time."

The frown on Meteh's face remained. She didn't take disobedience lightly and her petite build belied the strong will held inside the small frame. Meteh demanded respect and received it without question. Her deep-set eyes glowed darker than normal as she looked up into the girl's face.

Meryhken continued to babble. "We walked farther than I had intended and before I knew it we were near to the river. You know how much I love being at the Nile and the sun-set was so glorious shining over the water and I couldn't leave and…"

Meteh laid a hand across the girl's lips, stopping the rapid flow of words. Disentangling herself from the girl's embrace, she pierced her with an angry glare. "You know that you're not supposed to venture out of the royal grounds without permission," she admonished. But the anger in her eyes began to dissipate as they rested on her only child, thankful that she was home without having suffered any mishap. The woman shifted her attention to the silent boy, "as for you Psarta, you know you should not have taken her so far but…"

"Please Meteh," the girl interrupted. "Psarta is not to blame. I told him where I was going and he tried to stop me but I insisted."

The woman shook her head in exasperation. The graying mane of dark hair swayed restlessly with the movement. Now as always, her daughter's stubbornness left her feeling as if she had come up against a brick wall.

For a few seconds she held her steady gaze on the girl, then giving a helpless shrug of the shoulders waved her dismissal to the pair. "Go and freshen yourselves," she ordered. "The evening meal is about to start." With a scrutinizing perusal of her daughter she added, "your father wishes to visit with you this evening, so make yourself presentable." Once more, the piercing eyes turned on the boy. "I will be watching you, Psarta," she warned. "This must not happen again."

The boy bowed his head in obeisance and made a hasty exit to his own quarters, silently thanking the gods for his good fortune in not incurring more of the woman's wrath.

After a quick kiss to Meteh's cheek, Meryhken made her own escape, not wanting to give her a chance to say anything else.

Hastily stripping the dusty cloak from her body, she let it drop carelessly to the floor. Unwinding the lightweight gown that swathed tightly around her figure, she mindlessly dropped it on top of the cloak. *Thanks be to Aten that she didn't question me further.* Stepping over the shed clothing she walked to her bathing pool - kicked the sandals from her feet and stepped into the water. It felt good swirling around her ankles.

Meryhken realized all too well that her mother's preoccupation with the pharaoh's request had saved them from disciplinarian action. A momentary sense of guilt bothered her conscience at having involved Psarta in her escapade.

She was well aware of the reason why he could have been punished for her transgressions. Her status in the harem was so well placed that she rarely received any punishment. Instead, whenever she didn't behave according to her mother's rules, Psarta was usually blamed for not taking care of her.

Although Akhenaton already had six daughters by Queen Nefertite, he had sired numerous children among the lesser "wives" of the palace harem. Even so, because Meteh had served the pharaoh longer than any other woman, she'd earned the respect of her position.

Meryhken resembled her father, especially in mannerisms and carriage. Naturally, this pleased the king. Her olive skin was flawless and whereas the fleshy lips seemed to be somewhat petulant on Akhenaton, that same fullness became seductive on his daughter. Black kohl around the rims of almond shaped eyes emphasized the greenish flecks within the brown. The aquiline nose wasn't quite as broad as the pharaoh's but the shape of her face with its high forehead was definitely his. Of course her features were more delicate, as a woman's should be.

By no means was Meryhken as flawlessly beautiful as the Queen. Even so, she presented a striking figure with her height and abundant blue/black hair that hung in many small braids half way down her back. At almost sixteen years of age, she was only half-conscious of her sexuality. Her personality complimented her father's so that Akhenaton indulged this daughter of his heart. The girl could usually get anything she wanted from him, whether it was a piece of finery, or jewelry - or the boy, Psarta.

He'd been given to her by the pharaoh some ten years past as a companion and playmate. When Psarta had become old enough to join the palace servants Meryhken had quickly intervened, not wanting to lose this boy who had become a loyal friend. It really hadn't taken too much persuasion for Akhenaton to give in and allow Psarta to stay. Slaves were plentiful and easily replaced, but the father shrewdly surmised that the boy's loyalty to Meryhken, coupled with his cautious nature, would hopefully keep this headstrong daughter out of harm's way.

Pinning her braided hair on top of her head, Meryhken was unconscious of the perfect tableau she presented with her sculptured body posing naked against the backdrop of the waning light. Many openings set high in the walls of the room allowed the remaining weak sunlight to enter, bathing her in its warmth as she sank down into the water.

All of Amarna's buildings were open to the sun, as Akhenaton had built his new city in honor of the one true god, Aten Ra. His religious changes didn't please everyone, but the beauty and lifestyle of his city lulled his people into complacency. Gone were the gods and goddesses of the past. Under his rule the Spirit of Aten had replaced them all and Akhenaton's god could be seen in all aspects of Amarna's structures. From the glorious, gem-encrusted temple to the smallest home, Aten's sunlit effigies dominated.

Meryhken's rooms were no exception. As well as her toiletry room with its sumptuous bathing pool, there was a sleeping room with a large balcony that opened on to the harem grounds. A small anti- room led to the building's vestibule. These three rooms were the extent of her privacy. Even so, privacy was more than many of the other harem inhabitants enjoyed. Although Meryhken and her mother shared the community dining area and common room with everyone else in the harem, they each had their own separate quarters. The girl appreciated her privacy and guarded it jealously.

Securing the last tendrils of hair in place the girl lowered herself into the pool, breathing in its aromas of myrrh and sweet-rush oils. Her thoughts turned to her mother and the troubling problem of keeping her secret love from that woman's probing eyes.

Sighing heavily, she slid down into the perfumed water until only her head emerged. Languidly, she stretched out her long, sleek limbs and floated on the surface. It had been a few tense minutes when her mother had caught them returning from the river. *I must be more careful.* Deliberately clearing her mind of disturbing thoughts, she allowed the buoyancy of the pool to relax her mind as well as her body.

Tropical flowers grew in abundance around the balcony sending their perfume into the room. Familiar sounds of a bird's mating call could be heard and from a distance, an answering call was returned.

Meryhken closed her eyes, mindlessly allowing her thoughts to drift. Inhaling deeply, she relived the events that had brought her and Oedimus together. It felt like they had been together forever yet, paradoxically the time had passed rapidly. Lazily sponging her body she savored the picture of that 'special' day. Although a year had almost passed, that meeting remained as indelibly clear to her as if it had just taken place….

"Good day to you Meryhken. May I ask what is absorbing your attention so intently?"….

She smiled to herself as she lazily relived that memorable encounter on the garden's path. She'd felt so gauche and childish….

Abruptly jolted out of her mindless absorption of the pharaoh's gift, she'd looked up to see Oedimus standing in front of her. Her height usually gave her an advantage when meeting people but this man always seemed to tower over her.

"Oedimus! You startled me." He was standing too close. The hooded eyelids looked as if their owner were half-asleep, which was deceiving as the eyes themselves were sharp and knowing. His arms and bare chest were tanned a deeper bronze than normal from spending most of his life in the sun.

Lowering her head to hide her discomposure, she couldn't help but notice the rippling muscles of his legs that showed beneath the hem of his short skirt. The sandaled feet were firmly planted in the stance of a soldier - and he wasn't moving.

Raising her eyes once more, they locked with his. They held a kindly expression, but she could see suppressed laughter playing around the corners of his mouth. Acutely aware of the closeness of their bodies, her legs felt like they didn't want to give her support.

Meryhken raised her head higher in an unconscious effort to regain her composure. Tossing her hair away from her shoulders, she spoke the first words that came into her mind, "I have just left our pharaoh's company. See? This is the birthday gift that he presented to me." She held out the arm that bore the new bangle. "Is it not beautiful?" Encircling the delicate roundness of her limb, its' uniqueness showed to an advantage.

Oedimus lifted the outstretched hand, peering exaggeratedly close to look at the gold bracelet. "It is truly beautiful," he remarked as he let his fingers run slowly over the piece of jewelry, deliberately touching the soft flesh in the process.

With an abrupt movement she drew back her arm. Trying to keep her voice steady she said with fake unconcern, "I must go. Meteh will be waiting for my return and will be cross if I linger too long."

Meryhken made a motion to step around him on the narrow path - but Oedimus didn't move. Instead, he bent to pluck a yellow flower from a musk-scented bush and giving a deep bow, presented it to her. "May you have many more joyful birthdays, Meryhken."

It wasn't until she'd taken the gift that he finally stepped to one side. Still with the teasing smile on his face, he gestured for her to continue on her way.

She felt his eyes boring into her back as she hurried away from him, but she didn't turn around. Her stomach fluttered and her pulse beat rapidly. It wasn't until she'd rounded a bend in the path and knew that he could no longer see her that she slowed down. Her breathing came in short gasps as if she'd been running a race. Unconsciously, she'd crushed the flower in her clammy hand….

Merykhen climbed out of the pool and wrapping a bathing sheet around her body, absentmindedly began to rub herself dry. The sound of the apartment door opening and her mother calling out brought her back to the present. Without waiting for a response, Meteh entered the room and seeing the girl still unclothed, lifted her arms in a gesture of supplication. "Prayers be raised!" she exclaimed. "You're not ready for the evening meal yet, and you will be late for your meeting with the king." She continued to chide her daughter, "he will not be kept waiting. Even by you!" Fluttering between the two rooms, she fussed and chattered as she picked up the discarded clothes from the floor. "You will have to wait to eat until later. Hurry now. Finish with your toilet and attend the pharaoh's bidding."

Meteh bundled up the dirty clothing and placed it on a chair before concentrating on the task of searching through her daughter's robes. Finally settling on a pale green gown that was not too formal but appropriate for a palace visit, she wrapped it with expert movements around the girl's torso. Stepping back she gave a nod of satisfaction. Straightening wisps of hair that hung from the braids, she added a tight fitting, gold hat.

The woman knew that Meryhken disliked wearing the traditional head wear but it was mandatory when visiting with the king, or the temple. Sitting high on the girl's head and covering most of her hair, the effect was regal. It emphasized the slanted eyes and perfectly straight nose. Scrutinizing the results, Meteh nodded in satisfaction and picked up the garments from the chair to take them to the cleaning rooms. "Now hurry to the pharaoh," she urged as she made her exit.

Straightening the sides of the hated headgear and slipping her feet into sandals, Meryken put the finishing touches to her apparel. Adding an elaborate collar of beads around her neck, she checked to make sure that the gold cobra bracelet was in a position of prominence on her upper arm.

As usual, Psarta was sitting on the floor outside her apartment entrance. The boy uncrossed his legs and arose to follow, but she stopped him with a raised hand. "There's no need for you to have to wait to eat, Psarta. You know where I will be for the next hour so enjoy your meal. When you're finished you may come and escort me home."

Psarta's face held a quizzical expression as he watched her retreating figure. He knew that with Oedimus' absence he didn't have to worry about where she was and this gave him the extra freedom to do as he pleased. He was hungry but if he hurried with his meal he could spend time with his friends in the servant's courtyard. *Maybe I can talk them into playing a quick game of Stones and win back those that I lost the other day.*

Psarta loved this game of skill that required one to shoot colored pebbles across the dried, mud bricks of the courtyard with the intent of knocking his opponent's out of the game. The person that managed to remove the most pebbles from the pre-set boundaries was declared the winner. The smoother and more colorful the stones, the easier it was to trade them for other articles that might attract his pleasure.

At the last game he had lost some of his most valuable pieces that had come from other places, even as far away as darkest Africa. This night he intended to win them back. Feeling those that lay in the pouch at his waist, Psarta rolled them together in anticipation. *I feel lucky tonight.* And, he didn't have to concentrate on Meryhken's welfare. At times she really worried him. Psarta was fully aware that there were instances when she was lying and he also knew why.

As he headed for the servant's quarters, his thoughts dwelled on the girl's foolhardy behavior. How many times had he seen her eyes light up when she encountered the pharaoh's Chief Guard? *Thousands*, he muttered to himself. And, in return Oedimus would go out of his way to make excuses to 'accidentally' meet with her.

14

He realized that Meryhken was still as foolhardy and impulsive as she had been when they were children. But, this situation wasn't some childish prank. He wasn't protecting her from being caught at playing in forbidden areas. This was a much more serious game she was playing. Psarta shook his head in exasperation, then smiled at thoughts of his free evening. *At least, tonight I can relax.* He hurried through the doors of the servants' hall, knowing he could enjoy his meal in peace, as the soldier hadn't yet returned from the far reaches of Upper Egypt.

He'd heard through palace gossip that messengers had arrived earlier this day, bringing good news to the pharaoh. Apparently the Chief Guard's mission had been successful. *He will be home soon enough.* Psarta didn't know what was worse, having Oedimus here so that his mistress could keep her clandestine meetings with him or - having her take the risky sojourns to the Nile's docks to wait for his return. *Forget Meryhken and her worrisome ways.* He shook his head to clear it of the negative thoughts.

The boy scanned the room full of noisy people, looking for familiar faces that would be only too happy to join him in a game after they'd eaten. From the far end of the hall, he caught sight of a waving hand and recognized a friend. Grinning and acknowledging the gesture, he made his way across the room. Thoughts of his charge were forgotten.

From her balcony, Meryhken watched the full moon as it slowly rose higher in the sky. It was almost as bright as daylight and dimmed the surrounding stars. Moonlight shone on the golden dome of the temple that stood out amidst the royal compound's smaller buildings. The place of worship shimmered in the glow as if alive.

The night air was turning cool and the hour was late. A sudden breeze wafted across the balcony and Meryhken turned her back on the view to re-enter her room. Quickly climbing into her bed, she pulled the warm covering around her naked

15

shoulders. Thoughts whirled around in her restless mind as she repositioned her body into a more comfortable position. Eventually, she succumbed to sleep.

Moonlight streamed into the room to bathe the girl's face as if guarding this child of Egypt.

That same moon watched over a lone ship, sailing the Nile. Oedimus stood in the prow, only vaguely aware of its silver reflection on the waters around him. As it went behind a cloud millions of stars took its place to light the velvet night. It reappeared as the cloud drifted away. Moon rays cast an eerie blue light over the soldier's features, giving him the appearance of an unearthly phantom. Deep in thought, he stared at the fanning waves as the ship's prow cut its way through the waters.

All was quiet except for the rhythmic swishing of oars and sounds of the pacing gong that kept time for the oarsmen. Each stroke reminded Oedimus that they were bringing him closer to Amarna - and to Meryhken.

As he looked out at the vastness before him, images of his love whirled inside his head. When had she left child-hood behind and become a vibrant young woman? The unabashed adoration in her eyes when she looked at him, made him acutely aware of his own manhood.

Oedimus had joined the palace staff when she was only a child of eleven, or so. The soldier's tact and loyalty had rapidly elevated him to Chief Guard and one of the pharaoh's trusted advisors. Of course, it was inevitable that he and Meryhken would see each other around the palace quarters. And, the more he saw of her the more he found that he wanted to be in her company. A troubled frown creased his forehead. *What would the pharaoh say if he knew of my thoughts regarding his daughter?* Even worse, what would be the reaction of Akhenaton if he knew of his daughter's attention towards one of his soldier's? *Even if this soldier is a trusted protector?*

He'd been in his late twenties and full of a young man's vigorous love for life when he'd first met her. He smiled inwardly at the memory of the young girl's obvious 'hero worship.' *Was it such a short time ago that she'd follow me around like my own shadow?* He'd been somewhat amused by her admiration.

But as she grew into young adulthood, her open admiration appeared to subside and somehow, this caused him a feeling of regret. The more he saw the young woman the more he found that he wanted to be in her company, unconsciously looking for that certain expression in her eyes. *Surely, the pharaoh will look on me with favor now that I have successfully resolved his problems with the priests of Thebes.*

The monotonous boom - boom of the gong was soothing as it accompanied the rhythmic lapping of water hitting the sides of the ship. *Maybe he will be so pleased, that I can approach him and talk of Meryhken?* Shadowy figures of the oarsmen gleamed with sweat as they strained over their oars, their bodies swaying in unison with the paddles. *You must be mad! Even though he should find my efforts pleasing in handling the situation, he would consider it traitorous if he knew of my love for one of his own flesh and blood.*

The sturdy boat moved swiftly on its course, leaving a frothy white ribbon in its wake. A soft wind flirted with the sails, forcing them to billow and ease the small craft towards its destination. Smells of wet timber, mingling with odors of male sweat wafted on the breeze.

In spite of his somber thoughts, Oedimus felt good about the positive outcome of his mission. First and foremost he was a soldier. Once again, this latest uprising against Akhenaton's new religion had been quelled and although he felt tired, he was satisfied with his victory. Even so, he wondered how long the peace would hold? Would the changed religious laws last – or would the priests continue to use their power in influencing the citizens?

Shaking his head dourly, he dwelled on the pharaoh's seeming unconcern for the implications of his radical reforms. In his fanatical belief that Aten was the only true god, Akhenaton seemed blind to the fact that in the minds' of his subjects, the beliefs of his forefathers could not be eradicated so easily. This was especially so in the case of the priests.

Oedimus would never openly admit it, but although he'd been raised to honor all the deities of his ancestors, worshipping Aten, (or for that matter any of Egypt's gods) - didn't really affect him. He had always felt in control of his own destiny. Regardless, from ingrained habit and superstition he silently paid homage to all of the gods and goddesses, including the sun god.

Be as it may. Keeping peace in Egypt is conducive to keeping its strength. Didn't his pharaoh realize how his changes had affected the prestige and power of Egypt's priests? Why should the priests persuade the people to completely disregard their honoring of the ancient deities? *The priests have worshipped them for centuries and kept their control of the people through these beliefs.*

The farming communities especially revered the gods who controlled nature, therefore feared their wrath. *Besides, the temple priests feel the depletion of their wealth when the people cannot tithe to them because of crop failure.* He knew this added to their fear of having offended their gods. *I give thanks that I have been able to pacify them.*

With a sense of irony, he recalled the change in attitude as he'd promised the priests' compensation for their loyalty. *With the knowledge that their pharaoh's monetary support will now be forthcoming, they will be more co-operative.* Of course, he also knew that the dire hints he'd given of the pharaoh's retribution, should they fail to keep the people of Thebes under control, would make them to be even more willing to comply. *But how long can I continue to pacify them in this way?*

Dismissing his misgivings with a shake of his head, he inevitably turned again to thoughts of Meryhken. *Can I convince*

Akhenaton that I am worthy of her as convincingly as I persuaded his priests? Common sense quickly took over again and a scowl knitted his forehead.

His gloomy reverie was broken by the sound of the wooden planks squeaking beneath the weight of footsteps. Turning his head, he saw Calphus approaching.

"We should be arriving early in the morning," said his friend as he came alongside. Oedimus nodded as they stood in companionable silence, looking toward the direction of Amarna.

The two men were the same age but unlike his friend, Calphus already had a wife and child waiting for his return home. The Ethiopian was not as tall as Oedimus, being much stockier in stature. Broad shoulders supported a thick, powerful neck and his barrel chest was matted with curly, black hair.

Calphus' usual, amiable features showed concern as he turned his attention from the sky above him, to look into his friend's face. Instead of looking satisfied, as well he might after his victory in Thebes, Oedimus' features were set in grim lines. Calphus guessed at the reason, and it had nothing to do with his clever handling of the problem priests.

In admiration, Calphus had observed how diplomatically his friend had handled the holy men. He'd made them feel that they were in control, yet subtly reminded them that Akhenaton was their pharaoh, and therefore would not look kindly on the people being allowed to break his religious edicts. He continued to watch in silence as his companion stared ahead of the ship, unmindful of the horizon.

They had been together since childhood and there were few if any secrets between them. Although his friend had been reticent to talk about it, Calphus was fully aware of his passion for the harem girl. Oedimus was like a brother to him and it caused him worry. His devil-may-care persona had taken on a subtle change in the past few months. More often than not, Oedimus' countenance wore a sober expression, as was the case now.

19

At one time, he seemed to enjoy visiting Calphus' home of an evening. As he shared a meal and good conversation with Calphus and his wife, he had delighted in relaying stories of his latest female conquest. Sadly, his visits had become less and less frequent of late.

His talk of Meryhken had changed too. The pleasant banter between them, concerning the adolescent girl's idolization of Oedimus had stopped. In fact, he'd become reluctant to talk about the young lady. *She is not one of the town girls from an inconsequential family.* She belonged to the king. *She is still of his seed albeit from a lesser union than that of the queen.*

The two men remained quiet as the ship carried them through the night. Calphus spoke not a word of his concerns, as he knew from past experience that it would be useless to try and discuss the girl. He'd tried broaching the subject earlier during the journey, hoping that being in each other's close company would bring back some of their old intimacy. It had been a mistake. Oedimus had curtly interrupted him in mid-sentence. "I don't wish to discuss Meryhken. She and I are only friends." After a minute of awkward silence, he'd draped an arm around Calphus' shoulder and smiled in silent apology for his terseness. Forcing a grin to his face, he'd changed the subject and jovially queried Calphus about his wife. "So, are you and Thehta planning to start another child when you return home? I'm sure she will be more than ready to comply after such a long absence!" Matching Oedimus' jovial banter, he'd adopted his mood to his friend's and answered in the same vein. But, Oedimus' laughter sounded strained. After that, Calphus didn't mention Meryhken again. He puzzled over Oedimus' contrary nature. Although he had the innate ability to handle people and situations diplomatically, he seemingly lost all discretion when it involved his relationship with Meryhken. *All I can do is to stay close and keep alert for any trouble that he may bring upon himself.*

The moon drifted behind a cloud again, temporarily leaving only the stars to lighten the darkness. To the Ethiopian, the moon's disappearance was a bad omen. The hiding of its light seemed to be a message of foreboding.

But Oedimus' eyes were searching out the more well known star clusters, thanking them for guiding him home to his beloved.

CHAPTER TWO

*H*is heart was hammering so loudly that its thump-thump felt as if the temple's gong was resonating against his rib cage. He kept his head lowered as he hurried along the palace hallways, so that people who passed wouldn't see his enraged countenance. Knotted veins bulged at the temples of the priest's flushed face. Fury boiled inside Hytoph's guts. *How dare he chastise my judgment! Has he not forgotten that I was priest to his father when he was nothing more than a seed planted in his mother's belly?* Reaching the sanctuary of his apartments, Hytoph curtly dismissed the servant who bent to remove his sandals. Seeing his master's foul mood the boy hastily poured a goblet of wine for him and retreated. He had no wish to be the recipient of the priest's wrath!

Hytoph half emptied the goblet in two quick swallows as he paced the floor in frustration and anger. Absentmindedly raising a hand to his face, he brushed away a trickle of wine that ran down his chin. He stopped pacing. Forcing himself to take slow, deep breaths he began to gain the upper hand of his emotions.

The priest wasn't one to lose control but it took a few minutes for his pulse to stop racing. Finally it slowed to normal speed.

Slumping into a chair, Hytoph slowly sipped on the rest of the wine. In a more detached manner (albeit still with annoyance) - he considered his recent conversation with Akhenaton. *I must keep my composure.* The piercing dark eyes still expressed anger, but his hawk-like face was beginning to return to its usual calculated deliberation.

After a few minutes he arose to refill his goblet from the jar sitting on his ornate wine-table. Mindfully, he savored the potent liquid's smoothness as it slid down his throat. In irritation he brushed at the long skirt that clung to his hot clammy skin and loosened the gold sash that tied it together. He breathed a sigh of relief as the folds of material dropped away. Sinking back again into the chair, Hytoph stretched out his long, skinny legs in relaxation. The coolness of the marble stones underneath his bare feet felt good. *I need an orderly mind-set to take care of this matter without any emotions to influence my actions.*

The priest dwelled on the pharaoh's exulted expression as Akhenaton had revealed his plans to him. Deliberately keeping his mood detached he relived his pharaoh's news.

Apparently the Chief Guard's mission in Thebes had been very successful. This had naturally elated Akhenaton, but it hadn't pleased Hytoph. It had taken all of the priest's self-control not to show disappointment.

After a few minutes of listening to the ruler's praising of Oedimus and the glory of Egypt, Hytoph learned why he'd been summoned. He could hardly believe what he was hearing! The pharaoh had requested, *no ordered me*, to set forth a special day of celebration in the temple for the citizens of Amarna. The priest was to lead a ceremony starting at dawn and ending at sunset in worship of the one and only Sun God. Denying all the other gods their rightful honor was bad enough, but opening the inner sanctuary to the common folk was blasphemous!

Instead of his usual appearance on the balcony with his queen and the royal daughters so that the people could honor their pharaoh from a reasonable distance, they were to be allowed into Akhenaton's private sanctum! Such an act was unheard of.

"This way, my people may give praise to Aten-Ra while in my Almighty presence," Akhenaton had reasoned. "In this intimate atmosphere they may thank our god for his goodness towards them and bring them closer to my fold."

Hytoph had been speechless his shock was so great. *He is mad! Does he not realize the amount of dissatisfaction that rumbles throughout Egypt? The citizens will feel strange and uncomfortable inside the temple, especially being so close to their pharaoh. Besides which, they will resent having to leave their work in the fields for a whole day.*

Apart from this breaking of tradition, the harvesting was at its height and people were busy gathering the crops before the rainy season began. Dockworkers too would lose a precious day of loading perishable cargo. The situation was not good. Normally, the people enjoyed an excuse to idle their time away, but not in the middle of the busiest season of the year. Especially having to worship none but Aten, ignoring all the other deities that protected them and their crops.

Hytoph was well aware that most of the people still paid secret homage to their old, familiar gods and he understood and sympathized. To ignore Egypt's powerful gods, who controlled nature and the seasons, was extremely foolish. He feared that should the gods become angry, it would prove disastrous for Egypt. Hytoph's frustration was high at being forced to organize this charade.

After recovering his equilibrium he'd tried to dissuade Akhenaton from the plan, but had been strongly rebuked for his carefully worded attempt at a rebuttal.

"What is this, Hytoph? Do you not understand the significance of this celebration? Aten, our almighty god has cast his blessings upon Egypt and we must give thanks for his favor. You, as my priest and as my servant should be aware of this honor instead of questioning your pharaoh's decision!" Akhenaton's usual affability was gone. "Thus, heed my words and remember well. Even though I allow you many privileges, as your pharaoh I am still to be honored as Aten's chosen one. It is not for you to question my wisdom!"

The pharaoh's countenance was dark and his annoyance obvious. As if his priest were nothing more than an irritating fly, he'd waved his hand in a curt dismissal and ended the audience. "As it is, so it will be done." Akhenaton had walked away so that Hytoph had no other choice but to leave….

The priest's blood started to rise again as he relived the embarrassing chastisement and he could feel his face growing hot. He took another sip of wine to soothe his nerves. *I need to keep a clear head and proper perspective.*

Deliberately changing his focus to an image more pleasant, he dwelt on the recent journey that he'd taken to the island of Delos. A faint smile of satisfaction began to dawn and his quietude slowly returned at the remembrance of the powerful oracle. Ever since the significant omen had been revealed to him, he'd become increasingly reluctant to adhere to Akhenaton's reformed religion. The foolish ruler had even audaciously abandoned the name that his father had passed down to him. Such was his recklessness.

The ample amount of wine had the effect of quieting his nervous energy and Hytoph's thoughts became less emotional. What would his old friend, Akhenaton's father, have done to curb his son's impetuosity? Pensively tapping his pursed lips with fingers weighted down with jeweled rings, the priest's clever brain mulled over the situation. Precious stones flashed fire with the movement of his long hands. *What can I do to bring him back to the bosom of all the gods?*

The shaven head lifted thoughtfully to the heavens as he dwelled on the plan that was germinating in his brain. The tapered fingers moved to play with the chain of office that hung around his shoulders. Studded with lapis and garnets, the chain's grandeur competed with the brilliance of his bejeweled fingers.

The priest's love for rich adornments was his one weakness in his otherwise disciplined nature. Although Hytoph would never admit it even to himself, the loss of power and prestige he'd enjoyed under the rule of Amenhotep III rankled within him, even more than the loss of the old religious rites. His head lowered and his shrewd eyes narrowed to black slits as he dwelled on the recklessness of the old pharaoh's son. In privacy, he still paid homage to the greatest god of all- Amun.

Not that Aten is not a true and powerful god, he hastily concurred. He didn't wish the Sun God to become angered by his thoughts. Regardless, deep down inside he knew that Aten-Ra did not have complete power as Akhenaton wished to believe. His young pharaoh's misguided worship of only one god worried the priest greatly.

Hytoph's sharp mind returned to the Delos' oracle he'd been privy to experience and the co-incidental meeting with the Hittite dignitary, Castuss. *How very similar in context were our visions.*

Of course, Castuss' own gods had delivered the Hittite's omen but the significant link between Anatolia and Egypt had been very clear. Not only would Akhenaton's careless flouting of the gods prove to be disastrous to Egypt, but the gods of the Hittites also seemed to support the same prophecy. According to Castuss, his gods did not look favorably on the politically planned marriage of their prince to the pharaoh's third-born daughter.

The separate prophecies that he and Castuss had been given were too profoundly similar to be mere co-incidence. *Surely Amun and the Hittites' god, Sothe, have joined to bring Castuss and I together for the good of both countries?*

The vivid remembrance of his stay in Delos uplifted the priest and a glow of satisfaction transformed his frowning face into an almost beauteous expression…

Hytoph could still see the child-like form of the temple priestess with the eyes that had blazed with a red fire. In her delirious state she had brought forth the warning message that had been for him alone.

In awe, Hytoph observed the virgin as she lay writhing in ecstasy at the temple altar. Fascinated, he watched her shaking body in the diaphanous gown; her limbs stretched as if reaching for the unknown.

Then, Holy of holies, it happened! As the maiden slumped in a stupor, the phantom snake of Amun appeared. Slithering towards her, its reptilian body coiled around the virgin and ignited the fire within her soul. *Did not the reptile's all seeing eyes look directly into mine?* Even now he still trembled at the memory.

The intensity of light radiating from Amun blinded him, so that he covered his face with shaking hands and prostrated himself before the snake. Oblivious to the unconscious priestess' body, now in the throws of a seizure, Hytoph supplicated himself for an eternity.

That's when the vision appeared to him.

Hytoph's face still paled at the memory of the message he'd been given.

He saw his beloved Egypt with its river no longer full and flowing with life-giving water. Instead, the Nile was a mere trickle as if a tear of despair were escaping its source. Hytoph's own tears seemed to wet the riverbed. This riverbed showed nothing but dried black silt where the waters had once meandered. Fields that lined its banks were almost barren.

Almighty horror of horrors! The vision showed a swarm of locusts arriving to plague the dying crops and feast on what remained. Pestilence covered the land of Egypt. The glory of his country was gone forever and ever. Just when Hytoph thought he couldn't stand to see anymore, the sands of the desert appeared and blew over the Valley of the Kings, burying it for all time.

Shaken to the core of his being at the enormity of this message of doom, his body broke out in sweat. Hytoph felt as if he'd been plunged into the fires of hell and the images had sent him reeling. Tears rolled down his cheeks at the ghastly vision. In a state of shock, he left the temple. Yet, the gods weren't done with him.

As he stood on the temple steps attempting to control his shattered nerves, he saw a huge ram appear with its mighty, curling horns. It stood like a sentinel on a distant hill, gazing steadily in his direction.

Not only had Amun appeared to him in his sacred form of the snake, now he came in his most holy image – the Sign of the Ram. This was a privilege to be oh, so honored and given to few. This was truly a dire message from the almighty god. *Amun is telling me that it is my responsibility to redeem the religions of our forefathers, so I may save my country from self-destruction. Like the snake I must be all knowing and empowering, yet stand as invincible and steadfast as the Ram. Amun has spoken to me.*

Since that time, his mind had been gradually forming a plan…

Hytoph straightened up in his chair. His clash with Akhenaton had re-enforced his determination to take the action that he knew he must take. Recalling his 'accidental' meeting with Castuss and the intimate concerns that the dignitary had shared with him, he knew that for the good of both countries, the Hittite was destined to be his helpmate…

Still reeling from the impact of his experience the priest walked around the peaceful courtyards of Delos' temple, absorbing the message of the omen, and the responsibility that the lord god, Amun, had lain upon him.

He'd come upon the Hittite sitting on a bench in the gardens. The man sat with head bowed, oblivious to his surroundings and with an expression of deep brooding on his face.

They had met briefly the day previously and had exchanged pleasantries; talking of the marriage plans between the royal families and making the obvious politically correct remarks. However, the observant priest had sensed a false note in the dignitary's voice when Castuss expressed his pleasure at the forthcoming joining of their countries.

As he approached the bench where the Hittite sat immobile, the priest could see that all was not well with the man. And, it didn't take too much tactful probing on Hytoph's part to learn of the reason for his discomfort.

Castuss was normally a reticent man. Yet the burden of the omen he'd received from Sothe lay heavily within him, especially as it focused on the planned marriage between the daughter of Egypt's pharaoh and his royal prince. *Will not this sympathetic priest also have concerns for his own country's welfare?*

Through gentle persuasion, Hytoph won the man's confidence and by sharing his own vision with him, Castuss was encouraged to do the same. Of course, the priest was careful not to divulge his own true feelings regarding Akhenaton's new religion. It was dangerous to appear disloyal, especially to a foreigner.

Castuss opened up to reveal the omen that he'd also received, which was astoundingly similar to Hytoph's. Both visions were damning for their respective countries should not divine intervention take place.

Hytoph was quick to note from Castuss' cautious words, that not everyone in Anatolia was happy about the marriage of their prince to Egypt's princess. There was apparent discord within the Hittite royal palace and as Mussilli's advisor, Castuss obviously felt the weight of his role as the king's confidante. He had come to Delos hoping to find a solution. Instead he had also received an omen of doom, for Anatolia.

The two dignitaries quickly came to the same conclusion. The gods had brought them together for a reason. This was no accident. Both men realized that the almighty gods, Amun and Sothe, had orchestrated this meeting between them. Fate had intervened. The priest and the royal advisor had apparently been chosen to save their countries from certain disaster. The will of their gods must be obeyed.

Hytoph and Castuss parted with vows to work together for the good of both countries. Their royal sovereigns may be misguided but thankfully - - they were not.

CHAPTER THREE

*W*orkers scurried back and forth between the ships, carrying heavy burdens as they unloaded freight. Excited children playing around the docks got in the way of the adults, while women with babies straddled across their hips waited patiently for their men to disembark. Fishermen who were concentrating on unloaded their own small crafts were throwing their smelly catch onto equally odorous tables, in readiness to be cleaned.

A few old men sat observing the commotion from their improvised seats of empty, upturned kegs. As they reminisced about bygone days of their own youth, they naturally made critical comments at the lack of expertise on the part of the river workers, compared to their own superior skills when they were younger.

The sun beat down on the bustling industry. Its reflection bounced off the Nile as it lapped against the shoreline. The ground felt solid and warm underneath Oedimus' feet. It was good to be home again. The hour was early, but he knew that it was going to be a very busy day and his impatience to get started was palpable.

Once he'd performed the duty of reporting to Akhenaton, there were other neglected tasks that would need his attention after his long absence. But, the evening would be his - free to meet his beloved. Oedimus knew she would be waiting for him in the old temple ruins and most of his impatience was due to his eagerness to see her once more.

They had long ago found a secret place in which to meet. The ruins were secluded and private. Years past, the public temple had held people who had honored the old religious gods such as Horus, Thoth, Osiris --- all the many deities that their forefathers had worshiped. But, since Akhenaton's building of Amarna and his religious changes this particular temple had fallen into disuse.

Once, it had stood proud and magnificent but was now a crumbling mass of decay. Only a few of its stately columns still remained, rising up through the undergrowth tall and proud. Deteriorating walls inscribed with past glories defied extinction. The entrance vestibule still retained some of its former splendor and held an intact public bench.

Ornate flagstones of the inner sanctuary were almost indistinguishable under layers of rubble and dirt. Weeds grew between the flagstones' cracks. Nothing remained of the steps that had led to the sacrificial altar, except a pile of smashed stone slabs. The altar itself had long since gone. Only two objects were left -a huge stone ankh that lay on its side and a head of Horus. The latter had one brilliant red eye that pierced intruders with a disturbing glare.

The old temple was an ideal place for Oedimus and Meryhken to rendezvous.

Protocol was strictly enforced as the harem women along with their numerous children, gathered together for the evening meal. Homage was paid to the approaching night and salutations were given to Aten as they thanked their god for this day's benevolence.

Prayer blessings were just a formality, prior to relaxing and sharing the day's events with each other. The breaking of bread at the end of the day was an important social time for the people of Amarna and the harem was no exception. Naturally, the recent announcement that there was to be a royal marriage was attractive fodder for gossip and speculation.

Meryhken could hardly stand the ritual. *I'll scream if this incessant chatter doesn't stop!* Taking a nibble at the seasoned rice, she was unaware of its palatable taste. *What would Meteh do if she knew where I was going to be this evening?* She deliberately dismissed this unsettling thought.

"I hear that our pharaoh plans wondrous festivities, prior to his daughter's discharge to Anatolia." Meryhken was only half aware of the woman sitting across the table, talking to her mother.

"This is true," Meteh responded. "However, I do not envy the princess having to leave all that she is familiar with to live in a strange land."

Meryhken crumbled a wafer of bread, trying to block out the noise of their prattling. Talk of the marriage arrangements had been going on for weeks, and it only made her more conscious of her own problems concerning her unsettled state. She certainly didn't envy the royal princess' arranged, loveless marriage. But, she did envy her status that made marriage possible. *Even should Oedimus gain Akhenaton's approval for marriage, it would still be difficult. It would take a miracle of the gods to have our pharaoh give blessings to the marriage of a harem girl. Especially when that girl is myself.*

Her thoughts drifted, inevitably turning to the day when they had first confessed their love for each other….

After the incident of her birthday it seemed that they would 'accidentally' see each other almost every day. Each time, Oedimus would make an excuse to delay her and to keep her in conversation, until she'd met him thus for almost two weeks. It soon became clear that he was deliberately going out of his way to cross her path.

Oedimus had obviously learned her daily routine. His manner would always be as casual as if their meeting was a coincidence. And yet, she'd notice the eager smile and delighted expression in his eyes.

Although the encounters elated Meryhken she managed to keep her reserve, forcing her conversation to be just as casual as his. With an air of nonchalance, she acted as if he had no more effect on her than if he had been one of the limestone statues that adorned the royal grounds. That is, until that fateful evening when their well-preserved composure had finally succumbed to the intense attraction between them...

The hum of voices in the room receded. Clatter of dishes diminished. She became oblivious to the diners....

Dusk had begun to settle. She hurried along the path, concerned with thoughts of reaching the harem before night had completely fallen. She'd stayed longer with the pharaoh than normal and didn't like to dawdle in the waning light. As usual, she'd dismissed Psarta, not realizing the lateness of the hour. Meryhken worried about Meteh finding out that she'd traveled home, alone. Her mother always visited her after an audience with the king, wanting a detailed account of all that had passed between the father and daughter. If Psarta arrived first without her, there would be trouble!

Shadows from overhanging trees caused the waning light to become even darker and she increased her steps. Every sound made the girl nervous. She hurried faster. A soft rustling came to her ears. She swiveled around. The rapid movement caused her sandals to catch in a loose rock and before she could recover, Meryhken lost her balance.

Flinging out her arms to stop herself from tumbling, she felt a pair of strong arms grabbing her. Instinctively, she flung her own arms around the neck of her savior - - only to realize too late whom that savior was. She was looking into the face of Oedimus, who was holding her firmly around her waist.

As her startled eyes met his, Meryhken became acutely aware of his body close to her own with his warm breath touching her cheeks. Oedimus didn't attempt to loosen his hold and neither did she. Her arms seemed to be glued around his neck as those heavy lidded eyes looked into hers, asking a question and searching for the answer.

She was no longer capable of hiding her feelings and Oedimus caught his breath as he saw the expression on her face. He drew her closer. His gaze dropped to her mouth that was slightly parted and expectant. As if drawn by a magnet, she tilted her head and his lips met hers. A thrill swept through Meryhken as she tasted his lips and responded to his ardor.

The days of sidestepping their emotions could no longer be checked and any final reservations between them broke down. She felt as if she were drowning as Oedimus' hands caressed her and his mouth hungrily searched her own.

After an eternity, he raised his head and lightly brushed her eyelids with tender kisses. He moved down to softly kiss her cheeks before traveling down to her neck, murmuring endearments in her ears. Meryhken clung to him as if she were falling again, not wanting him to stop, yet knowing that this was dangerous madness.

But, it was Oedimus who finally took control. Pulling back, he held her away. The obvious struggle he was having with his feelings showed in his face.

With an effort Meryhken came back to the reality of their surroundings. Not fully comprehending just what had happened between them, she realized that they had stepped into a new dimension of their relationship with each other. And, there was no turning back.

Remembrance of her mother waiting for her brought her back to earth. "I must go before I am missed," she whispered. She needed time to regain her composure before meeting with Meteh. Oedimus reluctantly dropped his arms from around her but remained standing close. "Of course you must," he said as he gently stroked her cheek, "but we must meet again my beloved and very soon."

Her heart leapt at the sound of the endearment. Moving into the circle of his arms again, she laid her head on his shoulder. Raising her chin, he looked into her eyes questioningly. "We need to talk Meryhken, without being interrupted by others. When can we be alone together?"

Meryhken tried to steady her whirling mind and think clearly. How were they to meet without arousing her mother's suspicions, or without having Psarta as her shadow? Taking the hand that still rested on her cheek, she brought it to her lips and gently kissed the palm.

On opening the door and entering her building, she saw Psarta anxiously pacing back and forth outside her rooms. "Is mother inside waiting for me?" she asked in a panic.

"No mistress. She left these fifteen minutes past and luckily did not enter your apartments." He stopped his pacing and explained. "I told her that you were tired and resting before preparing yourself for the evening prayers. I took the liberty of telling her that you had left word with me that you would meet at the dining hall, later this evening."

Meryhken blessed him for his foresight! A sigh of relief escaped her lips and she thanked him profusely. He'd handled the situation so cleverly. Of course, she knew that Psarta was serving his own interests by lying for her, but she still felt grateful for his quick thinking mind....

"MERYHKEN?" Startled out of her witlessness, she came back to the present to see her mother staring across the table at her. Shaking her head as Meteh offered her a plate filled with fruit, she changed her mind on seeing the expression on the older woman's face. She reached across and took a pomegranate from the platter.

Her mother's scrutinizing gaze got Meryhken's attention. She couldn't afford to put her mother on guard and knew that if she didn't eat, she'd believe her to be ailing and take remedial action. Peeling the pomegranate, Meryhken took a bite of the fleshy fruit. Juice ran down her fingers and she absentmindedly licked them. Her focus was drawn to the maiden sitting by her side, realizing guiltily that the girl had been attempting to talk to her. She forced herself to listen.

"… and I told her that I didn't think that she should do that," the girl was saying. Meryhken tried to appear as if she was really interested in the girl's conversation, but not having followed the trend of thought she had difficulty in responding. Nodding her head in apparent understanding, she uttered a murmur of sympathy. Still conscious of her mother's eyes upon her, she tried answering the girl with a question. "So, what do you think she should do?" she said, hoping that the answer would provide a clue as to the girl's discourse.

Meteh relaxed. Rearranging herself for comfort, she turned her attention back to her table companion. Dismissing the misgivings that Meryhken's behavior of late caused her she concentrated on what her neighbor was saying. She soon forgot about her daughter as with relish, she listened to a tasty piece of gossip that the woman was relaying about the Hittites prince.

Lounging diners were either absorbed in their food or their neighbors' prattle, relaxing in the atmosphere of congeniality. Mothers' scolded their bored and fidgety children, while the young girls exchanged giggles and secrets. Meryhken had to physically stop herself from squirming like one of the naughty children. Her facial muscles ached from having to keep an idiotic smile in place as she continued to converse with the girl at her side.

People began to rise and leave. It was finally over. *Thanks be to Aten!* She couldn't wait to get out. Starting to rise, Meryhken remembered her manners and quickly sat back down, glad that her mother wasn't looking her way. Although Meteh seemed to be listening to her neighbor, Meryhken dare not attempt to escape before her parent was ready. It would be a breach of etiquette that wouldn't be tolerated.

Unbeknown to her mother, she had told Psarta that he was free to his own devices for the rest of the evening. Although he'd been reluctant to leave, as always his strong-willed mistress had insisted. He'd had no choice but to obey. Naturally, he knew why she'd dismissed him. Still, Psarta had battled with his sense of duty, versus the thought of having the freedom to gamble with his friends. Of course, the latter was too hard to resist.

Casting a glance at her daughter and nodding, Meteh arose. The two females left and walked in the direction of their building, the younger one listening dutifully as the woman relayed bits and pieces of gossip that she'd gleaned from her fellow diner.

None of it was important. It was just more of the endless speculation about the forthcoming wedding and the inevitable pomp and glory surrounding the event. Nevertheless, Meryhken forced herself to give her undivided attention, asking appropriate questions and giving the right responses. She steeled herself not to show any change in her demeanor when her mother's talk turned to Oedimus.

"I heard that the Chief Guard's ship has returned from Thebes," she commented. "The king will be well pleased to see his favorite soldier returning from such a successful journey." Meryhken didn't respond as her mother continued, "they say that he completely won the priests' confidence and abated the peoples' discontent. Of course, it was a blessing that the rainstorms came to water their crops. It was a fortuitous omen for the pharaoh's envoy."

Meryhken murmured in agreement, making her tone noncommittal. Reaching their apartments, her mother paused outside her rooms, looking around the outer gallery. "Where is Psarta?" she queried.

Meryhken reacted fast. "Oh, I needed him to run an errand for me after he had eaten. The cloth merchant has my new garment finished and I forgot that I was to collect it today. So, I sent him to fetch it for me." The ease with which the lie came to her tongue amazed her.

"You should have waited until tomorrow and collected it yourself." Meteh's voice held a hint of disapproval. "You know how that boy loves to dally with his friends of an evening. It's for certain he'll not return before another hour has passed."

Kissing her lightly on the cheek, she bade her good night. "Retire to your bed at an early hour daughter," she advised. "You look pale and need to get more rest."

Watching the figure as she walked along the corridor towards her own quarters, Meryhken felt an urge to run after her, but checked the impulse. How she would love to feel the security of her mother's arms as she had as a child when she'd hurt herself. Meryhken longed to confide in the older woman instead of having to lie. *It would be madness to even think of revealing myself, especially to Meteh.* Instead of being able to openly celebrate her love for Oedimus in an honorable marriage, she was being forced to lie and deceive.

Guilt at having to abuse her mother's trust weighed as heavy as if the lid of a tomb had crushed her heart. She watched as Meteh continued along the corridor, her figure eventually disappearing through the alcove that divided their quarters. Turning slowly, Meryhken entered her own place.

She crossed the floor to the balcony and looked up at the darkening sky with unseeing eyes. Like the evening star, they shimmered with unshed tears. *If only I could confide in someone.* Standing in the pink streaked twilight she saw nothing of the beautiful view as she willed the time to pass. Soon it would be dark enough for her to steal away to the ruins - - and to Oedimus.

The cold, marble column felt good against his back as he sat leaning against it - waiting. Darkness enveloped the crumbling entrance and the place smelled of musty neglect. The night sky was visible between the skeletal remains of the temple and through the entrance he could see shafts of silver moonlight illuminating the path outside. All was quiet - so quiet that he could hear himself breathing.

Oedimus shifted his body, impatiently. A fat lizard passed in front of his feet and scurried across the broken stones of the ruins. As it flit through the opening, the man laconically watched its movements. The lizard stopped abruptly in the middle of the path. It raised its head. Something had disturbed the reptile.

Caught in the ethereal light, its alert eyes shone like yellow beacons. Its long tongue flicked in and out in rapid movements. The lizard was nervous. All at once, it made quick dart into the shrubbery, vanishing from sight.

A few seconds later, the sound that had alerted the reptile came to Oedimus' ears. It was music to his soul! The tread of approaching footsteps brought him to his feet and he quickly moved towards the entrance.

Moonlight bathed Meryhken in its iridescence as she emerged from the shadows of overhanging trees. Oedimus' breath caught in his throat. *She looks like the Goddess Sati!*

Catching sight of him, she ran the last few yards and flung herself into his outstretched arms. They stood holding each other in a tight embrace as if afraid to let go. Like prisoners released after having been deprived of human contact, they soaked up each other's energies. Where her head lay against his chest, Meryhken could feel the rapid beating of his heart.

Oedimus placed his hand underneath her chin, gently raising her face. His searching eyes seemed to need reassurance that she was really there and not a figment of his imagination. Full of adoration, Meryhken's gaze mirrored the longing in his.

Gently, he bent to kiss her as if he were afraid she were a vision and would vanish. Meryhken eagerly accepted his lips, meeting his rising passion with her own. The weeks apart had been too long. Overcome by the intensity of their love, their pent-up emotions finally broke loose.

A dam burst and all remaining barriers between them disappeared. Their absolute need for each other swept away any final residue of restraint as the lovers were caught in a current of unleashed passion.

Meryhken and Oedimus were completely unaware of their surroundings. The problems created by their world were forgotten as the connecting of mortal bodies anointed their souls.

Nothing stirred. The head of Horus stared with its one, red unblinking eye. The stars continued their nightly vigil just as they had for millions of years. They blanketed the lovers who were in their own world. It seemed that for a moment in time the old temple stood in its former splendor as the cosmos bathed the ruins in glorious light.

The lovers were oblivious to anything except each other. Time had ceased to exist. The man and his woman had entered that rare, timeless space where separate spirits joined and returned to Oneness.

CHAPTER FOUR

*B*ack and forth- back and forth - - the pacing continued across the stone floor. Oblivious to the serving boy who stood at a discreet distance, the priest strode with his head bowed in deep concentration.

Chenkiop didn't know why he'd been summoned. Regardless, the boy didn't dare leave without permission. The silent pacing continued.

Coming to an abrupt halt, Hytoph lifted his head and noticed him standing by the entrance. "What is it you want, boy?" he barked.

"You sent for me, master."

Hytoph dismissed the quaking servant with a perfunctory wave of his hand as he remembered. He'd entered his abode with the intention of taking a leisurely bathe after the long and fatiguing temple prayers and he'd summoned Chenkiop for assistance. But, no sooner had he rung the gong than the messenger had interrupted with the letter.

Hytoph hadn't recognized the rough texture of the missive, as it was so unlike the sophisticated, Egyptian papyrus. With curiosity he unscrolled it and saw the reason why it was unfamiliar. It was from the Hittite, Castuss.

Once more, he read the words and shook his head in disbelief - yet no longer with the initial shock that the first perusal had caused. The contents were surprising and impressive. And, it was obvious that the Hittite advisor was desperate. *Why else would he have divulged such knowledge to me?*

To Hytoph, (the letter began) –

Most exulted and all-seeing guardian of Egypt's powerful and glorious gods.

Since my fated meeting with your holy personage when we shared our deepest and most significant thoughts regarding our divine experiences, I have had much time to reflect on the common concerns that we share - namely the welfare of our countries.

My disquiet has greatly increased since returning to Anatolia from the Island of Delos. As you know, the marriage plans are going forward with much verve, and the arrangements to unite our countries through wedlock are accelerating. Naturally, I would not be sending this most confidential communication to you, should I not be of the certainty that your concerns for Egypt's welfare are the same as mine for Anatolia.

With the utmost faith in your discretion, I feel that it is necessary for action to be taken to avert what could be a disaster to our respective homelands. It is imperative that the strength of our countries be preserved.

Please understand that what I am about to divulge is done so with the utmost confidence that this communiqué will remain with you, and you alone. No other eyes must see this missive. With the knowledge that you are a like-minded man of undisputed honor and unwavering faith in our respective gods, I trust that you will understand the need for secrecy. Should I not feel that the great lord, Sotheh is guiding me to reveal my secret to you, I would not be venturing to do so.

43

As you know, I am profoundly disturbed regarding this planned marriage between our royal families. You are also aware of the omen that was given to me at the Island of Delos, confirming that my fears were justified. My dread is that due to circumstances that are known only to a very few, should this marriage take place it would be the undoing of Anatolia and adversely impact Egypt.

Explaining the reason for my fears regarding this matter is an absolute necessity as only your eminent personage is in a position to avert possible disaster.

I know that you feel as I do that divine order has ordained that we alone have the burden of saving our precious homelands. Therefore it is with the utmost sadness and difficulty that I impart the following well-guarded secret to you – regarding our prince.

Tragically our prince, who is the true bloodline of our king, has a medical affliction of dire severity. This defect is not physical but of a mental nature. Our royal physician has confirmed that this imperfection has been carried through the royal seed. Consequently, there is no doubt that this dis-ease will be passed to the prince's offspring, should he marry and father a child.

To further exacerbate this problem, our King Mussille"s adoration and indulgence of his only son cause his eyes and heart to be blind to this cruel condition that fate has dealt Anatolia. No one dare discuss the prince's lack of mental capacities with our lord and master - not even myself, whom he respects above all others. On the contrary, he indulges his son and his uncontrollable fits of madness, unwittingly compounding the situation. Furthermore, our good physician fears that eventually, his seizures will no longer be controllable with apothecary remedies.

As reluctant as I am to divulge this knowledge to you, I know that it is most imperative that I do so. Sotheh has spoken. This marriage must not take place. For the sake of Egypt's future as well as my own country's well being, you Hytoph, pious nurturer of Egypt's royal family and the gods' chosen servant, have been chosen to stop this marriage.

I cannot emphasize more strongly that my revelations to you are of a profoundly, sensitive nature. I understand that as a priest of Egypt, any confidences shared with you are sacred. Therefore I know that you will keep your priestly vows and keep silent as to my confessions.

I will await your response with the utmost faith that your most wise council and love of Egypt will assist in finding a solution to this dilemma. It would prove to be tragic indeed, should we not intervene as the gods have ordained.

Knowing of your personal concerns regarding your Lord and Master, the glorious Akhenaton, and the disquieting religious reforms that he has commanded you and his people to follow, make me realize that we have a common need to save the peace of our countries. Without Egypt's power and support of Anatolia's strength, our nations will crumble. The gods have spoken.

The letter was not signed, except for the letter "C." Of course, Hytoph knew who had sent it and as he read it again a smile of satisfaction played around his mouth.

Neatly rolling the stiff parchment, he walked over to an ornate desk that was placed in an obscure part of the room. Hytoph opened a tiny drawer, almost hidden at the back of the elaborately carved writing desk. The priest was about to place the scroll in the drawer with his other private papers, but something seemed to be telling him not to save the missive. *His message is clear so why do I need to keep it?* He hesitated. Drawing back, he shut the drawer firmly.

He continued to stare at the incredible message in his hand. After a few minutes, he moved across the room to a sconce that burned with scented oil. Hytoph held the scroll over the strong flame and watched the blue smoke thicken and rise to the ceiling as it seared the letter. It took a long time to dispose of the hard material but Hytoph stayed focused. The smell of burning parchment mingled with incense but he was barely conscious of the cloying smell. Thoughts of what Castuss had revealed left him more elated than he had been in a long time.

Again, he marveled at the workings of fate and blessed Amun for bringing the Hittite to him. *With Castuss' assistance I shall bring Egypt back to the folds of all our gods and their blessed protection.*

Hytoph dwelled on the past glorious days of paying homage to Isis, Seth – Hapi - - Nut - - - all the many gods and goddess' of Egypt. And, the greatest One of all, Amun.

Like a man needing sustenance, the priest hungered to openly display his dedication to his gods as he had done underneath the rule of Amenhotep. He needed the temple rites and ceremonies of old as much as a child needs to suckle at his mother's breast. Hytoph visually preened as he fantasized on the power and esteem that would be his once more, when his country had returned to the folds of all their almighty gods.

Then, his thoughts turned somber. Castuss' revelations concerning the king's son were dire. He weighed the advisability of telling Akhenaton. *Of course not.* Naturally, the plans for this disastrous marriage had to be stopped. A daughter of Egypt could not be wed to one so incapacitated. *Even so, I may use this opportunity to my advantage.* His wily mind started to spin. Becoming allied with Castuss would not only serve the Hittite advisor's purpose but also his own. Akhenaton would thank him later when he realized that his priest had saved him from such folly. *And, he will finally come to know that Aten alone cannot protect Egypt. The day will arrive when he will be grateful to me for saving him and our country!*

A light rap on the door interrupted Hytoph's grandiose imaginings. Hastily brushing away the ashes of the scroll he called out. "Enter." He looked questioningly at his servant.

"Would you have me take care of your bathing requirements now, master?"

Remembering his initial intent, he shook his head. He was

too elated to bathe, besides which he was hungry. *This wondrous news has whetted my appetite.*

Ordering the boy to bring him food along with more wine, he sank back into his chair feeling pleased with himself. For the first time in months he felt as if he were in control of the pharaoh and Egypt's destiny.

Hytoph methodically went over his ingenious plan. Ever since his visit to Delos it had grown, developing like a child in a womb. *My brilliance surprises even myself!* His face glowed with self-satisfaction.

CHAPTER FIVE

*M*eteh had never felt so exasperated in her entire life! She couldn't decide whether it was worse to have her daughter subdued and pale of face, or acting like a mute imbecile. "Meryhken. ANSWER ME!"

The girl looked up with a blank expression, forced out of her reverie by the loud command. The half smile playing around her mouth vanished. "I'm sorry Meteh. My mind was elsewhere. What were you saying?"

"Never mind what I was saying. Whatever is wrong with you girl? You're as vacuous as the town idiot! I've been talking to you for the past five minutes and all you've done is to sit there with a silly smile on your face as if you had drunk too much wine!"

Once more, Meryhken apologized. "I was thinking of my forthcoming birthday and wondering what surprise the pharaoh will have for me this year." It was no longer an effort to lie so glibly.

Giving a derisive snort, the mother's voice turned scathing. "Your birthday doesn't take place for three more weeks and already you're thinking of what fineries and baubles you will receive. You are coddled too much for your own good, miss." She pointed a long, slim finger at the barely strung beads that the girl held limply in her hands. "I need that adornment completed while I'm still on this earth, not when I'm dead. It is not meant to adorn my burial chamber! You've been attempting to thread those beads for the past hour and you don't have half of the necklace finished."

Dropping the string to the floor, Meryhken arose from her chair and knelt in front of her mother's seat. Her arms encircled the irate woman's waist. "Don't be cross with me, mother," she coaxed. "You know it hurts to have you angry with me and I promise to have your baubles finished very soon. It won't take long to finish." She stroked her mother's abundant tresses. "Just a few more red beads and it will look lovely entwined in your hair." She bent her head to kiss the delicate hands that lay in the woman's lap.

Meteh's annoyance melted. She couldn't stay angry with her daughter for very long when she was being affectionate. Giving a sigh of resignation, she arose. Looking down at this child of her flesh, the mother wondered how she happened to be blessed with such a loving, yet complicated daughter? The child worried her constantly. But of course, she knew why she loved her so much. She was so much like her father and Meteh adored the pharaoh.

"I was trying to tell you that I have to go and help Petenahti with preparations for the food preserving. Meet with me this evening when we dine and try to concentrate on what you are supposed to be doing," she chastised. "Stop this day dreaming about fripperies." But the sting had gone out of her words and she smiled once more as she left the room.

Settling back in her seat, Meryhken picked up the unfinished string of beads. Concentrating on blending the colors, she chose a small and dainty red bead and carefully threaded it on to the thick twine. Next, she picked a coral stone shaped like an egg. *His arms are so strong, yet his hands are gentle when they caress me.* Deliberately trying to concentrate on her task, she picked out an onyx and painstakingly threaded it on the bead. For a few more minutes she kept her focus but inevitably it started to wander again. *The days are so long when I'm not with him.* Absentmindedly selecting another bead, it slipped from her fingers and rolled across the floor. In resignation she lay down the unfinished necklace. Arising, she called out to Psarta who sat outside the open door. The boy entered the common room with a questioning look on his face. He'd been dozing, having slept fitfully the previous night.

Like many other nights of late, Psarta had spent most of it wide-awake waiting to hear footsteps creeping back over the balcony's low wall. His mistress thought that no one was aware of her nightly escapes. *Ah! Does she think I am deaf and blind?* Now, she'd rudely broken through his dream of flying through the desert as free as a bird. "You called, Mistress?"

"Psarta, I need you to finish threading these beads for me." Her voice held a note of pleading. "My fingers are so clumsy today that more of them are being lost than threaded onto the cord. Please help me. Mother needs them by the end of the day."

He didn't say a word. Psarta took the bag of beads and cord from her outstretched hands but his face spoke volumes. *This is a female's chore.* Like her mother before him he pondered on her attitude of late. *She acts like a sheep during the mating season.* Unlike Meteh however, he was all too aware of the reason for her odd behavior.

Ever since Oedimus' return from Upper Egypt there had been a subtle change in the girl. That is, she wasn't a girl anymore but a vibrant woman. *At least she is when she isn't acting as if she'd been struck by the silly magic of the cow-headed goddess, Hathor!* Quickly, he sent a silent prayer of forgiveness to the love goddess in the event that she had heard his thoughts.

Resigning himself to the task, he settled down onto the floor, crossing his legs for comfort. Nimble fingers began to work on the beading while keeping one eye on Meryhken. Barely looking at his work, he selected another bead from the bag and expertly slipped it onto the strand. With deft fingers, Psarta worked on the adornment. It was an easy task and he didn't need to look at what he was doing. Instead his pensive gaze followed Meryhken, noting her mindless state. Why was she pacing the floor like a restless panther? Just when he thought he couldn't stand it any longer she stopped and plopped into her chair. Crossing her legs underneath her buttocks, she rested her elbows on her knees. Meryhken then cupped her hands underneath her chin and stared at her companion in silent contemplation. The steady gaze continued until Psarta began to feel uncomfortable under the hard scrutiny.

She finally broke the silence. "Psarta. Do you have a favorite female companion?"

Taken aback by her unexpected question, Psarta hesitated before replying. "I have several female friends mistress, but no particular favorite," he replied evasively.

She persisted. "You know what I mean. Is there a special female that you really care about a lot? Someone who warms your heart?

Psarta didn't like the way this conversation was going. He stalled to answer. *What is behind this strange questioning? Does she not realize that I'm a Eunuch?* It dawned on him that she was even more naïve than he had realized. Cautiously, he countered her question with a question. "Why are you asking this, Meryhken?"

She was quiet for a moment, staring off into space. Starting to open her mouth to say something, she seemingly changed her mind. After a long pause she answered. "No reason really. I just wondered if you care a lot for a girl and if so, how it makes you feel? What would you do about it if you cared enough to want to be with her forever?"

Psarta tried to think of what to say in order to put a stop to this talk. Instinctively, he knew that Meryhken was about to reveal something that she might later regret. He decided that the best way to handle her rashness was to make light of her too personal questions.

"Actually I enjoy the company of many girls," he lied. "You see each one is uniquely different. For example, one female friend has an ample figure and dimples to her cheeks. She likes to be cuddled a lot and laughs at my banter. She makes me feel manly." Warming to his subject, he continued in the same vein.

"Another female with whom I spend time, has the most beautiful eyes and she looks at me like I'm the most important person in the world while she whispers to me of her devotion. One voluptuous young lady talks to me of past Egyptian glories, while she sooths my sore muscles and …"

Enough!" Meryhken interrupted, laughing, "I understand perfectly what you are trying to tell me. You are a man of many pleasures and slave to none."

Psarta grinned, glad to have sidestepped a tricky situation. He didn't want Meryhken to reveal to him the depth of her involvement with the pharaoh's guard. He knew that this is what she had intended but had decided against it.

Already he suspected that the two of them were more deeply intimate than he cared to know about. *I don't need the burden of a confessional.* If the two of them were so minded, they could visit a temple and pay sacrificial homage to Aten. Or, confess their sins to a priest to try and salve their consciences. He definitely wasn't the person to confess to. *I could be burdened enough with my own sins if I wanted to give serious thought to them, which I don't!* As it was, he was already unwittingly too involved in their lives. The less he knew the better it was for all concerned.

Each night, Meryhken left her room and today it had been almost dawn before he'd heard her returning through her balcony opening. Psarta sympathized, yet was afraid that she was becoming too careless. It also irritated him that she obviously wanted to involve him even more than he was already. *Doesn't the foolish girl understand the seriousness of her entanglement?*

Standing up, he walked over to where she sat and held out the completed adornment. "Now Meteh won't have any more reason to scold you, will she?" His voice was heavy with meaning. The girl reached to take the finished necklace but Psarta held on to it.

Raising her head to look at him, her eyes held a question. Peering down at her, Psarta's tone was serious. "Take care Meryhken. Don't give Meteh reasons to discipline you. For that matter, don't give her an excuse to punish myself. Remember this. Her eyes are even sharper than her tongue. Very little goes unseen by her, especially when it concerns your welfare." With this, he placed the adornment into her outstretched hands. A somber expression covered his normally bland face.

Meryhken had the good grace to look abashed and understanding his meaning, squeezed his hand in gratitude. "Thank you Psarta. You are a good and loyal friend." Bowing his head in assent, he turned and left the room.

She sat in quiet contemplation, considering the subtle warning he had seen fit to give.

Oedimus remained quiet as she repeated Sparta's words of caution. For a few moments a heavy silence hung between them. "We will have to be more careful, my love. If Psarta has suspicions, there may be others who are also wondering about our relationship."

He placed his arm around her waist, feeling the familiar warmth of her body beneath her lightweight gown. Meryhken drew closer. They sat on the bench that had once held people seeking peace at the temple and she wished she could feel some of that same tranquility. Oedimus was still talking, trying to allay her fears but she knew that he was also concerned.

"I know that Calphus is aware," he was saying, "but I have no doubts concerning his silence. He's like a brother to me and as such is most loyal. He will keep his council, but will Psarta do the same?"

She quickly reassured him. "He is as loyal to me as Calphus is to you. It's Meteh that I worry about." Laying her head on his shoulder and nestling into the crook of his protective arm, she felt safe. "She only has my interests at heart but even though she loves me, she would never understand. Meteh will never permit us to be together. In desperation she asked the question that was constantly on both their minds. "Oedimus, what is going to become of us?"

Pulling her closer, he felt the trembling of her body and held her tightly. "Don't fret, dear heart. I will find a way I promise. Someday we'll be together as man and wife."

Lifting her head, Meryhken searched his face to find the reassurance that his words had evoked. His smile was tender yet there was a tightening of his jaw-line and his eyes were clouded as he looked into hers. "You are my life Meryhken, and we'll be together for as long as we live. And if the gods are kind, we'll also be together in the After Life."

In the shadows of the ruins they clung to each other, trying to find hope. Oedimus was all too aware of the obstacles that were in their way. Akhenaton was a kind and fair ruler, but Meryhken was his property. With a sinking heart he realized it would take an act from the gods for Akhenaton to consider a marriage between his child and his Chief Guard, even though he knew the king was well pleased with him. *How long would his benevolence towards me last if he knew of my love for Meryhken?*

It was ironic that he was being called to escort the royal princess to her wedding in Anatolia; two young people who were betrothed for political reasons and entering into a loveless marriage. Whereas that same royal blood running through Meryhken's veins, prevented him from taking her as his wife, because of the circumstances of her birth.

Thebes had calmed down significantly since his disarming of the radicals. However, as much as the pharaoh favored him, when it came to Meryhken there was no question as to what his reaction would be if he learned of their involvement. *I must find a way.* Oedimus held her as if there was already a force stronger than his own attempting to separate them.

If only I could confide in Meteb. Meryhken dismissed the thought almost as soon as it had entered her head. As for telling the pharaoh, that very closeness they shared was a deterrent. *We will find a way. We have to.*

Darkness had crept over the old temple and covered the surrounding landscape. Somewhere else in the world the stars shone, but not on Egypt. Clouds scurrying across the winter sky hid them from view.

In the distance, an animal gave a long lonely howl that reverberated mournfully against the eastern hills.

CHAPTER SIX

*S*he sat in the corner as still as a mummy. Blank eyes stared towards the balcony, an occasional blink of the eyelids the only indication that she was alive.

The hours dragged painfully slow, yet the woman was unaware of the night's passing. Dispassionately, she watched the nocturnal sky turn to cobalt - eventually giving way to dawn's soft pink light. Birds in the trees began to chirp as they heralded a new day.

Meteh was vaguely aware of a sound outside the door and knew it was Psarta turning in his slumbers. Last night as she'd quietly stepped around his inert body to enter the apartment, the faint snoring had indicated that he was in a deep sleep. Tumultuous thoughts had bombarded her brain all night long, but only one thought stood out sharp and clear. Staying calm and rational was a necessity.

At last! Above the bird's chirping came the sound that she'd been waiting to hear. The soft thud of feet landed on the balcony's mud bricks, followed by the light tread of footsteps entering the bedroom. In the still darkened room, Meteh saw the outline of a familiar figure. The girl had come home.

Earlier that evening, a well-meaning friend had disclosed a tale that Meteh could hardly comprehend, yet instinct had told her that the woman spoke the truth. She had entered Meryhken's apartments with the intention of confronting her daughter. Instead she'd found an empty bed. Its emptiness had screamed at her far louder than any of the alarming words that had been whispered into her ear.

Meteh's emotions had ranged from shock to disbelief, to an impotent rage against the pharaoh's Chief Guard - her daughter – Psarta. But most of all she'd raged against her own person. How could she, the girl's own mother, not have seen that which was so apparent to other people?

Throughout her endless vigil, Meteh had relived the many incidents that should have alerted her to the truth. In hindsight, everything that had taken place in recent months seemed to fall into place and should have aroused her suspicions. She'd relived her daughter's episodes of unbridled gayety without apparent reason. There had been times when she was pale and withdrawn, acting as if she were a walking, talking specter.

How many times had Meryhken made excuses to visit the royal palace when the king had not summoned her? How often had the girl gone missing and returned with a glib excuse on her tongue?

Meteh wondered how many nights Meryhken had sneaked from her room to meet this man - like tonight? What a blind fool she had been!

Meryhken automatically began to shed her clothing, barely able to stay awake. Once again, they had spent hours racking their brains in order to find a solution to their dilemma. Time spent in the old temple ruins discussing their options, had failed to produce anything of logical value.

Irrationally, they had considered the idea of running away together to some friendly country but quickly realized the stupidity of such a plan. No other country would openly risk defying Egypt's pharaoh by harboring them. And, should they be caught, they were doomed. For now, they had to be satisfied with a few stolen hours in the night.

Her body ached from lack of sleep and her spirit was heavy. Yawning, she kicked off her sandals and started to unwind her robe. *What was that?* She stood still. Her skin prickled icily. There was something - or someone in her room.

Fear gripped the girl. Clutching her raiment, Meryhken crept closer to the bed. Her frightened eyes tried to pierce the gloom as her heart beat in terror. Something stirred in the corner.

A black image uncurled itself and arose from the chair. Stifling the scream in her throat, Meryhken gasped as the figure came closer. "Mother!"

The woman said nothing as she stopped mere inches in front of her daughter. Without warning, she raised a hand and swung. Meryhken felt the vicious slap sting her cheek and a welt immediately formed across her face. Tears sprang to her eyes, but they weren't from the impact of the blow. The tears were for the look of cold disgust on her mother's face.

In spite of her good intentions Meteh's anger exploded. "You don't have to tell me where you have been all night," the tone was denude of feeling. "You've been with him, haven't you." It wasn't a question but a statement of fact. "You were with the pharaoh's guard."

Meryhken started to protest and was stopped by a raised hand. She flinched, expecting to receive another blow. Instead, icy fingers were placed across her mouth to still her tongue.

"Be quiet!" the voice hissed. "Don't lie to me, Meryhken. No more lies." Her voice started to mount uncontrollably. The long sleepless night of worry had been too much. "I know that you've met regularly with this soldier, Oedimus."

Again, the girl started to protest, "Psarta wouldn't"------

"Stop!" The voice cracked like a whiplash, " Psarta did not inform me." Meteh's voice took on a sarcastic tone, "his loyalty to you is beyond reproach."

With a wave of her hand she dismissed thoughts of the boy as if he were nothing but an aggravating flea. "Anyway, it is not important how I found out. What is important is the fact that you've lied and deceived me. Your behavior has been that of a street slut!" Meryhken's face paled. "Even worse, your lover has taken advantage of the pharaoh's goodness to him by dallying with his daughter. Oedimus is much older than you and should have shown more restraint. However, you have behaved no better than one of the lowest females that inhabit the dens of Amarna!"

Meteh was full of angry bewilderment as she continued with her tirade. "How could you bring such shame on me? And, what concerns did you have of the pharaoh's reaction to this whore mongering? Did you not bother to think of how he would react to his child laying down her body to a mere soldier?"

Meryhken felt numb. In her entire life she had never been spoken to in such a way. Never! She stared dumbly at this stranger in front of her, unable to believe that her ears had heard such condemnation.

Her mother had spat at her like an asp releasing its venom. Her face stung sharply from the impact of Meteh's blow, yet even though her ashen face showed an ugly red hand print, it didn't hurt near as much as her mother's words. Meryhken trembled as the terrible words continued to ring inside her head.

For a few seconds she stood in a state of shock. Then, a slow burning anger began to form. It crept upward from her bowels like an awakened monster. "How dare you," the voice was barely a whisper. Meryhken's quiet tone belied the eruption that was rising within.

A rage equal to that of her mother's sizzled and exploded. "How dare you defile the love that Oedimus and I have for each other? YES, HE IS MY LOVER! And, we would have wed these many months past if it had have been possible. But no one knows more than we do how utterly unacceptable our love is to this world that we live in."

Despair laced her tirade, "that is the tragedy that we have to live with. It is <u>not</u> your tragedy, <u>not</u> the pharaoh's but OURS! How can you possibly feel the anguish as we do? Our lives are joined in body and soul and it makes it all the more painful to know we cannot be united in law."

"Can you possibly understand how we feel, knowing that we cannot be together in wedlock?" The angry voice shook with desperation. "Of course not! Nobody can. We are unable to fulfill our lives as the gods intended and THAT is the real sin."

She ran out of words. As quickly as her tirade had erupted, it stopped. Her shoulders slumped and she sank to the edge of her bed, bowing her head. All life seemed to have drained away. Her exhausted brain finally refused to function. All she wanted to do was to seek oblivion through sleep. At least sleep would bring her a few hours of respite from this world of insanity.

Meteh didn't move. The room crackled with tense energy. Shocked into silence by the unexpected harangue, she stood observing her daughter.

What had she expected in response to her accusations? More lies, or pleadings for forgiveness? Certainly she hadn't visualized this rage against herself. It seemed impossible that her reserved, lovable daughter had turned into this hysterical raging stranger!

Hearing a slight movement from beyond the apartment's door reminded her of Psarta. There was little doubt that he still slept. Their voices had been loud enough to disturb the slumbering ancestors in the After-Life! She knew full well that the boy had to have been aware of Meryhken's comings and goings, but she would deal with him later.

Right now she didn't know what to do, except to take care of her daughter who sagged like a broken effigy. The delicate hands lay in her lap, grasping at her loosened gown with which she'd attempted to cover her nakedness. The mother was reminded of the young child that her daughter had once been. How often she had seen her thus, when as a little girl she had disobeyed her authority. But this was more serious than any child-like mischief. Her own anger subsided as she looked at the troubled face of the girl.

Moving to sit by her side, she placed an arm around the bent shoulders and pressed the girl's head down to her breast. Meryhken leaned against her mother, neither acknowledging the consoling pressure nor rebuffing the gesture. Both sat in silence within their own thoughts, bonded by blood ties but strangers in minds and deeds.

She was so exhausted. She couldn't think straight. Now that Meteh had learned her secret it would bring its own difficulties, but it also brought relief. The burden of guilt and fear of discovery had vanished.

Meteh's familiar body felt secure and safe. Not even Oedimus' loving arms could make her feel this safe. Even though their love bonded them, fear of disclosure had made it so desperate. They knew not a moment's peace.

In a sudden burst of wild imagining, she thought that her mother might help. *Now that Meteh knows the depth of my feelings, perhaps Akhenaton can be convinced that marriage would be a suitable arrangement. If she assures him of this, surely the pharaoh will give his consent?* Even as she dwelled on this, she mentally shook her head. As tired as she was she realized that her thoughts were more hopeful than logical.

The two females sat thus for the longest time, before exhaustion finally took over. Meteh observed the girl's eyelids beginning to droop and the body leaned heavily against her own. Gently, she eased the girl away from her. "You need to sleep, daughter."

Meteh laid the unresisting girl across the bed and smoothed the coverlet around her as she had done so many times during Meryhken's childhood.

Her even breathing and the occasional flutter of the eyelids reminded Meteh of her own tiredness. No matter, she had too much on her mind to sleep now.

Observing the sleeping girl, she struggled with her own feelings of loyalty to her daughter and anger at Oedimus. Her daughter's outburst was proof that she cared for this soldier. *It is immaterial whether Oedimus returns her feelings, or not.* What was important was to make the best decision for Meryhken's well being.

The sounds of dawning activity outside reminded her that there were things to take care of. Life must continue normally, so as not to arouse suspicions and more damaging gossip.

Arising stiffly, Meteh walked out of the apartment. Pausing outside the door she eyed Psarta who sat in his usual place, waiting for his mistress. He didn't meet the woman's eyes. Nothing in his face gave away the fact that he must have heard the angry commotion. Without uttering a word, she turned and headed for her own quarters.

Psarta was worried. Riddled with guilt at not being awake to warn Meryhken, he knew he couldn't have prevented the encounter, even if he had have been alert. It was inevitable. *There is nothing I could have done*, he thought glumly.

While frustrated at not being able to protect his mistress, he was fully aware that she'd brought this misfortune onto herself through her own actions. What Meteh would do now was uncertain. All Psarta knew was that he was an intricate part of Meryhken's life and whatever Meteh decided, it would affect him too. The woman would not easily forgive him for his role in the affair, even though he'd been a reluctant accomplice. Psarta's chin sank to his chest as his ruinous imaginings overcame his usual positive outlook.

CHAPTER SEVEN

*T*he atmosphere was stifling. Although the heat of the day had subsided it had left behind an airlessness that was oppressive. Not a breath of wind stirred.

Meryhken couldn't shake the uneasy feeling that gripped her. She'd been waiting for over an hour and he still hadn't arrived. *The pharaoh has probably delayed him.* Even as the thought came to her, she knew she was just trying to find comfort in rationalizing his absence. Akhenaton had never kept him so late. Once the royal family had retired for the night, Oedimus' evenings were free. *Maybe he's been detained with a problem concerning one of his soldiers.*

She tried to stay calm. Regardless, no matter how much she tried not to be upset, she new his absence was not a good omen. Oedimus never left her waiting. In fact, most evenings he was the first to arrive at their rendezvous.

The vestibule was dark tonight and in her imaginings the shadows came alive. Even the path's border of night jasmine with its sensuous fragrance, couldn't bring her its usual pleasure. Spirits of the temple seemed to be trying to communicate with her. In spite of the sultry air, Meryhken shuddered as if a cold hand had stroked her body. She was sure that the ominous presence of the old god Set was near.

Mentally chastising herself for being so silly, she nervously shifted her position on the bench. Her lips murmured a silent prayer to Aten - and to Isis for good measure.

Sitting on the seat for so long had become uncomfortable. Arising, she walked back and forth in the dimness of the ruins, her face showing pale in the faint light of evening.

Nervously licking her lips she tasted the bitterness of salt. The lightweight gown clung to her clammy body.

He isn't coming. After restlessly pacing for another few minutes, her mind accepted this fact. Leaving the temple ruins to retrace her steps, anxious thoughts bombarded her. At least there was no fear of Meteh waiting for her tonight, which was a small consolation.

Since their catastrophic encounter two nights previously her mother had been quite reticent in her communications with both herself and Psarta.

Surprisingly, the disciplinarian action that they had both expected had not occurred, yet. She'd expected to be confined to the vicinity of the harem and was surprised when this didn't happen. Meteh had also not taken any action towards Psarta. Meryhken felt a sense of relief, hoping that her mother's attitude was an indication of her acceptance of her lover.

Psarta's thoughts were not as optimistic. The tension inside him was building, as he knew that the woman was just biding her time. He sat at his post outside Meryhken's rooms fanning his hot body with a palm frond. *I'm not the one that suffers from the insanity of love.*

An unforgiving heat had settled over Amarna that blanketed the city with a heaviness that sealed like the stone in front of a burial chamber. For the past two days Psarta had been in a state of nervousness, waiting for Meteh's inevitable punishment. One thing was certain. Whatever that woman was planning to do, he knew that it wasn't going to make him happy!

Waving the frond over his perspiring face did little to relieve his discomfort, or the dire thoughts going through his mind. Absentmindedly picking a grape from the bunch he'd brought back from the dining room, he popped it into his mouth, only to spit it out in disgust. It tasted moldy. *Even fruit cannot survive in this heat.*

Oedimus was having difficulty controlling himself. His frustration boiled over and he thumped the side of the doorway. The bruising pain to his knuckles went unnoticed. *The gods can't do this to me! I must see her before I leave.*

He stood in the entrance to his quarters and peered in the direction of the temple ruins, knowing it was too far away to be seen from his billets. Even so he willed his mind to mentally contact her, hoping she'd understand that his absence wasn't intentional. *Hopefully she will not have waited too long.* He certainly didn't want the mother to find her daughter missing again.

Only yesterday, Meryhken had managed to visit the palace on the pretext of visiting the pharaoh. As discreetly as possible, she had sought him out. There had been no opportunity for them to speak in private without being overheard by people around them, but imploring eyes had sent him a silent message of communication. "I need to return to my quarters and take care of my duties," she had remarked to the room in general. She looked straight at him and added, "the walk through the gardens is so pretty that I think I'll stop and gather some flowers to adorn the harem's common room."

Oedimus had understood. After a few more moments of casual conversation Meryhken had left, deliberately heading in the direction of the garden. After allowing an appropriate amount of time to elapse, he'd excused himself.

He'd found her waiting for him halfway along the path. Straight away he'd known that something was wrong. The tears that shimmered in her eyes before she flung herself into his arms had sent cold chills through his body. He'd held her protectively, until she was able to gain control and talk. It was just as he had feared.

She had tried to sound so hopeful, describing the confrontation with Meteh. "It will be alright, Oedimus. I'm sure that she will help us, now that she knows the truth. She is my mother. She loves me and wants only the best for me." In spite of the reassuring words, Meryhken couldn't hide the desperation in her voice. By trying to convince him, she was really attempting to convince herself. "She has influence with Akhenaton and I know that he will have my happiness at heart."

He'd agreed with her in an attempt to satisfy her need for reassurance. "I'm sure that you are right, Meryhken. Maybe this was meant to be. Maybe Meteh will help now that she is aware of how truly we love each other. If she intervenes with the pharaoh she may influence him on our behalf. Surely the Spirit of Aten will shine upon us and give blessings."

The words that he spoke rang false to his own ears. How could he tell her of the dread that he felt? Oedimus kissed the top of her head as she rested it against his chest, smelling the familiar scent of her hair and feeling its silkiness under his lips.

She pressed her lips to the softly throbbing pulse under the hard jaw line. Reluctantly, she raised her head and stepped back out of his arms, knowing that she must leave and return to the harem before she was missed. They had parted after this brief encounter with a promise to meet this evening.

But the fates had taken over. Earlier in the day the pharaoh had sent for him. He was to leave immediately for the land of Syria.

"This act of aggression by these Hittites will not be tolerated! It needs your immediate attention," declared Akhenaton.

Over the years, the Hittite nation had become quite powerful in the Middle East. Their superior skills as metallurgists combined with their access to Anatolia's copper and iron, were a necessity to Egypt. The Hittites were experts at making swords of steel, whereas the Egyptians were still using bronze for their weapons, which did not hold an edge as well as the stronger steel. And, in battle a steel sword could cut a bronze one in half.

Even so, Egypt still retained most of the dominance and control over the trading routes. Because of their sources for precious gold and ivory, their power remained unchallenged. Regardless, in order to keep stability, an alliance between the two countries was greatly valued. It was imperative that the two countries remain allies. Hence the recent plans for the royal marriage to cement that relationship even further.

Now without any provocation, Hittite soldiers had attacked an Egyptian caravan! The pharaoh had been advised to curb his natural outrage, to await an explanation from the Hittite king. It was politically expedient to keep the peace between the two countries and find out why Mussilli had ordered this terrorist attack. Whatever the outcome, the action would not be tolerated and needed a thorough investigation.

In recent weeks, rumblings of a few skirmishes by a band of Hittite radicals had reached the pharaoh's ears, but the peace-loving ruler remained unconcerned. As long as their marauding didn't affect his country it was not his problem. If they chose to flout Anatolian laws let Mussilli take care of it. But, this latest incident was a different story. Not only had an action been taken against Egypt, but also the marauders were not mere outlaws. They were Hittite soldiers.

Akhenaton was at a loss as to the reasoning for such a debacle. Naturally, the wedding arrangements were to be postponed. Why had the Hittites done this?

Could he believe Mussilli's claim that he had not ordered the attack? And, if this were true, then who had given the soldiers this order? And why? It didn't make sense.

Within the hour of the messenger bringing news of the attack, another man sent by Mussilli arrived, carrying a personal message from Anatolia.

He had traveled swiftly from Anatolia's capital city of Hattushash, to reassure the Egyptians that Mussilli was not responsible. "Anatolia's most gracious king sends his felicitations to the great god Akhenaton, almighty pharaoh of all Egypt and lands beyond."

"Let it be known that our most illustrious ruler is most angered by this treacherous act. Rest assured these attackers were not from Anatolia's army, and the king is most innocent of this unfortunate incident. He wishes to assure the most glorious of pharaohs of his loyalty and support in this matter. Any and all decisions that are made by your wise counsel will be met with his blessings."

Akhenaton was at a loss for words and upset that his peace had been disturbed. He didn't want to have to admit even to himself that he disliked conflict and avoided it at all costs. As much as the pharaoh abhorred losing his Chief Guard even for a few weeks, he realized that Oedimus was his most able man to handle this troublesome incident.

Because of this fiasco there were also problems in his beloved city. The rippling effect had heightened the dissatisfaction of the people. This very day, his priest had brought him the news that there was disturbing restlessness among the inhabitants of Amarna. Why had his god, Aten, allowed this upheaval?

The dead caravan guides had been popular citizens. They were fifth generation camel drivers with good reputations among their peers. And, they had been mercilessly slaughtered. Not only were families and friends mourning their loss, but Hytoph had also brought more disturbing tales.

People were saying that the old gods were angry. By neglecting to honor their earth god, Seb and the all-wise Horus, revenge from these gods was been taken against Egypt.

"Because of their unrest and fear, they are even proclaiming that Osiris has come from the Underworld to demand retribution!" Hytoph had declared ominously.

Akhenaton had ordered the priest to pray to Aten for guidance in settling the unrest, and to perform an hourly sacrifice to the almighty god at the temple altar.

The pharaoh shook his head in disbelief. He'd thought that with the quelling of the problems in Thebes, all would be well. Now this! It seemed that overnight his serene and tranquil world had erupted like a volcano, spewing forth its destruction over him. He needed Aten's protection now more than ever. *Have I offended my lord?* There were too many unanswered questions.

"Make yourself ready," he'd instructed Oedimus, "and take however many of your men that you think you will need. I wish you to start immediately. This matter <u>must</u> be resolved. Verify whether Mussilli is telling the truth. And if so, unmask these fiends that dare to attack Egypt's might!"

Oedimus had no choice but to obey. But his mind had been in a tumult as he left Akhenaton's presence. How could he get word to Meryhken of his impending departure? He had no time to seek her out before the evening, and he couldn't trust anyone to send in his stead. Calphus was the only one that he trusted completely but he couldn't place his friend in such a position.

Beside which, Calphus had his own personal matters to take care of as he planned to take him along. His friend would need the evening with his family to say his own good-byes.

Throughout the long and busy day he'd pushed his personal worries to the back of his mind. The innate discipline of the soldier took over as he took charge of the immediate necessities of organizing his men and seeing that his orders were properly executed. He planned to take no more than half a company.

Even so, he needed to designate various duties and oversee the supplies needed for the journey. Primarily, they would need an ample supply of drinking water, as the oases in the arid deserts of Syria were few.

The garrison of Beth Shean was on the trading route but still a substantial distance from Amarna. It would be nothing but desert once they left Gaza. Fighting tools had to be checked and replaced if needs be, in the event that they ran into trouble. The attack on the caravan had been most deadly, apparently killing all three guides.

He was as surprised and as puzzled as the pharaoh. What was the reason for the pillaging? Why would the Hittites' king jeopardize the peaceful co-existence of their countries? He seemed to be most eager for this marriage to occur, so why would he anger our pharaoh in this way? There was something to this catastrophe that didn't make sense. *But why does it have to be myself who is given the responsibility to solve the mystery?*

Of course, he knew the reason why. He hadn't been elevated to Chief Guard for nothing. Apart from his soldier's disciplined training, Oedimus knew that his unquestionable loyalty and ingrained astuteness had not gone unnoticed by his king.

This was the reason why he'd become as close to the pharaoh as any of his advisors. Without any sense of egotism, Oedimus knew that he was the best man for this job.

The problem was that he'd been given such short notice that he'd been kept busy well into the night. Eventually everything was completed and the men had been relieved to get a few hours of rest before their early departure. Now he could relax and think of Meryhken. *Relax? Ah!*

Oedimus leaned against his doorway, too frustrated to be aware of his tiredness. *She will have long since left the ruins and retired to her bed.* For a wild moment he had the idea of going to Meryhken's rooms to see her, then shook his head and gave a mirthless laugh. *I must be mad to even entertain such a thought.* He could only imagine what would happen to him, if he were caught visiting the king's harem. Even worse was the thought of what such stupidity would do to Meryhken.

Looking up at the night sky, he judged by the position of the stars that there was about three hours left before daybreak. The only consolation was that he knew she would learn of his departure through the inevitable palace gossip. *Certainly not the most ideal way to find out why I did not meet her,* he thought darkly. *By that time I will be well on my way to Syria.*

For a brief moment he regretted not having asked Calphus to meet Meryhken for him, but dismissed the thought almost as fast as it had entered his mind. Already he was feeling a sense of guilt regarding his friend. Calphus' wife was with child again and he doubted that they would return in time for him to be with her during her confinement.

Calphus hadn't hesitated, or shown any sign whatsoever that he was reluctant to leave. If he had, Oedimus would have relieved him of his duty even though he was his right hand man. But, when he'd learned of Akhenaton's wishes, Calphus hadn't hesitated. "When do we to leave?" he had asked. Such was his loyalty.

In the shadows Oedimus saw the outline of a figure approaching and as the person drew closer, he saw that it was the man of whom he'd been thinking. "What brings you here, friend? Should you not be at home with Thehta?"

Calphus shrugged. "My wife and I talked for a long time, until she could no longer stay awake" adding laughingly, "even for her husband. I believe that this latest child must be a boy, as he demands his mother's attention even before he has entered this world. She is sleeping so soundly and obviously doesn't need me, so I thought maybe you might want to talk over some last minute details before we leave." They both knew without it being said that the man's real reason for being here was to try and take Oedimus' mind off his personal problems.

Calphus and his wife had discussed this, agreeing that Oedimus needed his support at this time. Kissing Thehta 'thank you' for her understanding, he'd left to seek out his friend.

Returning inside, Oedimus removed two drinking vessels and a jug of wine from a shelf. Setting them down on a table, he poured a generous amount of the ruby liquid into a goblet and handed it to Calphus. After filling the other container, he raised it in salute to his friend. "To you Calphus. Truly a most loyal friend whom I love as my own brother."

Calphus returned the salute. "May the Great Aten shed his light and wisdom on you during our travels and, also when we return."

Psarta didn't know how to tell her. He watched and waited for an opportunity as she and Meteh sat talking with a few of the other women who occupied the common room. It was a quiet time of relaxation for the harem inhabitants before retiring to their quarters for the mid-day resting period. Meryhken had been looking increasingly pale of late and today there were dark blue shadows underneath her eyes, emphasized by the black kohl ringing the rims.

Of course she had slipped out again last night but had surprised him by returning much earlier than usual. He now knew why. He'd only just learned of the Chief Guard's departure and doubted that she had yet been made aware of this. He hoped to speak privately with her before she learned from some other source.

Too late. He heard one of the women talking. He listened, wishing that he could stop the woman's wagging tongue!

"It was so sudden," the gossip was saying. "He and a few of his soldiers left before this dawn had risen." The woman was relishing being the center of attention. "The wedding has been postponed until this unfortunate situation has been resolved."

Without thinking, Psarta moved to stand protectively by his mistress' side. The stiffening of her body was the only indication that this news had affected her. Even this was so slight a movement that Psarta was sure he was the only person to have noticed the change.

Not quite. Meteh was faster in her response than Psarta. "This room is so unbearably hot," she declared. "Meryhken, will you accompany me to the courtyard? We will sit awhile under the shade of the trees, before taking our rest." She arose and holding a hand out to her daughter, assisted her to her feet. Taking the girl firmly by an elbow she turned to the women in the room. "My apologies to all of you, but I feel the need of some cooling air."

Meryhken allowed herself to be led out with Psarta following close behind. Once they were outside Meteh nodded to him, indicating that he was to leave them alone. He headed for their quarters.

Underneath the low branches of the almond trees, the woman sat down on a bench. Patting the seat beside her, she indicated that her daughter should also sit. A long drawn out silence prevailed, but eventually the girl broke it. "Mother, did you have anything to do with Oedimus' departure?"

Meteh shook her head. "No daughter. Even I don't have that much influence with our pharaoh. Admittedly, I did know that the Chief Guard had left for Syria." She hesitated, choosing her words carefully, "I was waiting for the right opportunity to tell you. He has been ordered to search out the details of this business with the caravan. The loss of the cargo and death of the drivers has impaired the wedding plans."

Meryhken stared at the ground.

Pausing for a moment, the mother continued in the same vein. "I can't say that I'm sorry that this has happened. It is most opportune that this unsettling situation with Anatolia has arisen and I cannot but believe that Aten orchestrated this. It has forced the pharaoh to act accordingly." She tried to be tactful. "This is a delicate situation for our country and needs to be handled with the utmost care."

"I can't help but feel that the Great Lord Aten has looked kindly on our personal problem and seen fit to intervene on our behalf," she said. "Unknowingly, our pharaoh has solved the situation without my having to reveal your involvement with his Chief Guard." She spoke earnestly as she turned to face the girl. "I'm sure that you must realize that he would have been extremely angry if he had have been made aware of this. Akhenaton would have taken immediate action against him."

Meteh didn't add that she had mulled over the advisability of discussing the situation with her king and had decided against it. She wasn't sure what his reaction would have been if he were to learn of the affair. Whatever it was, it would not fare well for her daughter. As loving as he was towards their child he would not condone such behavior.

For hours Meteh had struggled with the problem and each time she'd decided to confide in the pharaoh, she'd changed her mind. The mother was afraid that because of his strong feelings for Meryhken, his reactions would prove to be extreme. *Fate has surely stepped in to find a solution for me and I thank almighty Aten for his benevolence.* Having being in a dilemma, she felt very grateful that her problem and fears had been eliminated.

Clasping Meryhken's hand between her own two, she tried talking sense into the girl's head. "You must realize that this has happened for the best. You may not think so at this moment but surely you can see that your relationship with Oedimus is impossible?" Emphasizing her next words she continued, "you know that our pharaoh will never allow such a thing."

And neither will I, she thought to herself. "You are still very young, and in time you will come to realize how impossible it is." Her tone changed to patronizing self-confidence. "The day will come when you will make an appropriate match with a man of Akhenaton's choosing. Trust me, you will then live a life of contentment. I have lived longer than you and I know these things." Meteh patted the hand that still lay in her grasp.

Meryhken's heart sank lower with each word that she heard. The last hope of any intervention by Meteh on her behalf, died.

How can she speak such meaningless platitudes? It was inconceivable that her mother really believed that she could forget Oedimus. *Does she think that I'm still a child who can be consoled with words and coaxed with promises of delights?*

Meryhken knew with a certainty that it would be useless anymore to try and make her mother understand. *It would be as if I were trying to change the course of the Nile*. Biting her lower lip, she swallowed the lump that arose in her throat. Her mother had no concept of the depths of her feelings for him. And, Meryhken knew that Oedimus shared those same feelings. Only death itself could separate them.

Raising her head, she studied her mother's countenance long and hard. In an expressionless voice she finally answered, "I'm sure that you are right, mother. Anyway it is immaterial now, isn't it? Oedimus has gone from Amarna and there is no telling as to his return. So, you don't have to be concerned that I will be meeting with him. You no longer have any need to worry about my welfare."

"I feel a need to rest so please excuse me." She stood. "This heat has tired me." Turning her back on Meteh she walked across the courtyard, heading for her rooms.

Meteh remained seated, observing the girl as she walked with head held high and her tall body straight as an obelisk. She didn't understand Meryhken. She never had. There had not been the expected response to her dissertation. She wasn't really sure what she had expected, but certainly not this quiet compliance. To be honest with herself, she'd thought that her daughter would shed tears and plead or, heaven forbid throw another angry tirade against her person!

Instead, the words that Meryhken had spoken had sounded mechanical, almost as if she were pacifying her elder. Had she really decided to give up the infatuation with her lover?

Giving a dismissive shrug, Meteh arose to retire to her own rooms. *It doesn't matter anymore*, she thought philosophically. Her step took on a jauntiness as her mood lifted. *Hopefully the next time that a man warms her blood, he will be a more appropriate choice of the king's choosing.*

Smiling in self-satisfaction she entered her quarters. *I believe that I will attend the temple today and pay a sacrificial homage to our glorious god, Aten. He has answered my prayers and I need to show reverence to him for having removed this aggravation from my life.*

Sitting on the edge of the bed she stared blankly at nothing. Meryhken hadn't slept well. All night long, unsettling thoughts of Oedimus' unexpected departure had swirled through her mind, disturbing her rest. How long would he be gone? Had he tried to send her a message before he'd left? Did he miss her already as she missed him? There was a physical ache inside her being. The land of Syria was so far away!

Automatically, she arose to dress for the day. Securing a garment around her body she reached for her toothed bone from her dressing table, perfunctorily straightening the wisps of hair that hung around her face.

Her eyes came to rest on her vanity box that held scents and unguents. It had been a gift from the pharaoh when she was just a child of twelve. She recalled how excited and grown up she had felt when he'd placed it in her hands. Made of a rich dark wood, the lid was embossed with elaborately placed gems that formed the letter "M".

She picked it up and studied it thoughtfully. *I'll send it to him. It will surely remind him of me as he travels, and reassure him that my love for him is constant.* She would give it to Psarta to pass along to one of the messengers.

Meryhken knew that regular communications were sent from Amarna to the Egyptian outposts. Now that Oedimus and his men were on this mission, the communiqué's would be even more frequent so that Akhenaton could be apprised of his soldiers' progress.

Walking onto the balcony, she bent over the low wall and picked a yellow bloom from one of the bushes that grew close. It was the same kind of flower that he'd given to her on that day of her fifteenth birthday. Emptying out its contents, she placed the flower in the box. It still held a heady perfume. Meryhken closed the lid, firmly.

CHAPTER EIGHT

 *T*he desert storm was trying its damndest to stop them. Sand whirled like canting dervishes, stinging the soldiers' faces as they struggled through the Syrian Desert. It was vicious. Penetrating the scarves that covered their jaws, it left grit clinging to parched lips.

Oedimus squinted red-rimmed eyes in an attempt to see ahead but except for thick, orange clouds of dust, he couldn't see a thing. Turning his head to check on his men he dimly discerned the straggling band pulling their horses through the dunes. Alongside him, Calphus guided his chariot horses through the drifting sand.

Every few yards the chariots would sink into sand and have to be tugged by the traces to get moving again. The animals suffered more than the men from the wind's fury and the only recourse was to place blinders over their eyes and lead them.

Gritty particles clung tighter than a centipede to Oedimus' sweaty skin, causing his body to itch. Fortunately the markers along the trade route had stood the test of time against such weather. They were still intact.

He'd been told that the caravan had come under attack not too far from the garrison of Beth Shean and was hoping the storm hadn't covered the remains so completely as to be undetectable. Oedimus and his men moved one tired foot at a time towards their destination.

It seemed like forever since they'd left Egypt. They had stopped at Gaza to replenish their supplies, before continuing on their journey. Here, Oedimus had left details of their progress with Gaza's commissioner, to be sent back to Akhenaton.

The commissioner had told him that it had been less than a week since the caravan had stopped to rest the camels and drivers. The attack must have happened shortly thereafter, therefore the remains should not be too disturbed. The messenger, who had carried news to Amarna of the plundering, had been very thorough in supplying details of its location.

Apparently, soldiers from Beth Shean had been on a routine patrol of the trade route and had come upon the remains along with the bodies of the drivers and a lone camel. The messenger had also said that the main guide's young son, who had been accompanying the caravan, had miraculously been found alive. Barely conscious, the soldiers had hastened the young survivor to the garrison to have their physician minister to him.

Oedimus was anxious to talk with the boy. From Gaza, it should have taken little more than two days for he and his men to reach the garrison. But, because of having to stop and shelter until the worst of the storm had subsided, it had already taken three days.

The first day out of Gaza their progress had been uneventful. But that evening, luck had left them. The storm had arisen. Had they not been so far away from the community Oedimus would have considered turning back. As it was, they had traveled too far into the desert for this to be an option and they had no alternative but hunker down behind a sand dune for protection, until it subsided. Covering themselves with blankets, they sheltered between the chariots and animals while the storm raged around them. By early morning of this day, its ferociousness had weakened. It was starting to abate and Oedimus felt it safe to make their way towards Beth Shean.

After another hour of slogging against the gusts, it was easier to move forward as the blowing sand became less dense. Looking upwards, Oedimus saw glimpses of blue sky beginning to show amidst the heavy clouds of dust. And, he could actually take a breath of air without inhaling sand.

In the act of wiping sweat from his face something caught his attention. His hand stopped in mid-air as his peripheral vision caught sight of a moving object. A few yards away to his right, something bright fluttered in the wind. Raising his arm to halt his men, he handed the reigns of his chariot horses to Calphus, bidding him wait.

Oedimus left the trail and grappled through the dunes for several yards. His eyes never veered off the fluttering object. Reaching it, he bent down to inspect it closer. It was a ragged piece of multi-colored cloth, dancing in the wind. *If it hadn't have had such bright colors I might never have seen it.* A large piece of splintered wood was sticking up out of the sand and the rag had caught on it. Oedimus removed the piece of cloth and on closer inspection, saw it to be the remains of a blanket.

A gust of wind blew his way, bringing with it an unpleasant odor. Sniffing the air in disgust, he clambered over a large dune. The smell was becoming stronger. Oedimus held his kerchief to his nose - then saw the reason for the putrid stink.

At the bottom of the dune a camel lay on its back, its cloudy eyes with its beautiful spiky lashes staring sightlessly at the sky. From a gaping wound in its side, stomach entrails and sickening clots of blood spilled onto the sand. The surrounding area was dark with seepage.

The huge bloodstains mixed with fecal matter and urine

spread from underneath the animal. The spillage looked so incongruous against the undulating cleanliness of the desert.

Oedimus clamped his kerchief even tighter over his nose as he inspected the animal. The stench was overpowering. Obviously the marauders had taken the rest of the camels to sell on the open market, so why kill one of them?

Above him a vulture screeched in protest and lifting his head he saw the creature circling, waiting for him to leave. Already the camel showed signs of having been gnawed. He knew that the bird's companions would return once he had left, but they must wait for their feast while he searched the area. Once the birds continued their meal, nothing would be left of the camel, except bones to be bleached by the sun. Nature would begin its cleansing process.

His search further afield didn't reveal any human bodies. *I suspect the soldiers from Beth Shean buried the drivers and their graves will have been covered by the storm.* He hoped that in the process they hadn't disturbed the site too much, so that clues might be found. The wind still blew but at least it wasn't as strong as it had been. Oedimus could see what was left of the caravan.

Very little remained. Turning over bits and pieces of broken caskets, he scanned the debris. Containers lay strewn all over the area, stripped of their contents. A broken piece of ivory tusk - - wind-blown blankets - - cloths of silk. Precious oils of myrrh soaked the wood of a broken box, giving off its pungent aroma. Why such carnage? It was a careless robbery to have ruined so much merchandise, instead of taking it all.

Muttering an angry oath, he kicked an empty sack out of his way as his eyes took in the senseless destruction. He needed his men to thoroughly search the surrounding area.

Turning to head back he saw a remnant of fine spun silk fluttering across the sand as the dying wind played with it. As he watched the piece of material being carried on the air, something bright caught his eye. A sudden shaft of sunlight was glinting and

Star   ᏆᏏᎾ   Marie Friend

flashing on an object. Oedimus covered the few yards to where it lay and bent to retrieve it.

It was a steel axe head. Apparently it had broken off from its handle. A few inches away lay the broken wooden handle. Holding them, Oedimus turned the two pieces over and over in his hands and saw that they were Hittites weaponry. Finely honed and smooth, the sunrays had glinted off the steel axe head. He was familiar with the Hittites' tools, as their expertise at producing such weapons was well known. Oedimus had always admired their unmatched skills and artistry. Yet, something about this broken handle and head wasn't right. *What is it that seems so odd?* A puzzled frown knitted his forehead. As he continued his inspection, rolling them over, he felt their smoothness. His scrutiny scoured their perfect form. There wasn't one blemish to mar their perfection... *That's it!* It suddenly hit him. *This is not a Hittite soldier's fighting tool!*

The weapons of the Hittites' army were much more ornate than this. The head was always inscribed with the individual's rank. Also, the handles were carved with Hittite deities; images that denoted the strength of the soldier such as the lion and bull in combat - the griffin - the tree of life. All Hittite weaponry was decorated with their power gods. Sometimes they even held carefully crafted prayers to honor the deities.

Oedimus continued to stare at the handle. Although well made and obviously of Hittite origin, the pieces were clean of any such carvings. This was not a soldier's weapon. It looked more like a common worker's tool.

A thoughtful frown covered his face as he retraced his steps back to his waiting men. Calphus looked at him questioningly, his eyes going from Oedimus' somber countenance to the objects in his hands.

Without a word Oedimus handed the two pieces to his friend.

Calphus took them, noting that the superior workmanship and shaping was indicative of the Anatolian skills.

"Do you find anything unusual about this weaponry?" Oedimus' questioning nudge caused Calphus to look closer. They appeared to be an ordinary axe and handle. He looked in puzzlement at the other man. "Are they not the remains of a soldier's axe?"

His friend stared pointedly at the broken tool in Calphus' grip. "Look again. Did not the Hittites' king deny knowledge of this affair?" He paused, meaningfully, "did he not declare that his soldiers were not the attackers? "

As Oedimus had done earlier Calphus turned them over, curiously scrutinizing the pieces. A dawning light began to creep over his face. "This is not the weapon of a Hittite soldier!"

Oedimus' face showed triumph and giving a satisfied nod he declared, "King Mussilli spoke the truth, which leaves even bigger questions. Who was it that murdered our caravan drivers if not his soldiers? And, of more importance- why?"

The two men stood looking at each other. The same thoughts whirled around in both their heads. There was more to this than the obvious marauding of a caravan.

His soldiers scoured the rest of the area but found nothing else of significance. Besides, the vultures were becoming restless. Intermittently they would swoop down and tear a piece of carcass from the camel then fly away screaming their victory.

"There is nothing more to be gained by searching this place." Oedimus was sick of the stench and becoming angrier by the minute at the senseless slaying of a camel and destruction of the cargo. "We must make haste to Beth Shean so I might talk with the boy that survived. He might be able to shed more light on this treachery." He gave the command for his men to move on as his brain tried to sort out the seemingly illogical act.

CHAPTER NINE

*H*e couldn't remember when he'd ever been so exhausted, yet sleep eluded him. Turning over onto his back, Oedimus propped his arms underneath his head. He lay staring up at the view through the wall opening high above his head. The storm had finally ended its mad flight over the land leaving behind a cloudless sky that was lit by every star in the heavens. Their brilliance danced into the room as if celebrating the soldiers' safe arrival. The display reminded him of the many nights that he and Meryhken had been together on similar star-studded nights.

Leaning over the side of the garrison's cot, he reached for the bag that lay on the floor. He felt the wooden box and pulled it out. Oedimus traced the letter of gemstones in the lid, as if he were caressing her face.

This was the first time since leaving Amarna that he'd allowed himself to dwell on Meryhken and the emptiness that he felt at being without her. He raised the lid and was met by the faint aroma of the familiar scents that she used, mixed with the musky smell of the faded flower.

Beth Shean's commander had handed him the papyrus wrapped parcel as they had sat relaxing after a satisfying meal. "This came for you this morning," Metenhab had explained.

Puzzled, Oedimus had unwrapped the covering and seeing the initialed box had quickly rewrapped it. Glancing up at Metenhab, he was relieved to see that the commander was too absorbed in reading his own communications to have noticed his guest's reaction. As soon as he'd been alone in his room he'd taken the gift out of it's wrapping and hungrily inhaled its scents.

Closing the lid, he slipped it back into his bag. He lay down again, thinking of the many times that they'd been together, whispering endearments to each other and planning their future. He groaned to himself, *what future?* Recalling the disastrous events following their last time together, his thoughts turned dour. *Is she all right?* Had Meteh informed the pharaoh of their relationship and if so, what had taken place?

Negative worrisome thoughts raced around inside Oedimus' scull. Taking the cushion from beneath his head he thumped it into a ball, rearranging it before replacing it. The cot felt hot and uncomfortable. He threw the covering off his body and turned over, away from the view of the sky. Determinedly closing his eyes against the starlight they abruptly came wide open again. His mind had returned to thoughts of the boy. *Hopefully he can supply me with a clue as to who these fiends are who dared to attack Egyptian property.*

They had arrived at the garrison so late that Medenhab had suggested waiting to see the boy until the morning. Oedimus had readily accepted his advice and had welcomed the evening of relaxation. But now he was having difficulty quieting his mind.

Earlier this evening, the commander had shared information with him that had confirmed his suspicions regarding the find at the caravan site. Apparently, the boy had been very near to death from dehydration when he'd been found. It had taken him time to recover. Just this day the commander had been able to talk with him briefly, and the bits and pieces that the boy had recalled were disturbing. When the attack had occurred, he'd been out of sight behind a sand dune and had the wits to hide under the cover of a blanket.

"He's still in a state of shock from his experience as he witnessed the slaughtering of his father," Medehab had commented with a grave shake of his head. "It sounds as if they were taken by complete surprise during the night. The boy was unable to determine how many there were, but says that they were soldiers and had many weapons." His expression was grim. "It was a terrible slaughter for the boy to witness." He gave a heavy sigh.

Oedimus shook his head in sympathy as he listened. "I have my doubts as to the murderers being Hittite soldiers." He told Medenhab about the axe and handle and the commander agreed with his conclusions.

"The boy couldn't understand the language that they spoke, except for some common Hittite words," said Medenhab, "but he says they roared with laughter at the screaming of their victims. He was terrified. Apparently it was all over within less time than he could tell, then they were gone."

Medenhab's face looked pained as he continued to relate the horror. "He stayed under the blanket, even though he heard the galloping of the horses fade away as he was too traumatized to come out of hiding. No doubt this shelter kept him from being scorched alive by the heat of the sun. Even so, he could not have lasted too much longer had my soldiers not found him. It was his good fortune that the sharp eyes of one of my men saw a foot sticking out of the covering."

Oedimus now lay thinking of Medenab's conversation, hoping that there was more that the boy could tell him. *Tomorrow I will find out.*

Exactly when he had fallen asleep he didn't know, but came instantly awake at the sound of several sharp raps on his door. For a few seconds he couldn't remember where he was. Sun streamed into the room and he stared blankly at the strange surrounding. Then, his brain finally cleared. "Enter."

A serving man carrying a bowl and a pitcher of water appeared, with drying clothes draped over an arm. The man crossed the room to a small table and laid down his burden before turning towards Oedimus.

Placing one hand across his heart the newcomer bowed, murmuring a salutation in a strange tongue. Returning the greeting in his own language, Oedimus took in the man's appearance. From his dress, he surmised that he was an Arab. He wore the long flowing robes of the desert people and a scarf covered his head that hung down the back to his shoulders. Although his raiment was of a plain, rough textured material it was held together around the waist by a bright red and black sash. His face was of a swarthy complexion. That is, what could be seen of his face as the blackest of curling beards joined sideburns that grew below his ears, hiding the lower half.

The man's beard reminded Oedimus of the bristling growth on his own jaws and he ran a hand across the stubble. "I feel that my face is in need of that hot water," he remarked, ruefully.

The Arab gave him a smile and answered in fluent Egyptian. "The water is very hot master and I am sure that along with your sharp razor you'll soon discover your face once again."

Oedimus chuckled. "What is your name, friend? Your humor is welcome after spending the last two days fighting weather sent from Hell."

"I am El Bet Ammon," the Arab answered. "My duties are usually dedicated to the commander but he felt that you would be in need of my assistance this morning and so, I am at your service." He finished this last statement with a slight bow and flourish of a hand. "Are there any other needs that you have master, with which I might be of help?"

Oedimus swung his legs over the side of the bed ready to make the most of the water before it cooled. "Thank you, El Bet Ammon. I do need to replace my clothing with clean garments. Could you see that my dirty clothes are cleaned?"

The man bowed his head again and answered with a wide smile, showing teeth that sparkled whitely against his dark hairy face. "Your clothing is already being taken care of master and here, there are clean garments for you," he gestured towards a wooden bench that lined one wall of the room.

Still feeling sluggish, Oedimus hadn't noticed that the bench was no longer as empty as it had been the night previously. It held neatly folded clothing. In surprise, he wondered how the man had managed to enter the room to leave them without having disturbed his sleep?

As if reading his thoughts, El Bet Ammon explained, "I knocked on your door over an hour ago, and as there was no response I took the liberty of entering. The commander instructed me to make sure that everything was all right, you understand?" Oedimus nodded. "You were sleeping so peacefully that I did not wish to disturb you," the servant explained. "When I reported back to Medenhab, he told me to allow you to sleep a while longer as your journey through the storm had been so exacting."

As the Arab talked, Oedimus had arisen and procured his razor from his leather pouch that he'd left on the washstand. He began the ritual of shavings, flinching as he slapped a stingingly hot wet cloth onto his face. Needless to say the effect was to get rid of the last remnants of sleep from his head. El Bet Ammon stood watching the ministrations then handed him a fresh cloth to wipe his smoothly shaven skin.

Donning the clean garments, Oedimus continued to talk to the friendly manservant. "You are right about the extent of my tiredness. Fighting through that storm was a grueling experience. I give thanks to our great god, the almighty Aten, for having kept us safe during our passage" He continued in the same vein as he fastened his knife belt around his waist, "even though his light didn't penetrate the desert madness, his great goodness still shone upon ourselves and I felt his protective presence."

"Even my strongest brothers would not venture into such weather as you experienced, master." Underneath the Arab's subservient tone, there was a faint note of criticism, "the desert is very treacherous during such storms and a man can become lost very easily." El Bet Ammon was walking towards the door as he continued talking. "I have no doubt that our great and magnificent Allah who is well aware of our fickle deserts, also watched over your journey." At the door he turned and looked at Oedimus, "therefore, you and your comrades were doubly fortunate to be protected by not one, but two glorious and watchful gods."

Oedimus had an uncomfortable feeling that the man was subtly reminding him that the Arab's god was equally as powerful as Egypt's.

El Bet Ammon opened the door. "I will leave you to finish master, and then the commander asked that you join him in breaking bread before you meet the survivor." He left the room as unobtrusively as he had entered, quietly closing the door behind him.

The boy's face was ashen but the serving woman attending him was motherly and gentle. She was feeding him from a dish of steaming rice and goat milk. Propped up against cushions in his cot, Oedimus saw that in spite of his frail appearance he was wolfing down the food as fast as the woman could bring it to his mouth.

The Chief Guard smiled encouragingly as he approached the bedside, yet he noticed that the child was staring in fright at his waistband. Looking down, he realized that the boy's wide-eyed gaze was directed at the hilt of his dagger, protruding from its scabbard. Removing it, he slowly placed it on a table. "Have no fear young man. I am your friend not an enemy." To put the boy at ease, he spoke in the common dialect of the working-class people of Amarna. The boy's steady gaze moved from the knife on the table to the man's kind face and his small body visibly relaxed.

"I have been sent by our illustrious pharaoh to see that all is well with you" said Oedimus as way of explanation. In a friendly manner he made himself comfortable, sitting on the stool that the woman had vacated. "Our Lord Akhenaton is most concerned for your welfare and has sent prayers of thanks to Aten, for having saved you from certain death."

The boy visibly shuddered at the terrible memories still fresh in his mind. "I too have given many prayers of gratitude for my safety, master."

Oedimus gently prodded. "I need to learn as much as I can of these murdering dogs from the Underworld. My soldiers need to capture and deal with them so that they'll not harm anyone else." In the same reassuring tone, he pursued. "Can you tell me what happened?"

Silence lay heavy over the room. Oedimus saw emotions playing over the young face as the boy tried to focus on the fearful event.

"Take your time." Oedimus voiced his patience. He knew that the boy couldn't be rushed.

Haltingly, the youth began to recount his ordeal. It was much the same as Oedimus had already heard, but hearing it first hand made it all the more horrifying. The caravan had been taken by surprise while the drivers slept.

At the sound of the commotion, his father and he awakened. Startled, they leapt to their feet and ran from their tent, only to be confronted by a ghastly scene.

The blaze from the burning campfire showed several horsemen wielding deadly weapons at the drivers. One of them was cut down as he exited his tent. The body lay with the partially severed head hanging at a grotesque angle.

"My father grabbed me and hurled me out of the light of the fire, so that I was hidden in the shadows." Choking on his words, the boy relived the horrendous events.

Even now, he could still hear the screams of the men and a camel's bellows of agony as it got in the way of an attacker's weapon. It was meant to penetrate a driver who was making an effort to escape on its back, but had entered the animal instead. The camel's knees buckled, shedding its rider and rolling to its side, flailing in an agony of death. The rider was sliced down before he could arise. Time and time again, the murderers swung axes at limbs and thrust swords into flesh. One murderer turned on a camel driver, severing an artery in his neck. Blood gushed like a fountain from the wound. In utter terror, the boy watched from his hiding place behind a dune, unable to move.

"One of those Hittite devils slit my father's throat." He hastily wiped his running nose with the back of his hand as tears trickled down his cheeks. The boy's emotions were pathetic to see.

Oedimus hated having to make him relive the tragic events. *But he is the only witness left alive to tell what happened.*

Waiting for him to regain his composure, Oedimus turned to the woman who still hovered by the bed. "Bring him warmed wine," he ordered quietly. "He has had enough food and needs stronger sustenance." The woman left to do as she was bid.

Giving a trembling sigh, the survivor sank back into the cushions. In short order the servant returned and handed the goblet of wine to the Chief Guard. A pungent steam arose from it and the boy straightened up as Oedimus held the spiced wine towards him. With trembling hands the boy hugged the goblet as if for support as he took a long swallow of the liquid.

Taking one of the small hands in a firm grip, Oedimus squeezed it reassuringly. Once he saw color return to the patient's cheeks, he continued with his questions. "Did you get a good look at the soldier's?"

"I clearly saw the one that killed my father as he was the closest," the answer came haltingly. "He was a big man and had a cruel, bearded face. His eyes were those of a monster."

With his next words his voice shook in anger, "he laughed loudly when he slit my father's throat! I wanted to run out of hiding and kill him with his own knife!" The boy's chin sank into his chest and in a voice laced with shame confessed, "but I was too afraid to move."

Oedimus continued to hold on to his hand firmly. "Do not feel shame, my boy. You could not have saved your father and would have met the same fate, had he not hidden you. It is Aten's will that you live to take care of your mother and siblings. This, your father realized and wanted your life to be saved. You are now the head of your household. You must not forget that."

Gaining strength from the encouraging words, the boy's tear-filled face took on an expression of determination. "I want to be a soldier like you, when I become a man. I will not be a murderer like those Hittites!" The simple declaration born of tragedy was impressive.

"Tell me. What did this soldier wear? Did you recognize the soldier's helmet as being of the Hittites?" The boy nodded his head.

"What did his breastplate look like?"

The innocent eyes looked questioningly into his.

"You know what I mean," Oedimus urged. "Was it the same breast armor that our Egyptian soldiers wear when they go in to battle, except with different markings? Were you able to see any particular design on it? Was it designed like our Egyptian soldiers' and made of a strong metal, or was it different?

"He did not wear a breastplate, master. He only wore his helmet."

Oedimus caught his breath.

The boy continued. "I remember seeing the Hittite soldiers

when some of them accompanied the Hittites' ambassador on his visit to our city last year. And, I also remember the heavy breastplates that they wore."

He is sharper than I realized. Oedimus' flesh tingled.

"Remember when they came to visit our pharaoh?" The boy asked.

Oedimus nodded, listening closely. He well remembered the Hittites' ambassador arriving to discuss the details of the planned marriage.

"The murderers' helmets were exactly the same. I remember well," the youth affirmed, "but that was the only armor they wore."

"Are you sure of this?"

"Very sure master. I remember because the one who killed my father was sweating a lot. That is how I know he did not wear armor. His bare chest was covered with ugly black hair and it was soaking with sweat." The boy made a grimacing face. "It glistened in the camp fire's light and he looked like a wild boar. But he smelled like camel dung!"

In spite of the seriousness of the disclosure, Oedimus couldn't help but smile at the description, but his brain was busy digesting this piece of information. *No soldier would go into a fight without his breastplate.*

Combined with the unadorned axe and handle he had found and the boy's account, his suspicions were confirmed. These murdering Hittites were not from King Mussilli's army. Whoever these demigods were, they were not Hittite soldiers. *But, who are they and, why did they try to disguise themselves as soldiers?* Oedimus' mind whirled.

What had happened as a result of this attack? It has caused the marriage between the two royal houses to be postponed. That was a major catastrophe to the peaceful relationship between Anatolia and his country. Even more significant was the fact that the deaths of the caravan's drivers had rekindled the unrest in the people of Amarna. Murmurs of dissatisfaction had spread throughout the streets only hours after the tragic news had arrived and was already seeping further into other cities. People were whispering fearfully that the old gods were angry and seeking retribution. Conclusion? For whatever reason, somebody - or some people in the Hittites' camp didn't want this marriage to take place. Also, it seemed that these same forces wished to undermine Egypt's strength by causing its people to look upon their pharaoh with dissatisfaction.

Oedimus didn't have all the answers, yet, but it was obvious that this had taken careful planning. *I must get word back to Akhenaton.* He would have to inform Mussilli of this development, so that the Hittites could investigate the problem within their own domain.

Standing up, he saluted the boy as if he were saluting one of his soldiers. "Thank you, young man. When you are older you must come to see me and I will gladly recruit you for Egypt's army."

For the first time since Oedimus had entered the room, a smile came to the young victim's face. With a look of pride he returned the salute, imitating the Egyptian soldier to perfection.

CHAPTER TEN

*A*khenaton looked up from the report he was reading. His face registered a mixture of surprise and irritation at the girl's query. The pharaoh wasn't used to having his womenfolk ask questions concerning Egyptian affairs of state. On the contrary, they were discouraged from speaking of anything but that which met their role as women of his household.

Even Meryhken, whom he indulged as much as one of his legitimate daughters, usually would not take such liberties. Of what relevance to her was this communication from his Chief Guard? "Why are you so interested in this unfortunate event, daughter? It should not be of any concern to you."

"Please excuse my boldness most gracious lord. I did not mean any disrespect towards my most exulted father. Yet I am always concerned for your peace of mind and your brooding countenance causes me to worry for your welfare." Meryhken hurriedly continued to explain herself, before her parent could object. "I know how hard you work to keep our country and its people free from trouble." She chose her next words carefully, "it is just that on my way to see you, I heard that a messenger had brought you news from Beth Shean and my lack of propriety is due to your seeming preoccupation." Meryhken bowed her head low in deference. "Please forgive me, oh Great One."

In an attempt to cover her rashness by questioning him, she deliberately made her tone submissive, "your usual composure seems to have been disturbed, my lord, and this troubles my heart. My mortification for not remembering my place in your presence is overwhelming."

She paused and lowered her head even further in a manner of supplication. "I forget myself, Master. My only excuse is that it hurts me to see your concern." Meryhken continued in the same vein, "although I am very young and but a lowly female, I realize that Egypt depends on its most glorious pharaoh's ultimate wisdom to keep it strong and powerful. When you are troubled my own heart is troubled."

She lifted her eyes and saw his features starting to relax. Meryhken exhaled in relief.

A satisfied smile replaced the frown and taking one of her slim hands, Akhenaton patted it gently. "You are maturing faster than I had realized, Meryhken. Your interest in my welfare and that of our country pleases me. Nevertheless, you have no need to think on such matters," he said condescendingly. After a contemplative pause, he seemingly changed his mind and decided to enlighten the girl.

Although Akhenaton wouldn't admit it, her words had flattered his ego. Even though she was only a female her intelligence reminded him of his own youthful questioning of his father. Whenever Meryhken was in his presence, Akhenaton became conscious of the child's similarity to himself and his pride in her expanded, even though she wasn't a son.

Moving closer, he placed a benevolent hand on her shoulder and lifted the girl's chin to look into her face. "So be it. Since you have expressed such a desire for my peaceful state of mind, I will reassure you and tell you that the news is good. The messenger brought word that our troops are returning to Amarna."

Meryhken had to force herself not to jump for joy!

"My Chief Guard has found that the king of Anatolia has spoken the truth. The caravan was not attacked by King Mussilli's soldiers, but seemingly by unknown insurgents from Anatolia."

He continued as if thinking aloud, "I must notify Mussilli of this and let him know that the sanctity of marriage between our kin, will go forth. Our empires will be joined as ordained by Aten." Once more he perused the message "however, it seems to me that Mussilli has traitors in his midst and must be made aware of this."

With an affectionate motion he stroked Meryhken's hair, "your concern for my peace of mind is comforting to me, child. Regardless, this unfortunate incident with our caravan must be forgotten and forgiven. The problem is Anatolia's and does not concern Egypt. I feel confident that King Mussilli will handle it as he sees fit."

Bringing the discussion to an end, he held a hand towards her so that she could pay homage before leaving. His parting words were a gentle chastisement. "Your thoughts should be of girlish pleasures and the tranquility that the harem brings you, daughter, not on thoughts of state affairs."

She bent to kiss the extended hand, keeping her head bowed to hide the frustration that she felt. *How can I possibly feel tranquil when he's away from me? My pleasures are with Oedimus.* Even so, Meryhken realized her impulsive questioning had been a mistake. In the future if the gods ordained for Oedimus to be away from Amarna, she would have to be more careful in acquiring assuredness of his safety.

Meryhken was fortunate that she knew her father's personality so well and could respond appropriately. *At least, he is coming home!* Leaving the palace her spirit sang in spite of the difficulties with her mother. *We will find a way to be together. Surely now that he has done his pharaoh's bidding the gods will look kindly upon us and assist us in our need?*

In the hallway she saw Akhenaton's priest hurrying towards the royal quarters. His manner was preoccupied as he gave Meryhken a perfunctory nod in passing. He looked upset. For a brief moment she wondered as to what had disturbed the king's spiritual advisor, then mentally shrugged as she dismissed the holy man from her mind. Her thoughts were too wrapped up in the pleasure of seeing her love again.

CHAPTER ELEVEN

*L*ike a deep-rooted tree, the soldier's muscular legs were planted slightly apart with the feet firmly grounded. A thick sinewy neck supported very broad shoulders and the features were definitely Egyptian, with high cheekbones and slanting dark eyes. The broad face was expressionless as he listened to the priest.

Hytoph had long since learned that Nekute not only had the warrior's ingrained methodical thinking, but he also knew that behind that bland face was a sharp mind.

He'd done well in recruiting him. Mindfully he listened as the soldier relayed the news he brought concerning Anatolia. It was much as he'd suspected. The pomp and circumstance taking place within Mussilli's palace, was much the same as it was here.

According to Casstus, the marriage arrangements were well under way and in spite of the Hittite ambassador's stalling manipulations, all was going well - too well. The young prince was being closely watched and his physician was constantly at his side. His behavior was acceptable and the hopes of those close to him were high, except for Casstus. This dignitary knew that it was only a matter of time before he would succumb to one of his fits, then one could imagine the effect this would have on his marriage! Casstus was desperately looking to the priest to thwart the plans, once and for all.

Hytoph thoughtfully stroked his chin as he reread the message that Nckute had handed to him. *I must be more careful this time and depend on no one but myself. Nothing must go wrong.* He squirmed uncomfortably at thoughts of the caravan fiasco.

Leaving so much of the planning to Casstus had been a mistake. The priest had hardly dared to breath for days until he'd received word that the marauders had reached the safety of the Anatolian underground. Hytoph refused to think of what could have happened, should any one of them have been captured. Hytoph laid a hand on Nekute's shoulder in a comradely fashion. He trusted this man's abilities.

The priest had been very careful in his search for the right person. Keeping his ears and eyes open to the gossip of the palace, he'd listened to the whisperings of dissatisfaction that filtered into the compound from the streets of the city. Of course, his role as a confessional advisor had also helped. This, along with his innate ability to 'hear' what people did not say, had stood him in good stead when he'd sought a suitable accomplice. Body language sometimes was more revealing than words.

The priest had long since realized that in his spiritual zeal, Akhenaton was oblivious to the fact that not all of his people were happy with his new religion. The pharaoh's misguided faith in Aten Ra's power alone would be his undoing.

Observing Nekute's quiet demeanor, Hytoph felt pleased with his own astuteness in judging character. Over a period of time, he had scrutinized him most carefully and his patience had paid off.

Even though the soldier had hidden his discontent very well, the holy man's shrewd perception had picked up on telltale signs. As it was, under Hytoph's clever probing the man had soon revealed his displeasure with the pharaoh's radical beliefs.

Through conversations with him Hytoph had been pleasantly surprised to learn that there were more dissenters among Egypt's army than he'd realized.

Nekute's eyes were full of trust as he listened to the priest's orders. "Once we have rid ourselves of this farcical union and the pharaoh is left vulnerable to his peoples' growing discord, he will naturally turn to me for advice," said Hytoph. "The people will see his misfortunes as omens from the gods." He began to warm to his subject, "then I alone will be in a position to remind him of our great and almighty Amun's displeasure at having being ignored for so long a time. Akenaton will gladly come to see the drastic error he has made." He lifted his arms in exultation as he continued in the same vein, "in his blind worship of non other than Aten Ra, our pharaoh has incurred the wrath of Amun and all our glorious Egyptian deities."

Now he was really feeling his own importance. "Our almighty and glorious pharaoh must be brought back to the gods of his forefathers." Grabbing his apt listener by an arm, his enraptured voice continued. "You and I friend, with the help of the Hittites, will save his soul! We will once again be able to openly enjoy the luxury of Amun's blessings along with the benevolence of all of Egypt's gods." The cadence of his voice resounded against the walls of the room as it rose and fell with emotion. "Every temple in every city will resonate with the glory of Egypt and bask in the powers of our great and Almighty gods!"

Hytoph's fervor was contagious and Nekute beamed with pride that he could serve such a man as this! A holy man was as close to the gods as any human could be, and this personage was Akhenaton's own High Priest, no less. To have been chosen as helpmate by such a man was indeed an honor. He bowed awkwardly and taking the hand that held his arm, kissed it in adulation.

Acknowledging the gesture as his due, Hytoph dismissed Nekute with a benedictory prayer, followed by his own flattering words. "You have served Egypt well and your loyalty will not go unrewarded." He continued, emphasizing his next words carefully. "This time, I alone will set forth all the plans for saving Egypt's glory. We will pray to our gods that our superior strength and proficient Egyptian skills will succeed. Let it be known to the ambassador that I will send prayers to his god Sotheh for guidance, as well as our own mighty lord of Egypt, Amun."

Activity in Amarna had intensified. As people went about their daily tasks they talked excitedly of the marriage and how it would affect the power of Egypt.

Within the palace, seamstresses and handmaidens worked industriously with the finest silks and threads, creating gowns embroidered with exquisite jewelry to adorn the princess and her retinue. Workers were checking and re-checking the royal barge for any needed repairs, while craftsmen worked on a special palanquin to carry her royal highness from the Nile, across the desert to the land of the Hittites.

Since the incident with the caravan Mussilli had increased his vigilance around the borders of Anatolia, ordering searches of any activity that appeared to be suspicious - brooking no mercy when he found any Hittite who showed signs of dissension.

Unfortunately the renegades who had attacked the caravan couldn't be found, but Akhenaton was satisfied that Mussilli was innocent of the plot and the pharaoh brushed away any lingering concerns from his mind. Gratified that the defection was within Anatolia, he relegated it to being the Hittite king's problem to solve.

Akhenaton was fully aware that Mussilli wanted this marriage to take place as much as himself. The Hittites' ruler knew that it was in his country's best interests to cement this relationship with Egypt. Didn't they need access to Egypt's bountiful gold and ivory supplies, as well as their precious frankincense, myrrh and such? Trading was a necessity. But even more important,

Mussilli knew that being under the powerful protection of Egypt was even a bigger necessity.

As for Egypt, this union would re-enforce their dominance in the world, beyond question. And most satisfying, the peace-loving pharaoh would not have to resort to war to keep that power. The Hittites had much to offer Egypt in the way of needed metals and their horse breeding was of the finest. Trade would be solidified and at the same time Egypt's trading routes would be doubly protected.

At last, everything was going smoothly. An atmosphere of festivity prevailed among Amarna's inhabitants that infectiously spread like a tidal wave to the cities beyond. Even those who resented the new religion couldn't help but get caught up in all the gaiety. Dissatisfactions were temporarily pushed to one side and even the cities of Thebes and Karnack were in a lighter mood. All of Egypt was enjoying a holiday atmosphere.

They sat in the shadows, each within their own thoughts. She grasped his hand tightly as if needing reassurance that he was actually beside her. It was becoming so much harder to meet. This was the first time since his return that they'd been able to be alone together. Since learning of their 'affair' (Meteh's scathing word for their relationship) - her mother was watching her more closely.

She had persuaded Akhenaton that Meryhken needed the stability of a suitable marriage. Her words, along with the wedding of his legitimate offspring had made him conscious of the fact that Meryhken was no longer a child and needed to be taken care of appropriately. Not so subtly, Meteh had started to present suitable men to her daughter and was becoming increasingly annoyed at the girl's lack of response.

Oedimus squeezed the delicate hand that lay in his own. "I know that Akhenaton is pleased with my service and is depending more and more on my judgment," his tone was full of confidence as he talked, "and given time, I'm sure that he will not be averse to our wedlock."

She shook her head in doubt, thinking of Meteh's dogged persistence. "Even should he feel you worthy my love, Meteh does not. She still has influence with him and is still searching for an appropriate match for me, a match that will have the approval of our king."

Drawing her closer, he lifted her chin, "look at me, Meryhken." Oedimus' tone matched his solemn expression. "I will not allow any man to take away my rightful place beside you. I plan to become so invaluable to our pharaoh that Meteh will have no choice but to look upon me as a suitable husband for you."

Hearing the spark of determination and noting the stubborn set of his jaw, she felt secure. She drew closer to feel the strength of his body and Oedimus held her as if he'd never let her go. But although his words were reassuring and Meryhken trusted him completely, deep inside her being was an unease that couldn't be denied.

CHAPTER TWELVE

egotiations were finally complete. All the niggling but important wedding details had been worked out. Now, the caravan that was to take the marriage dowry to the Hittites' capital of Hattushash was ready to leave. More gold and ivory than Egypt had ever dispatched before weighted down the caravan, so that extra camels were being taken along as reserves. Exquisite jewels and exotic silks were among the bounty. Even the harem girls had joined in the making of colorful baubles and spinning of fine threads to make into gowns for the bride's adornment.

Meryhken was so sick of listening to the constant gibble-gabble and childish giggling that she had begun to dread having to enter the common room. "What do you think he looks like? … Do you think she is nervous? … The princess is pretty - but will she please him?".… On and on it went. The harem sounded as if a herd of squawking geese had inhabited it! All the jabbering only emphasized Meryhken's own problems.

For weeks, communiqués had gone back and forth between the Egyptian pharaoh and the Anatolian king, as to what was a suitable amount that the princess should bring to the marriage table. Akhenaton had been more than generous and Mussilli was well satisfied.

Every precaution had been taken to ensure the caravan's safe delivery. Besides the usual company of rear guards and Officers of State, Akhenaton had ordered that a dozen of his best, hand-picked soldiers were to also escort the caravan, for prudence' sake. Oedimus had personally selected the men according to their length of service and expertise.

Although Oedimus knew little of his men's personal lives, he did know that they were twelve of his finest warriors and the soldier to be in charge was known to have the strength of a bull.

After replenishing themselves at the garrison, the caravan planned to make their last stop at Damascus. The route had been well planned and the safety instructions strongly emphasized.

Mussilli had promised to send some of his own men to meet them in Damascus and help to escort the caravan for the remainder of its journey. It was but a short distance from Damascus through the mountain pass to Anatolia. Every precaution was taken for the safe arrival of the caravan's cargo.

Beth Shean's commander met them at the gates to personally oversee their stay. Giving the orders for the cargo to be secured within the inner courtyard, in plain view of the soldiers' billets, he cordially invited the drivers to share a meal and cots in his servants' building. His own soldiers were ordered to guard the caravan while the rest of the travelers were led to the dining quarters, where the tantalizing aroma of food met them.

In Damascus they were welcomed in much the same way by the governor, Apophi. Well known for his extravagant tastes, the governor's hospitality was no less expansive than his person. His booming and eloquent speech bidding the caravan, "welcome citizens of Amarna, our almighty Akhenaton's own, blessed city," was echoed in much the same fashion when the Hittites entourage arrived, shortly thereafter.

After a few days of replenishments and rest, the caravan was on its way with its gifts for King Mussilli. A messenger was dispatched from Damascus to Akhenaton, stating that all was well. The journey had been uneventful and smoothly completed. No problems were expected now that they had double the amount of protection with the Hittite personnel. Hattusash was but a short distance through the mountain passes.

Arriving at the palace, the caravan was unloaded and its Egyptian entourage feeling relieved that they had delivered the cargo without mishap, left to return home.

A commotion outside his doors rudely broke through the pharaoh's meditation. Loud voices penetrated into his private salon and before he could summon his servant to investigate the cause, the doors were abruptly flung wide open. A harried looking messenger rushed in with a guard at his heels.

Breaking free of the guard's restraining arm, the man rushed to Akhenaton and threw himself at the feet of the bemused king. "My Lord and Master, on the threat of death I have been ordered to hand this missive to you alone, and no other." With an imploring gesture he thrust a scroll into Akhenaton's hands, just as the guard was about to strike him with his sword. The pharaoh gave a slight shake of his head and the sword was reluctantly lowered. "You may leave," he informed the guard. "This man is too frightened to be a threat." The guard retreated but left the door slightly ajar in case he was needed.

Unrolling the heavy scroll, Akhenaton began to digest its contents. The frown on his face deepened with each word that he read. His cheeks slowly turned a deep rosy hue. His generous lips compressed to a mere slash. Anger exploded as he came to the end of the letter and a sound like the wrath of gods erupted from him.

"GO!" Flinging the scroll to the floor, he ordered the frightened messenger to arise and leave.

The man didn't need any second bidding as he scrambled to his feet but stopped in his tracks as his pharaoh's voice roared again. "STOP!" The poor man quaked. "You will stay close by and alert in order to take a reply to this – this – devil of a so called king!" Akhenaton was striding back and forth in fury. Flinging an arm wide, he once again addressed the terrified man, "now you may leave." The messenger fled the room heaving sighs of relief; thanking the gods for protecting him from certain death.

Fury engulfed Akhenaton. He turned his attention back to the missive, his brain unable to believe what his eyes were reading.

He yelled for his servant who scurried into the room and stood at a safe distance. "Send for my Chief Guard." Before the hapless man could leave to do his bidding, another command came. "WAIT!"

The man stopped.

"I also wish to consult with my priest."

He sank into his official chair to await the two men but abruptly arose again, too upset to follow the protocol of receiving subjects while seated.

Hytoph was the first to arrive and found the pharaoh striding back and forth in a state of agitation. The priest said nothing, eyeing his king with bland curiosity.

"Read this." Retrieving the scroll from the floor, the pharaoh unceremoniously handed it to the priest, yet before Hytoph could read its contents the door opened to admit the Chief Guard. Immediately, Oedimus felt the loaded atmosphere in the room.

Akhenaton's anger couldn't be contained. "What manner of person is this ruler of Anatolia?" he stormed. "He has addressed me in such a way as to accuse me of underhanded deceit! I, the ruler of all Egypt!"

Oedimus stared, mystified. The pharaoh pointed to the scroll that Hytoph was now carefully reading. "This outrageous missive has just arrived from him. His words to me are so blasphemous that it is hard to discern exactly what has happened." He started to pace again, his body trembling with agitation. "But, the message is very clear," once more he stopped and pointed a shaking finger at the scroll. "He is accusing me of dishonesty by not sending him the promised amount of gold and ivory! He claims that half of it is missing."

His voice continued to raise several octaves with every word he uttered. "This Hittite scorpion of a king is demanding that I, blessed of Aten, give him an explanation!" Veins bulged on Akhenaton's forehead and his eyes blazed fire. "How DARE he question my integrity and honor? Does he not realize whom he is accusing?" His feet resounded on the floor as he stomped back and forth. "Did I not give him MORE than he asked for? These words written by him are diabolically TREACHEROUS!"

His two companions watched in shocked silence as their enraged pharaoh gave vent to his feelings, his angry words mixed with confusion. Once again he turned to his Chief Guard who still looked perplexed. "Did you not personally oversee the loading of the caravan?"

Oedimus nodded, "most emphatically my lord pharaoh. Everything was checked by myself personally not once, but twice and my soldiers had strict orders to watch the cargo closely and not to rest, except for the designated stops at Beth Shean and Damascus." He reminded Akhenaton of the message received from Damascus, "as you know most illustrious one, you personally showed me the message received stating that the caravan was on its way to Anatolia without mishap."

Without a word, the priest handed the scroll to Oedimus. Incredulity crept over him as he read the missive.

Akhenaton stopped his pacing and rubbed his head in a gesture of befuddlement. He turned to his priest. "What do you make of this strange event, Hytoph?"

The priest was slow to answer, choosing his words carefully. "Most adored pharaoh, I believe that you should demand an apology from this Hittite king. Inform him that this marriage will not be taking place until he does so. Mussilli has blasphemed not only against your personal integrity but in dishonoring you, he has dishonored Egypt's benevolent and almighty Aten."

The priest paused before proceeding, choosing his words delicately. "May I suggest that it might be fortuitous to pray to Aten for guidance and, if I might venture a further suggestion, possibly ask our most sacred and powerful Sun God if it would please him to communicate with Egypt's former gods." Before Akhenaton had time to react he hastily continued, "so that Egypt may have benefit of Aten's almighty wisdom, supported by all the power possible? Maybe the former gods of your most revered father, from whom you inherited such wondrous insight, will help to enhance our one and only sun-god and assist in this delicate matter."

The silence was deadly.

Hytoph hurriedly continued, "with the blessings of our almighty Aten-Ra giving permission for the gods of your forefathers to join with his power, surely Egypt will rejoice in such protection?" He bowed his head. "Of course, we must have Aten's unquestionable consent and guidance." Hytoph held his breath.

Akenhaton's eyes had narrowed to black slivers as he listened to his priest.

Hytoph opened his mouth to say something else but Oedimus threw him a warning glance and quickly interceded. "Reacting with more anger towards Mussilli will only exacerbate the seriousness of this problem. It would be wiser to investigate this matter further; find out exactly what has taken place before making any impulsive decisions of an adverse nature."

Akhenaton looked as if he were ready to explode. But, he remained still as he took in Oedimus' calming words.

"There is no doubt that the Hittites are angry and thus, if all of the cargo did not arrive in Anatolia, they have reason to feel violated. There has to be an answer that we are not aware of yet." He turned his attention back to the simmering king, "with your permission most holy one, I will personally investigate this matter and find the truth. I'm sure you will also agree that it would certainly be wise to offer prayers for guidance," adding, "without question it will be to our one and only illustrious god, Aten-Ra."

Akhenaton's face still looked murderous, but he motioned for Oedimus to continue. The Chief Guard kept his voice calm and unemotional, "might I suggest that a ceremony and sacrificial homage to Aten be conducted in a public manner? I believe that as High Priest, Hytoph should conduct public prayers from the temple's balcony, led by you and the royal family." He now had the pharaoh's attention.

"Conducting a public display of piety would have a strengthening effect on the people. In this way, not only would the citizens of Amarna feel honored to share the prayers of their pharaoh, but it would encourage the populace to also offer sacrifices to our Sun God." Both men were listening and Oedimus saw that his words were having the desired affect on Akhenaton.

"Our granaries are full. It would be no hardship to the people to offer sacrifices of grains to please our beloved and all powerful Aten." Oedimus' logic couldn't be denied. "We could even offer a sacrificial lamb to show our earnest intentions." He was now warming to his subject, "this gesture of good faith would spread to the other cities of our country and may also be carried to Anatolia. When Mussilli hears of Egypt's solidarity he will be ill advised not to believe in our lord pharaoh's good-will. But first and most important, we must inform the Hittites of our willing intentions to recover the lost dowry."

The room was as still as the Sphinx. Warm sunbeams played over the floor, seemingly attempting to dispel the chill atmosphere.

The priest shifted from one foot to the other as Oedimus ended his diatribe.

Akhenaton slowly sank into his chair. After an eternity, he spoke. "You are right."

His companions visibly relaxed. "This grievous matter needs to be investigated. I do not owe this miserable Hittite king an apology. Before long he will be apologizing to me! As for a public prayer ceremony for the people, that is an excellent idea."

Directing his full attention to Hytoph he spoke slowly and softly. There was no mistaking his meaning. "Egypt has but one almighty god, and one pharaoh blessed by Aten's power. He and I are one! This you know, and this is all my people need." His black eyes pierced his priest.

"The all wise and all knowing Aten Ra needs no assistance from any other gods and neither do I. As a priest of my realm you should be fully aware of this. No more words of other gods will be spoken! He stopped to let his message sink in, before adding. "See that the prayer arrangements are taken care of."

Hytoph once again shifted his stance. Nodding his head in assent he started to open his mouth to try and salvage the damage he'd incurred, but changed his mind. Silence was in order, at least for the time being. He gave a low bow of obeisance.

Once more, Akhenaton turned his attention to Oedimus. "You will leave for Beth Shean and Damascus immediately. Retrace the steps that our caravan took and see what you may learn. This missing cargo must be found." With a wave of his hand he dismissed the two men. His expression was still grave but his anger had dissipated.

Oedimus bowed and the priest bent even lower. Hytoph kept his body doubled over as he backed out of the pharaoh's presence. His shaven head shone with an aura of deference, his arms crossed in a pious manner. Needless to say, his thoughts were far from pious as he exited behind the Chief Guard.

Oedimus headed straight for his billet. He needed to think. Methodically he went over the serious implications of the letter. At the same time, his brain was organizing his plans. A sound strategy had to be implemented before making any move.

He hadn't risen to his present position by being impulsive and irrational. It wasn't in his nature. *Except when it comes to Meryhken.* The thought automatically flashed into his head and he gave an inward groan. Telling her the news of his departure was going to be very difficult.

Deliberately forcing himself to dismiss his personal problems, he mulled over the disastrous events. Apart from the Hittites obvious anger there was little pertinent information to be gleaned from the missive, except that Mussilli had not received the entire promised dowry. So how did it disappear? And, where did it go? That's what he needed to find out.

The Chief Guard went over the facts that he did know, but nothing out of the ordinary jumped out at him. It seemed impossible that the cargo could have been tampered with – but it had. This was not a random act of robbery. It had to have been well planned for it to take place without arousing any suspicion. *Did I not personally oversee the loading?* He'd even waited around until the lead camel driver and his assistants had left Amarna. He'd also handpicked the soldiers that were to escort them. *My men are unquestionably trustworthy.*

Too restless to sit any longer, he arose to stride around the room. His mind refused to believe the conceivability of someone stealing the cargo. His gut began to hurt from pent up fury. This act had affected his pride, as it had taken place underneath his nose and undermined his sense of infallibility.

Sitting down again he deliberately cleared his mind of the anger and bewilderment that Mussilli's words had created. The Hittites' king had every right to be angry. Yet, Akhenaton had been accused of dishonesty. That was of more concern to Oedimus.

Realizing that he needed to think rationally without allowing his emotions to interfere, he forced himself to calm down. Inhaling deeply, he slowly let out a breath. Once more he repeated the slow breathing that controlled his mind and body. The deliberate, calming technique began to have the desired affect. After a few minutes his pulse slowed and the tenseness drifted away. *Instead of worrying about things that I don't know- I must start with what I do know.*

He methodically retraced every step of the caravan's journey, from its departure from Amarna to its arrival in Hattushash. The only stops that they had made were Beth Shean and Damascus. These places were always well guarded by adequate soldiers from Akhenaton's army, as well as those that had accompanied the caravan. He had no reason to believe that they had stopped elsewhere.

The Egyptian trading routes were long and wearisome, having only certain stations whereby it were possible to stop and refresh camels and drivers. The princess' dowry was too valuable for the drivers to even consider making any unauthorized stop.

Beth Shean was their first major layover. The number of guards there made it impossible to tamper with the cargo. Oedimus eliminated the garrison as being the sight of the devilry. Damascus was their next destination where Mussilli's soldiers had joined the caravan. Even more trained men protected the cargo. Could it have been the Hittites that somehow, infiltrated the cargo? Not possible.

Oedimus shook his head in frustration. After the fiasco with the previous caravan, Mussilli had instigated too many rules and regulations to stop any further mishaps between his country and Egypt. It was very unlikely that any Hittites would dare risk such a venture. They would be too afraid of the consequences if they were caught. He was well aware of the Hittites predilection for unique torture techniques. A Hittite soldier who was found to be disloyal would be blinded, deafened or even castrated and turned into a woman! Just the thought of such a thing made him flinch. *No matter,* he thought wearily, the clever execution of this act had to have taken place somewhere, but where and by whom? As much as he hated to think so, the only logical conclusion was Amarna and their own people.

He arose and opened his door, inhaling fresh air. As if in sympathy, a cooling waft fanned his face that softened the energy of the sun's rays. The oxygen helped him to focus. After a few minutes, he closed his door and moved to pour himself some wine. Taking a swallow, he sat again to think anew.

Whoever had instigated this foul act had to have had help within the ranks of the caravan's crew. But for what good reason would the workers jeopardize their lives by incurring their pharaoh's wrath? *Greed.* That was the obvious answer. Camel drivers were not paid well, but would they be so stupid as to steal from the pharaoh? He shook his head in doubt as he took another slow sip of wine. Such a large amount of gold and ivory was too hard to get rid of without bringing attention to the thief, or thieves. *This was not an ordinary act of robbery.* His orderly mind categorized that which did make sense and that which didn't. *Someone in charge had to have money to be able to bribe the workers.* A clever plan had to have been devised in order to steal the cargo without arousing suspicion.

Sitting up straight, he finished off the wine. The scowl on his face started to clear. What he did know was that the lead caravan driver hadn't been in service for more than a year, having replaced old Narkheph who had passed from this life on earth. *Even so, Kuhteti is Narkeph's son by marriage.* He doubted that he was the culprit. He'd come with excellent credentials, having been one of the father-in-law's assistants since childhood. Oedimus rubbed his chin thoughtfully. *But I don't know anything about his assistants.*

Coming to a decision, he arose and left his billet. He walked purposefully to the soldiers' common area and found a young recruit. He told him to find Calphus and let him know that he was needed immediately.

The urgency of his message brought Calphus to his billets in less than fifteen minutes. Even so, he found Oedimus impatiently pacing his floor.

After listening to his friend's logic, Calphus agreed with the conclusions. Oedimus' theory that the robbery had to have taken place before the caravan left Amarna was the only plausible explanation.

"Go into the city and see if you can learn anything that might seem suspicious." Oedimus' tone was urgent. "Ask questions. Listen to the locals. Pay for information if necessary, but find out what you can, especially concerning the backgrounds of the camel driver's assistants. We may yet learn something from the vermin that inhabit Amarna's dens of iniquity." With feeling, he added, "be careful." His manner was somber. "Whoever is responsible for this, is very clever and will be dangerous once they find out that they are being tracked. These people would probably cut your throat before they've finished smiling at you"....

"Don't you see, my beloved? This will place me in a position where I may ask the pharaoh's indulgence. Once this task is successfully completed and the rift with Anatolia has been mended, Akhenaton will be in a frame of mind to grant me anything that I wish. The successful marriage of the princess will make his feelings so benevolent towards me that I'm sure he will grant me a holy betrothal to you."

Standing in front of the stone bench, Oedimus looked down at his love. He'd dreaded this meeting and having to tell her his news. Sitting down beside her, his arms wrapped around the girl, trying to bring her reassurance.

He could feel her body trembling. Gently, he kissed the top of her head that lay on his shoulder. "Your fears are unfounded, Meryhken. No harm will come to me. This journey is just an investigation, not a journey into battle." Oedimus was trying to make her see the possibilities that Akhenaton's dependence on him was creating. "I have no doubt that he will offer me any favor after I have averted this break with Anatolia."

"And what if you are unable to resolve this problem?" Raising her head she looked at him questioningly, "obviously some person, or persons were able to steal from the caravan, even though it was well guarded. Whoever these mercenaries are they will be desperate when they learn that you are tracking them, therefore you will be in danger. They will have nothing to lose if they can kill you, and everything to gain," her voice ended on a note of distress.

Oedimus said nothing, but gently rocked her back and forth as if she were a child. How could he tell her that apart from not being able to ignore his orders he didn't want to? Meryhken was but a woman, unable to understand the thinking of a soldier.

Didn't she realize that this was an opportunity to show the pharaoh how indispensable he was? There was no doubt in his mind that this would prove to be a favorable situation for them. *I intend to take her as my bride and the only way that I can see for this to happen, is to have Akhenaton look upon me as being worthy.*

Carefully holding her away from him, he looked into her face. "My love, you know I cannot disobey Akhenaton's orders. I am his Chief Guard and as such, must fulfill my duty to him. Once I have investigated this affair and cleared the way for this marriage to take place, my position will be firmly set. Not only will our king view me with dependency, but will also see me as a suitable husband for you. Trust me, Meryhken. This is a great opportunity and one that I cannot deny."

She remained silent. *What can I say?* Her thoughts were dismal. Mentally she shook her head. *This man of mine is to place himself in danger, in order for my father's legitimate daughter to marry.* Yet because of her station as a concubine's daughter they could not wed.

With an effort she straightened her back and took control over her emotions. Oedimus didn't need the added concern of worrying about her welfare. She attempted a smile and gently kissed him. "Take care, my heart. You have to do what you have to do. Perform this duty to our pharaoh and come back to me." The relieved expression on his face caused her heart to ache.

Meryhken couldn't explain the fear that lay deep within her being. It sat in the pit of her belly and refused to be stilled. The nagging fear lay as restless as the unseen bed of the Nile that shifted back and forth underneath its waters. She could no more change fate than she could change the flow of the life-giving river. The weight of her destiny felt as heavy as her heritage.

Oedimus sat idly watching the play of shadows that the flickering light of the sconces threw over his room. But his mind was far from idle. *Where is he?* Calphus had been gone all the afternoon and evening and still had not returned.

The soft rapping at the door brought him instantly upright. He hadn't meant to fall asleep, but he'd finally succumbed to exhaustion. It was well past midnight and on opening the door saw a shadowy outline, barely recognizable against the blackness beyond. Oedimus stepped back to allow his friend to enter the dimly lit room. Calphus' tight curly hair was plastered to his head with perspiration, and his normally neat person looked unkempt.

He had fallen asleep brooding over his friend's safety. "By all that is holy, I am glad to see you!" Impulsively, he grabbed his friend's body to his own.

Calphus grinned and returned the gesture, then abruptly stepped back. "Has your sense of smell deserted you?' He gave a ruthful laugh, "even I cannot stand my own stink!"

"Now that you mention it there does seem to be something putrid about you," Oedimus' rejoinder was met with a scowling, faint punch. The camaraderie between them relieved the tension. "No doubt you need this more than you need to bathe," said Oedimus as he handed him a goblet of wine. Calphus gratefully took the proffered drink and slumped into a chair.

Going around the room, Oedimus carefully closed the shutters to the wall openings. The act eliminated outside air from entering, but did allow more privacy. Even though it was late, he didn't want to take a chance of been seen, or overheard. Lighting another sconce he carried it to the table, noting in its glow that the man sitting across from him looked excited, in spite of his obvious tiredness. Oedimus guessed that his hours spent in Amarna's city center had produced something fruitful. It was hard to stay silent but he allowed Calphus to unwind before asking questions.

Calphus sat back in his seat, somewhat revived. "My venture into the inner city proved to be most satisfying," he said, pausing to drain the rest of his wine before continuing. "Our friend Kuhteti is not all that he seemed."

This piece of news didn't surprise Oedimus. The more he had thought over the unexplainable events, the more he'd become convinced that they had originated in Amarna. And, he'd soon realized that Kuhteti would have much more access to the caravan's cargo than his assistants. He listened as his friend went over his hours spent among the lower denizens of Amarna.

Calphus hadn't learned anything from the inhabitants of the marketplace. His casual questions, regarding the activities of the caravan's assistants, produced nothing of significance. They were all young boys, coming from simple family backgrounds except for one; a stranger recently arrived in Amarna from Upper Egypt. Calphus had meticulously questioned the local people about his background, but found nothing out of the ordinary. It was a wrong lead and a waste of time. The young man lived with a relative and, like the rest of the boys was making money to help support his family. Calphus was beginning to feel frustrated. Just when he was about to give up, his persistence paid off.

A scruffy looking beggar accosted him. Feeling hot and grimy from hours of wandering the crowded streets, he was about to curtly dismiss the creature when the man mentioned Kuhteti's wife. The seedy individual got Calphus' attention.

After handing over the expected payment, he'd followed the man out of the city's center towards a less populated lower class neighborhood. Staying alert and resting his hand lightly on the dagger at his waist, Calphus followed the beggar into a small narrow street that led away from the main thoroughfare.

Poor class dwellings lined either side with a few small shops mingling in between. The non-descript place looked much like all the other working class streets that surrounded the center of the town. Here, venders catered to the local inhabitants, selling their left over wares at bargain prices.

The vagrant led him to a mediocre store that sold women's cheap fripperies, run by a man who gave the stranger an ingratiating smile along with a calculated inspection. Obviously the shopkeeper thought he was a prospective customer looking to spend money, possibly a trinket or scarf for a mistress. The smile disappeared when the beggar enlightened him as to Calphus' reasons for being in his establishment. But, it quickly resurfaced when the stranger reached into his pouch and came out with a handful of coins. After being promised a generous payment he was eager to be of assistance.

Meanwhile the muckworm sidled toward the door. As if ready to leave now that he had performed his duty, he hesitated. The beggar stood pointedly staring at the pouch that was still in Calphus' grip.

Muttering an oath the vendor pushed him out the door, shutting it firmly behind him. Calphus suspected his reasoning for the rough dismissal. Should more money be forthcoming the storeowner didn't intend to share it!

Once the merchant had his visitor alone, he began to talk. It seemed that the locals had found something new to gossip about - Kuhteti's wife.

"For sometime, she's been spending extravagantly in the

merchant's store," said Calphus, "as well as other places." His tone was full of meaning as he addressed his friend.

Oedimus sat up. He refilled the empty goblet and the tired man paused to take a drink before continuing. "Not just the usual necessities either, but expensive items for women's adornment."

He leaned forward to emphasize his next words. "A fellow merchant had gloated about her having purchased costly bathing milk from his store, the special kind of goat's milk that is only affordable to women of the upper classes." He took another sip of wine and gave a derisive chuckle, "the old lecher relished sharing his confidences with me. He really believes that the driver's wife has taken a rich man as her lover. His comment was that she had more money than Kuhteti ever gave her. In fact, Kuhteti is apparently a notorious miser and his wife publicly complains that he's more tight fisted than a temple priest with the coffers." Calphus paused and leaned across the table towards Oedimus. He spoke slowly and distinctly. "Interestingly, her husband has yet to return home."

"Of what importance is this?" Oedimus looked perplexed. "Maybe the drivers have been delayed on their journey?"

Calphus sat back and smiled knowingly. "Because the rest of the drivers returned hours past."

The silence was pregnant.

Calphus continued. "They told his wife that Kuhteti had remained behind to 'take care of other business' and she should not be concerned as he would be returning later."

As Oedimus digested this bit of news he saw the enigma falling into place. "The drivers would have been escorted to Mussilli's palace and made sure that the delivery reached the royal residence." He was thinking aloud rather than addressing his companion. "After helping the soldiers to unload the cargo into the Hittites' care, Kuhteti and his assistants should have been free to return with the camels. Why would he have reason to be delayed?"

"Why indeed." Calphus wasn't finished, "that isn't the half of it. I paid the vendor to have his son take me to Kuhteti's home, to meet with his wife. She didn't want to talk with me until I told her that I had been sent expressly on our almighty pharaoh's orders. I 'tactfully' mentioned the fact that if her husband were involved in breaking the law, she also would be under suspicion, unless she co-operated. Reminding her that the pharaoh's wrath would come down on her head too if she were also responsible, was most helpful in gaining her cooperation."

Under Calphus' threats the frightened woman had talked. It seemed that for the past several weeks Kuhteti had welcomed an unexpected visitor in his home. Calphus hesitated in his story. He still had difficulty in digesting the last piece of information the woman had revealed. "The visitor was non other than our own comrade, Nekute."

The room seemed to tremble. Oedimus' face waxed pale in the flickering light.

"Is she certain that it was Nekute?"

His friend nodded emphatically. "She described him perfectly. Besides which, during one visit she heard her husband call him by name, whereupon Nekute sharply rebuked him. At this point, Kuhteti abruptly handed her a few coins and told her to leave. Later she questioned her husband but he cuffed her and told her to guard her tongue."

Oedimus' incredulity slowly turned to an impotent anger. He'd trusted Nekute implicitly. *My own man a traitor?* Didn't it make sense? *Of course it does!* His escorting soldiers had just as much access to the caravan as the camel drivers and were trained to be sharp and calculating. Even so, why would he want to rob the caravan? *Akhenaton pays his soldiers well so I doubt it was for money.* But, where did Nekute obtain enough money to pay off the camel driver? Even his pay would not be enough to cover a bribe. Oedimus' mind was racing. *The money had to have come from someone higher up who does have access to large amounts.* Someone in a higher position than his soldier had to have organized this. *When I find out who this traitor is, I will learn <u>why</u>.*

Calphus was still talking. "After that, whenever Nekute visited her husband would give her two or three girsh to spend and order her to leave. She told me that before he left with the caravan, he'd seemed uneasy. She'd asked her husband what was troubling him and Kuhteti had promised to explain everything she needed to know, on his return."

"She is very worried," said Calphus. "He never told her that he wouldn't be returning with the others. She is most frightened and begged me not reveal her secret to anyone. Of course, she suspects that her husband has done something dishonest."

Calphus' tone changed to astonishment. "Amazingly, the woman is more terrified of her husband's wrath than she is of the pharaoh's possible punishment, if he finds out that she has spoken of this!" He gave a sardonic laugh, "I won't repeat the name that she called Kuhteti but she's convinced that the only reason he keeps her alive is because he doesn't want the funeral expense. Naturally, she was so delighted by his unexpected generosity that she would always stay away from the house until she'd spent all the money he'd given her."

Oedimus stood abruptly, having come to a decision. "We must leave at daybreak for Beth Shean. I must see whether or not Kuhteti and Nekute have stopped at the garrison on their return journey. Although I suspect that we'll not find them there. Regardless,, they must be found and made to talk."

Seeing his friend's extreme fatigue, he allowed that he needed his bed. "Get some rest. You deserve it after all that you have accomplished this day. It is but a few hours to dawn and you need to say your farewells to your wife." Calphus arose.

Thinking his friend's wife, Oedimus automatically envisioned Meryhken and how much he would miss her, but he didn't have time to dwell on his personal feelings. "I need to glean what information I can from the garrison's soldiers, before their memories of what took place have faded." Calphus agreed and arose to leave. Oedimus clamped his friend's shoulder in an embrace of thanks as he left.

He stood in the doorway, watching as Calphus disappeared into the darkness. *I need to get some rest myself.* But the troubling memory of Merhyken's face automatically reappeared. He doubted that he would sleep well.

CHAPTER THIRTEEN

*T*he familiar stone structure loomed into view, only this time his mission was different. Also, Calphus was the only one accompanying him and as the weather stayed pleasant their journey hadn't taken long. It was as if nature sensed their urgency to reach Beth Shean quickly, and was co-operating.

Oedimus was eager to find out if the caravan driver had ever returned and if not, track him all the way to Anatolia if necessary. He also doubted that Nekute had made an appearance and intended to find this betrayer.

The first attack had appeared as if it were Mussilli's problem. Now, this latest upset had changed the picture. It had obviously been engineered in Egyptian territory and the blame lay at Egypt's feet. Oedimus meant to find out who was attempting to undermine Akhenaton's power.

The meal that he and Medenhab shared was satisfying; the wine being of the right temperature and well aged. Feeling refreshed, he was now ready to hear whatever information the commander could give him. Of course there was no news of either Kuhteti or Nekute.

Oedimus had deliberately asked that Calphus be allowed to spend the night with the garrison's soldiers, so that he could keep his ears and eyes open to anything that might sound suspicious. He sat back in the chair slowly sipping from the goblet, but his mind was sharply alert, listening while Medenhab began to talk.

"The camels and all the merchandise were in clear sight of the soldiers throughout the night," the commander declared emphatically. "I made certain that they were in a position to see and hear anything that might be unforeseen. The courtyard is so close to the billets that the slightest noise would have alerted them."

Medenhab reiterated what Oedimus already knew, but the commander's feelings of guilt were obvious. Oedimus felt that he was trying to somehow assuage his sense of being responsible for the theft.

"You took all the precautions necessary, Medenhab. Our pharaoh does not lay any blame at your feet. The treachery may have taken place in Damascus. As it is, in order to learn where the responsibility does lie, I need you to tell me every tiny detail. Even should it seem so small as to be insignificant."

In spite of the reassuring words his host's face remained troubled. "Something is bothering my conscience, although at the time I did not think the matter of any importance."

"What is it?" His guest fixed him with a steady gaze.

Medenhab hesitated, seemingly trying to make up his mind as to what he was about to disclose. "It may, or may not mean anything but it did perturb me when it happened." He shifted uncomfortably in his chair.

Oedimus sat up straight. He was certain that the commander was now reviewing a piece of information that he'd held back. "Speak! Let me be the judge as to its importance."

With some reluctance Medenhab continued, "after the caravan had left for Damascus, I learned from my officer in charge that your escorting soldiers had enjoyed much revelry the previous night." Hesitatingly he began to reveal his story. "It seems that their leader - he glanced enquiringly at his companion – did you say Nekute was his name?"

The Chief Guard nodded, listening.

"He allowed them to indulge in drinking excessively," Medenhab stated. "They were joined in their billets by a few of the women from the garrison's brothel and apparently were entertaining all night." The commander frowned and his face showed his disquiet.

The anger Oedimus felt towards Nekute sizzled anew and he was having a hard time controlling himself. "So. What happened?"

"It wasn't until the next morning after the caravan had left, that I learned of this revelry. I berated my officer Phut, and asked why he had not reported this to me when it was taking place, knowing that these escorts were supposed to be alert to their duties. Phut explained that he was about to notify me, but first voiced his concerns to the soldier in charge. He wished to assess the situation first before disturbing me unnecessarily."

"After conferring with Nekute, he felt that the man was acting on good faith and was reliable. Apparently your man was concerned for the men's welfare, as their journey had been exacting. They had been forced to stay awake day and night while traveling with the cargo. He told Phut that he felt they needed some relaxation from stress before continuing their journey."

As he related the incident the commander was becoming increasingly ill at ease. Giving Oedimus an anxious glance he continued, "and so, Nekute released the men from their duties." As if trying to reassure himself as well as Oedimus, he explained his officer's actions. "Your man assured Phut most sincerely that he planned to personally stay on watch all night in their stead. His plan was to sleep in his bedroll by the caravan. The camel driver and he would take alternate watches throughout the night."

Sagging into his chair, Medenhab bowed his head as if confessing his sins to a priest.

Oedimus said nothing.

Mednenhab looked up, his expression somber. "As it was Phut made it his business to see that this was indeed a fact. He personally watched that Nekute and the driver did remain with the caravan all evening and did not imbibe any liquor. He checked on them intermittently until the early hours of the morning, at which time the revelry had stopped and everyone was sleeping. So he left to get some sleep."

"At dawn, Phut checked on them once again. Nekute and the camel driver were walking the perimeters of the cargo. He expressed his admiration for the conscientious vigilance of the two men."

Medenhab was looking more upset by the minute, realizing the importance of this information in the light of what he now knew. "At the time I was annoyed at learning of this laxness. But as Phut is one of my finest men, I trusted his judgment and dismissed the incident from my mind." Spreading his hands in a helpless gesture, he tried to explain his rationale. "After all, when they left the next morning all appeared to be well."

Oedimus' mind was whirling as he digested the significance of this story. He ran his hands through his hair in frustration, mentally lashing himself.

Medenhab looked on in disquietude, noting the angry spark to the eyes under the deceptively sleepy looking lids. He remained silent waiting for Akhenaton's Chief Guard to speak.

Oedimus was too busy with his own thoughts to mind the commander. He'd trusted his selection for this significant task. Hadn't he personally without reservation, chosen the man for the task of leading the caravan? *What a fool I was! Yet how was he to know?* Nekute had been part of Egypt's army for years. In fact, he'd spent most of his life since boyhood as a soldier for Akhenaton.

Doubling up his fist in impotent anger, he stood up and thumped his thigh in frustration. *Holy gods of my fathers! What did I miss?* There had been nothing in the man's character to indicate that he was not a staunch and loyal Egyptian. What caused him to turn traitor? Instinctively, he knew it wasn't money. Then what?

"Do you think that maybe your soldier deliberately encouraged his men to become drunk?" The ridiculous question broke through Oedimus' thoughts. *Medenhab's mind has become soft from spending too much time at this haven of rest!* Trying not to sound scathing he answered. "Most definitely! It is the only explanation."

He strode around the room like a confined animal trying to find an escape. "I personally chose Nekute to ensure the caravan's safety. I made a drastic mistake." He hit the side of his head in disgust. "He had ulterior motives for his seeming thoughtfulness towards his men."

He was thinking aloud as the plot became clearer in his mind. "It was an ideal situation in which to be able to tamper with the cargo, without being observed. The soldiers were either too drunk, too involved with the prostitutes, or both to be aware of anything beyond their own pleasures."

His pacing continued. "Nekute and the camel driver had to be working together. But they did not plan this alone." His mouth twisted sardonically as his voice took on a note of sarcasm. "As clever as they were in the execution of this theft, both their brains put together aren't brilliant enough to devise such a calculated scheme." He shook his head. "Someone, or some persons with much more sagacity are responsible for this. Kuhteti and no doubt my soldier, were paid to steal the dowry."

Placing his hands on the edge of the table he leaned towards Medenhab, who looked as if he wished the ground would open up and swallow him, "and it must be a person, or persons who have something to gain by disrupting the alliance between our country and Anatolia."

In trepidation the commander listened, realizing that the situation went far deeper than just an act of robbery. "I should have known better and stayed more alert."

Oedimus didn't have time to indulge the commander's feelings of guilt. Straightening up his stance, he spoke decisively. " I must consult with Calphus and make sure that he is ready to leave by the first light. Too much time has already been wasted and we need to find these traitors before they can burrow deeper into hiding. Until we do, we cannot apprehend the real perpetrators of this crime," adding meaningfully "we have no time for self-recrimination."

At the obvious rebuke, Medenhab arose and took control of his deflated ego. "You are right. What can I do to help?" The soldier's training came to his stead.

Oedimus felt a twinge of compassion for the man's obvious need to redeem himself. "My friend, you have helped by telling me of this occurrence and not keeping it secret. Granted, my soldiers should not have been allowed to let down their guard and make merry, but unfortunately you and your officer were cleverly manipulated."

He placed a hand on the commander's shoulder, "now that we know that there are dark forces afoot, we must be alert to any suspicious behavior and deal with it accordingly. You can help by keeping me informed via your fastest messenger, should anything else unusual occur. They must have hidden their ill-gotten gains around here somewhere, as carrying it on their persons to Anatolia would have been too foolish. These evil doers whoever they are, will not catch Egypt unaware again"

CHAPTER FOURTEEN

*P*raises be to the Great and Glorious Aten for bringing him back to me! He's returned and I give thanks to all my ancestors and all the gods for watching over him!

Meryhken ran along the pathway in the semi-darkness. She could hardly wait to reach the figure standing in the entrance to the ruins. With arms outstretched he was ready and waiting to hold her. She felt as if she were flying as she drew closer to him, yet illogically, it seemed to be taking her forever. Her legs felt heavy and she had difficulty raising her feet. Blessed joy! She'd finally reached him.

She felt his muscular arms close around her, holding her as if he'd never let her go. Hungrily breathing in his familiar scent she knew she'd come home to where she belonged. How their bodies melded as if they were one person! Raising her head to meet his lips she looked in to his loving eyes.........Oh GOD! NO-o-o-o!

Her breath stopped. She tried to scream - but couldn't.

Instead of Oedimus' eyes looking at her, a monster stared out of a mummy's lifeless mask! It was a sickly gray image with garishly bronzed lips, unnaturally thick and unsmiling. An unholy terror filled her being as she slowly backed away - -and backed away.

This wasn't her love, this was - - DEATH!

Jolting upright Meryhken gasped for air, her heart pounding like the beat of a drum. The bed's coverlet had slipped to the floor and she shivered uncontrollably. The cool night air blew through the open balcony. Yet her trembling was not from the cold. The horrific nightmare closed in on her like the cover to a sarcophagus.

The dregs of the dream clung as if it were wisps of a shroud clinging to her spirit. Numbly, she arose and picked up the cover. Wrapping it around her body she walked into the ante- room. With shaking hands she poured herself a goblet of wine from her carafe, slopping a few ruby droplets onto the marble topped table. The drops glistened dark and sticky against the white of the stone. For a moment she stared at the spillage, then downed a generous gulp of the wine.

Warmth slowly began to seep through her limbs and Meryhken gained control over her shaking. Making her way back to the bed she sat on the side, sipping at the wine. She found comfort in her familiar surroundings. The bed felt soft but firm under her buttocks, while the coverlet that she pulled closer around her naked body felt protectively warm.

Looking beyond her open balcony Meryhken felt the gradual, calming effect that the tranquility of the star-lit sky had on her emotions. Mentally shaking her head, she tried to eliminate the terrifying dream from her mind. *It was just a dream and doesn't mean anything.* The images began to fade as the wine did its job. *It was just because I miss him so much*, she rationalized.

Finishing the wine with one final gulp she returned the empty goblet to the anti-room. She opened the door and checked the entrance hallway to make sure that all was well. She missed Psarta.

Her mother had relegated her companion to lowly kitchen duties, as punishment for his part in aiding the lovers' deception. "Be thankful that I do not send you away from the palace quarters to work in the fields with commoners," she'd stated. "You can no longer be trusted to watch over my daughter's welfare, therefore will be better employed as a kitchen helper."

Meryhken had begged in vain for Meteh to reconsider. "He is my most loyal friend mother and it was my fault entirely that he did not tell you of my meetings with Oedimus."

"Too loyal for your own good miss," the older woman had retorted. "He is fortunate that I don't banish him from the royal enclosure. The only reason that he isn't in the fields with the peasants is that it would arouse too many questions and may likely get back to the pharaoh's ears." They both knew that they couldn't afford to have Akhenaton asking awkward questions.

Closing the door firmly, Meryhken returned to her bed. Lying wide-eyed she wondered what Oedimus was doing? Had he found the person who was responsible for the missing caravan cargo? Could he bridge the chasm between the two countries, so that the thwarted marriage could go forth?

In spite of this setback the excitement in the city was still as intense. In fact, the looting of the caravans, especially the one carrying the royal dowry, had only served to increase speculation and gossip.

Meryhken was so tired of the frivolous conversations in the harem. All that the mothers and girls talked about was this proposed marriage and the intrigue involved. How could they be so naïve and stupid? Didn't they realize the dangers involved, especially to Oedimus? Of course they didn't. They were so rapped up in their own little world that they couldn't comprehend anything beyond their delights at being involved in all the glamour and romance of this 'escapade'. Added to the emptiness at being without Oedimus was her fear for his life.

Meryhken knew that this fear had caused the nightmare. *Hopefully the temple ceremony will have helped to appease the gods and he may return in safety.*

The grandiose prayer ceremonies at the temple had been well received by the people of Amarna and she'd witnessed the uplifting energy of the citizens. In fact, the gossip was that celebrations and sacrifices had spread as far as Thebes and even Karnack where the empty temple of Amun still stood. But even the priests in those cities had followed the lead of Amana and celebrated with sacrifices to Aten.

Thinking of Egypt's priests her thoughts turned to her encounter earlier this day with Akhenaton's priest, Hytoph. *What a strange person he is.* Meryhken didn't know the pharaoh's spiritual advisor well, but whenever they met around the palace she always felt an aversion to him – such as today.

She'd been waiting to be admitted to the king's presence for her usual visit. A servant had apologetically told her that Akhenaton was in an audience with his priest. Naturally, she hadn't minded the wait. In fact as it turned out it had served to her advantage. She had gleaned unexpected knowledge of Oedimus' progress, without having to ask revealing questions.

The servant had unknowingly left the door to Akhenaton's salon slightly ajar and she could hear the voices beyond quite distinctly. Meryhken hadn't meant to eavesdrop, but when she heard Oedimus' name mentioned she couldn't resist moving closer to the door.

" ……The message from my Chief Guard is very clear and there is no mistaking its import." Akhenaton's voice was raised in excitement. She couldn't hear the priest's response, but whatever it was, Akhenaton interrupted him before he could finish. "Oedimus does not make mistakes, Hytoph! His communication clearly expresses his conviction as to the perpetrators' identities. From the evidence that he has unearthed it is clear that we have found at least, two traitors within our midst. You have read his report to me. It couldn't be more thorough."

His next words were muffled as they moved across the room but from the sound of the raised voices, Meryhken surmised that they were having a heated discussion.

Again, the conversation grew more distinct. She realized that Akhenaton was walking around the room and had once more approached the entrance.

"This camel driver is most certainly one of them," he was saying, "but, it is hard to comprehend that one of my own soldiers would act so treacherously. Regardless, Oedimus has command of this situation. Have no fear. He will find them."

Meryhken caught Hytoph's soft-spoken voice and caught a few of the words. " ...on his way to Damascus? ... think he ... Hattusash?" From the pharaoh's reply she surmised that he was asking about Oedimus' plans.

"He must be well on his way to Damascus by this time. The messenger said he handed him this report to deliver as he was about to leave Beth Shean."

Footsteps were coming closer. "I will offer prayers for his safety and success in his endeavors, most wise and benevolent pharaoh." Hytoph's words sounded as if they were right behind the door.

Reacting like a startled bird she flew to the far end of the anti-room and sat down - just in time. The door to the salon was flung wide and Hytoph appeared. The priest barely glanced at her, being absorbed in his own thoughts. He hurried across the anti-room.

Just as he was about to pass her chair, something dropped from underneath his robes and landed at her feet. Automatically Meryhken bent to retrieve it for him, thinking that it was one of the multiple pieces of jewelry that adorned his wrinkled old neck.

The gold chain was heavy, with an intricate looking medallion hanging from its center. The priest snatched it from her hands -

but not before Meryhken had seen the medallion's emblem. She recognized it as the standard symbol of Amun, worn for centuries by Egypt's priests and priestesses. Surprised, she looked up and met the priest's eyes. The look of malevolence in them shocked her.

She quickly composed her features and spoke in a voice full of innocence. "The clasp on your adornment must have become loose, Holy One. I have always admired your taste in jewelry and it would be a pity to lose even one such fine piece."

Hytoph visibly relaxed. "Thank you, Meryhken. Your admiration is appreciated. May the blessing of Aten be upon you."

She stood and bowed in acknowledgement, looking demure and pious. The priest left, clasping the chain with its sacrilegious image in a tight fist.

As she tried to settle herself back to sleep, she puzzled over the incident. Why would the pharaoh's High Priest be wearing the medallion of Amun? Akhenaton had long since banned all religious symbols not pertaining to the one true god of the sun, Aten- Ra. Even though he had hidden it beneath his robes, Hytoph was still guilty of a sin for wearing it.

Of course he was priest to Akhenaton's father, so no doubt still felt a sense of loyalty to the old gods. She shook her head dismissively. *If he wants to risk his pharaoh's displeasure by wearing a forbidden religious symbol, that is his problem, not mine.*

Meryhken's thoughts were too wrapped up in Oedimus' safety to have a care about a priest's religious preferences. The information that she had learned from her eavesdropping both elated and worried her. Could he be so close to successfully solving this problem, that her father would look kindly upon them? Was Oedimus right in believing that Akhenaton would allow then to marry? *Will Aten protect my love from danger?*

The vivid nightmare still weighed heavily on her mind. *Surely it is not an omen?* She wouldn't allow herself such a thought! *I'm worrying too much.* She turned her head on the pillow to peer through the balcony opening. The star-lit sky seemed to calm her mind.

Deliberately forcing herself to dwell on Oedimus' loving personality she closed her eyes tightly, willing herself to return to sleep. Her last thoughts were of his sultry eyes looking at her with love. Meryhken felt safe.

CHAPTER FIFTEEN

*S*oon they were passing outlying farmland with crops of ripening wheat gleaming white in the moonlight. He calculated that they would be reaching Damascus' city gates within the hour. They passed dark shadows of olive orchards and Oedimus inhaled the smell of olive oil coming from unseen vats.

The desert night was turning cool and he urged his horse to go faster. Calphus followed suit, digging his heels into his horse's flanks. Only the sound of the animals' hooves could be heard thudding rhythmically over the hard ground.

One more night and then we will be heading into Anatolia. In spite of the thought of a warm bed waiting for him at the governor's house, Oedimus was anxious to get to Hattusash and find his traitors.

Calphus broke the silence between them. "The thought of resting in comfort tonight instead of the hard ground, does my heart good."

Oedimus grinned. "You must have been reading my mind."

Looming high in front of them was a wall of stone that encircled the town. Iron gates leading into the city faced the two riders. Numerous torch flares were strategically placed within recesses, lighting the night sky. At the sound of the galloping hooves stopping outside, an indistinct figure peered through the bars of the gate. After identifying themselves the gates were swung open.

"Our governor is awaiting your arrival." As he spoke the gatekeeper beckoned to someone who stood a few yards away. "Take our visitors to the governor's house." A man came out of the shadows and beckoned for them to follow him.

They passed through a large square that seemed to be the community center of the city. Many roughly built homes surrounded the outer edges and although they were made of Egyptian sun-dried bricks, they were not as finely constructed as Amarna's newer buildings. These houses were so close together that there was barely any space between them. An occasional tent occupied what little space there was left between the dwellings.

Families sat outside, obviously enjoying the coolness of the night air after the day's heat. Heads turned curiously, watching the two horsemen as they followed the man walking a few steps ahead. The only sound was the soft thuds of the horses' rhythmic gait, and a few surreptitious whispers made behind hands.

After meandering for a while through non-descript streets, their companion finally stopped outside another smaller gate situated in a wall much like the one that surrounded the town. Their guide opened the gate wide to allow them to pass through. They found themselves in the courtyard of a house that looked grand in comparison to those of the other city homes. Their horses had hardly come to a halt, when the door to the house was flung open and a tall, thin man appeared on the steps. Standing silhouetted against the light from within, his voice loudly bid them - "WELCOME!"

Alighting, Oedimus moved forward to introduce himself, but before he could open his mouth the man had reached him. Long, bony hands clamped his shoulders in a grip of steel. "You must be the mighty soldier known as Oedimus, the great and almighty pharaoh's chosen guard!" the man exclaimed. "I am Apophi, governor of all Damascus and honored servant of Akhenaton, glorious ruler of Egypt. And, I am now your most humble host and honored servant while you abide under my roof." He ended this effusive speech with a deep flourishing bow, one hand brushing the air theatrically.

There is nothing humble about this man that I can perceive! Oedimus was having difficulty hiding his amusement at this overt display of grandiosity. Casting a swift glance at Calphus, he could see by his friend's expression that he was similarly impressed.

The governor's flamboyant personality exuded an energy that reminded Oedimus of a mythical giant. Thick hair fell around his shoulders and framed the elongated face. *Those tresses would be the envy of any woman.* A pair of expressive eyes bridged a prominent nose that was not quite as broad as that of an Egyptian. However the well-shaped, full mouth was definitely indicative of his race.

"It is good to be welcomed with such pleasure, Apophi," said Oedimus, warmly. In spite of the exaggerated welcome from this man there was something very likeable about him. Oedimus turned to introduce Calphus who was standing at a discreet distance. "May I present my friend and right hand man?"

Calphus stepped forward and was given the same effusive welcome that Oedimus had received. "My most sincere greetings to you, Calphus. May your stay in Damascus prove to be most pleasurable. Come," he beckoned them to follow him into the house, "allow me to open my modest home to you. Refreshments are being prepared, also soft beds in which you may rest this night and replenish your energies."

Oedimus interrupted him. "Excuse me Apophi, but I have a small request. Might my friend share a room with your soldiers? As you know our business here is most serious and it would help to hear first hand what your soldiers have to say." The governor nodded in understanding and gave a flourishing bow. "But of course. A very wise decision."

He turned to the silent man who had accompanied them. "Show Calphus to my officers' billets," he instructed, "make sure that he is well taken care of and that all his needs are met."

Calphus followed the man's lead across the courtyard and back through the gateway.

They entered a large living area that seemed to take up most of the space in the house. Its grandeur was almost as imposing as the royal palace in Amarna, even though on a lesser scale. The red brick floor had two or three fur rugs scattered on it that looked to be the black coats of sleek panthers. Around the room were various ornate, but softly cushioned chairs. A matching pair of huge ivory pedestals holding golden busts, dominated one wall. Appropriately, the effigies were of the pharaoh and his queen, Nefertiti. Above them centered in the middle of the wall, was the sun disk of Aten. Its golden rays shimmered in light from the inevitable sconces that lit up the room. *Why should I be surprised at such a display, after having met the owner?* His eyes finally ended their perusal as they came to rest on a long, wooden table surrounded by matching chairs that dominated the center of the room.

He returned his focus back to the governor. " Have you seen anything of my soldiers yet? By this time they should have returned from Anatolia."

"Yes. They stayed but one night and left yesterday," Apophi confirmed. His story was similar to that given by the camel drivers. "They informed me that their leader had been ordered to stay behind to finish some business. His men didn't question his decision, being that he was in charge. There was no longer any need for caution seeing that the caravan had arrived safely."

If only I had arrived sooner. "Did the men give any further details of Nekute's change of plans? I would have liked to have personally questioned them."

Apophi laid a hand on his shoulder. "Naturally I asked if they had any idea as to what this unforeseen business was. Believe me, they knew nothing." Staring intently into Oedimus' face he sensed the man's anxiety. "Tomorrow, you may continue your journey to the Hittites country and solve this situation for yourself." In a firm voice that brooked no argument he continued, "tonight however, you must rest and replenish your strength." With this, he clapped his hands and immediately a young girl of about thirteen, entered the room. "I will have my serving girl show you to your room, where you may freshen yourself before we dine." The girl had entered so quickly that Oedimus suspected that she had been waiting outside in anticipation of being summoned.

"Show our guest to his rooms, Shasa." With a smile and a flourish of the expressive hands, he turned his attention once more to his guest. "At your convenience and after you are freshened, it will be an honor for me to share a modest meal with you."

Oedimus followed the girl along a narrow hallway that was inconspicuously hidden behind a hanging gold and red embroidered drapery. The way her body swayed as she walked and the abundance of dark braided hair, reminded him of Meryhken. The memory caused him a pang of loneliness. At the end of the hall she stopped and opened a door, inviting him with a delicate wave of her hand to enter.

Stepping over the threshold, he found himself in a small room that was almost as elaborate as the one they'd just left. The largest bed that he'd ever seen, piled with colorful cushions, took up most of the space. A heavy looking fur skin was thrown carelessly across the end. Damascus nights were notoriously cold and he mentally thanked the servants for this thoughtfulness. He noticed steam arising from a washbowl that sat on a beautiful ivory stand. It gave off an odor of pungent incense.

"Is there anything else you may wish, master?"

He dismissed the girl with a grateful smile, "thank you, but no. Your assistance has been appreciated, Shasa." The girl bowed and left the room.

Finishing his absolutions, he walked to the bed and sat down to test its comfort. It sank under his weight and after sleeping on the hard desert floor, it felt as soft as a woman. Thoughts of Meryhken resurfaced again and he quickly forced his mind to dismiss them. He needed all his concentration on finding the camel driver and his treasonous soldier.

They are not in Damascus, as Apophi would have known if they were hiding anyplace in the city. He instinctively knew that nothing happened in Damascus without the governor's knowledge. This meant that he and Calphus would have to continue on to Hittite territory.

He wasn't familiar with Mussilli's country and didn't look forward to seeking out the traitors in a foreign place. Nevertheless if it were necessary, he would do it. *They can't have just disappeared without leaving any trace behind.* Oedimus' self-confidence in his own abilities was unwavering. Even so, there was a nagging sense of foreboding that he couldn't dispel. *I've let Meryhken's worrying influence me.*

A light knock at his door broke through his morbid mood. He turned to see Shasa entering. "I have been instructed to see if you are ready to dine, master?" He arose and followed the girl back along the hallway.

Tantalizing aromas coming from the vicinity of the main room, reminded him that he was hungry. His eyes grew wide at the sight that confronted him when he entered. *If this is what our host thinks is a modest meal, I wonder what he considers to be a banquet?* The table was heaped with dishes full of appetizing selections of rice and lentils, all smelling of palatable spices. Two huge platters were weighted down with a shank of lamb and a curried goat.

Other dishes held fruits of every description accompanied by creamy looking yogurts.

Oedimus stared in amazement at the bounty. A door at the opposite end of the room was suddenly thrown open to admit his host. *He comes and goes like a whirlwind!*

Striding across the space that separated them, Apophi clasped his guest's shoulders in greeting, much the same as he'd done on arrival. "Come, my friend. Share my food and let me have the pleasure of your company this evening. We have much serious business to discuss but first - we need to regenerate our energy with sustenance."

Oedimus shook his head at the offer of more wine and sank back in his chair, feeling satiated. He regarded the governor with purpose. "So Apophi, do you have any thoughts to share with me regarding these traitorous dogs?" His host's hospitality was boundless, but now he needed to get to the business that had brought him here.

Apophi studied the face across from him. "Your message arrived just this very morning and to say that I was most surprised by your revelations, is an understatement. Naturally, I knew that the caravan contained a valuable cargo and was supposedly well protected. My concerns had been centered on the possibility of a band of desert rats marauding and pillaging, not our own people."

The governor leaned forward in his chair, looking at the Chief Guard in concern. "I was most relieved when the caravan arrived here without mishap. Amarna's soldiers were extremely conscientious in their guard duties as well as the Hittite soldiers, and I felt proud to be of service to them during their stay." He sat back again and his expression was incredulous as he recalled reading the missive from Akhenaton. "It would never have occurred to me that there would be thieves amidst our own, trusted people!"

"Excuse my bluntness Apophi, but I have no time to dwell on our laxness in being taken unawares. The damage has been done and the future of this marriage merger depends on my clearing Akhenaton's good name. Egypt cannot afford to lose the Hittites as allies." Oedimus comments were spoken politely but the message was clear. He wasn't here to dawdle over regrets. He needed to get to the business of finding Egypt's traitors, before it was too late.

The governor said nothing but fixed his guest with an intent gaze. A subtle change came over Apophi's demeanor and when he finally spoke, his words were slow and deliberate. "My friend, I am all too aware of the seriousness of this situation. King Mussilli's nation is closer to Damascus' borders than Amarna's. Therefore my city is more vulnerable. I know the Hittites well and they are not the kind of people to cross swords with - - yet neither am I."

He paused to let his next words sink in, "I have already set in motion an investigation of my own." Oedimus looked taken aback, causing the man to give a small chuckle. "You see I have not been idle."

"Immediately after receiving your correspondence, I dispatched one of my most trusted men to find out what he could of these rebels. Even as we speak, he is backtracking the route of the caravan to Anatolia and following any leads he may find. If anyone can unearth these miscreants he can, and I feel sorry for them if he does!"

Apophi sat back in his chair as if he didn't have a care in the world. "I have learned from experience that like the deadly asp, it pays to be inconspicuous and watchful. When the prey is certain that he is out of danger and has let down his shield, then the reptile strikes."

Oedimus mulled over this logic. *This man is more than just a pretty adornment for Damascus.* The change that had come over the governor was subtle but enlightening.

145

The exaggerated gestures had disappeared. The voice had taken on a timber of authority that brooked no nonsense. Oedimus' respect for him increased. "Excuse my former bluntness, Apophi. It is a relief to know that I have such wise council in your person."

The governor acknowledged the compliment with a nod. "You have no need to excuse yourself, Oedimus. Your anxiety is understandable and I admire your tenacity in this situation." Considering his next words, Apophi spoke carefully, "for many years, I have been in the position of needing to make some difficult decisions. Whenever possible, I have learned not to act without first giving careful deliberation to the problem. Acting while in the heat of passion is counter-productive."

Seeing that he had his guest's undivided attention he elaborated, "your soldier's training teaches you to immediately fight back when being attacked. This of course is exactly what your enemies expect of you. However, you also know from your involvement in the politics of Egypt, that weighing a situation first, is imperative."

"Waiting until you are certain of all the facts and knowing the right time to act on those facts, is of the utmost importance. And, you know the importance of strategy. If your enemy doesn't know what you are planning to do he is left to guess. Confusion is then your friend. This is when you make your move."

Oedimus digested Apophi's words for a few minutes, then arose and saluted him in the Egyptian form of respect. "Thank you Apophi, not only for the comforts of your home but even more so for your valuable and most wise counsel. I will now retire and think on your words."

Loud raps on the door brought him instantly awake. It took a few seconds for his disoriented brain to remember where he was. Calling out to whoever was knocking, he sat up straight. The door opened to admit Shasa. "Excuse my intrusion at such an

early hour master, but our governor has asked me to awaken you."
Oedimus could tell by the urgency of her voice that there was
something wrong. "He wishes to confer with you, immediately."

He swung his legs over the edge of the bed, wide-awake and
alert. The room was barely light and glancing up at the opening
in the wall he saw that a few stars still remained in the paling sky.
"Tell your master that I will join him as soon as possible."

The girl was already closing the door as he scrambled for
his clothes. Pouring water from last night's jug into a bowl, he
vigorously splashed his face. Its tingling coldness drove the last
remnants of sleep from his head. His bristly jaw scratched against
the cloth as he wiped his face. Brushing a hand over the prickly
growth he scowled but decided to ignore it. The urgency of the
girl's message was more important than shaving his face.

As Oedimus approached the dining room's area, he caught
the tale end of a question…. "able to determine how long he'd
been there?" Apophi was asking. Parting the hallway drapes, he
was just in time to see another man answer with the shake of his
head.

Apophi stood with his hands leaning on the edge of the
table, head bent. The other man's dark swarthy face was grim.
For a second, Oedimus thought it was the Arab servant from
Beth Shean but he quickly saw that it wasn't. The same type of
scarf was wound around this man's head in the Arabic fashion.
The difference was that black beetling eyebrows sheltered eyes
that were startlingly light, instead of the usual dark brown of the
Arabic race.

"Oedimus! I am glad you have joined us and please accept
my abject apologies for disturbing you at such an early hour." As
usual, Apophi's manners were gracious.

The governor gestured towards the Arab. "This is Ben Abheeb,
my most trusted compatriot." Ben Abheeb responded with a deep
bow. "I have heard much about your tracking expertise from my
soul brother, El Bet Ammon." He spoke the Egyptian language

with only a trace of his native dialect. "His words for you were very admirable."

Oedimus felt at a disadvantage. The man seemed to know of his personal activities, whereas he knew nothing of this stranger. Yet, making a mental observation of the man, he liked what he saw and could tell that whatever it was that had brought him to Apophi was obviously of serious concern. The two men were tense.

"Sit with us, Oedimus." Apophi sat down in a chair and pulled it closer to the table, indicating for his guest to take the one next to him. Ben Abheeb pulled out a chair to face them across the table.

"My friend has information…" The governor was interrupted by a knock at the door, followed by Calphus' entrance. Bidding him welcome, Apophi introduced his companion to the new comer. "I took the liberty of having Shasa alert Calphus," he explained. "I thought that no doubt you would also wish for him to hear the news that Ben Abheeb brings."

Oedimus noticed that his friend looked as surprised and hastily dressed as himself. His jaw-line looked decidedly blue and rough against his mahogany complexion.

No sooner had Calphus taken a seat, than Shasa entered loaded down with a tray of refreshments. Even though the food and drink were welcome, Oedimus was beginning to get restless. Hearing the news that this Arab had brought was more important than sustenance. Regardless, he had to curb his impatience while the serving girl performed the ritual of serving bread and fruit. Finally she left, and Ben Abheeb began to talk.

Oedimus had already guessed that this was the man that had been sent to track the thieves. Ben Abheeb was saying that he'd not traveled too far out of the boundaries of Damascus, when he had made a gruesome discovery.

"I had just reached the base of Phoenicia's mountains and was preparing to camp for the night. In the act of searching for wood for my fire, I saw something protruding from underneath a bush." He stopped talking to quench his thirst with his goat milk and wiped away a few creamy dregs that clung to his beard. "On closer inspection I saw that it was a body, carelessly hidden underneath the bush." Ben Abheeb hesitated, "the man had been strangled." Oedimus' attention was riveted.

"Although there was nothing to identify who he might be, I strongly suspect that it is your camel driver as he…"

Calphus broke in. "Where is the body now?"

"Ben Abheeb carried the body here on his horse," announced Apophi. "It has been placed in one of my servant's homes that is currently unoccupied." Oedimus came to his feet. "I have need to see this body, immediately. Take me to this house so that I may verify whether or not this is indeed Kuhteti."

In the dimly lit room, he pulled back the cloth. Underneath the shroud was a sight that made the hardened soldier draw an involuntary gasp. Calphus stood alongside and Oedimus felt rather than saw his friend's body tense. Bloodshot eyes bulging out of their sockets stared blankly back at him. The face of the corpse was bloated. Purple lips were pulled back in a grimacing sneer. Protruding grotesquely, the black swollen tongue reminded Oedimus of an over ripe avocado. The head lay at an unnatural angle.

Oedimus took in the bruised and mottled neck with a thin wire encircling it. The wire had cut into flesh, so that dried crusts of blood caked the strangling device. It reminded him of a garish string of rust colored stones. In meeting death, Kuhteti had experienced Hell.

Flies hummed around the ceiling and the smell of rotting flesh was nauseating. Bile arose in Oedimus' throat and he quickly placed the cover back over the body. Moving to the doorway, he inhaled several gulps of air.

Apophi came up behind him. "Is it your camel driver?"

Nodding, he walked away from the house, the smell still lingering in his nostrils. The governor drew alongside, keeping in step. Calphus and the Arab were the last to leave. Nobody spoke as they made their way back to the governor's home.

"We must bury the body before the day becomes too hot." Apophi was the first to speak as they once again sat around the table, each man deep in his own thoughts.

Of course we must. Oedimus realized that the body was too decomposed to have it taken back to the man's family. "We must send a messenger back to Amarna and advise Akhenaton of this latest development." he declared. His mind was jumping into action. "His wife must not learn of his demise, yet." Oedimus was emphatic. "This news must not become public. We do not need our enemies to know that we have discovered the body."

"Consider it already done." Apophi was in command of the situation. "What are your plans now, Oedimus? You no longer have the opportunity to question this camel driver and, it's obvious that someone wanted to make certain that he wouldn't talk." He eyed his guest speculatively.

Oedimus was already thinking along the same lines. Kuhteti's untimely death was a set back but only a temporary one. "Nekute still has not been accounted for and even if he may not be the instigator, he is just as deeply involved."

Calphus agreed, "no doubt even more so than the camel driver." He directed his attention to Apophi, "Last evening I talked with your men at length. They all agreed that our lead soldier and camel driver seemed to be unusually close. They were seen more than once conversing in private."

Ben Abheeb spoke for the first time since they had left the corpse. "I suspect this other infidel to be still alive and in hiding. If he had met the same fate as the camel driver, I would have also found his body." He paused, looking at the questioning faces turned towards him. "Someone of intelligence wanted to make sure that nothing incriminating was found on this man. I found none of the stolen articles on his person. In fact, there was nothing on the body that would identify who he was. This alone is significant. And - - what happened to his camel?"

They all looked at each other, before turning their attention back to Ben Abheeb. "If he were returning to Egypt, surely he would have had his camel with him?"

"How do we know that Nekute wasn't also killed, and both their animals taken?" Calphus queried. "Maybe the person who killed Kuhteti also killed Nekute and took the animals as contraband."

Apophi interjected, "you did say that you found Kuhteti's body hidden underneath a bush. Calphus could be right. Maybe the other body has also been hidden someplace, or even buried."

Oedimus leaned his elbows on the table, supporting his chin with his hands. He was listening to all the suggested theories, but his mind was racing ahead.

Ben Abheeb gave a self-satisfied smile. "I thought of all this so I made a thorough search of the area, even traversing some miles further a-field in every direction. There were no signs of any disturbance, no mounds that might have been a grave or even animal droppings. There were no vultures in sight. Nothing," he asserted. "Everything was as untouched as a virgin in Paradise."

Oedimus remained deep in thought, thinking of the horrific way in which Kuhteti had been murdered. Whoever did this deed wanted to make sure that his victim would not be questioned and reveal his cohorts. "It seems to me that whoever this person or persons might be, they have become desperate," he said, quietly. "If and when we find Nekute we will learn who the brains are behind this treachery. In any event, if he is not dead then where is he?" The question was rhetorical. "I agree with Ben Abheeb. Traces of the act would have come to light if the same people that killed Kuhteti had killed Nekute. Maybe Nekute killed Kuhteti to make sure he didn't talk."

Before anyone could voice an opinion, he continued to expound on his logic "Nekute has not returned to Egypt, that is obvious. He is not lying dead in the desert. Therefore, he must be in Anatolia. Someone there has to be protecting him." He had his companions' full attention.

"On the other hand, if he has met the same fate as Kuhteti then it must have taken place in Hittite country, otherwise he would have been found by Ben Abheeb. All this leads me to believe that this scheming is not only being contrived by someone of importance in Egypt but has a similar ally in Anatolia."

"There is no doubt in my mind that the attack on the caravan of a few weeks past and this latest attack, were planned and executed by the same people. And, whoever these terrorists are their quest has cast suspicion between Egypt and Anatolia." He had everyone's attention. "This can mean only one thing. These acts have not been about the stealing of goods. Stealing the caravans' cargos was just a means to an end. No my friends, there is much more to this situation than first appears." His companions remained silent. "This whole upheaval has been a very clever political endeavor by people in power who may lose something of importance to them, if this marriage alliance takes place. When we find out what is so important as to jeopardize our country's peace, we will find the perpetrators who planned these foul deeds. Nekute and Kuhteti have been nothing but tools used to enact this scheme." No one said a word.

He came to a decision and stood

"The longer I wait, the deeper these traitorous rats will burrow into a sewer pit! Nekute must be found and made to talk." Looking at Calphus, he nodded, "my friend and I will leave for Anatolia immediately."

CHAPTER SIXTEEN

*P*sarta almost fell through the partially open door, which would have been his undoing. Through the small crack he took in the unbelievable scene inside the room. He cautiously backed away a little, keeping his eyes glued to the slit in the opening. He couldn't believe what he was seeing. The strong odor of incense wafted to him from the room beyond. This in itself was insignificant. After all, this was a priest's apartment.

Chenkiop had inadvertently left the door slightly open when he'd entered the room. Psarta could see the serving boy standing a few feet behind the priest, waiting uncertainly to gain his master's attention.

Hytoph was sitting cross-legged, chanting unintelligibly before a huge magnificent icon that Psarta couldn't identify. His back was to the entrance and with his head thrown back and body swaying from side to side, he was oblivious to anything but his own bliss. Multiple torches flared around the effigy. It was without a doubt superimposed on some sort of an altar – but not an altar that Sparta had ever seen before. The Holy Man's voice rose and fell in cadences of passionate worship. Every few seconds he would prostrate his upper torso to the floor, and kiss some object that he held in his hands. The white eyes of the huge black marble figure seemed to bore into his body. The fiery glow of the torches smoldered in the marble eyes.

Psarta shivered for no reason.

Alas, the priest paused - seemingly sensing someone behind him. He turned his head and saw Chenkiop. Leaping to his feet, he screamed - "GET OUT!"

Chenkiop backed away closing the door tightly behind him, but not before Psarta had seen all the details of the black, marble image. It finally hit him! The icon was that of the old god, Amun.

"I had no idea that he didn't wish to be disturbed." The tray full of refreshments rattled in Chenkiop's shaking hands. "I thought he meant for me to bring them to him immediately, instead of at his usual time." The boy's voice shook almost as much as the tray he held.

"What is he doing in there?" Psarta's curiosity couldn't be curbed. "Why is he worshipping the forbidden god, Amun?"

"What?" The boy's vacant look was genuine. His widely set eyes in the flaccid face, looked even more puzzled than usual. "He is always on his belly worshipping," he replied. Chenkiop's tone turned scornful, "it would seem that from the amount of time he spends praying he would be a god himself. Instead, he acts like a screeching parrot!"

Psarta impatiently repeated his question. "Why does he pray to a god that is no longer honored by our pharaoh?"

The boy's expression was even more idiotic than it already was. Exasperated, Psarta dismissed his query with a wave of his hand. "Never mind. It's none of my concern." He realized that Chenkiop lacked the intelligence to comprehend anything about the old gods.

Hytoph's serving boy was not a friend that Psarta associated with very often, unless there was no one else with whom he could find to play a game of Stones. Absorbed in the priest's strange behavior, he'd temporarily forgotten that the boy's mental abilities were not the sharpest.

Although Chenkiop was an easy prey for Psarta's gambling expertise he really found it boring to match skills with him. He liked a challenge and Chenkiop's retarded brain made it too easy for Psarta to cheat. This evening had not been very conducive to fulfilling Psarta's pleasures. In fact, it had deteriorated rapidly.

Being sent to the lowly kitchen duties had proven to be an unexpected asset, even though the heat and smells of sweating bodies weren't pleasant. To his surprise he had more free hours than he'd had when being at Meryhken's beck and call. It was good not to have to worry about her all the time. And, he could sleep undisturbed all night. Of course since the Chief Guard's departure there was no need to have to stay awake all night. But, the cot in the servants' quarters was more comfortable than a pallet on the floor outside her room. Psarta tried to dwell on the positive aspects of not being with Meryhken every day, so that he'd not be reminded of how much he missed her.

He'd left the kitchens this evening looking forward to meeting with some of his friends and passing away a few hours of gambling. Unfortunately, the fates had not been with him. Either his usual companions were still working, or had other plans. Turning to Chenkiop had been a last resort.

Some people said that Chenkiop had been touched by the magic of the Evil Ones when he was born. He was a nice harmless simpleton and could be relied on to do anything menial for anyone - including Psarta.

Working for Hytoph was considered a blessing for the boy, as being under the priest's guardianship ensured that he was protected from any further evils. If the truth were known, working for the volatile priest was an evil unto itself! So be it that no one was aware of this except Chenkiop. Because of his slow mental capacities the boy never questioned that there might be something better in life.

Psarta had felt a twinge of guilt at the boy's eager acceptance of his offer to play a game of Stones, but only a twinge. The boy explained that he needed to take care of his master's needs first, so would Psarta please wait for him? He was pathetically afraid of upsetting Psarta by keeping him waiting.

Now, Psarta was wishing that he hadn't waited. His mind was uneasy at what he'd just inadvertently witnessed. There was no doubt in his mind that the priest had been paying homage to the highest of the forbidden gods. That brief one or two minutes of seeing him prostate in front of the icon along with the incantations, had been unnerving. *Our pharaoh would bring his wrath upon the lowliest of citizen for such a breach of his laws. I dread to imagine what would happen, if he knew that his own priest was sacrilegious!*

Meryhken was uneasy. What Psarta was telling her had reminded her of the incident when Hytoph's medallion had dropped at her feet. "Did he see you waiting outside the door?" she asked, anxiety lacing her voice.

He shook his head. "No. I jumped out of sight when he started to scream at Chenkiop."

All day he'd pondered over the disturbing scene from last evening. And so, when he knew that Meteh wasn't close by he'd sought out Meryhken. Having shared the experience with her made him feel better. "Even more disturbing were the strange prayers that he chanted," he said.

"What do you mean?"

Psarta had not understood the priest's ranting. "I'm not really certain. They were not the standard prayers of worship to Aten-

Ra. And, I didn't recognize the name of one of the god's that he was calling upon." He was having difficulty in trying to find the words to convey his impressions. "Most of the prayers were to Amun, but he also prayed to a god that sounded foreign to my ears. His words of praise were so puzzling and he called out as if possessed!"

"Can you remember any of his words? Were they the old rituals used by the ancient pharaoh's and priests?" Meryhken felt increasingly disturbed. She had always instinctively felt that the priest was not what he appeared to be. Even so, Psarta's account did not sound like the persona that Hytoph usually presented, that is the submissive religious advisor to his lord pharaoh and Holy of Holies, Aten-Ra. "You must tell me everything that you remember." Her voice trembled with urgency. "This may be more important than either of us realize."

With a pensive motion Psarta closed his eyes in an effort to concentrate. Rubbing a hand across his forehead, he tried to recall the details. "I know that he was at times prostrate. Some of the words that he uttered were indecipherable because of his low tones. But others were loud and full of fervor."

"The priest began to raise his voice in adulation, beseeching Amun and several of the old gods for their help." Psarta opened his eyes once more, staring into space. "Just before he realized that he wasn't alone, he began a different supplication to a god that I've never heard …" He scowled with the effort to recall.

Biting his lower lip, his furrowed brow showed the strain of trying to remember the name. "At first, I thought he was calling on Soth but it wasn't Soth's name…. It was more like Sat-ee- or maybe Sote -eey."

"Are you trying to say Sotheh?" She held her breath.

"THAT'S IT!" Psarta exclaimed in triumphant. "Who is he, or she?"

Meryhken felt as if she'd been hit.

She was taken back to her childhood when she'd spent many hours with the pharaoh listening in rapture as he read to her from the ancient writings. "Sotheh is a great and powerful Hittite god," she answered mechanically.

In her mind's eye she could still see the ancient tome in Akhenaton's hands. The child sat on his knee as he taught her the ancient wonders of the world. Meryhken loved to learn and the king was delighted to find that his concubine's small daughter was such an eager pupil. Her love of learning everything about ancient worlds and gods empowered him. Her sense of spirituality was so like Akhenaton's own.

Meryhken never lost her taste for learning and still studied avidly. The drawings in the tome were as fresh in her mind as if she'd seen them yesterday. She'd sat listening to the pharaoh's explanations of all the world's many gods and goddesses. Fascinated, she'd studied the pictographs of the Ancients' temples. They including the Hittites' temples and their gods, especially their most exulted god - - Sotheh.

"Why would an Egyptian priest be honoring one of Anatolia's gods?" Psarta's question echoed her own.

Why, indeed? "Did you see, or hear anything else?"

He shook his head. "It was then that Hytoph realized someone was standing behind him. He acted as enraged as if Chenkiop had been caught in the harem! I've never seen a priest act in such a manner!" Psarta exclaimed. "I left the ante-room a lot faster than Chenkiop."

Mystified, he searched Meryhken's face for answers. "What does all this mean? Why is Hytoph acting in such a strange manner?"

How could she answer him when she didn't understand herself? "I'm not certain, but whatever his reasons he is breaking the laws of Egypt."

Her brain sped as she picked over all the unforeseen events that had taken place in recent weeks. From the first attack on the caravan, to Oedimus' discoveries of the strange events surrounding that incident - to the medallion of Amun that Hytoph secretly wore - the stealing of the marriage dowry that culminated in Oedimus' departure, once again.

Now this. She felt a heaviness encompassing her spirit that wouldn't be dispelled. It wasn't just missing Oedimus that was causing her present melancholy, although she missed him as she would a limb. *No. It is more than that.* Yet, she couldn't pinpoint her unrest.

This incident that Psarta had witnessed was just one more thing to nag at her. *It is like a stone that has caught in my sandal and digs into my foot.*

"Do <u>not</u> say anything about this to anyone." she ordered sharply. "I am certain that there is more going on than just the forbidden wailings of a priest."

"But, what will you do? Shouldn't Akhenaton be made aware of this blasphemy?" he asked.

"Not yet. He would ask how I had come by this knowledge and I have no plausible lie to give. Your involvement cannot be revealed." She was still thinking. After a few seconds she came to a decision. "I must get word of this to Oedimus as fast as possible."

Whatever was happening (and she wasn't sure what) - there was one thing of which she was certain. This strange behavior of Hytoph's was somehow linked with the discord between Akhenaton and the Hittites. She didn't know what that link was but her instincts were shouting at her as loudly as the priest had screamed at his servant.

"Do you know any of the messengers that are trustworthy and speedy?" she asked.

Her friend smiled knowingly. "I have access to many channels mistress and some owe me favors."

159

The governor eyed the missive with curiosity. The letter wasn't sealed with Akhenaton's official mark, yet it had come from Amarna. Apophi looked again at the unfamiliar seal. It was meant for the Chief Guard who was no longer in Damascus.

As he held the small delicate scroll of papyrus, he caught a whiff of its seductive scent. Smiling, he held it to his nose and inhaled. Who was this female sending a message to the Chief Guard? *Probably a maiden who has succumbed to his charms and wishes not to be forgotten.*

He addressed the waiting messenger. "It's too late to deliver this to him. He is already on his way to Anatolia. However I doubt it needs his immediate attention, so I will keep it and give it to him on his return journey. My senses are that it is not of too much importance and can wait."

Chuckling to himself, he placed the letter in an urn used specifically for important papers. *He'll no doubt appreciate it even more on his return from that god- forsaken country!*

CHAPTER SEVENTEEN

𝒯 he first thing he noticed was the litter. Unlike Amarna, Hattushash' city streets were not as clean as they could be. Granted, Egypt's capital was a newer city and there were sections even there that were less than desirable. Even so, the shabbiness in his hometown was confined to the poorer places. Everywhere Oedimus looked in this Hittites capital appeared unkempt.

The clip- clop of their horses' hooves echoed rhythmically on the hard dirt roads. It was still early morning and few people were about, except for those that had manual labor to do before the heat of the day was upon them. Both men had purposely dressed in nondescript clothing and had chosen Hittite horse-gear, so as not to look conspicuous.

They needn't have bothered. People they passed were too intent on their own affairs to take any notice of them. To the citizens, they were just another pair of strangers in a city used to foreign visitors. Even so, Oedimus didn't want to draw any attention that might run the risk of alerting their prey.

It had been no problem to obtain the Hittite king's permission to seek out their traitorous soldier. Apophi had made sure that a message had been personally delivered to Mussilli asking that their visit remain as private as possible, for obvious reasons. King Mussilli had given his blessings and offered any assistance that they might need. The ruler was as eager as Akhenaton to find the culprits before the wedding took place. But Oedimus had declined his offer of help. He wanted to remain as inconspicuous as possible and the fewer soldiers to arouse suspicion the better.

Calphus' Ethiopian features were not unusual in this place of busy commerce. As for Egyptians, like the Phoenicians they were almost as common as the Hittites, being on such friendly terms with these countries.

Oedimus stared at the numerous grand looking temples they were passing as they made their way through the city. It seemed that almost every area had a square designated to one of these places of worship. Temples in honor of the Hittites gods and goddesses were everywhere. Intricate architecture denoting their many deities were carved into the temples' wall spaces, while huge statues dominated their facades. Streets going off the squares showed red mud brick dwellings and businesses, all closely packed together like so many ants in an anthill. Some were newer and cleaner than others.

Ben Abheeb had supplied them with the name of a contact supposedly having access to the Hattushash underground. For a price, this person would get information for them.

Oedimus stopped his horse to consult the rough sketch that the Arab had drawn and Calphus drew alongside. So far Ben Abheeb's details of the city's streets had been very accurate. Now, they needed to locate the house of their connection.

Calphus pointed a finger along the thoroughfare. "That is the square and the temple to Anus. See? It is open to the sky like our temples. The street that we are looking for should be close by"

Oedimus saw that the temple his friend was indicating had no roof.

Between towering columns stood an effigy of the Hittites sky god. Legend told that Anus had removed his father Alalus from the throne and opened up the sky to the earth, so that the sun could endow its glory upon Anatolia.

"The house should be located on that street, at the back of the temple." Calphus indicated a spot on the sketch. Looking at where his finger was pointing, Oedimus saw an arrow going south towards a short street. As his friend had said it seemed to be going off the back of the temple building.

It was almost as narrow as an alley and the houses looked murky, in stark contrast to the magnificence of the temple that stood guard at the entrance. The massive house of worship obliterated the sun's light from penetrating the street, making the way appear grey and gloomy.

A black cat darted out of nowhere into the path of their horses, causing the animals to shy. Automatically the two men tightened their hold on the reigns and gripping the horses' flanks with their knees, calmed them. They continued slowly, looking for the house of the man that Ben Abheeb had called Teluza. A young boy came towards them. Oedimus stopped and getting his attention, asked directions. The boy pointed to a house situated almost at the opposite end.

The home of their contact was not much different than his neighbors. Some of the bricks were broken and were a dirty black instead of their original ochre. The wooden door was rotting from use and neglect. Both men alighted from their steeds and tied them to a horse ring situated on the side of the house's wall.

They approached the entrance. In response to Oedimus' sharp rapping the door was opened a crack by a small girl who peered at them from around its edge. "Is this the house belonging to Teluza?" Oedimus' query was met by a nod, while the eyes that stared up at him grew to the size of large, round onyx.

From somewhere inside the house a voice called out, asking who was there? Before the child could reply, Oedimus answered in a voice loud enough to be heard, "my name is Oedimus." He spoke haltingly in the Hittite language. "I have come from Damascus, sent by the Arab, Ben Abheeb."

For a few moments there was silence from within, then the sound of a chair being scraped across a floor. Oedimus detected the shuffling of feet coming closer. He waited. Calphus stood with a hand resting lightly on his scabbard. Their tethered horses snuffled and tossed their manes.

The girl disappeared as the door was flung wide to reveal a man who's bulk filled its width. His body was huge. Underneath the man's beard, a double chin disappeared into his neck and shockingly thick eyebrows sheltered small, penetrating eyes.

He stood appraising them with a suspicious glare. "Why do you come here?" The soft-spoken voice didn't fit the man's size.

"I am Chief Guard to Egypt's pharaoh, the almighty Akhenaton." Indicating his friend, he added. "This is Calphus, my friend and right hand man." He pulled a parchment from his waist belt pocket. "Ben Abheeb of Damascus sends his regards."

The man took the proffered note, opening it swiftly with hands that looked too big to be so dexterous.

Oedimus scrutinized his appearance while the man absorbed the message of introduction. He was clothed in the raiment of the desert people and his thick neck supported a large head. Oedimus noticed an ugly red scar went from his chin to his ear, almost as deep as the lines in the rest of his florid face. He watched as the man's moist red mouth silently formed each word as if he had difficulty in reading the Arab's writing. His bushy moustache wiggled with the movement of his lips in his effort to read the words.

The man finally finished. "How do I know that you are the person that Ben Abheeb says you are?" Looking up, his small eyes locked with Oedimus' own before turning to scrutinize his companion. His cold stare dropped to Calphus' hand resting on

164

the scabbard. "What proof do you have that you are this emissary of Egypt's pharaoh?"

"I have none, other than Ben Abheeb's seal at the bottom of the message - and my word as a loyal Egyptian. I have been sent by Akhenaton to find the traitor who would destroy the peace between our countries. Ben Abheeb assured me of your assistance and we have your king Mussilli's blessings. This matter is of grave importance."

He met the man's gaze unflinchingly. "I do not know you, anymore than you know me. However, I trust Ben Abheeb and have to believe that his confidence in you is well founded. My hope is that you will take his word with regard to me."

The man hesitated for a few seconds longer, his eyes still searching Oedimus' own. Seemingly coming to a decision he stepped back, allowing them to enter. "I am Teluza," he said unnecessarily as he beckoned them to follow him.

They entered a small room that looked surprisingly cozy with its simple wood furnishings. Woven hair rugs covered the dirt floor. A plump woman was taking oaten cakes out of a big stone oven that occupied most of one wall. They smelled delicious and suddenly, Oedimus realized they hadn't eaten since the previous evening.

As if reading his mind, the woman placed several of the wafer thin oatcakes onto a platter and laid them on the roughly hewn table. The child came through a door that led out of the back of the house, carrying a dish of fresh goat curd. Teluza pointed to chairs at the table and invited them to sit, while he poured goat milk into small earthen jars and placed them in front of the two men.

The child stood silently ogling the two strangers but after a few moments the woman spoke a few unintelligible words to her and she moved to sit on a stool by the oven.

The food tasted as good as it smelled and Oedimus watched Calphus help himself to a second oatcake, slathering it with the curds. Teluza sat eyeing them as they ate, while every so often he glanced at Ben Abheeb's note that he still held in his hand. It was as if he was trying to make up his mind about his two visitors, while attempting to gain reassurance from the message.

Oedimus knew he needed to win the man's confidence. "Ben Abheeb spoke highly of your skills, Teluza. He shared with me the time that you both worked together in solving the problem with the Bedouins concerning the ownership of some camels." He didn't reveal the fact that Ben Abheeb had told him very little about the skirmish with the desert nomads, except to mention that Teluza's help had been invaluable. "His obvious gratitude towards you is profound."

The man's expansive body relaxed slightly and his eyes grew less wary. "Ben Abheeb and I have been comrades for a very long time." He considered his visitors for a while longer. "So. Exactly what is it that you want of me?"

The two friends glanced at each other, a wave of unspoken relief passing between them. Oedimus leaned towards the man to emphasize his words. "We need your help Teluza in penetrating the dens of Hattushash." Oedimus told him of his mission and the man listened without comment.

"We believe that this treacherous soldier of Egypt never left your city, and suspect that he is being well hidden. He is the only one that knows who the perpetrators of this foul act are and we need to find him." His tone became passionate. "We <u>must</u> find him. It's imperative that we make him talk. The marriage between our royal houses is in jeopardy. Anatolia and Egypt need to remain allies or else our countries will lose prestige in the eyes of the rest of the world."

Teluza remained quiet as he digested Oedimus' words. The woman busied herself flattening more dough into cakes, while the child sat nibbling on her food. The silence grew as the two Egyptians sat waiting.

Without warning, Teluza raised his bulk from the chair. "Return this evening when the sun has started to set," he stated flatly. "I will make enquiries as to this cur's whereabouts." His face took on a ghost of a smile. "Even rats have to come out of their holes occasionally to breath fresh air." His companions gave audible sighs of relief.

Teluza wasn't finished. "Stay out of sight. Although you are dressed as common citizens you exude the smell of foreign soldiers." Turning to Calphus he stared pointedly at his scabbard. "Displaying your weapon so obviously is not wise. Hide it," he advised - adding. "Do you really think you would have had a chance to use it should I have been an enemy?" The question didn't need an answer.

Dark shadows thrown by the waning light partially hid them as they walked along the street. They had agreed it probably would be less conspicuous to return to the Hittites' house on foot. A stable had been found that smelled of fresh hay, where a lad cleaning manure from the floors had offered to take care of their horses for a reasonable price. The manner in which he'd handled the animals had reassured the two men that they were being left in capable hands.

This time, they didn't have to wait to be admitted. As they approached the house, they saw that Teluza himself was already at the door - waiting. On entering they saw a man sitting by the oven. He looked to be about the same age as Oedimus and Calphus and as athletically built.

Their host introduced him. "This is Kumrab. He brings news that you will want to hear." The young man didn't rise but gave them an Egyptian salute with a bare arm that showed hard biceps and taught knotted tendons.

"Kumrab was in the service of Mussilli's army until an unfortunate accident befell him." For the first time Oedimus noticed that only one leg showed beneath the skirt of the man's short tunic. The other limb was severed just below the knee and showed nothing but a scarred stump. A long, walking stick with a padded block on the top leaned against his chair.

Teluza motioned towards the table that was set with refreshments. "Let's sit in comfort," he said, as he poured wine into mugs. The woman and child were not around.

Kumrab arose and with admirable expertise maneuvered the stick underneath his armpit, to glide smoothly to a seat across from them. Without preamble he began to talk.

Immediately after the two Egyptian's had left his house that morning, Teluza had contacted Kumrab. Apparently, the man still had connections within the Hittites army and also knew the workings of the inner city. From the highest officials to the scum of the earth, Kumrab appeared knowledgeable in getting favors and information from anybody.

He had learned from his army friends that Nekute had left Mussilli's palace along with the rest of the escort. "But after that nobody saw him. He disappeared as swiftly as a bat at sunrise" said Kumrab.

"Lucky for him." Oedimus interjected dourly.

"Of course he has not vanished." Kumrab ignored the interruption and continued. "Nobody disappears at will except the gods, and even they leave behind tell-tale vapor."

He has a wry sense of humor. Oedimus smiled to himself, liking the man already.

"The last time that he was sighted," Kumrab was saying, "he was riding through the city's center. However, he was not heading in the direction of Damascus but towards the inner city." He paused to sample a date.

Oedimus waited while the man selected a yogurt and dipped the fruit into it as delicately as if he were a bee selecting nectar from a flower. Calphus couldn't contain himself. "So, where is he?" he asked impatiently. "If you know, tell us!"

Frowning, Oedimus gave an imperceptible shake of his head. Calphus got the message. "Forgive my seeming rudeness, Kumrab. It is just that we are anxious to find this Son of Darkness before more mischief occurs."

"Your concern is understandable, but care must be taken if you are to catch this man." Kumrab leaned across the table to look directly at Calphus. "As you know, he has not acted alone. Nothing must arouse his suspicions - or those of his compatriots. Acting rashly without a plan would be foolish." Swallowing the date he savored its gritty sweetness before continuing to give an account of the day's events.

It hadn't been easy for Kumrab to gain information on the man's movements. No one seemed to have seen where he went after he'd left the royal grounds. After hours of seeking out his known informants and learning nothing, he was at a dead end. "Then, by a lucky chance that could only have been orchestrated by the gods," said he, "I overheard bits of a conversation between two men who stood outside a brothel."

Kumrab had picked up enough of the conversation to realize that they were talking about 'the Egyptian soldier who had escorted the caravan.' "Their manner and speech led me to believe that their indiscretion in talking so publicly was due to an over indulgence in wine," he said sardonically.

He'd waited and watched as the men entered the professional establishment, then after a discreet amount of time had elapsed followed them. "I know the woman who runs this house of pleasure. She is a good friend."

From the tone of his voice, Oedimus guessed that the woman was more than just a 'good friend.'

While pretending to be a customer, Kumrab had managed to talk with her in private. It had been so easy. When the two not-so-bright men were offered a selection from her available ladies, she'd maneuvered them into picking two of her sharpest. After advising her girls as to what they needed to find out, they were led to her finest boudoirs.

"The prostitutes had little trouble in finding out what I needed to know," said Kumrab. "Expert flattery and promises of sexual delights soon loosened their bragging tongues. After indulging in more liquor along with the girls' amorous attentions, they divulged more than they realized."

It seemed that the two men had been paid a goodly amount to escort the fleeing Egyptian to safety and had apparently been taken to a house that lay at the outskirts of the city. The house belonged to a merchant who supplied serving maids to grand households. Kumrab paused in his narrative –deliberately emphasizing his next words. " This <u>merchant supplies servants to a palace official.</u>"

Odeimus drew in his breath. "Did they reveal the name of this official"?

"Unfortunately they did not."

He slumped dejectedly in his seat.

The one legged man gave him a sly grin. "But, they did let slip the name of the merchant who is harboring your soldier."

Oedimus sprang to his feet. "We must go there immediately!"

"We must leave right away!" Calphus followed suit.

"Stop!" Teluza had risen and held up his hand to stay any further commotion. "This seller of servants is but a player being used in this game." Oedimus sat back down. "It is going to take more than valor and a soldier's strength to get to this man," Teluza spoke with emphasis. "Very wily minds along with careful planning have obviously gone into this venture." He now had his guest's full attention. "One false move and you will loose him again."

He leaned across the table so that his face was close to Oedimus'. "Not to mention the possibility of losing both your lives if you act impulsively." Leaning forward, he scrutinized the the two men, making sure that they heeded his words.

The Egyptians looked abashed. "What do you suggest?" Oedimus questioned, turning to look first at Teluza and then Kumrab.

For several moments the question hung in the air. The two men exchanged knowing glances. "I have already begun to devise a plan and discussed it with Teluza before you arrived," said Kumrab.

CHAPTER EIGHTEEN

*H*is body was cramped from standing in one position for so long. And, from Calphus' fidgeting, he could tell that he too was feeling the results of their long vigil. Kumrab seemed to be the only one unaffected by the strain of waiting. The street was deserted. The sun had not yet fully risen and they'd been here since the stars were still at their brightest.

He gave a start as he felt a sharp nudge to his ribs. Calphus motioned with his head towards the house of the merchant. The door had opened and a shadowy form was coming out. The figure closed the door softly behind him and began to walk down the street. He was approaching the spot where they were standing.

Kumrab beckoned hastily and they backed into the confines of the alley, tromping on a pile of stinking refuse. A rat squealed in protest and scurried out of the way of their feet.

In no time at all, the merchant was hurrying past the entrance to the alley, oblivious to the three sets of eyes watching his progress. Creeping forward, they were just in time to see him reach the end of the street, turn the corner and disappear from sight.

They waited a few more minutes just to be safe, before emerging from the hiding place. The street was still empty and as somnolent as a tomb. A sliver of moon in the periwinkle sky was reluctantly giving way to a rosy dawn. The three men left the alley and walked purposefully towards the house.

Kumrab had taken great pains to ensure that his plan would work. For a few days he had cased the house, watching the comings and goings of the merchant and any other person from the household. Apart from the man of the house there appeared to be no one of significance around the place. Except for servants and an occasional tradesman coming by, nothing of a suspicious nature occurred.

"He leaves early each day and is gone for several hours," he'd informed them when they'd discussed their strategy. "They must be very sure of their hiding place for this soldier, as I did not see any sign of a guard outside the house."

"Maybe they are deliberately leaving the house unguarded so that no attention is drawn to the location," Oedimus commented. "Whoever is orchestrating this concealment is being both cautious and clever. Having someone standing guard would look too suspicious."

Teluza agreed. "Even so, over confidence may prove to be their undoing," he said. "Too much presumption of one's superior abilities has a tendency to make one careless, in which case," he added sagely, "we may have the element of surprise on our side."

Oedimus and Calphus stood back as Kumrab approached and hammered on the door. It was opened almost immediately by a petite, oriental girl. Her waxen complexion emphasized the narrow slitted ebony eyes that stared at Kumrab.

Without preamble, he spoke. "We wish to see your master. Tell him that we have news of the greatest importance regarding his guest from Egypt."

The girl became flustered. "I am most sorry, my master is not here. Was he expecting you?"

173

Kumrab moved closer, his voice ringing with authority. "Of course he is expecting me, stupid girl! When will he return? Did he not tell you that we were to be here today?"

He took a step forward, ready to walk in. "Our illustrious master will be extremely angry if we return without our Egyptian 'merchandise.' We will await his return." Before the girl could react he'd pushed his way into the house, followed closely by the others.

The girl's loud protestations echoed in the hallway and seemingly from out of nowhere, a burly looking individual suddenly appeared. . "What is it, Min Lu? Your cat- a- wailing broke my… he didn't finish what he was about to say as he caught sight of the three strangers.

Before his hand could reach for the dagger at his waist, Calphus had him pinned to the wall with a knife pressed to his throat. "Do not move." The shocked lout gulped, causing the knife's point to prick his Adam's apple. A speck of blood surfaced and his face broke into a sweat. It was clear he thought he was doomed.

Kumrab already held the girl bound with one strong arm, leaning on his walking stick with the other. "Don't make me have to use my sturdy stick on you, girl. I do not wish for it to be sullied with your brains." The girl went limp and he laid her unconscious body gently on the floor.

Oedimus was already checking the room off the entrance. It was empty, but another hall led from it. Approaching the hapless man he got in his face. "Where is the room of the soldier from Egypt?" he hissed. His knowledge of the Hittite language was scant but his expression didn't need any interpreting. Calphus looked as if he wanted to penetrate the man's jugular, while Oedimus' cold expression was a study in murderous intent. The lout didn't utter a word but his eyes veered towards the hall, off the empty room.

Oedimus nodded grimly at his friend. With the tip of his knife, Calphus slowly traced a line from the man's throat to his hairy chest. " Speak." His tone dared the man to remain silent.

"He's in the room at the end, to the left." The choking whisper was barely audible but it was enough for Oedimus, who moved swiftly.

Calphus' dagger scratched out a delicate circle on the man's sternum, nicking his chest in the process. Saliva escaped from the man's mouth as he looked down at the circle. His body slid down the wall, landing on the floor with a thump. Abject terror showed as he looked down at the tiny beads of blood appearing like garnets in the middle of his chest. "Move, and I'll carve a hole through that circle all the way to your heart," Calphus promised. A stench of urine arose as the lout lost control of his bladder.

Kumrab remained on guard as Calphus followed Oedimus to the door at the end of the hall. Oedimus tried the handle but the door didn't budge. Scuffling noises came from inside. Dropping back, Oedimus lunged with a shoulder. The door creaked and began to give way. *Thanks to the gods for its poor condition.* Again, he pulled back – and lunged. There was a sound of splintering wood as the door crashed open - just in time to see a half- dressed figure attempting to climb out of an opening in the opposite wall.

With a flying leap, Oedimus covered the space that separated them. Grabbing the man's legs he hauled him back into the room and Nekute fell heavily. Calphus pinned the flailing arms and legs and even the soldier's undeniable strength couldn't combat the ferocity of his two captors. They had him pinned down and Calphus sat across his body with his dagger at his throat.

Oedimus leaned over Nekute with his knife poised above his face. "Give me an excuse to carve your face into shreds, you disgusting excrement of a dung beetle" The eyes that pierced those of the soldier's were full of cold rage. This was one of his own men that he'd trusted and honored. He badly wanted to slit his throat but he needed him alive. Nekute's eyes flickered then dropped under his commander's contemptuous glare.

He was absolutely exhausted. Oedimus' body ached from lack of sleep and his eyes felt gritty. There was a bitter taste in his mouth that wasn't completely due to lack of hygiene. He still couldn't believe all that Nekute had revealed.

Slumped in a chair across from him, Calphus bloodshot eyes showed the same exhaustion and shock. Only Kumrab and Telluza still looked human.

Catching Oedimus' speculative glance, Kumrab spoke, as if reading his mind. "My friend. You should realize that even the all-powerful Egypt is not immune from devilry among her own people, especially those who are closest to your pharaoh." He arose and took a piece of leavened bread from the dish that Teluza's wife had left on the table.

Teluza nodded in agreement. "Complacency has been the downfall of many nations. Both Anatolia and Egypt would do well to learn from this experience. No land is inviolate and the higher a country climbs in power, the harder it falls." Teluza turned and looked significantly at the merchant and his cowardly abettor, sitting on his floor with hands and feet bound.

He speaks the truth, thought Oedimus. *Egypt is the most powerful country of all - but she is only as powerful as her citizens. If the people lose faith in their pharaoh, they lose their strength.* Rubbing at his stinging eyes, Oedimus looked at the merchant who appeared to be more angry than afraid as he glared back. The circular mark on the other man's chest was an angry red, in sharp contrast to his pasty face.

They had spent the hours of waiting for the merchant's return in questioning the traitor. Oedimus grudgingly admired Nekute's stamina. Their most 'persuasive' physical endeavors hadn't loosened his tongue. Of course, as an Egyptian warrior he'd been trained to endure pain, besides which the man realized that they wouldn't allow him to live whether he talked, or not.

The bombardment of interrogation and torture had produced nothing. Even when Nekute's right arm hung broken and lifeless by his side he stayed silent, gritting his bloodied mouth against the agony of his beaten body.

Kumrab had suggested even worse inducements than those already inflicted. Everyone in the room knew that the Hittite wasn't making idle threats and only Oedimus' intervention had stopped him from carrying them out. After all the man was still an Egyptian.

Oedimus needed Nekute to be coherent enough to tell the truth, not so insane with pain that he'd say anything they wanted him to say. Anyway, promises of blinding with red-hot sticks did nothing to faze him. Even the threat of slicing off his penis had little affect on the man.

Nothing seemed to be working. Finally, Oedimus changed his tactics. He started to talk of the repercussions to his family in Amarna. He pointed out that even his children weren't safe from the pharaoh's wrath. After hours of persecuting the man the Chief Guard didn't care what happened to Nekute, or his kin.

He was ice cold in his anger and Nekute saw in his face that Oedimus meant what he said. At mention of his family, the man's face turned grayer than it was already. To his physical agony, this new fear had been added. Oedimus saw the change come over him. He moved in for the kill.

"Can you imagine the retribution that Akhenaton will take on your wife and children?" He stared at the soldier with eyes as merciless as a wild animal that teases its prey. "And, after our pharaoh is through with them, if there is anything left I will personally finish them off with the most delightful trimmings I can think of."

Nekute made a feeble attempt to lurch to his feet but Calphus casually kicked him back down. Through swollen, pain filled eyes he looked pathetically at his captors. "My family has done no harm," he whispered. "The pharaoh would not take revenge on them." The words sounded thick through bruised and cut lips. Underneath the fearful tone was a ring of anguished pleading.

The two friends exchanged merciless chuckles, but Oedimus' expression remained as hard as granite. "Are you willing to take that risk?" His voice was deadly calm. "Our king is a benevolent ruler- but Aten is unforgiving. Even the great Akhenaton himself would not dare dishonor Aten-Ra as you have." He leaned over the man's body, "do you really think that any gods will give you and your family salvation, even should your pharaoh show mercy?"

Nekute crumbled. Except for the tremulous movements of his chest as he breathed, he appeared lifeless. "Liquid. My mouth is parched." The request was barely audible.

Oedimus nodded to Calphus who left the room, returning with wine. Calphus knelt by the man and held the cup to his lips while he drank greedily, slurping as he gulped at the refreshment. He began to choke and splutter but his mouth still tried to cling to the rim. Oedimus took the goblet from Calphus' grip.

"Enough." The man raised his head and looked at him pityingly. "Talk. Then you may have more." Sobbing quietly, the broken soldier began his tale of deceit and deception.

Oedimus would never forget the look on Nekute's face as he'd raised his dagger and sealed the traitor's fate. He'd looked almost relieved, as if happy to be going to the After Life.

It was still difficult to grasp the amount of scheming and devilry involved. Even more incomprehensible was Nekute's revelation concerning the pharaoh's own priest! Oedimus was still having difficulty in accepting the Holy Man's diabolical mind-set. Not to mention this Hittite official who apparently was as close to Mussilli as Hytoph was to Akhenaton. He mentally shook his head. How did they know each other? *It doesn't matter.* What was significant was how they were able to find so much weakness among Egypt's people in order to devise such a plan? *How could they even consider getting away with such a scheme?* But, they almost had.

He shrugged his shoulders, thankful that it had been stopped. What was important now was to leave this pesthole of a country and get back to Amarna. Akhenaton needed to be apprised of this mad act of treason so that he could take necessary action.

Without question, Akhenaton needed to confer with Mussilli as soon as possible. Whatever the Hittites would do to their traitorous official was not his business. Egypt's peaceful existence was, not to mention the pharaoh's safety.

Rolling his head from side to side, he attempted to loosen the stiffness in his neck and shoulders. The sooner they could deal with this priest from Hell, the better he would feel.

"What shall we do with your soldier's body?"

Teluza's question brought him back to the present. "We need to bury him where he cannot be found" adding, "apart from not letting our enemies know he is dead, he does not deserve the honor of a warrior's burial."

"I will take care of it." Kumrab's smile was not pleasant. "This man is garbage and needs to be buried with garbage." He nodded towards the two bound men sitting on the floor. "Should we dispose of them also?" Two pair of eyes looked horror struck at Kumrab's dispassionate question.

"No. There is no need to kill them." Oedimus' tone was equally unfeeling. "They were nothing but hired help."

He already had too much blood on his hands. The death of Nekute had been as much as he could stand. He eyed the prisoners with unconcern, "deliver them to Mussilli and let their own people do what they see fit."

Kumrab grinned. "They will wish that you had ordered their slaying before Mussilli is through with them."

His wife laid a platter of food in front of him, but he ignored it. The mouth- watering aromas emitting from the dish did nothing to stir Teluza's appetite. *What is taking him so long? He should have returned hours past.* Kumrab had left with the two prisoners shortly after the two Egyptians had departed.

Teluza's thoughts momentarily switched to the Egyptians. Both had earned his grudging respect. *They are not soft, even though Egyptian.* He'd suggested they rest a while before leaving but the Chief Guard had been adamant. He needed to return to Amarna as fast as possible.

Where is he? Once again Teluza's mind grappled with his dire thoughts. What had happened to his friend and compatriot?

Like the two soldiers, Kumrab had refused to rest before leaving for the center of the city in order to turn the two prisoners over to Mussilli's palace guards. Teluza had offered to travel with him, but he'd scoffed at the idea. "Do you think that I cannot handle two insects such as these?"

This had been hours ago and still no sign of his return. Picking up his goblet, he raised it to his lips only to find it empty. His hand stayed in the act of reaching for his jug as a faint rap came to his door.

Teluza was on his feet before his wife and child could move from their seats. "I will answer it," he barked. "Go into the other room and don't come out until I call you."

Cautiously he cracked the door open - immediately flinging it wide at sight of his friend. Kumrab leaned against the door jam, barely standing on his one good leg. Caked blood streaked his face and the man hung heavily onto his stick. His body started to slide down.

Before he hit the ground Teluza had grabbed him and lifted

him like a baby, carrying him into his house and slamming the door shut with his foot. Kumrab's face was ashen underneath the blood oozing from a deep gash across his forehead. One eye was closed and swollen shut. The color was that of overripe meat. His stick thudded to the floor as his head fell back in a faint.

"WOMAN!" Teluza's wife came running. "Boil water and fill it with your strongest medicines. NOW!"

She took in the situation at a glance and didn't need any further bidding. "Place him on our bed," she stated. Teluza moved quickly to a room off the main one, lowering his burden onto the big bed. The man lay limp and lifeless, his blooded face a ghastly color.

A tightly wrapped bandage swathed Kumrab's head and for the first time in three days, it wasn't reddened with seepage. His head turned on the pillow and through a haze, he caught sight of the man sleeping in a chair.

"Teluza?" At the faint sound the man came upright. His brain had picked up the soft-spoken call even though he'd been dozing. Kumrab's eyes were open and staring at him.

Forgetting the cramps in his body, Teluza arose quickly and leaned over the figure. "My friend, you don't know how glad I am to see you awake." Teluza wasn't a man to show emotion but his voice sounded gruffer than usual and his eyes glistened.

Tufts of hair sticking out around the bandage were matted with dried blood. Kumrab's face was still as white as the dressing, except for the discoloring bruises that splotched the area of his swollen eye. The eye was no longer closed, but broken blood vessels made it look like a pomegranate.

"Can you see me clearly?'

"Yes." With a semblance of a smile Kumrab added, "how could anyone not see your massive bulk?"

A chuckle born of relief arose from deep within Teluza's belly.

"Thanks be to our goddess, Hannahannas. And, to our glorious Teshub for watching over you so that you did not die at the hands of the dragons from Hell!"

He hadn't been sure that his friend was going to live. In spite of his wife's expert ministrations, Kumrab had developed a horrendous fever. He'd tossed and turned, moaning unintelligible words while Teluza sat vigil at the bedside for what seemed like eternity. Occasionally, he'd wet Kumrab's mouth and wipe his perspiring body with cooling water loaded with medicinal herbs.

The dressings to his ghastly wound had to be changed constantly, and he'd wondered how much blood a man could lose before dying? Kumrab had thrashed in his delirium when Teluza's wife ministered to the gash with her salves and pastes.

Gradually the fever had appeased and on the morning of the third day, his breathing had become less labored. He'd slept solidly throughout yesterday and all through last night.

Morning light was beginning to steal into the room. Turning his head, Teluza looked through the opening set high in the wall. He saw Venus' strong light shining in the paling sky. It was a good omen. Kumrab's light hadn't been extinguished.

His wife fed him the nourishing broth and in between slow sips, he told what had happened. It was just as Teluza had feared.

Kumrab had been almost to the palace entrance with his two prisoners in tow. Feeling good at having successfully helped in thwarting the plan of destruction, he rode along the streets with the creatures shuffling behind his horse. Although they were not as well bound as they had been in the house, their hands were still tethered. A long rope fastened them to the horses' neck and he was making them walk as fast as his animal moved. Kumrab's self-confidence was high and he didn't concern himself with the occasional, curious glance that was thrown his way.

Few people were about at this time of the day as the noontime sun was at its hottest. Besides, people were used to seeing prisoners being escorted to the palace's barracks. Shoplifters – vagabonds – gypsies – anyone who had broken a law or two, were often escorted thus.

Kumrab was too elated to notice the three non-de-script characters that kept appearing behind him. One by one they stayed at a discreet distance as he made his way through the streets.

Eager to reach the palace grounds, he took a short cut through a narrow alleyway. Normally used only by trade's people for the unloading of their wares, the alley was full of garbage – and empty of people. Dust arose from his horse's hooves as they trotted over the hot, dried mud and stinking refuse. There wasn't a breath of air in the narrow passage and heat bounced of the brick buildings. Kumrab took his kerchief and wiped sweat from his face and neck, feeling relieved that he was near to unloading his 'burden'. Carelessly he looped the damp kerchief into his belt.

The horse whinnied and came to a halt, tossing his head and gingerly raising a front hoof. Cursing underneath his breath, Kumrab planted his stick on the ground for support, before swinging his one good leg to the ground. Making sure that his prisoners were still secure, he knelt and lifted his horse's hoof. He saw the problem. A sharp rock had wedged in between the foot's padding.

A shadow fell across his bent body and he started to turn his head. Automatically he reached for his dagger. It was tangled in his kerchief and even as he struggled to set it free, he knew it was too late. Instinctively Kumrab bent sideways in an attempt to avert the blow but a searing pain across his forehead left him gasping for air. He fell backwards as blood gushed down his face.

Through a sickening haze, his eyes discerned activity going on around his prisoners. A blurred image bent over him and fumbled at his waist. Making an attempt to get up caused another explosion of pain as a foot landed brutally in his side followed by a fist slamming into his face. His head felt as if it were exploding - before everything went black.

"When I regained consciousness, night was falling and no one was around. My horse stood nibbling on stinking food-waste. Luckily those fire breathing sons of Illuyankas had not taken my walking stick, being hidden underneath me." He stopped talking and shook his head as Teluza's wife offered him more broth. His head sank into his pillows. "I feel as helpless as a new born infant."

"I'm amazed that you were able to get back," said Teluza. "Your blood loss was so great that I feared for your survival."

"I don't remember how I got here." Exhaustion threatened to overcome Kumrab but with an effort, he forced himself to continue. "I do vaguely remember seeing an empty crate close by and thought to use it to pull myself across my horses' back. A youth passing the alley saw me and ran to my side. I thought he was looking to rob me, but the gods must have sent him as he asked if he could help. After assisting me in clambering onto my horse, I managed to tell him where you lived and asked that he lead my horse to your house. Everything else is a blur. He must have led me as far as your door and helped me down." Kumrab suddenly remembered his steed. "What of my horse?"

Teluza reassured the invalid. "He is in much better condition than his master. I saw to his stabling" He picked up the bowl of broth. "You have talked enough. Finish this and then you will rest."

Obediently, Kumrab drank from the spoon that Teluza held to his mouth but shook his head when offered more. "I think I gave the boy my coin pouch for his goodness and told him to go on his way. If he had not led me here, I doubt that I would have made it on my own. My life is owed to a stranger."

Teluza replaced the bowl with a wine goblet and lifted his head so that he could take a drink. After resting for a minute,

Kumrab continued to talk. "I know the cowardly vermin will have long since gone underground and won't be found." Weakness showed in his tremulous voice as frustration and anger contorted his features.

"You are not to blame," Teluza gently reminded him. "How were we to know that our enemies were so close at hand? They must have been watching the house and saw you leave with the curs."

Kumrab shook his head in regret. "Even so, I should not have been so careless as to make my presence on the streets so obvious." He tried to raise himself into a sitting position but fell back helplessly.

"Do not exert yourself. Fretting will not help your recovery." The big man fussed to rearrange the cushions for comfort and straightened his bed covering. In spite of his condition, Kumrab gave a wan smile of amusement.

Straightening up, the big man caught the look on Kumrab's face and scowled. "Your life is no laughing matter. I believe you think yourself as immortal as the gods!"

The amusement left Kumrab. "You have saved my life friend and I am forever indebted to you." His next words voiced his anxiety, "how are we to alert the two Egyptians that the prisoners have escaped?"

Teluza looked thoughtful, "hopefully, they should be well away from Anatolia by this time and they know who their Egyptian traitor is. By now they are probably nearing the safety of Damascus. As insurance though, I will personally ask an audience of Mussilli and advise him of all that has taken place. The faster our king is made aware of the enemy that is close to him, the quicker he can act before the perpetrator is able to escape."

"Through Mussilli's messengers, my words will reach Amarna faster than Oedimus and his companion. In this way, Akhenaton may take immediate action against his own traitorous conspirator, long before his warriors have returned. You know how swiftly our own king will act against enemies. I'm sure that no matter how deeply the cockroaches have burrowed, Mussilli's soldiers will find them."

Teluza stopped talking. His compatriot's face was beaded in perspiration and he arose. "You must rest now and no more worrying about what you should or shouldn't, have done. You will live another day and if the gods are willing, you will get your revenge."

Kumrab's eyes had begun to close before he had vacated the room, but his breathing was easy.

CHAPTER NINETEEN

"Are you not listening to what is being discussed?" Meteh looked annoyed and the girl shifted uncomfortably, "I am sorry mother, my mind was elsewhere." The girl brought her mind back to the common room.

I know where your mind was! Meteh could barely keep a blistering response from escaping her lips. *That man has not only taken your body, but has taken your brain and turned it into romantic slush!* In exasperation she repeated herself, "we are discussing the celebrations for the forthcoming wedding and need your help in organizing the dancing girls."

Meryhken's dancing expertise was generally known by everyone and especially admired by Akhenaton. "But mother, the wedding plans are still unsure." Under normal circumstances, teaching the harem maidens knew steps were a task she enjoyed.

With a dismissive wave of her hand the woman responded. "It will take place, you'll see." Merykhen tried to curb her frustration. *Doesn't she realize the seriousness of this problem?* Obediently she forced herself to listen as Meteh talked. "As soon as the pharaoh's Chief Guard has found the people who stole from the wedding

187

dowry, everything will continue as before. That is his job." Grudgingly she added, "and in the past he has performed it well. There is no reason to believe that he won't be successful again."

Her manner is as casual as if she were talking about getting rid of a blemish on a harem girl's face! Meryhken clamped her mouth to stay her tongue as Meteh continued to talk.

"Once all these minor difficulties have been resolved, the princess will leave for Anatolia to meet her betrothed."

She wanted to scream at her mother's complacency! *How can she be so casual when he has placed his life in danger? Is she blind and deaf to this situation?* With an effort she forced herself to sound composed. "Of course, mother. Tell me what you would like me to do?"

As mindlessly as if she were a spool of thread spinning on its wheel she half listened to the women's plans for celebrations, injecting her own appropriate remarks when asked. It was useless to try and explain to Meteh the seriousness of this breach between the two countries. Like all the harem women, Meteh was only interested in that which pertained to her role as the pharaoh's concubine.

By this time her warning message to Oedimus should have reached his hands. *At least, I hope this is so.* Ever since Psarta had shared his revealing story, Meryhken had kept her eyes and ears open, deliberately going out of her way to 'accidentally' come into contact with the priest. So far she had seen nothing of a suspicious nature in his attitude. *Except for the fact that he causes my skin to crawl.* Although his behavior around her was nothing more than 'priest-like' she didn't trust Hytoph.

"What colors do you think the girls should wear, Meryhken?" She turned to the person who had spoken, "I believe that each one should wear white, for purity." Her voice held the right amount of interest and the woman looked pleased. All the women began to give voice to their own ideas. The common room began to resound with high-pitched squawking as each female tried to be heard above everyone else. Meryhken retreated into herself.

Psarta couldn't wait to tell her. His usual composure had taken flight as he paced outside her room, hoping that Meteh wouldn't catch him there.

As soon as she saw him, she knew something had happened. The harem discussions had been mentally exhausting but her spirit lightened at sight of her friend.

He hurried forward as she came along the hallway, casting a quick glance towards the entrance. "Is Meteh nearby?"

"No. She left with one of the women to select cloth for the wedding celebrations - - Psarta, what is wrong?" He started to speak but she stopped him. "Wait." She opened her door, "come inside where we have privacy."

They stood on the balcony, just in case her mother should make an unexpected appearance. If needs be, it would be easy for him to hop over the low wall and escape discovery.

"I have just spent the morning with Chenkiop." At Meryhken's request, Psarta had deliberately been seeking out the boy as a means of learning about the priest's daily activities.

"And?" She sensed his excitement and her own eagerness grew.

"His master had a visitor yesterday - - a most uncommon visitor." He stood silent with a knowing smile on his face.

Meryhken wanted to shake him! " Stop playing with me!"

He leaned forward and whispered in her ear as if afraid of being overheard, even though there was no one in sight. "It was a stranger. A Hittite delivering a message to Hytoph."

A huge Macaw sat on a low branch of a tree that overhung the balcony. The bird eyed them balefully. Flashes of brilliant color contrasted against the yellow sky as it ruffled its feathers in disgust at being disturbed.

Meryhken stared wide-eyed at her friend. "How do you know he was a Hittite?"

Placing his hands on his hips and looking pleased with himself, Psarta's answer came with an air of confidence, "because I saw the message!"

An involuntary gasp escaped the girl. "What are you saying?" She sat down on the wall. "Surely you were not in the priest's apartments?"

He lowered himself to sit alongside her, "no one saw me in there." Smiling smugly, he continued. "Chenkiop showed it to me while his master was with the pharaoh and his family in the temple, performing the daily prayers."

She sat in stupefaction as he began his incredible story. He had learned from Chenkiop that on several occasions, Hytoph had received messengers bringing him communications from various places. This in itself was not unusual. Being the pharaoh's Holy Man meant that messages frequently went back and forth between the temples of Amarna, Karnak, Thebes - as well as cities beyond Egypt.

But, when Chenkiop had started to tell of the messenger 'who was dressed in funny clothes and talked strangely' he'd gained Psarta's attention. "He said that the man spoke our language with great difficulty and Chenkiop couldn't understand what he wanted. He finally gave up and fetched Hytoph. Fortunately, the priest had been in a good mood and didn't reprimand his serving boy for disturbing him."

"Hytoph must have known the visitor, because he immediately invited him into his private rooms and dismissed Chenkiop. Before the priest closed the door, he heard the man say the word 'attack' and the priest answering, Chief Guard... becoming too much of a nuisance."

Meryhken gripped the edge of the wall for support. Noticing that her face had paled Psarta quickly interjected, "I'm sure that

Oedimus is alright. We would have heard through Akhenaton's messengers if he were not."

Meryhken straightened her back. "Please continue." Apprehension filled her mind as she listened, wondering what Oedimus and his friend Calphus had learned - and if they were safe?

Psarta had questioned Chenkiop extensively and the simple-minded boy had been proud to show how clever he really was. He knew exactly where Hytoph kept all his correspondence. Psarta wanted to embrace the boy but curbed his enthusiasm, knowing that Chenkiop didn't need more encouragement. The simpleton already idolized him and followed him around like a shadow. His adoration was embarrassing.

Psarta did however promise him one of his best stones if he would show him the priest's hiding place. Chenkiop was eager to please, and revealed the hours when the priest would be away from his apartments and in the temple. Psarta thanked the fates for the boy. "Chenkiop isn't as senseless as most people seem to think he is," he stated. "It's surprising how much he really understands."

Meryhken couldn't speak. Her heart was hammering against her chest and her hands felt clammy. *They invaded a priest's apartments!* She felt as if she were choking. "How could you have been so foolish? What if you had been caught?" Meryhken had never felt so much panic in her life. Images of what could have happened had they been discovered, raced through her mind.

"But we weren't," he answered flippantly. His face was a picture of jubilation.

She stared at him, feeling impotent in the face of his seeming lack of fear. Psarta's attitude was such that he thought the risk he was taking was just a game. Guilt overwhelmed her for having placed her friend in such danger. *I should never have involved him.* Not to mention the danger to Chenkiop.

"You should have talked to me first Psarta, before taking such a risk," she admonished.

The smile left his face. "Why? So that you could have advised me against such actions?" He didn't wait for an answer, "Egypt is as much my country as it is yours. If there are people trying to undermine our security, then it is also my concern." He laid a hand over hers reassuringly, "don't worry, Meryhken. I took every precaution and would not have attempted it had I not known that I was safe."

"The other servants are used to seeing Chenkiop coming and going from the priest's rooms and would not think it unusual. He was very good at sneaking me in without being seen. We only stayed long enough to check the drawer, and look at his correspondence." He grinned wickedly, "besides don't you want to know what I found?"

In spite of her fears Meryhken's curiosity got the better of her, "tell me."

"Actually, I couldn't read the letter as it was in the Hittite language. Even so, I could tell that it had come from Anatolia as it was written on the rough material they use. There were several such letters in the hiding place of his desk." Half to himself, he added wonderingly, "I still haven't any idea how Chenkiop opened the drawer."

"It was locked?"

"Yes. But he used a strange piece of metal to open it without damaging the lock. I told you that Chenkiop isn't so dumb!"

Meryhken couldn't believe what she was hearing, but Psarta remained unperturbed. He was as nonchalant as if invading a priest's privacy was an every day occurrence! Psarta continued his tale, "a few of the words were recognizable - that is, the words 'Chief Guard' and 'Akhenaton' and also a phrase containing words that looked like, 'wedding stalled.' It also was not signed, but had the letter 'C' at the end."

192

"I know of no one of importance with a name beginning with C." Meryhken's thoughts were spinning. "Then, I do not know the people of Anatolia's palace except of course, the king and his name does not begin with that letter."

Psarta leaned forward conspiratorially. "The letters weren't the only item in his drawer." Meryhken held her breath, wondering what else he was going to reveal.

The Macaw suddenly gave a series of loud squawks and flew out of the tree, seemingly in protest at the invasion of his peace by the whispering people below.

She looked questioningly and Psarta leaned even closer. "There was a thick binder and I opened it. They were obviously notes from Hytoph to himself, written almost daily according to the recorded dates." He grinned at sight of her incredulous expression. "One item in particular was very significant." Emphasizing his next words, he spoke slowly and deliberately. " It gave the very day that the 'two Egyptian trackers' had left Damascus and were headed for Anatolia. Also, that he must notify 'C' of this."

A slight breeze moved the hem of Meryhken's dress and rustled the fronds of the tree that shaded the balcony. Flowers swayed in unison. The motionless figures could have been a part of the natural scenery.

"He has to be referring to Oedimus and Calphus."

Psarta nodded, "there has to be someone in Anatolia who is working with Hytoph against Egypt."

"Praise to the gods that I had the foresight to send that message to Oedimus." Her tone changed to uncertainty. "But what can we do now?"

Her first reaction was to tell Akhenaton of his priest's treachery. There was now no doubt in her mind that Hytoph was the traitor behind the recent catastrophes. She didn't know why he had turned against his pharaoh, but this damaging evidence had proved her instincts to be right. *How can I inform the pharaoh without revealing Psarta's part in these discoveries?* Akhenaton would want to know how she had come by her information.

If it became known that Psarta and the serving boy had invaded Hytoph's dwelling, the repercussions didn't bare imagining. Even though that priest was not fit to wear the holy robes, invading his home was akin to invading the tombs of the pharaohs in the Sacred Valley of Kings.

Mentally shaking her head, her thoughts grew increasingly somber. *It would be seen as blasphemous as if they had defiled the temple.* The fact that they had disclosed Hytoph's deception would not be an excuse for their foolhardy act. Even so, it would not bide well for Hytoph if Akhenaton should become aware of his priest's treason. He needed to be stopped before he could do more damage. Meryhken's mind was in turmoil.

" I dare not inform Akhenaton of your find." She was adamant and Psarta understood her reasoning all too well. "Yet it's imperative that I get word to Oedimus of this." Her voice filled with desperation and knowing of her deep involvement with the Chief Guard, Psarta felt a wave of sympathy for her.

Anticipating Meryhken's request, he didn't hesitate. "I will contact the same person who delivered the last message to Oedimus. He is trustworthy and fast."

Meryhken took his hands in her own, "you are more than my friend, Psarta. You are like my own blood kin." Her eyes were bright with tears. "Promise me this. Please do not take anymore such risks. If anything happened to you I would never forgive myself."

Psarta didn't answer. He couldn't trust himself to speak. The boy's own emotions were equally as full as he squeezed the hands that grasped his own.

CHAPTER TWENTY

$\mathcal{T}$he sky was ablaze with stars, some denser than others. Clusters joined together in a magnitude of never-ending splendor. No moon was visible so that the glory was displayed in all its fantastic perfection.

Even though the thick blanket cushioned his body against the hard ground, Oedimus couldn't sleep. The only sound to break the deep silence of the night was Calphus' soft snores as he slept nearby. One of the horses gave a snuffle. All was quiet.

Although his eyes were focused on the sky above him, Oedimus' mind was elsewhere. They were almost to Damascus and should reach the city by mid-morning of the morrow. From there, he would have the governor send a messenger ahead of them to apprise Akhenaton of the devilry he'd unearthed. His whirling thoughts would give him no rest.

It would be difficult for the pharaoh to believe that his own priest had instigated this plot. *I have difficulty in believing it myself.* Even so, it was too incredible for Nekute to have made up such a story. He had nothing to gain by doing so, especially knowing that he was about to die anyway. The soldier had been desperate to try and save his family from harm, so that accusing the priest would not have served any purpose. On the contrary, if it wasn't true it could do his family more harm than good. Did Hytoph really think he could gain more power and the people's trust, by breaking their pharaoh's laws?

His brain refused to think logically anymore. He knew that Akhenaton would take necessary action for the priest's grievous sins. Now let Amun save Hytoph from his pharaoh's wrath!

Yawning, he turned over and bunched the blanket under his head into a more comfortable position. Deliberately closing his eyes, he willed himself to relax. The campfire's dying light was the last thing he saw before he fell asleep.

The horses' fretful winnowing broke through his dreams. Bolting upright, he saw that Calphus was already on his feet. Oedimus grabbed his dagger and sprang upright as the smell of danger hit him.

In the faint pre-dawn light, he discerned three shadowy figures on the other side of the campfire's smoldering embers. No longer creeping stealthily, the figures charged with raised weapons.

Adeptly side-stepping a swinging axe, he spun his heels and slashed at his attacker, his knife connecting with the man's face. Howling curses, the Hittite clamped a hand to the slit on his cheek, at the same time attempting to fend off further attack. Abruptly, the man fell to his knees as Oedimus' foot made heavy contact with the man's groin. Not waiting to see him double over in agony, he dashed over to where his friend was frantically warding off blows from the other two attackers. Blood trickled down Calphus' left arm from a nasty looking gash. With his other hand he was waving his dagger back and forth, desperately trying to avert certain death.

Oedimus leapt onto the back of one of the murderous thugs and bringing his arm around the man's shoulder -thrust his dagger into the middle of his chest. He felt it sink into muscle and cartilage as he plunged upwards through the middle of the rib cage. The man gave a grunt and arched backwards, toppling Oedimus off his back in the process. He fell to the ground, landing next to the man. Oedimus crouched in readiness for further attack, but saw that the man lay still. A trickle of blood ran from the corner of the open mouth and the lifeless face was set in astonishment.

Oedimus scrambled to his knees and looked up in time to see Calphus straddling the other man, cutting his opponent's jugular as neatly as if he were slaughtering a pig. Quickly noting that his friend was safe, he bent to roll over his victim and remove his dagger embedded in the chest.

"LOOK OUT!"

Startled by the warning cry, he instinctively ducked. A glint of metal caught his peripheral vision - - as an explosive pain shattered his head and traveled down his body. He never heard Calphus scream his name.

The Hittite with the gash on his cheek stood over Oedimus' still form. Calphus' knife sank deeply into flesh as he flung himself at the murderer. The dog didn't realize what had hit him as he toppled over, landing atop of Oedimus' inert body.

Dropping to his knees, Calphus shoved aside the Hittites' carcass as if it were so much excrement. Unbelievable panic gripped him. The opaque eyes in the strangely peaceful face stared up at him unseeing. Thick, dark blood slowly seeped from underneath Oedimus' head, forming a widening puddle on the ground.

He can't be dead! His brain refused to believe his eyes. Wasn't Oedimus a brilliant fighter and invincible? Wasn't he one of the gods own protected people? *He's alive – he has to be alive.* One second Calphus had seen him kneeling over the corpse and in the next moment the Hittite from Hell was towering over him. It had happened so fast.

Comprehension began to dawn. A seeping agony began to spread through him like the spreading pool of blood on the ground.

"OEDIMUS!"

By sheer force of will, Calphus tried to make his friend respond. The body didn't move. In a stupor, he stared at the still form of the man he loved as a brother.

He'd been too busy battling for his own life to see the other man. Slowly rising like a viper, the murderer had slithered towards Oedimus' kneeling form. By the time Calphus saw him the devil's weapon had found its victim.

As a new day began to dawn, the still figure of the man sat as if mesmerized. Blank eyes stared up at him. The black hair was sticky and matted with blood. The man finally moved. Calphus gently turned his friend's head to one side, hoping to stench the flow. His shocked mind still refusing to accept what his eyes were telling him.

He swallowed down the bile that arose in his throat. The axe lay firmly embedded in Oedimus' skull and the back of the head was cleaved into two parts. As he ineffectually tried to remove the axe, gray matter spilled from the cavity. Horror filled his being as he stared at the clumps of bloodied brain lying in his hands.

A terrible wailing reverberated across the Syrian landscape, echoing back from the mountains like a responding dirge of sympathy. The man was unaware that the lamentations came from deep within his own guts.

The rising sun bathed the distant mountains in a deep orange glow. Sunlight stole across the land and gently stroked the man cradling the lifeless body. Calphus rocked back and forth, holding his friend like a baby.

CHAPTER TWENTYONE

*M*eryhken was so elated she felt like bursting! How long had it been since they'd been together? It seemed like forever. Every waking hour of her days had been spent in waiting for Oedimus' return. The time had dragged slower than the temple priests' droning incantations of worship. Blessed be the gods! He'd finally returned home.

Word of the arrival of 'the soldier back from the mission' had arrived around noontime.

The news had spread like wildfire throughout the palace grounds and most important, Oedimus was being hailed as a hero.

Ever since hearing the glad tidings she'd been unable to contain herself. She'd counted the minutes until she could be with him. Maybe now that he had pleased the pharaoh they could approach Akhenaton and ask for his blessings in marriage? Surely her father would not refuse them after his Chief Guard had served him so well? Her mood was lighter than it had been in months.

So much had taken place and she could hardly wait to tell

him. Since the pharaoh's personal priest had unexpectedly died, everyone wondered what next the gods had in store for Egypt. Rumors had flown throughout the palace after Hytoph's servant had found his master's body.

No one knew what had caused the priest to kill himself but Meryhken had her suspicions. Chenkiop had found Hytoph slumped in his chair as if asleep, except his face had been the color of blue dye and set in a distorting grimace. It was said that his hand gripped a wine goblet so tightly that the physician, who had been hastily summoned, had to break the fingers to get them unclasped. Chenkiop saw the medic sniff the wine goblet, then murmur the word - "Poison."

Meryhken felt such a sense of relief, as she hadn't experienced in weeks. For days her mind had wrestled with the advisability of telling her father what she knew about his Holy Man. But, trying to devise a way to unmask the priest without involving Chenkiop and Psarta was impossible. She had tried and tried racking her brains, but no feasible explanation was forthcoming. *I should have trusted that the gods would take care of the problem as they saw fit.*

Shortly after the Hittite had unexpectedly arrived with a message for Akhenaton, Hytoph's body had been found. According to gossip, after the pharaoh had read the missive he'd roared loud enough to shake the pyramids! People had thought that it was more bad news from King Mussilli but apparently not, as Akhenaton had immediately ordered a continuance of the marriage arrangements. It was when he'd sent for his priest that Chenkiop had made the discovery.

Meryhken had to stifle the urge to seek out her father and learn first-hand the news he'd received. Of course, she didn't dare. As close as the bond was between them, even she would not be so foolish as to approach him when his mood was so black. After learning of the priest's death, Akhenaton had secluded himself for hours and no one dared disturb him. She would just have to be patient and learn from her love what had taken place.

She paced back and forth amidst the temple ruins, unable to sit still. *Where is he?* For the thousandth time she questioned his absence. Glancing up through the columns at the crescent moon, she noticed that it had risen even higher since she'd first arrived. *Be calm Meryhken.* She silently chastised herself for her impatience. *Of course, Akhenaton has much to discuss with him and no doubt wishes to keep him in celebration.*

Almost an hour later she dragged her way back along the path. *He isn't coming.* With head bowed she slowly walked home, a puzzled frown knitting her brows. *Surely he is as anxious to be with me as I am with him?*

The well-worn path was partly shrouded by ornamental trees that had been allowed to go wild. Soft sounds came from the bushes alongside the edges, as her footsteps disturbed nocturnal creatures going about their nightly business. Mechanically, she retraced her steps along the path that a short time before she'd seemed to fly over. Reaching the outer edges of the harem courtyard, she stopped. Peering intently in the direction of a stone seat, she saw a shadow move underneath the trees.

A dark silhouette arose from the bench. Shadows masked the figure, but she made out that it was a man. Her heart leapt. For a wild moment she experienced exquisite joy. It must be Oedimus!

The figure started to come towards her and as he left the shelter of the trees, she could see him more fully. It was Oedimus' friend, the one known as Calphus.

Meryhken couldn't move. An ominous feeling washed over her. *Why is he here and not Oedimus?* It suddenly struck her that the gossips had only mentioned one man's return.

As he drew closer she noted the tight set of his jaw. Trembling with a dread that she couldn't comprehend - or didn't want to, she hugged herself in protection.

201

Calphus came to a stop in front of her. He seemed to have difficulty speaking and when he did, his voice shook, "Meryhken, I bring you terrible news." He gulped as his throat constricted.

Looking into his eyes she saw agony written there. Her heart plummeted. She waited for him to continue.

But Calphus didn't speak. He couldn't. Instead, he held out an object. Bewildered, she took it from him. It was her box that she'd given to Oedimus. Trancelike, she opened the ornate lid. Inside were brown and withered flower petals and a dried twig that had once been its stem. A smell of decay arose from within.

Why do I feel so cold? She looked at Calphus questioningly.

"Oedimus is dead, Meryhken." An agonized whisper was all he could manage.

There was a ringing in her ears. Calphus' image began to blur. The next moment, she felt strong arms supporting her body. Gently, he half carried her across the courtyard to the stone bench. Her body sagged limply against him as he sat her down on the cold slab, chafing her hands between his warm, callused palms. She was unaware of anything except a sense of unreality. Her body didn't seem to exist.

Calphus was talking to her, but his voice seemed to come from a great distance and she couldn't comprehend the words that he spoke. What had he said about Oedimus? Dead? No, she'd been mistaken. Oedimus would never leave her. Never! He'd promised to find a way for them to be married hadn't he? He had promised!...... But where was he? Why hadn't he met with her tonight? Meryhken gripped the box tightly, as if hanging on to life.

The man looked on in desperation, wishing that he could call for assistance - or at least had some warm wine to give her.

For the longest time Meryhken sat, her face completely devoid of color. Finally she spoke. "What happened?"

He couldn't tell her how Oedimus had met his death. It was

too hard even for a hardened soldier such as himself, to relive those circumstances. His friend's death scene haunted his sleep every night and had been with him constantly throughout the days since. "One of those wild beasts of darkness took him unawares and cut him down," he answered. "I should have stayed closer to him, but there was so much confusion."

The voice was full of guilt as he continued, "Oedimus had relaxed his guard and was bending to retrieve his knife. This murdering barbarian was suddenly behind him. I rushed to help him. But I was too late." Tears swam in his eyes as his words recounted a softened version of Oedimus' death. He had to stop and swallow several times as he spoke.

She sat watching his face as he told the story, and Meryhken's breaking heart was filled with sympathy. Wasn't there also this same gut wrenching pain inside her belly? It seemed to be consuming her with its energy.

Her chest felt constricted. Words came from her mouth as if spoken by someone else, "do not punish yourself Calphus," she took his hand in her own. "Oedimus often spoke of you as if you were his brother. He loved you dearly." He bowed his head in anguish as she tried to comfort him. "The fates were against him. Just as his life was not ours to control, his death also was not for you to determine."

Calphus listened to her words and gained new respect for the girl. "Oedimus had good reason to love you," he murmured quietly. *She is so young and yet has the wisdom of an older woman. Her own heart is breaking, yet she tries to comfort me.*

From his skirt waistband, he took out a small folded package and handed it to her. Opening it, she recognized the letters that she'd sent to Oedimus. They were un-opened. She looked into his face enquiringly.

"Regretfully, they reached Damascus too late. He never received them."

Reflexively, Meryhken crushed them in her fists.

Calphus arose from the seat and searched her face. The color had started to return to her cheeks and her body no longer trembled. In fact, it looked stiff. He could tell that she was making an effort to regain her composure. There was a subtle change in her demeanor. It was hard to analyze exactly what the change was, but a light had gone from those lovely eyes and there was a hard lift to her chin. It was as if she were defying the world. The only indication of emotion was the tight grip of her curling fingers on the letters. Innocence had left Meryhken.

Calphus sighed heavily, not wanting to leave her alone but knowing that he must. He had taken a risk by coming into the harem grounds and although luck had been with him so far, he couldn't afford to linger any longer.

When he had told Thehta what he planned to do, she had tried to dissuade him, worrying for his safety. "I must go," he'd stated. "If it were I who had been killed, Oedimus wouldn't hesitate to tell you before you found out from unfeeling strangers." His wife had understood and reluctantly agreed with his decision, but he knew that she would be awake and worrying until his safe return.

"I must leave, Meryhken, and you need to rest." He was still concerned. "Can you manage to make your way back to your apartments without assistance?" he asked.

She nodded and standing up to face him, laid a hand on his arm. "Thank you Calphus for thinking of my welfare before your own," she murmured. "I am grateful to you for personally bringing me this news. May Aten bless you."

Picking up the box from the bench, she opened it. Placing the crushed missives inside, she closed the lid firmly. Without another word she turned and walked away.

The man watched. With her back straight and her head held high, her posture reminded him of the mighty pharaoh. *She is truly of royal blood*, Calphus thought in admiration and pity. He stayed until he saw her entering her building, then left the courtyard the same way that he had entered. Cutting through the trees and bushes so as to run less risk of being seen, tears ran freely down the staunch Ethiopian's cheeks.

Entering the gallery to her apartment she saw Psarta sitting outside her door. Seeing him there was like old times. He jumped up as she walked towards him, anxiety spreading across his face. Meryhken looked at him not saying a word. He could tell by her expression that she'd heard the news. "You know don't you?"

She answered him in a controlled voice. "He was slaughtered by a beast on two legs as he was making his way back to me." The tone was flat. "Calphus was kind enough to tell me before I learned of it through the palace gossip. I couldn't have born that." Meryhken steadily eyed her old friend and the bitterness left her voice, "is that why you are here instead of in your quarters, sleeping?"

"I came as soon as I was able to do so, without Meteh finding me here. I was hoping that I could reveal the news to you before you heard it from strangers."

Meryhken managed a weak smile. "Thank you Psarta. It is good to know that you are still my friend, even though I have caused you many problems. For this, I am sorry."

"Do not concern yourself." He gave a nonchalant shrug of his shoulders, "working in the kitchens is not as bad as expected." Psarta's tone became more serious, "if there is anything I can do to help you mistress, please remember that I am always near at hand."

Grasping his hands she whispered her gratitude before abruptly turning her back and entering her rooms. She closed the door firmly behind her.

Psarta stared at the closed door for a few seconds and sadly shook his head. He turned and slowly left the building.

Alone in her rooms Meryhken allowed the tears to fall as

she stared unseeingly at the walls. Automatically her feet carried her to the balcony where she had so often stood idling the time away until it was dark enough to meet her lover. Through her tears she gazed in the direction of the temple ruins. It seemed incomprehensible to her shocked mind that he wasn't waiting.

Remembrances of the many times that they had sat in the ruins, speaking of their love and planning a future together were vividly planted inside her head. She could still feel the warmth of his body close to hers and the strength of his arms as they held her, as if he would never let her go. A sob escaped and she stiffened her back to try and gain control. Even now, the pleasant musk scent of his skin seemed to surround her. It was as if he were close by, and yet too far away to touch.

She recalled the times that they had walked in forgotten places and made love under trees that had once been cultivated orchards; trees that sprawled wild and free like their love for each other. Her body yearned to run through the night, back to the old temple. *Maybe he will be there*, she thought irrationally. *Suppose it was all a terrible mistake and he is still alive?*

Some time later her mother found her still standing on the balcony, not moving or making any sound. Meteh had knocked lightly on her door before entering, not wanting to awaken her if she was sleeping. She'd put off the inevitability of telling her the news, having not known how to approach her with it.

As soon as she saw the stance of her body, she knew that Meryhken had been told. There was no response when the woman called her name. Walking to her side, she touched her gently on an arm. The flesh felt icy cold. Meryhken's profile looked like alabaster. The girl gave no sign that she was aware of her mother's presence.

"Meryhken? Look at me!" The mother's sharp command got a response. The girl turned her head and stared expressionlessly. Dried tears stained her cheeks. "He's gone mother. Oedimus will never return." Turning back again she continued to stare at the nocturnal void above. "He couldn't come back to me you see, because he's left for the After Life." The words were spoken in a flat monotone.

"You must rest, Meryhken. You have received a terrible shock and you will need time to recover. Believe me, this sadness that you feel will eventually pass. Come. Let me take you to your bed and I will fetch wine for you."

She guided the unresisting body to the bed. Meryhken stood as she had as a child, allowing the woman to disrobe her. She sat on the edge of the bed while the woman knelt to take the sandals off her ice cold feet. Rubbing the extremities with her hands, Meteh eased the body underneath a covering.

Looking down at the inert form, Meteh felt an overwhelming sense of inadequacy. It was a new sensation for this orderly-minded woman. She realized that her child was in a state of shock, but didn't know quite how to handle the situation. *What else can I do to ease this sadness she is experiencing?* She felt helpless. *Her feelings for the soldier are obviously deeper than I realized.*

Meteh's sense of wonder at this discovery was completely genuine. She had never felt the ecstasy of love. Her love for the king had grown from childhood duties of a concubine, eventually to turn into a worshipping idolization as she reached adulthood. It was impossible for the mother to relate to her daughter's heartbreak.

Leaving the girl's bedside, she went to the small anteroom. From the jug of wine on the table, she poured a generous amount and returned to where Meryhken lay motionless.

Raising the girl's head, she forced the red liquid between her lips. Meryhken coughed as it went down her throat. She shook her head as Meteh put the cup to her mouth again. "Drink," the woman ordered. "You need this so don't be foolish." From force of habit Meryhken obeyed. Slowly the cup was emptied and natural color started to return to the cheeks.

For the longest time, Meteh sat by the bed until her daughter finally fell into a fitful sleep. She watched, feeling helpless as the girl's body turned restlessly. Intermittent trembling sighs escaped from her mouth, while blue-tinged eyelids fluttered. Occasionally she'd give a small cry, like a kitten mewing.

The woman awoke with a start. Her body felt cramped and cold. Shivering from the bad dream that she'd had, she looked toward the bed. Meryhken was sound asleep and not moving. She saw the chest slowly rising and falling underneath the cover.

She stood up and tiptoed across the room to the door, the dream still troubling her mind. She couldn't remember the details but knew that it had been something to do with Meryhken. She'd been a little girl and crying out for her mother, but something had been stopping Meteh from reaching the child.

Curled up in the chair by her daughter's bedside, she'd had her feet tucked underneath her bent legs and cramps in her limbs had awakened the woman. *I'm too old to sleep thus*, she thought irritably as she opened the apartment door.

Stepping across the threshold, she almost tripped over a pair of long legs. Startled, Meteh looked down and saw in the gloomy light that they belonged to Psarta.

A sardonic expression came over her face. *He must be as concerned as I about her welfare if he chooses to sleep on this hard floor, instead of the servants' comfortable sleeping quarters.* She stood for a second or two watching the boy as he slept.

Her methodical mind raced and she came to a decision. Tomorrow, she would bring him back to serve Meryhken. Now that Oedimus was no longer a threat, it served no purpose to have the boy working in the kitchen. He would be better equipped in serving her daughter's needs. She needed someone close to her at this time.

Meteh continued to observe the sleeping boy. *She trusts him, and his loyalty to her is beyond question*, she grudgingly admitted to herself. He had already proven this by his actions in aiding her in her foolish behavior. *He will certainly watch over her now during her emotional trials.* She smiled to herself in irony. *What better person to take care of her than this boy who knew more of the sad affair than anyone else? Including myself.*

She left the gallery and made her way to her own rooms, not even bothering to remove her gown as she sank heavily onto her bed. Worrying over her daughter had depleted her energies and all she wanted to do was to stretch out under her own warm, covering.

CHAPTER TWENTY-TWO

*A*marna was in a somber mood. Several cases of the dreaded disease of smallpox had been reported among the people of the lower quarters. At first no one had been too concerned. After all, almost every year there were a few deaths from this pestilence that usually attacked the peasant population. No one became too excited by its occurrence seeing that it usually confined itself to a small area, and lasted for a matter of a few weeks before dying away.

This year the outbreak was lasting longer, and now a case had been reported in the home of one of the government officials. A child of an assistant to a General had succumbed to a feverish rash and within hours, the telltale pustules had appeared. The pharaoh had sent Pento, his own physician to attend the child but to no avail. In less than a week the child was dead.

Everyone said that it was a blessing from the gods that the marriage party had left for Anatolia, before the disease had struck. The princess was well on her way to Hattushas and her new home with her prince.

There was also the good news of the missing dowry having been found. During his interrogation, Nekute had confessed to its hiding place not far from the gates of the garrison. For his diligence in locating it, and seeing to its safe passage to King Mussilli, the pharaoh had duly commended Beth Shean's commander.

At least all was well between Anatolia and Egypt again, thanks to Amarna's deceased hero. Oedimus had been given a burial ceremony fit for a prince.

Now, with this smallpox outbreak the festive atmosphere had disappeared. People were frightened and secluded themselves inside their dwellings. The streets of the city were practically deserted.

A heavy pall hung over the city and the cloying smell of incense was everywhere. Even the royal quarters were showing evidence of confinement, as Pento himself had cautioned residents within the royal enclosure to limit their contact with each other. Herbs were kept burning day and night to ward off the evil, causing buildings to reek with overpowering, medicinal odors. Daily sacrifices were made at the temple, while priests' mournful chanting echoed throughout the royal grounds.

Meteh was more concerned about her daughter's state of mind than the disfiguring disease. She had hoped that Meryhken would recover in time, from the trauma of Oedimus' death. Maybe two, or even three weeks seemed a reasonable amount of time to mourn, but this listlessness that engulfed the girl was beyond reason. It had been almost six weeks since the news of her lover's death and she still acted like a walking, talking mummy.

She has become too thin. Observing the girl with a critical eye as she sat across from her in the day room, Meteh noticed how her nose appeared too prominent between the sunken cheeks. The gown she was wearing hung too loose and revealed bony shoulders.

Meryhken sat with head bowed as she worked at her weaving.

She hadn't spoken for almost an hour. Fortunately the room was practically deserted, as most of the women were following the physician's advice and avoiding each other's company as much as possible. The few that were there were too busy with their tasks to notice anything unusual in Meryhken's somberness.

Meteh attempted to draw her out of the darkness that she seemed to dwell in, "I understand that the pharaoh is planning an evening of entertainment at the palace once this bad fortune has left Amarna." She was met with silence. She tried again. "We will need gaiety to uplift our spirits after this terrifying pestilence has passed." The mother continued to prattle in the same vein, "he talks of having our harem maids entertain with dancing and shaking of the sistrums. Do you plan to join in this?" Without waiting for a reply she continued, "you will need to practice your skills. Maybe I can help you in practicing some new dance movements later this evening?"

"I won't be dancing at any palace festivities, mother." Meryhken hesitated, "also, I will not be free to keep you company tonight as I have made arrangements for an audience with the priest, Sehnit. I wish to make a temple sacrifice to Aten, to honor our fallen hero."

Meteh didn't raise her head as she concentrated on the cloth she was weaving. Her fingers continued to work adeptly with the thread. *She doesn't look well.* Ever since the soldier's death her concern for her daughter had been increasing. But, she couldn't pinpoint any specific ailment. *If I could see some signs of a physical illness I would know how to medicate her, but there are none.* Nevertheless, she was all too aware that the girl's disposition was not normal. Meteh feared for her daughter's mental state.

It is good that she has decided to consult with a priest. Maybe he can advise her and comfort her, as I don't seem to be able to have any affect. Then her practical mind took over, *what she needs is to cultivate new social activities that will uplift her spirits, instead of having the time to mope throughout her days.* She remained silent while continuing to work on the cloth. Meteh was determined to take action. *As soon as we are clear of this irritating disease, I will consult with the pharaoh concerning young men that might be suitable for her. I will insist that she join in palace festivities.*

Meryhken climbed the steps leading to Akhenaton's great temple, arms loaded with flowers, incense and a small bag of grain to place on the offering table. Reaching the top step that led to the first terrace, she paused to catch her breath and sat for a few moments on a bench. She couldn't understand why she felt so exhausted.

The weakness made her realize that she'd hardly eaten all day. Breathing deeply helped. *Mother is right. If I don't eat, I will lose all my strength. But what do I need strength for? Life is useless anyway and everything seems to be such an effort of late.*

The only time that she felt as if her mind was at rest was when she was sleeping. For a brief moment when she first awakened of a morning, she would feel her old sense of wellbeing and purpose. Then, reality would set in and the all too familiar weight of her loss would close in on her being. Overwhelming tidal waves of grief would wash over her, knocking her off balance. Those brief moments of mindless contentment that she experienced on first awakening would be gone and inertia would set in.

Arising heavily from the seat, Meryhken continued her climb to the temple. The steps rose endlessly, broken by another terrace before continuing again to the massive double-door entrance. Standing eight feet in height and glistening with gold inlays, the doors to the temple led through a gallery that ran between rows of giant complex columns. Inlaid with red quartzite, blue glazed chevrons and black granite obsidian, the history of Akhenaton's glorious reign was inscribed on them for posterity, along with accolades to Nefertiti and their six daughters. Brightly shining amidst the rest was the newest of the inscriptions, relating to the daughter's marriage to Mussilli's son.

Meryhken entered the awesome building. Its silence seemed to vibrate with unseen spirits. Approaching the offering table she laid down her gifts, giving a deep bow in reverence to the many images of the Sun God and Akhenaton. It was difficult to distinguish between the king and the god, as both images seemed to encompass one and the same person.

Traversing the long hallways to the aisles of the inner temple, she approached the altar. Its resplendent gold sun disk, showing its myriad sunbeams with its hands of blessing, dominated the center. Prostrating herself on the ground she stretched out her arms in supplication.

She tried to praise Aten and thank him for his many blessings but couldn't. The loss of Oedimus so overwhelmed her that she could hardly breathe and uncontrollable sobs began to wrack her body. Raising her tear filled eyes, it seemed that the sun disk was shining down upon her, yet all she could see was her beloved's features superimposed within the sacred image. Tears flowed down her cheeks, dampening the ground where her face hovered close to the stone floor.

Meryhken felt the touch of a hand on her shoulder. For one wild moment she thought it was Oedimus! Lifting herself and sitting back on her heels, she turned her head in anticipation. She looked up to see Seneht standing over her.

Being the most senior priest, Seneht had temporarily taken over Hytoph's position in the temple, until the pharaoh had performed a sacrificial ceremony to choose a new Holy of Holy's.

Clothed in the priest's standard long white robes, his shaven head bore the gold band of Aten Ra. To the distraught girl he looked unreal. Yet, the eyes staring down at her were full of pity.

"My child, what is this? What grieves you so?"

Meryhken couldn't answer. She had requested to see him, hoping that she could receive his blessings and somehow, help to ease her intolerable despair.

Now as she actually facing the priest, she was acutely aware of the impossibility of such a confession. All at once she realized that even a priest would not be able to keep such knowledge from the pharaoh. This was especially so now that Seneht had taken Hytoph's exulted place as Akhenaton's spiritual advisor. *What made me think that I could confide in Seneht? He expects an explanation of my behavior.* She would have to try and explain herself, without revealing Oedimus' name. Meryhken's mind desperately clung to a thread of hope. *Surely he is a wise man and will help to relieve this terrible burden?*

Sighing heavily, she began a halting explanation, "I am weary Seneht and sore of heart. I love a man who is not fit to be my husband in the eyes of my father, the great pharaoh, so we have had to part. He is gone and I'll never see him again." Her voice trembled and she pressed her lips together tightly in an effort to keep control. Like a person who is drowning, Meryhken was crying out for a lifeline to rescue her from her abysmal grief.

Seneht gave an inward sigh of relief, *what a foolish child!* The priest would never have thought that the poised, self-assured Meryhken would have such feelings for any man. *Thanks be to the good Lord Aten, that it is not as tragic a problem as she seems to think it is.* She would soon learn that this was nothing more than a girlish infatuation.

Seneht hated to have to minister to life's really serious problems and would pass such counseling on to one of his subordinates, if need be. His new responsibility lay heavy on his shoulders and as much as it pleased him, he wasn't quite sure how to handle it. "Have you discussed this problem with our glorious pharaoh, Meryhken?"

She quickly assured him that she hadn't, "Akhenaton would be displeased with me. That is why I decided not to see this person again, as I do not wish to anger my royal father. But my heart is sorely aching and needs your wise counsel." She placed a hand on the priest's arm. Beseechingly, she looked up at him, "please do not reveal this conversation to our pharaoh. I couldn't bare his displeasure."

I also do not wish to face his anger by telling him such news. Seneht would never admit to himself that he was really a coward. He preferred to think of himself as a cautious and tactful man, who had found his ideal in the safety of the priesthood. He hoped to keep his position as Akhenaton's spiritual advisor and had no intention of jeopardizing that!

The priest patted the hand that lay on his arm, "I understand your concern, child. As long as you reassure me that you will not see this man again, I do not feel it necessary to upset our almighty king."

Meryhken bowed her head in silent compliance. *If he only knew how simple it really is for me to keep such a promise. I would give my life to be with Oedimus once more, but how can I when he is dead?* Tears started to well up again. She gripped her hands so tightly that her nails dug painfully into the flesh of the palms.

She must have cared a great deal for this person, the priest thought, feeling surprise and concern for her obvious, distraught condition.

Moving directly in front of the girl he placed his hands on her shoulders, gripping them firmly, "pray with me child, so that your heart may be healed of this hurt. Let us pray to Aten and ask his indulgence so that life may be pleasurable for you, once more."

Once again, she prostrated herself at the priest's feet. With raised hands and loud sonorous voice, the holy man began to chant prayers to the great and living Aten Ra.

"Bless this child, oh almighty god of all Egypt. Warm her heart with thy glorious and beauteous rays. Let thy benevolent presence ease the hurt that dwells within her heart. Make her worthy of thy goodness and strengthen her will against the temptations of mortal flesh."

Seneht began to warm to the sound of his own voice, "embrace her with everlasting love, and your almighty powers that rule over Life and the After Life. Banish all demons of the Underworld from her presence."

The voice grew more commanding as his thunderous tones echoed throughout the vastness of the temple, rising and falling in cadence as he called on the sun god. Chanting the deity's name along with Akhenaton's, the priest's verve increased. With each utterance, he became more carried away by his own exuberance. "Almighty god, Egypt's most exulted Aten Ra. Lay your warmth on this child and give her the strength to overcome the sins of the flesh. Remove all temptation from her path of enlightenment and guide her into your most loving presence." In ritualistic monotones the voice rose and fell, thundering on and on as the eager priest became engrossed in his feelings of rapture.

The voice hit Meryhken's ears like thunderclaps. She felt dizzy from the impact and tried praying silently, but couldn't. After a while she gave up, unable to compete with Seneht. Too exhausted to continue, she felt as if she'd swoon if he didn't stop.

After what seemed like an eternity, the sweating priest ended his ranting. For a few minutes the two were silent, the girl's prostrate body immobile while Seneht mopped at his perspiring brow with the sash of his robe. His energy had finally run down and he regained his equilibrium.

Seneht reached out a hand to the girl and helped her to her feet, "return to the harem my child. Aten will surely guide you in the days to come. Be joyful in his all-powerful wisdom, light and abundance. Time will heal your bruised heart and I know that soon, our wise and all knowing Akhenaton will select a suitable mate for you. Such a man will come to you at our great pharaoh's bidding. He will take you as his wife and bring to you the fulfillment of motherhood."

For a few seconds, Meryhken stood searching into the priest's face. Finally and without a sound she turned and walked away from the altar.

Seneht watched the tall straight figure, walking along the aisle that led to the outer galleries. He was exhilarated. *I should pray with such vigor more often*, he thought in self-satisfaction as he wiped his perspiring head with his hand. *The release of energy it invokes, is most strengthening to my body. My spirit feels lighter.*

He gave not a thought to the disquieting spectacle of the bereaving girl as he indulged in his own gratification. The idea that Meryhken might not have gained any benefit from his prayers didn't enter his consciousness.

She couldn't sleep. Tossing and turning, she threw the coverlet from her body. It didn't help. She was still too hot. Arising, she made her way to the anteroom and poured herself some wine. Surprised, she noticed that the jug was almost empty. Had she drank so much in one night? Even so, the wine did little to quench her thirst.

Since Oedimus' death she'd had difficulty in falling asleep and stayed awake most nights until the early hours. Eventually, her tired body would succumb and she'd sleep until the early morning light streaming into her room aroused her. Tonight she'd been awake much longer than usual.

Sipping at the wine, she carried it outside onto the balcony, grateful for the cool breeze that fanned her hot body. Clouds blanketed the sky and there was nothing but a black void. Returning inside, she swallowed the last dregs of wine and climbed back into bed.

Meteh came along the hallway, noticing that Psarta was still sleeping outside the door. Reaching his curled body, she gave him a sharp nudge with her foot and loudly commanded him to wake up. " Why are you still sleeping at such a late hour?" she asked. Psarta jumped, still groggy with sleep. "Where is your mistress?"

Still feeling the impact of her foot in his side he moved a safe distance away before answering. "She hasn't arisen yet, mistress

Meteh." He was as surprised as the mother that Meryhken hadn't
made an appearance. The sun had been high for over an hour. It
was long past the time when she usually awakened.

Meteh rapped loudly on the door and without waiting for an
answer, entered the ante- room. The place was quiet. The woman
made her way towards the bedroom, calling her daughter's name
as she entered. She saw her sleeping. Or, was she?

The coverlet was on the floor and her naked body lay sprawled
across the bed. Moving further into the room, Meteh saw that
Meryhken was moving her head restlessly from side to side. A soft
moan escaped her parted lips.

Meteh was across the room in an instant, dropping to her knees
by the side of the bed. Two rosy patches colored the pasty white
cheeks. She felt the girl's forehead and gasped, drawing back her
hand as if she'd been scalded. Her daughter's skin was as hot as the
sun god's rays at high noon. "PSARTA! Come, quickly."

At the urgent cry, the boy ran into the room. He looked down
at Meryhken's sleeping form and wondered why he had been
summoned when she was still disrobed?

"Bring cold water immediately and a cloth. No - bring a
goodly supply of cloths and water filled in the biggest bowl you
can find."

He didn't budge, staring at Meryhken in bewilderment.

"MOVE! Your mistress is ill. Bring the water and cloths.
NOW!"

He ran from the room, returning within minutes with the
required bowl full of cold water and several clothes. In disbelief,
he stood looking at Meryhken's restless body.

Meteh plunged one of the cloths into the bowl. Squeezing
out the excess water, she wrapped it around the burning forehead,
sponging the face and lips with the ends of the material. Meryhken's
head thrashed as if trying to shake off the weight of the cloth. The
woman took the face between her hands, holding it gently but

firmly, "Meryhken, you are ill. This cold compress will help to sooth your inflamed body."

The girl mouthed some words that were unintelligible.

"Psarta. Fetch the physician, Pento." The command came in a calmer voice but the woman was feeling far from calm. In fact, Meteh was having difficulty in controlling her panic.

Without a word, Psarta hurried from the room only to return a short time later, "the physician was not at his home, mistress Meteh. I left a message for him to come as soon as he returned." His voice was more emotional than Meteh had heard in all the years she had known him. Not taking her eyes away from her daughter, she nodded. "Get more cold water. We must try and cool her feverish body."

Pento arrived in the late afternoon, "I came as soon as I received your message." He looked from the woman's terrified face to the girl in the bed. Meryhken now lay still. Approaching her side he turned the girl's hands over to look at the palms. They were blotched with an angry looking rash that was creeping up towards her wrists. He moved down to examine the feet. The same condition marked the soles. The body was on fire and Meryhken's face was beginning to show the familiar red blotches of the rash. Grim faced, he turned to look at the woman who hovered anxiously behind him.

In a trembling whisper Meteh voiced a question. "Smallpox?"

Pento nodded soberly. She sank into a chair, her legs no longer able to hold her upright.

The good doctor sternly admonished her, "you must not give way to your emotions, woman. She will need all the care that you can provide. You must be strong."

His practical voice had the desired affect. *He's right. I cannot give in. I must stay in control.* Straightening her back, she asked, "what must I do?"

"We must wait and see what happens," he stated. "Trying to

cool her fever is all you can do at this time." He reached into the medicine pouch that he always carried with him. Taking out a small bundle of herbs, he handed them to the mother, "Steep these in liquid until the medicine has been thoroughly extracted. Make sure that she drinks it all. She will start to vomit and this will help to reduce the fever, as well as aid in stemming the infection."

As if hearing his words, the girl began to wretch. Pento immediately raised her head and shoulders, supporting her with his arms while Psarta grabbed the half-empty water bowl and placed it underneath her chin. Fowl smelling stomach contents spewed forth. Meryhken's body heaved convulsively as the retching continued. Eventually the spasm ended and she sank back, whimpering softly.

The physician looked at the contents of the bowl and shook his head gravely, "I will return tomorrow. There is nothing more that I can do." With a helpless shrug he turned and left the room, escorted by Psarta.

The hand that gently shook Meteh startled her into wakefulness and she immediately came upright in the chair. It was Psarta. "Why don't you go to your bed and sleep, mistress? I will stay by her side and keep watch until you have rested."

She looked around, staring blankly as she tried to clear her fuzzy brain. As Meteh's mind awakened, she remembered why she was in her daughter's room and arose to approach the bedside. In the first light of dawn she could see the nasty looking pustules that had begun to make their appearance. Meryhken's face was blotched with indented yellowish blisters. "Her flawless complexion will be so scarred that people won't want to look upon her face." Meteh refused to consider the possibility of death. She couldn't face such a thought. The woman turned her attention to the boy, "I will stay with her. When she awakens from this evil state she will need to see me by her side."

Psarta looked pityingly at the woman. She seemed to have

aged within the past two days. He couldn't believe that she'd sat by the sick bed for so long, without adequate sleep. This was the first time since Meryhken's illness that he'd actually seen her sleeping. "Pardon my boldness Mistress Meteh, but if you don't get proper rest you will become ill yourself. What will Meryhken do then, when she needs your help in regaining her strength?" He didn't add that he thought there was slim chance that she'd even regain consciousness, never mind need any more help. Psarta's heart was heavy, yet he couldn't give way to his feelings as long as the mother still had hope.

Meteh hesitated, digesting the logic of what Psarta had said. Her drained body desperately needed rest. "Maybe you are right," she agreed reluctantly. "When this pestilence has left she will need me to bathe and feed her. Maybe I will rest for a while, but call me immediately if she awakens." Wearily she dragged herself out of the chair and left the fetid room for her own quarters. Psarta watched her leave, shaking his head sadly. He knew that it would take a miracle of the gods to save Meryhken, but the mother refused to see this.

Turning his attention to his long time friend, he watched Meryhken's labored breathing. It was the only sign that she still lived. Taking a cool cloth, he patted her forehead and cheeks. He soaked another cloth in the water and methodically rung out the excess. He rolled it into a pillow and gently raising her head and shoulders, Psarta carefully placed the roll at the base of her skull. Her head fell limply against his arm. The hair clung moistly to the nape of her neck. The abundant black braids hung matted and lusterless.

Meryhken's eyelids fluttered open and he saw that the eyes were rolled back into her head. *How can she stay alive with so much disease racking her body? She must be suffering the hell of the damned.* Unbidden tears began to roll down the boy's face and he sank to his knees. Covering his face with his hands, Psarta sobbed.

She couldn't understand why everything seemed so unreal. Dizzying images rushed through her head and devilish loud voices seemed to be tormenting her brain - ebbing and flowing – ebbing and flowing. The pain was excruciating. Just as she thought her head would explode from the agony the monsters retreated and she'd fall into a black pit.

Sometimes, Meryhken thought she heard her mother's voice and Psarta's, but before she could grasp their words they would be gone. She swam in a dark void full of frightening images and throbbing pain. The darkness was burning her flesh.

Thanks be to the gods for blessed blackness! The nightmarish phantoms left and she became oblivious to everything, until the sounds of weeping aroused her to semi-consciousness. Hands touched her head and she wanted to scream, yet couldn't. Hammers pounded at her skull but she couldn't open her mouth and tell the hands to stop.

Praises to Aten! The torment had subsided. Meryhken wanted to reach out and try to comfort the person who was weeping, but it was too difficult. She couldn't raise her hands.

There it was again. The vice was squeezing her skull, tighter and tighter. Nausea swept over her and convulsions shook her body. Someone raised her head as pink tinged bile spewed out of her mouth. Sweet oblivion! The pounding had stopped. Her body no longer felt as if it were weighted down.

Who was in the room? Meryhken knew someone had entered but she couldn't see. She tried to force her eyelids to open but they wouldn't budge. Was she blind?

It didn't matter anyway because she detected a familiar odor of musk. Oedimus! He was here in her room. Her lover wasn't dead after all!

Turning her head, she saw him standing just inside the entrance to her balcony. He was smiling at her - that warm, loving smile that was for her alone.

Her eyes still refused to open but miracle of miracles!

Meryhken could see him quite plainly and he was beckoning for her to come to him. She arose effortlessly from the bed. Why had she thought she couldn't move? She felt as free as a bird in flight as she went to him. Eagerly taking the hand that he held out to her, she felt his firm grasp and thrilled at the touch. She had missed him so much!

Oedimus was finally here and Meryhken knew he wouldn't ever leave her again. How she had missed seeing his dear face! Looking up at him in adoration, she nodded without speaking as he gestured in the direction of their temple ruins. Hand in hand Meryhken and Oedimus left the balcony. They headed towards their sanctuary.

A wild scream rent the air as Meteh rushed to the bedside. Transfixed, Psarta stood immobile. Meryhken's lifeless body lay with the head turned towards the balcony as if looking at the sky. An enigmatic smile was fixed on the slightly parted lips. Her facial expression showed complete serenity.

Kate

LONDON, ENGLAND 1537
REIGN OF HENRY VIII

The ice-cold wind whistled down Cheapside, mindless of whatever obstacle stood in its path. Shoppers hurrying along pavements were buffeted unmercifully as they attempted to go about their own business. With heads lowered into hunched shoulders, folks made futile attempts to protect themselves against the blustering northerner.

Gusting over the swollen waters of the Thames it swept big and small boats alike in the river's rapid current. Few ferryboats were crossing from one side of the river's embankment to the other, being too hazardous to maneuver the crafts through the churning swells. Only those passengers who absolutely needed to get to the other side were going across, carried by ferry-pilots who were brave enough, (or foolhardy depending on the point of view) – to take the risk. Even so, these hardy boatmen grumbled among themselves at the sparse amount of fares they were collecting and cursed the vicious wind for their misfortune.

The stalwart London Bridge, busy as always ignored November's inclement weather as pedestrians as well as horse drawn vehicles traveled back and forth by the only bridge to span the river. Even the wealthy homes and upper class businesses that lined the bridge's expanse couldn't escape winter's fury. As the wind blasted through cracks around windows it howled like a soul in hell. Doors that were unlatched as people came in and out of buildings were slammed wide, banging against walls in protest.

High on the top of the three-storied Southwark Tower, the ghoulish heads of traitors stuck atop of pikes, stared sightlessly down at people passing underneath. The hair on the decapitated heads danced wildly in the wind as if still alive. The grotesque faces were twisted as if still in the throws of torment as the heads, streaked with black encrusted blood, hovered over the people below. The wind appeared to be enjoying a satanic ritual of death with them, while London's Tower seemed to hold unforgiving support for the blustering game from Hell. Strong men as well as women averted their faces as they passed underneath the pikes. A die-hard Catholic crossed himself in protection and kissed his rosary as he hurried underneath their gruesome burdens.

The wind continued to blow madly over the city looking for another victim to play with. Effortlessly skirting London's numerous church spires, it finally came to St. Paul's. It wasn't intimidated by this grand structure as it whipped dust and debris over the bottom of the steps, where Kate stood warming her hands over the hot coals in her barrel.

She'd been in the marketplace of St. Paul's Walk since sun-up, but her sales had been poor. Nobody wanted to venture outside into bad weather unless it was an absolute necessity. *Folk do not consider hot roasted chestnuts a necessity*, Kate thought ruefully as she poked and turned the roasting nuts. A tempting smell arose from the coals as she watched the brown shells blacken and pop open under the heat, revealing their creamy white nutmeats. She smelled their goodness and gingerly picked one from the white-hot coals. Tossing it from one hand to the other to cool it, she bit into the crackling shell and dislodged the nut to pop into her mouth. Mindfully she savored its smoky sweetness.

Taking the few coins that she'd collected from her apron pocket, she counted the amount. Kate shook her head dolefully, *just enough to buy a loaf of bread and a flagon of ale for supper.* She dropped the coppers back into the security of the pocket.

In spite of the fact that she'd worn both of her wool kirtles, she was still cold. Kate's shoes had holes in them and even though she'd lined the soles with brown paper, her feet were damp. Once more she tried warming her reddened hands over the heat, knowing that she'd regret it later when the chilblains on her fingers started to itch.

"Kate!"

Looking up, she saw Noll running across the church steps. "Where hast been all this day?" she called out crossly as her cousin came within hearing distance. The lad stopped next to her, panting from exertion - and something more. Noll's roguish face held a gleam of excitement.

"Thee were supposed to have returned to help me hours past," the girl accused, rubbing at her eyes that stung from the fire's smoke. Kate didn't know that she'd left dirty smudges streaked across her face.

Noll grinned cheekily. "Thee looks like a chimney sweep."

"I'll thank thee not to be giving me any lip!" she retorted, attempting to wipe the grime from her face but smearing it even worse over her reddened cheeks.

Kate wasn't pretty, but there was an aliveness about her that made folks think otherwise. Although her hair was abundant, it was a non-de-script mouse brown and its healthy sheen made it noticeable. That is, it shone when it was clean. At the moment it reeked of smoke from the fire and needed washing. In an attempt to keep it away from her face she'd tied it back with a piece of twine.

Kate blinked her watering eyes, trying to clear them of the stinging smoke. They were her best feature. Large and expressive, the color reminded people of warm green meadows turned slightly brown by the mid-summer sun. At the moment there was a faint trace of humor in them as she admonished her cousin, giving away the fact that she wasn't really as cross as she'd like to convey. Not having been very busy she hadn't really missed his help. "So. Am I to learn what's been up to all day, or shalt continue to stand there grinning like an idiot!"

Noll didn't respond but continued to smile showing perfectly white teeth, unusual in a working class lad. Unlike most of his kind, the boy took pride in his appearance and diligently cleaned them every day with soot and salt. He stood quietly observing as Kate began to place the newly roasted nuts into paper bags; feeling their weight to make sure that the same amount went into each one.

With hands on hips and lanky legs spread apart, Noll gave an impression of arrogance, albeit that his shabby black breeches had holes in the knees. The wind tussled his mop of raven hair and he unconsciously raised a hand to brush it out of his eyes. In spite of his poor clothing he was a handsome fellow with a charismatic air of self-confidence.

He finally spoke. "How much money hast made this day?" he asked.

Exasperated, Kate stopped what she was doing and turned her full attention on him. "Not as much as if thee had been here to help with share of t'work," she answered tartly. Noll's reticence in telling her where he had been was really annoying and she was losing patience with him. "Doest intend to stand there watching me work for t'rest of the day, instead of helping?"

What would say if I told thee I'd made more money than thyself this day?" His expression told Kate that he knew something that she didn't and was deliberately holding back. As if slowly sucking on a sugarplum to prolong its pleasure, her cousin was definitely savoring a secret.

Kate's irritation was rapidly increasing. The chilblains on her feet were beginning to sting and her chapped hands smarted uncomfortably. She was in no mood to play guessing games. "Stop with t'nonsense and tell me why thee be grinning as if thou had inherited a fortune."

As the thought of a fortune entered her head a suspicion slowly began to form. *He surely hast not succumbed to gambling again, after he promised?* Aloud, Kate asked the question that she hoped would be answered negatively. "Tell me, our Noll. What hast really been doing all day? Hast been playing with t'dice again?" She leaned into his face, "or was it cards this time?" Kate's heart sank as she saw the look of triumph transform his countenance. "Thee promised Bessie that woulds't not!" she exclaimed, realizing that her suspicions were well founded.

Noll's biggest weakness was gambling. It didn't matter whether it was a deck of cards, playing dice, or - the latest fad of betting on whether or not King Henry would marry again. The lad could never resist a game of chance.

A few weeks past, he'd almost ended up in jail. He'd been accused of using loaded dice and unfortunately, Noll's 'victim' had been a man of some wealth and importance. When the man had become suspicious of the boy's continuous winning streak, he'd sent for the local sheriff. It had taken all of Noll's wits and charm to convince the loser and the law that he'd just been lucky.

After returning the man's money, (he'd managed to pocket a sixpenny piece without being noticed) - the disgruntled fool was somewhat appeased.

Once he'd calmed down, the gentleman had given much thought to the repercussions at home should his wife become aware of his gambling escapade. *Should I follow through with charges against this rascal, she might question my reason as to the necessity to bare witness at the Old Bailey.* The toff had grown uneasy as he weighed the pros and cons of prosecuting the boy. *She really would rile against my person if she learned of my gambling - especially with the common folk, and I cannot stomach her sharp nagging tongue! My good woman hath no need of an excuse to nag at me, so why give her reason to do so?* All these thoughts had swiftly passed through the man's head and he'd come to a decision. *After all, the young scamp did return my money, didn't he?*

It hadn't taken very much to convince the sheriff that it had all been a terrible mistake and after a bit of haggling, the charges were dropped.

Noll's mother had been extremely upset at the thought of how close her son had come to being hauled off to Newgate prison. It had sent cold chills throughout Bessie's body and her heart had palpitated. Kate had worried that the woman was going to have an apoplexy. The girl loved her aunt and hated to see her so stressed. Recovering from her terror, Bessie had made her son promise that he'd not gamble anymore.

Now it seemed that he'd broken that promise. "I just knew that thee couldst' nare stay away from t'vices for long." Kate's tone was scathing. "What is thy ma going to say after thee made her a vow?"

"She'll say naught when I show her this." Noll reached into his breeches pocket and with a jolly grin on his face came away with a gold piece in his fingers.

"Blessed Virgin and all the saints! Tis a half crown piece! However didst' come by so much money?" Kate's shock turned to a mixture of awe and suspicion, "did'st cheat again?" Noll looked pained. "Of course not," he replied, indignantly. "I am the best player in all of London and hath no need to cheat," he bragged. "Everyone knows this, and t'gentleman that played with me lost his money fair and square."

Kate wasn't convinced. "Why would any fool continue to gamble until they had lost that much money?"

He gave a triumphant chuckle as he placed his wealth back into the safety of his pocket, "because dear cousin, after losing a shilling and thruppence to me he was foolish enough to bet me double that amount if I would play one more hand with him."

"Naturally I won and being the honest bloke that he was - even though a stupid one mind - he paid up." Slapping his sides, he laughed heartily at his own cleverness and impetuously grabbing Kate around the waist, began to twirl her off her feet in excitement.

His enthusiasm was contagious and in spite of herself Kate melted. A smile began to play around her mouth and pretty soon she had joined in his laughter as he danced her around and around in the middle of the street. Gasping and out of breath they eventually stopped and clung to each other, still laughing at Noll's good fortune, even if gleaned by doubtful means.

"Come, cousin. Pack up yon wagon for t'day and let's go home," said Noll. "We shall stop along the way and buy some cheese for supper and a loaf of hot bread from t'bakery. None of that day old muck either!" As he talked, he picked up a pale of water from alongside the wagon, meant for the dowsing of the coals in the barrel. Hissing steam arose in protest as he threw the water over the fire.

Grabbing padded mitts from the wagon floor, he put them on for protection before picking up the hot barrel by its sturdy handles. Clamping it to the back of the wagon with the steel fastener made just for that purpose, Noll stepped back and wiped his sweating brow. "We hast even got enough money to buy some meat," he said, puffing from the effort of lifting and securing the heavy barrel, "Bessie can make one of her good pottages for our dinner tomorrow."

At mention of her aunt's name, Kate hesitated in the middle of packing away the unsold chestnuts. A sobering thought had crossed her mind. "How must we explain to Bessie how didst come by so much money for food?"

Noll stopped in the middle of rechecking the barrel. A frown crossed his good-natured face. For a few moments he stood deep in thought then, his face cleared and a smile broke forth. "We'll tell her that thee found it," said he with an air of aplomb.

"What!"

"Of course." Not waiting for a reply, he continued, "we shall say that a wealthy looking bloke was purchasing some nuts from thee and while getting the change out of his purse, he must have accidentally dropped t'gold piece. No one noticed as t'wind was blowing so hard, and it rolled under the wagon wheels. Thee didn'st find it until we were readying for home."

Kate was dumbstruck. *His lying tongue never ceases to amaze me!* Still… she couldn't find anything amiss with his story. *He just might get away with it.*

Bessie raised her head at the sound of the door opening, but didn't bother to look around. The woman continued to stir the fire with a poker, methodically coaxing the coals into a blaze.

A blast of icy cold air entered hitting the fire and causing the flames to leap higher. "Shut the door, quick-like! The buxom body didn't turn from the task of coaxing the fire into giving out more heat. "That wind's colder than Sir Tom's body on yon chopping block!" she exclaimed.

Of course, Bessie was referring to the ill-fated Sir Thomas More who, having displeased the king by openly refusing to sanction his majesty's marriage to Anne Boleyn, had recently been executed. A lot of heads had rolled since King Henry had defied the Holy Catholic Church by divorcing Catherine of Aragon.

This latest beheading had taken place after Henry denounced papal Rome and declared himself lawful head of England's

Church. When Sir Thomas had publicly criticized his majesty's wedding to his mistress, Anne, he'd been sent to the Tower to dwell on his traitorous tongue. His refusal to sign the Acts of Supremacy that declared Henry to be the head of the Church of England was the last straw. The holy man's luck ran out and the king had recently ordered his head to be chopped off.

Not that being the new queen had done Anne much good, either. Only months before Thomas' beheading, that poor soul had made the same rendezvous with Tower Hill's chopping block. Henry had been so kind as to honor her last request for an expert swordsman to perform the act, rather than using the less precise axe.

Folks everywhere were now whispering that if the latest queen, the ill-fated Jane Seymour, had not recently died just twelve days following child-birth she would have eventually met the same fate. King Hal was a notorious womanizer and fell in and out of love (or lust some would say) -almost as often as he dined. Not a very good habit to have for promoting harmonious wedlock.

Finished with her concentration on the fire, Bessie straightened her ample body and turned her attention to her young charges. The woman's eyes grew as big as saucers as she finally focused on the young people standing by the door. The plump, rosy face took on a picture of astonishment. "Holy, Blessed, Mother of God! What hast got there? Hast robbed the money lender, or summat?" The woman's mouth gaped open.

Underneath an armpit, Noll held a loaf of bread that emitted freshly baked odors, while the hand clamped a goodly sized cheese to his waist. In his other hand, he gripped a flagon that smelled suspiciously like it was holding mead. Kate held a bunch of parsnips, carrots and leeks, crooked in the elbow of one arm while the other clutched a slab of fatty mutton. *We hath not seen mutton in this house in months!* Bessie was in a right state as she took in the sight, "where dis't come by all that food?"

234

Laying their spoils on the kitchen table they both started to talk at once, falling over each other's words as they attempted to tell the story that they'd concocted.

"Stop! One of thee at a time. I cannot understand either of thee with all that jabbering going on." Bessie's dark eyes so like her son's were full of bewilderment.

Before Kate had a chance to open her mouth again, Noll started to speak. "Thee would not believe what happened to our Kate, ma."

The girl stood back, observing her aunt's face as Noll told his tale of how they had found the half crown. *He sounds so convincing, even I almost believe him. And, by the look on Bessie's face, she hath been taken in by her son's lying tongue.* A twinge of guilt passed through the girl.

"Well I never! Fancy our Kate finding all that money. Might be sure thee couldn't locate t'man and return it to him, Kate?" The aunt's tone was full of concern as she turned her attention to the girl. Not trusting herself to speak, Kate shook her head.

"Don't fret none, ma," her son interjected, before Bessie could question Kate further. "If the man were so careless as to lose so much money, he must be rich enough not to miss it. What poor man hath a gold piece in his purse, never mind be so neglectful as to lose it?"

Noll's explanation seemed to console his mother, but her face still looked troubled. Biting at her bottom lip, she brushed away wisps of iron-gray hair that had escaped her mop-cap.

Kate hated to see her aunt so worried and moving to the woman's side, she encircled the generous waist in a tight embrace. "Please don't worry Bessie. I am sure that Noll is right in his thinking. Remember telling us that the Lord will provide, whenever we don't know where our next meal is to come from? Well, I do believe that this is one of those times when God hath seen fit to provide his bounty."

Bessie's face began to clear as she listened to the girl's reassuring words, *she's a good lass. More like me own daughter than me niece.*

Kate dropped her arms as she saw that her words were having the desired affect. Reaching into her apron pocket, she drew forth the small amount of money that she'd earned. "Look here aunt," she said, "we did naught use the chestnut money so this and a little more will pay our house rent for the next few weeks." She held the money out to the woman. Bessie looked down at the coins in the girl's outstretched palms and without a word, hesitatingly took them.

Her eyes were misty as she turned her back on the young people and reached for the moneybox that sat on the fireplace mantle. The tin was kept just for the purpose of holding the rent money and removing the lid, the woman dropped the coins inside. They clinked loudly in the stillness of the room. Keeping her back turned so as not to show her emotions, Bessie blinked away the unshed tears. Fumbling with the pins that held the fob cap in place, she stalled to regain her composure. After a minute, she lifted a corner of her apron to her nose, giving a noisy blow into it before turning back to face the young people.

With her small pointed chin thrust out Bessie straightened up and pushed her shoulders back. "Well, let's not stand around gawking when there's food to be eaten." She moved to take dishes from the hutch, bustling around to set the table. Kate and Noll stood quietly watching. "What do thee want to do? Leave it for t'mice to enjoy?"

The girl and boy looked at each other in relief.

"Go and wash thee dirty hands in t'rain-tub," Bessie ordered briskly, "and let's get to our meal."

The two young people left by the back door to do as she bid. Bessie had recovered from her moment of 'emotional weakness' as she was apt to call any show of sentimentality. *Ben would be so proud of the way they turned out.* She hadn't thought of her husband in a long time.

Kate's parents had been dead these past seventeen years. Her mother, (Bessie's sister) had died, giving her birth and within the year, the baby's father had been killed in a drunken tavern brawl. Bessie always said that if he hadn't died fighting, he'd have eventually killed himself anyway as the booze would have pickled his innards.

The aunt hadn't hesitated to take in the newborn after her sister's death. And, the ne'er do well brother-in-law had only been too glad to have the burden of a child taken from his shoulders.

Bessie's own baby son was less than a year old and like she had told her husband Ben, "there's plenty of milk t'feed 'both of 'em and what is one more mouth to suckle? If it were left to that drunken sot, the poor little mite would probably be put out to one of those baby farms and over me dead body will I let that happen! "

Ben had nodded in silent agreement, wrapping his muffler tighter around his neck as he was in the habit of doing. No matter what the weather was like outside, hot or cold, her husband always wore his muffler and if strangers were nosy enough to ask him why, he always gave the same stock answer. "I would rather go without me breeches than t'muffler." That usually stopped them from questioning him further.

He wasn't a man to talk much. Whenever he was at home he preferred to sit by the fire-earth and whittle away at a piece of wood, making toy soldiers for his lad Oliver, or Noll as they had got to calling him. Now, he would also be able to make dolls for the baby girl. They had baptized her Katherine, but called her Kate. As Bessie had said, Katherine sounded too good for the likes of themselves even though it was a good, honest Christian name.

Ben was a seafaring man and rarely at home. Only his wife called him by his proper name, as he'd gained the nickname of Muff by his fellow crewmen on account of his always wearing his muffler. He'd been called Muff for so long that some people didn't know that it wasn't his given name.

Most of Ben's time was spent at sea and after he'd been home for a couple of weeks, he'd become bored and itch to return to his ship. Not that he didn't enjoy Bessie's company mind you. After living on sea rations for months at a time he always looked forward to his wife's good wholesome meals, not to mention her warm ample body in their bed at night.

As for Bessie, she liked the security of her husband's sturdy and quiet nature. Besides which, he was a good provider. The sailor earned a decent wage and always turned almost all of his pay over to her. Being the thrifty soul that she was, she managed to make the money stretch until he came home again. At least, it paid the rent and bought food. She'd make a few extra pence cleaning out the butcher's shop, or wiping down the spills from the alehouse tables. Sometimes she'd find a farthing, dropped on the alehouse floor by a careless customer. The landlord always let her keep it. This way Bessie managed to save a bit for what she called 'a rainy day.'

Alas, that rainy day came sooner than expected. One day, Ben didn't turn up when he should have. One of the worst storms in the English Channel's history swept in from the Atlantic. Massive breakers boiled and crashed back and forth between the shores of Britain and France as if trying to escape perdition. The might of the storm took Ben's ship down. For weeks afterwards wood and other ship debris washed up onto the shores of France and England. Very few bodies were recovered. Some of the coastal fishermen sighted several lucky sailors clinging to a piece of the ship's side and braved the storm to go out in their fishing boats to rescue them. Ben was not among the survivors.

After the initial shock had subsided, the ever-practical Bessie had literally picked herself up and took stock of her situation. She grieved for her husband, but her grief was not so much for Ben but more for the loss of security that the man had provided. After all, he'd hardly ever been home so how could she miss him that much? Her biggest concern was how to keep herself and her babes out of the workhouse.

The neighbors liked Bessie. She was always willing to help out someone in need. Whenever anyone was ill, or needed someone to help in laying out a deceased loved one, she was there to give assistance. Why, only a few days before the storm, hadn't she saved the old widow Blocket's life?

The town crier had come rapping at her window in the late hours of the night to summon her help, after hearing a loud moaning coming from inside the widow's house. Luckily, they'd found the back door unbarred. The old lady was lying on the floor where she'd fallen out of her bed. The poor thing couldn't get up again as she had badly sprained her ankle.

Between them both, they lifted the old woman back into her bed then, Bessie sent the crier to fetch the doctor from his bed. She'd talked to widow Blocket and allayed that good woman's fears until the doctor's arrival. The doctor later told anybody who would listen that if it hadn't have been for Bessie's quick actions, the old lady would have probably lain there in the cold until she died from the filling up of the lungs.

No one wanted to see Bessie and her children going to the workhouse. Neighbors rallied around to help, and the business people found extra work for her to do for them so that she could earn more money. She'd cart the children with her to the alehouse or butcher's shop, while she did her chores. They were happy youngsters and customers enjoyed keeping them amused while she worked.

Occasionally, she was given mending to do by the merchants' wives, as she was handy with a needle and thread. She'd mend tears in gowns and bodices with such fine stitches, that they couldn't be seen.

As the children grew and it was safe to leave them by themselves for a few hours, she'd find more work farther away from their home. The children grew independent very early, and learned how to manage the house while Bessie was absent.

When Noll and Kate reached the age of a dozen years, (or thereabouts) the local milkman joined the list of contributors to their welfare. Silas, (as the milkman was called)- would leave jugs of milk on their doorstep. When Bessie would try to pay him he'd refuse, "nay Bessie, t'were ready to be thrown out anyway, as 'twas beginning to turn," said Silas. "T'young folks are growing quick like and they need the goodness of a drop o' milk occasionally. Thee can make it into cream cheese for them."

Her two charges would tease Bessie about the milkman's intentions as he had himself recently become widowed. "Stop t'nonsense thee young fools. Silas is a good man and he knows that I'll not be looking for another husband. He wouldn't take advantage, so keep thee silly tongues still and stop talking such gibberish!"

The years came and went and Bessie kept a good outlook on life even though it was a struggle. Most importantly – the family stayed together.

Supper was over. With their hunger satisfied, the three people sat around the fire hearth enjoying a comfortable silence between them. Bessie's fingers worked at mending a tear in one of Kate's threadbare kirtles. *She really could use a new one.* The woman eyed her niece critically as she sat on a stool next to her, *but we can't afford the material and besides, she needs a new bodice more than she needs a kirtle.*

The girl sat with her elbows on knees, hands supporting her chin, staring into the firelight. Her bodice had once been white but was now a grimy gray from age. The material had worn thin and stretched tightly across the well-developed chest. Strands of hair falling around her face shone with gold from the glow of the firelight. Bessie caught a whiff of rosemary as the girl tossed the strands away from her eyes. Before sitting down to eat, Kate had filled the big iron pot with water from the rain barrel outside and placed it on the hook over the fire to heat. After supper she'd taken the steaming pot out back and washed the grime from her hair, throwing in some rosemary to scent the water. No matter how much Bessie warned her not to wash her hair so much, Kate did anyway. "Thee will catch t'death of cold from so much washing of t'head," Bessie would scold, but it made no difference. Kate hated to feel dirty and especially dreaded the thought of catching lice. Fleabites were bad but lice were worse.

It looks nice in spite of all the washing, Bessie thought, as she returned her concentration to her mending.

Folks often remarked that Kate appeared older than her seventeen years, which was only partly due to her ripe figure. She had the self-confidence and dignity that one usually attributed to a more mature person.

At the moment, she was enjoying flights of fancy as she gazed into the red coals. Images of exotic dancing girls seemed to sway among the flickering flames, changing swiftly into dashing swordsmen with sparring weapons. The blaze seemed to take on a life of its own before her eyes. Her fanciful imaginings came from remembered stories from childhood that Bessie would tell. The stories were repeats of Ben's tales that he'd brought home from his many voyages and the little girl would listen in awe while sitting at her aunt's feet. Kate loved to hear the fascinating tales of strange, hot desert lands where it was never cold and people had never heard of chilblains. She envied those dark skinned people who dressed in scanty garments and didn't have to bundle all their clothes on top of each other to keep out the winter's cold. It was hard to believe that the sun never stopped shining in those faraway places.

Gazing silently into the flames, those stories resurfaced and Kate's imagination took flight. Indulging in her favorite pastime, she pretended that she lived in such places.

From his seat on the stool at the other side of the hearth, Noll gave a noisy yawn and arose. "Methinks it is time to retire to bed. The day hath been long and busy and I doest need my sleep."

Kate couldn't believe her ears! Coming out of her reverie she glared at him with a look that spoke volumes, *'Twas not honest work that caused thy tiredness, my fine fettled friend.* Reading her thoughts, Noll grinned and gave her a surreptitious wink behind his mother's back. "'Bout time thee got some sleep too, cousin. Thou looks fair done in."

Kate stifled the sarcastic rejoinder that almost escaped, not wishing to upset her aunt by arousing her suspicions of this day's events. Instead, she consoled herself by giving him orders for the morrow. "Make sure thee doest gets enough rest my lad as I shall be awakening thee bright and early in the morn," she promised. "We needs get t'market early so as to find a good sheltered spot, away from the cold wind." She deliberately emphasized her next words. "I doest not wish for thee to be exposed to bad elements." Kate was making sure that he understood what she was really saying. Her cousin wouldn't be indulging in his gambling games tomorrow if she could help it. Bringing home a gold piece one day didn't mean that she'd be letting him off from an honest day's work, the next.

Chuckling, Noll patted her lightly on the head, "I'm sure that thou will protect me from anything bad cousin, no matter how forceful it might be. I shall see thee bright and early on the morrow as thee command." Ignoring her baleful glare he went over to Bessie, still busy with her needle. He bent and kissed her cheek, "I'll bid thee goodnight, ma."

With adoring eyes, Bessie watched her son as he climbed the ladder in the corner of the room that led to his bed in the loft. She thought him a fine handsome lad, in spite of his reckless ways.

Full of pride, she continued to watch until his legs disappeared through the ceiling's trap door.

Turning her attention back to her niece she noticed the faint blue shadows underneath the girl's eyes. Not for the first time Bessie felt a sense of urgency in her need to protect the girl. She suggested that Kate go to her bed that was in the corner of the kitchen. "I'll just stoke up the fire lass, so t'will stay nice and warm in t'house, before taking off to me own bed." Putting away her mending, she continued to fuss. "Doest think thee might need an extra cover for thy bed? I can fetch one from yon chest if needs be."

Kate arose from her stool and bent to give her aunt a kiss, "'tis warm enough, Bessie. Not to worry 'bout my welfare so much," she chastised gently. "I'm a big girl now and can well look out for myself."

Stroking Kate's sweet smelling hair away from her face, Bessie looked up at the girl, her voice taking on a serious tone. "Thou knowest that thee be like my own daughter to me. I worry more about thee than I do about our Noll. He can take care of himself well enough, but thou art but a slip of a girl. I know thee doest work harder than he" adding sagely, "my son doth not fool me none."

Kate laughed, tossing her hair back over her shoulders and Bessie saw how the reflection of firelight in her eyes made them shine with a strange, otherworld glow. She watched the girl cross to her bed in the corner and begin to prepare for sleep.

Bessie put her workbasket to one side and arose stiffly. Methodically she went through the nightly routine of snuffing out the tapers on the mantle shelf, before crossing to the table and extinguishing those that lit the rest of the room.

The oily aroma of melted tallow hung in the air. Blue/ gray smoke wafted up to the ceiling like specters of the night, while shadows danced on the walls as if alive.

Carrying one remaining candle, Bessie made her way to her bedroom in the back of the house. Stifling a yawn she shed her outer garments before throwing a billowing, flannel nightdress over her head. It emitted a scent of the lavender that she'd dried and sprinkled in her wooden clothes chest. After letting down her hair and securing her nightcap, she climbed underneath the many covers of her feather bed. The woman was asleep within minutes.

Outside, billions of stars shone over the city of London and the meandering waters of the Thames reflected their silver light. The north wind had finally died. The river was once more calm and serene as it flowed to the sea. All was well. Nothing stirred in the city's streets - except for a few prowling cats looking for rodents.

CHAPTER TWO

Kate could barely contain herself! The excitement of the crowd was so contagious that she had little control over her jubilation. The gay atmosphere swept her up in its path as she stood at the side of the roadway along with the rest of the Londoners. Restlessly, the crowd waited. The king was expected to ride into sight any minute now. Kate felt like jumping up and down as she had done as a little girl when she'd been promised a treat.

This very day the court was leaving to travel to the king's summer residence in Woodstock, Oxford shire, while Greenwich Palace was vacated in order for the annual cleaning to take place. This spring ritual required much work, so that the monarch's favorite London home could be made habitable for when he returned at the end of the summer.

As soon as the winter's rains had stopped, the palace windows were thrown open wide to let in fresh air. Smells of new grass and sounds of birds twittering, accompanied the buzzing of servants as they rushed around halls and rooms like bees in a hive.

All over the city, servants and housewives alike could be seen leaning out of windows as they shook out bed linens and clothing, causing dust particles to shimmer like specks of gold in the sunlight. Thick dust arose from back yards where people were beating blankets and rugs hanging over clotheslines. The methodical thumping of the brooms seemed to be keeping time with each other as the sounds echoed from yard to yard. Dirty rushes were swept out of doors, to be replaced with new sweet smelling fronds.

As for Greenwich Palace, now that the court was leaving the accumulated debris from the long winter months could be discarded. Tapestries and eiderdowns were thoroughly shaken and all the royal pewter polished until it shone as good as new.

Woodstock Palace was an ideal place to escape to during this time. Nestled in the lush Oxford countryside, the king with his court would wile away the spring and summer days enjoying the outdoor activities that Henry loved so much. The monarch would spend hours of relaxation indulging in games of tennis-competing in jousting matches - or walking the gardens with a favorite mistress. The court would fill the lazy sun-filled days in myriad activities, while Greenwich was once more made habitable. Even more significant, they would be avoiding all the pestilence that the summer's heat inevitably brought to London's streets.

This day, King Henry and his court would be traveling by royal barges with all the usual pomp and circumstance, sailing down the Thames and on to Woodstock. The private road leading from the palace to the dockside had been temporarily opened to the public so that common folk, like Kate and Noll, could view the pageantry of the departure.

Out of the blue on the previous day, Bessie had made a surprise announcement. "His Grace and t'court will be leaving t'city tomorrow," she'd declared. "How would thee both like to go and watch the parade leaving?" Kate had paused in the middle of polishing a window and Noll, in the act of sweeping cobwebs from the ceiling stopped with the broom hanging in mid-air.

"What about all the cleaning that still needs to be done in t'house, aunt?" Kate was astonished.

"Doest think that I'm incapable of cleaning me own house in a proper manner, without help?" Bessie's annoyance at Kate's remark came from a woman that prided herself on her neatness. Noll quickly interceded, "Kate hast no mind to question thy housekeeping, Ma. She knows that thee be t'best in neighborhood. 'Tis just concern that she feels, as thee might overtire without our help."

Her son's quick thinking response soothed Bessie's rumpled feathers. "I was cleaning house long afore thee both were born," she said huffily, but the flash of quick temper had disappeared. "Our Kate looks right peaked and needs some sunshine in her cheeks. A day's holiday will do thee both good. Besides," she added tartly, "I can get more done without thee both getting under foot!"

Kate had been out of bed before sun-up and was surprised to see Noll make an appearance a few minutes later. They fixed themselves some left over cold pottage and were out of the house just as the sky started to turn light.

Arriving at Greenwich early they'd been able to get a clear spot at the edge of the roadside. The king's guards were already lining the street on either side, in readiness to control the expected crowds. Soon after their arrival people began to make trickling appearances, slowly filling up the pavements that lined either side of the long thoroughfare.

In the distance, Kate saw a cloud of dust arising in the middle of the road. A murmur passed through the crowd. Noll nudged her with an elbow. "See our Kate! Yonder are horsemen coming this way. "Kate craned her neck and stood on her toes, shading her eyes against the sun's glare. She could just make out the indistinct shapes of horses and their riders as the sun's rays flashed and bounced off silver and gold adornments.

The loud rumbling of carriage wheels became louder and the clip clopping of horses' hooves more distinct. Now, she could make out the bright colors of the riders' clothing as they drew nearer. Her excitement knew no bounds.

A noise like that of rumbling thunder began to ripple through the crowd, and then the crashing crescendo hit the people around her. "GOD SAVE OUR GRACIOUS KING!" The roar echoed along the road like a shot from a cannon, "HAIL TO HIS MAJESTY!"

In their eagerness to see the king, people behind her suddenly rushed forward. Kate felt herself losing her balance and Noll grabbed her arm to keep her steady. The guards swung into action. Grasping each other's hands, the king's men quickly formed a barricade between the crowd and the parade of prancing horses and rolling coaches. "STAND BACK!" a guard yelled, as he drew his sword and moved to stand between Kate and the roadway. Noll moved protectively closer, but the crowd had stopped pushing. The flash of steel and authoritative command had done the trick.

Soldiers gripped each other's hands tightly and as if by unspoken agreement, all of the guards along the parade route followed suit.

Kate couldn't see a thing. The bulk of the guard's body in front of her blocked her view. In frustration she moved from side to side, trying to see around him. Without thinking, she placed her hands against the man's back to steady herself as she raised herself on tiptoes. Turning his head and seeing her predicament, the soldier stepped slightly to one side and gently nudged her forward. "There now missy. Thee may see without being trampled underfoot." She now had an unobstructed view along the roadway and Kate thanked him for his kindness.

Raising a hand to her mouth, she gasped in awe. From the clear space that the guard had made the biggest most magnificent blue/black horse that she'd ever seen was slowly approaching. A tall and stately figure sat astride it and even if she hadn't heard about the blazing red hair, she'd have recognized King Henry from his regal bearing alone.

As he drew closer, she could see that he was very broad as well as tall in the saddle. Never before had Kate seen such a handsome man! In reverence, she stared at His Majesty.

Nearer and nearer he came. A small beard covered his jaw, being the same shade of red as his hair. Underneath a flat pearl embroidered hat the auburn hair was cut in a short bob that just covered his ears.

An audible sigh went through the crowd as the steed and its rider came within a few feet of where everyone was standing. The prancing horse held its head high, tail twitching as if showing off.

Kate's gaze took in the monarch's fine doublet made of dark green brocade with exaggerated puffed sleeves that made his broad shoulders appear to be even wider. Underneath this he wore a white shirt of the finest lorn, its sleeves edged with narrow lace ruffs at the wrists.

She stared at the big hands that gripped the horse's reins. She'd never seen such jewels! Every finger held rings of emeralds and rubies that flashed and sparkled in the sunlight. King Henry's skirt flared as he sat astride the horse's back and fell open at the front to reveal an elaborate codpiece.[1] Kate's gaze wandered down to the strong looking, muscular thighs that gripped the horse's flanks. Below the black and gold colored breeches she noticed that his sinewy legs were clothed in silk hose the same shade of green as his doublet, while his shoes in the stirrups were the same black velvet as his hat. Over all this was a russet waistcoat trimmed in ermine.

Kate absorbed King Henry's appearance as he drew closer and closer. She'd never seen such richness or grandeur in her life! Her eyes swept over his figure, studying his dress before rising to his face.

---

1 Codpiece: A pouch that men carried to hold small personal items, such as a handkerchief.

Her breath stopped. The king's steady gaze held hers. A pair of small, penetrating eyes wandered over her person in an appraising manner and Kate's face reddened. After taking in her appearance for a few moments, the king turned to speak to one of the knights, riding as guard alongside. Before she had time to recover, the man turned his head and stared into her face…

Their eyes locked. The parade became non-existent….The king disappeared. Everything faded for Kate - except this man. She felt herself being drawn into the unfathomable depths of eyes that were strangely familiar. An electrical charge flowed between them and she had the strangest sensation of knowing this person. *How could I? I hast not seen him before this day.* Kate shook her head as if to clear her brain of a disturbing fog. She couldn't possibly know this man - or could she? - - - The sensation left her as quickly as it had taken possession. Yet, their gaze still held.

In those few moments that lasted for an eternity, the pomp and glory surrounding Kate were forgotten. All she was conscious of was this man staring down from his horse as he slowly rode past.

He couldn't be called handsome, being too rugged of features. Still, his presence held her like a magnet. He rode a horse that was only slightly smaller than the one ridden by the king but its beautiful coat looked like a piece of tan suede. The man's dress was grand, but not ostentatious. No matter. Kate was hardly aware of what he wore as she stood with upturned face, looking into his. He appeared to be as tall as the king himself, but not as heavy in girth. Her brain unconsciously took all this in while her emotions continued to whirl dizzily…

LONG LIVE KING HENRY! The contact broke. CLIP CLOP. Sounds of hooves suddenly seemed loud to her ears. GOD BLESS OUR NOBLE KING!

The parade moved along the road – distancing the rider from Kate. But her gaze still followed his back. She stared at the proud tilt of the head underneath a hat of blue silk. Her focus remained glued as he rode further and further away. Just before he finally disappeared - he turned around in his saddle and looked back.

Kate was completely unaware of the horse drawn litters passing by. She didn't see the court's grand ladies in all their finery, smiling and nodding at the crowds. People shouted their appreciation as delicate hands could be seen waving through carriage windows.

The girl continued to stare blindly in the direction that the knight had gone.

As the parade rolled on, an occasional pretty face would lean forward to peer out at the crowd, looking to be admired by the gawking citizens.

Kate was oblivious. Other fine looking gentlemen rode past, smiling and bobbing their heads – but her mind was still on the man in the king's personal retinue.

She jumped as a rude jab in the ribs brought her back to earth. "What doest think our Kate?' Noll sounded animated. "Is it not grand to see all the primping and preening of t'royalty?" Kate's attention returned to her surroundings as her cousin continued to babble. "Yon court ladies are the fairest that I hast ever seen. 'Pon my word I do swear, but they look like angels!"

Kate's equilibrium returned. She gave a derisive snort at her cousin's words. "Pox on thee our Noll! Any woman may look like an angel if she hath all that expensive muck to put on her face. Not to mention all the servants that coddle and spoil them, catering to their every whim."

"My, oh my. I do believe thou art jealous." Noll raised his eyebrows quizzically, observing his cousin's frowning face.

With an abrupt swivel, she turned her back on the pageantry. "Let's go afore t'crowd starts to leave and we are caught in t'crush. It's too hot to make our way home through hordes of people." Noll's remark had hit too close to the truth, leaving Kate with a sense of disquiet.

She often daydreamed of having fine clothes like those she'd just seen. Before this day, she had only been able to see them in pictures that Simon, the street artist, would sometimes sketch. Simon sometimes sat nearby their wagon to take advantage of its warmth, while he made a few coppers by sketching portraits of people who visited St. Paul's Walk. He was a talented man and when he wasn't busy making money with his portraits, he would doodle and draw pictures from memory.

Whenever Kate wasn't busy she would stand and watch him, and especially loved his drawings of ladies and gentlemen in fine clothes. Now, after seeing those stylish clothes she was all too conscious of her own shabbiness. *Methinks those court ladies can probably wash their hair whenever they take a fancy to do so.* Kate felt envious and mentally tried to shake away the uncomfortable thoughts. She followed her cousin as he squeezed his way through the people, *and, they probably bathe all over more often than I can.*

They paused to catch their breath as they reached the end of the road. Now free of the crowds, her cousin mopped at his perspiring brow with his jacket sleeve. "Let's go and walk along the embankment to Cheapside and see the sights," he suggested.

"What might Bessie say if we do?" Kate queried. "She never said that we could go anyplace else."

"She never said that we could not either." As always, Noll had an answer for everything, "she'll not be expecting our return this soon, and as long as we arrive home in time for t'mid-day meal she'll not be concerning herself."

With some reluctance Kate acknowledged his logic and besides this, the thought of being confined to the house for the remainder of the day didn't appeal to her. She'd never seen the city outside of her own neighborhood and the opportunity of so much freedom was irresistible. "As long as we get home afore noon, I suppose it may be all right," she conceded. "But thee better make certain that we get back at a goodly hour. I doest not wish for Bessie to be fretting herself over us."

"Not to worry. Ma will never know." Before she could think of any more reasons why they shouldn't venture forth, Noll headed towards the river's embankment.

From Kate's part of the city, she had often let her gaze sweep over the grand looking homes that bordered the Thames. But, she'd had to be satisfied with a view from a distance. Now as they walked along the embankment, she saw them up close.

Low walls separated the private gardens from the public path but she could still see the huge, brilliantly hued rhododendron bushes in the gardens. Rows of tulips and daffodils grew in abundance on the other side of the stone barriers and she breathed in the musky smell of bluebells. Some of the flowers had crept outside the walls, as if curious to see what was beyond the boundaries of the gardens. Spring blooms grew in colorful mixtures and ivy trailed over the walls to overflow onto the embankment's walkway. Willow trees with their trailing veils helped to shade the young people from the sun, yet it was still unseasonably hot for the time of year.

I wish I were able to shed my petticoats. Shaking her heavy kirtle, she tried to create a breeze to cool her body. Even though Bessie had managed to buy material and make her a new bodice, the stiff boning of her stomacher was uncomfortable in the heat.

Noll loosened the collar of his shirt and licked perspiration from his upper lip. "If this be an example of t'weather in spring, what shalt be like in mid-summer?" He didn't expect an answer, but got one regardless. "It was thy idea to walk to Cheapside. Would thee rather be beating covers in the heat of t'back yard?"

Noll gave her a look of scorn. "Ye know better than that, cousin. Wait until we reach Cheapside and I'll buy thee a mug of cool cider from t'nearest alehouse," he promised.

"And, may I ask what thou plan to use for money?"

He gave her an impish grin before reaching inside his breeches' pocket, "with this 'ere copper." Peeling his hand free, he held up a penny between his thumb and index finger. It glinted in the sunlight as he waved it around.

"Where might I ask didst come by a copper? No. Thee hast no need to tell me. No doubt thee were gambling again."

"Wrong again, missy. I earned this by honest labor!"

Kate smirked, giving him a look of amused skepticism. "Since when hath thou done honest labor, willingly?"

"I earned this money fair and square I'm telling thee, and if t'stop deriding me, I may tell how I came by it." Scowling, he waited to see if she was going to continue with her sarcasm.

Curiosity finally got the better of Kate. "Come on our Noll. Do tell. I promise to stay quiet and listen."

He wanted to wait a while longer and keep her in suspense, but the pleasure of letting her know how clever he was won. "A gentleman that is one of my regular card-playing customers asked me to teach him a few 'tricks of the trade' so to speak, so he would know how to handle himself at his posh club's gaming tables. Doest understand?" Kate nodded. "So I obliged, and he paid me this 'ere copper."

Puffing out his chest, he bragged, "yon chap was unaware that he was learning from t'best! Of course, I only showed him one or two simple tricks, so he will feel the urge to come back and learn more." A mischievous grin spread across his face. "T'thing he doest not hath any mind of is that the next time it will cost him more than a copper!" He gave a hearty laugh and with a flick of his wrist tossed the coin into the air, expertly catching it as it came back down.

Kate shook her head, but couldn't stop herself from joining in his laughter. Her cousin was a right rogue – but a harmless one at that. He pocketed his money and taking her arm quickened his steps, pulling her along with him towards Cheapside. The thought of a thirst quenching drink encouraged Kate's steps.

The narrow streets were dirty and today because of the royal pageantry, were crammed full of people. Most people were making their way home but some, like Kate and Noll, were taking the opportunity to do some sightseeing.

Street beggars and merchants alike were taking advantage of the influx and were hustling anyone who looked like they could be hustled. Noll stayed close by Kate's side and taking the coin from his pocket, gripped it in his hand. He wasn't about to leave it in his breeches and run the risk of having a pickpocket lift it from his person.

Kate was hot and thirsty. She was beginning to wish that she hadn't agreed to Noll's impulsive suggestion. *Cleaning house might be better than being jostled and jabbed by this crowd.* Unconsciously she sidestepped a pile of dog dung that lay in the middle of the street.

"Cheapside is only a short distance from here," said Noll, giving her arm an encouraging squeeze. "See! There's t'cross of Eleanor that Ma told us about." They'd entered Ward Street and Kate looked curiously at the stone cross, placed long ago by a mourning king in memory of his lost queen.

It was told that following his wife's death this king would place a holy cross in every town that he visited, in honor of his love. Kate noticed a peddler sitting on the steps at the base of the cross's pedestal, calling out his wares to passersby. She felt as if he shouldn't be there, as if his presence was somehow, sacrilegious. But the tantalizing aroma of the sweetmeat that he held made her mouth water.

"How about a tasty morsel for yon sweetheart, my fine lad? The man addressed his question to Noll, but his eyes were on Kate. "Thee looks like t' be in need of some nourishment, missy." The seller leaned towards the girl with a leering grin and proffered the sweetmeat for her to take. "Tis worth all of tuppence," said he, coaxingly. Kate backed away and Noll hurriedly grabbed her arm and moved her along the street.

Finally, they reached Cheapside. The girl stood and gaped. She'd never seen such a marketplace! St. Paul's Walk was industrious, but Cheapside was much more crowded and also larger. It was double the width of the other streets and either side was lined with buildings that besides having two stories also had an attic. They looked as if they would have toppled over if they hadn't have been so close together!

Their overhanging thatched roofs seemed to dwarf the people below. Boxes on windowsills were weighted down with trailing ferns and flowers. The whitewashed walls of the buildings were crisscrossed with supporting, blackened wood beams. Each house was so intricately patterned with the oak beams that they seemed to be competing with each other.

Folks crushed together as they looked over merchandise that was on display at open stalls. Shopkeepers leaned through open-sided establishments, displaying their wares and calling out to would-be customers.

The smoky smell of pork-sides mixed with other mouth-watering odors, drifted towards Kate as they walked by a meat shop. The merchant leaned over the open counter, taking note of the girl with the eager expression. He held out a slab of bacon in one hand, while with the other he offered a spicy smelling pasty. "How about some bacon for thee young man's supper, lass? Or maybe a nice, hot pasty with a crust as light as any ye could make thee self?"

"No thank thee, kindly." Kate answered politely, wishing she had the price to make a purchase.

Noll steered her away from the shop. "Look Kate," he pointed a finger. "I do believe that is an alehouse yonder." She peered in the direction that he was indicating, and saw a red sign jutting out from the side of a building. It was only a few yards along the street.

The sign had an image of a man wearing a gold crown. In bold, black letters above it were the words, 'The King's Head'. She hastened her steps, anticipating a rest and a refreshing drink.

Kate was proud of her reading skills. Most people had to look at a picture to understand and guess at the name of a place, but for her this wasn't so. Bessie had been very diligent in making sure that they both received adequate schooling.

As soon as they were old enough to be accepted by St. Mary's Church school, that good woman approached the old priest and paid the required donation. The children were no more than three, or maybe four years old when the church school had started to teach them their letters and numbers. The priest was very strict and put the fear of God into infant minds. Any pupil who didn't learn how to add and subtract without using their fingers, or stumbled over spelling out their name on their slates, would feel the sting of the holy man's cane across their knuckles.

Kate was an eager student and rarely came to grief with the irascible teacher, but her cousin was a different story. Noll would easily become distracted and prone to devilment. Needless to say, he often felt that sharp cane whiz across his backside.

Reaching the alehouse, they passed through a narrow passageway that led into a small paved courtyard. An empty table and two stools were placed in the center of the enclosure. The main entrance also had a wooden bench conveniently placed alongside it with the inevitable flower box hanging from a window above. Noll told her to wait for him while he went inside, and Kate thankfully plopped onto the bench.

Only barmaids or whores went inside as it wasn't considered proper for a maiden to be seen in a public house. All pubs had a separate 'take out' entrance and these were the only rooms where a female could enter and purchase a flagon of ale.

Kate closed her eyes, breathing in the sent of the flowers hanging above her head. Lazily she relaxed in the quiet atmosphere.

She hadn't been there but a few minutes when a sudden commotion by the entrance disturbed her peace. Startled, she glanced over at the door and saw a scruffy looking man staggering out. He was attempting to stay upright as he grunted and cursed, leaning heavily against the doorjamb. The drunken sot gave a noisy belch and all at once, started to slide to the ground.

Without a second thought Kate jumped up and ran to assist him, but he'd already stopped his fall by clinging to the door's handle. The man straightened up and focused rheumy, bloodshot eyes on the girl standing ready to help him.

His inebriated gaze slid up and down her body. His slack mouth broke into a grin,   Before she knew what was happening the drunk lurched at her, intent on grabbing her body. In horror, Kate backed away but he fell against her and almost knocked her off balance. She gagged as his face closed in and she smelled the stench of his fetid breath. Desperately, she tried to disentangle herself from his grip.

She wasn't aware that Noll had returned through the door. He took in the situation at a glance and laid his tankards of cider down on the bench. Before the man new what was happening, Noll had the drunk's arms pinned by his sides and was easing him away from her body. "Wow there, friend. Let me help thee to get t'bearings, afore ye do thyself some harm."

As Noll talked, he moved the man towards the bench and had him sitting down before the foul bugger knew what was happening. "Rest thee self for a while, afore ye try to make t'way home."

 The befuddled tippler was only too glad to feel the firmness of the bench underneath his teetering body. He sat blinking, trying to focus on his surroundings but made no attempt to move.

Noll picked up his tankards and nodded for Kate to follow him to the empty table. Setting the cider down, he pointed to one of the stools. "Sit thee self down and drink t'cider. He'll not be bothering thee anymore I'm thinking."

Kate did as he bade, still feeling unnerved from the unpleasant encounter. Gripping the tankard with trembling hands, she gulped down half of her drink before setting it back down. She still held onto the mug, but felt more foolish than afraid at having allowed herself to get into such a situation, *I should not hath been so foolish as to approach the man.* Aloud, she tried to explain her actions to her cousin. "He was about to fall, doest understand? I was only trying to help him."

"Have no fear," Noll comforted. "Thee hast not had as much experience as I of the outside world and needs to be more cautious."

His condescending manner rankled and had the affect of removing Kate's last remnants of discomfort. "Thee is but a few months older than me and I hast more sense than thou credit me for!"

"Tut tut." Noll patted the hands that still gripped the mug, "no need to get riled, cousin. I was only looking out for thee as ma told me to do."

Kate had the good grace to feel ashamed for her outburst. *He did rescue me from a nasty pickle.* "Well he did frighten me some," she admitted.

"He's just a harmless old drunk." Noll turned his head to glance towards the bench. "Look at him now. He's not so frightening, is he?"

She turned around. The inebriated fool was laying half off, and half on the wooden seat. His eyes were shut and loud snoring escaped from his open, drooling mouth. Spittle ran down his chin. Kate turned back in disgust.

"Drink t'rest of yon cider Kate and let us be gone from here. Methinks ye hast enough excitement for one day."

Kate nodded her head in silent agreement as she raised the tankard to her lips.

CHAPTER THREE

*T*he artist frowned in concentration as his deft fingers made broad sweeps across the heavy linen. Simon maneuvered the piece of charcoal into doing his bidding; drawing a curve here and a fine line there. He paused to raise his head and scrutinized his subject's features. After a few seconds, his concentration returned once more to his drawing. Kate stood and watched with pleasure as he brought the man's image to life.

Shading the area around the eyes with a thumb, the artist proceeded to make feather light strokes to form the man's eyebrows. The subject sitting on the high stool kept very still, casting an occasional curious glance at the man with the delicate fingers.

Simon's light eyes looked startling against his swarthy complexion, as they moved between his easel and his subject. Back and forth –back and forth they swiveled as he concentrated on his drawing. He worked fast and industriously, pausing to make a stroke here and a shadow there. Leaning back to get a better perspective, he rubbed absentmindedly at his long hooked nose, leaving a charcoal smudge across the bridge. No one had to question Simon's Jewish heritage, as his features were indicative of his race.

Kate dropped hot chestnuts from the barrel into a bag, not bothering to look at what she was doing. She had performed the same procedure so many times that she automatically put the same amount into each bag, without having to think about it. Business in the Walk was slow this morning, which gave her all the time in the world to enjoy watching Simon. As usual, Noll had disappeared earlier in the day but Kate didn't really care. Her rapt attention was on the man's portrait that was being created.

"See James. See? That is the artist of whom Gwendolyn was so enamoured."

Kate turned around at the sound of the excited voice. She saw that a couple had approached and stood a few feet behind her. The woman was addressing a man by her side and continued to gush liltingly. "He produced such a beautiful likeness of her youngest daughter and her husband was most exceptionally delighted!"

Kate felt as if hit by a thunderbolt. Transfixed, she stared at the man. The woman's prattling continued - but she was only conscious of the person who had the woman's arm linked in his own. It was the man who'd been riding with the king in the parade, five months past. There was no forgetting that face - or that experience.

Her eyes remained riveted on him. Likewise, he was looking at her with an expression of puzzlement.

How could she forget those enigmatic eyes that had lingered on her person as he'd ridden past? They had held her then - and they were holding her now.

There was no response from him as the woman continued to extol the virtues of Simon's talents. His attention was locked on Kate.

"James? Thou hast not been listening to me! The woman tugged impatiently on his arm. James broke the contact and turned his attention back to his companion, "I am sorry my dear. What was it thee were saying?"

The woman pouted her perfectly shaped lips that formed a Cupid's bow. "You must ask if he mayest draw my portrait. Please dear." The tone was that of a child that is begging for a treat.

Kate finally turned her attention towards the woman. She saw a pair of eyes that were the bluest of blue turned upwards to look into the man's face. "We shall give it to my mama and papa as a gift," said she. They will be so pleased to have my portrait to look at each day, as thou knowest how they do complain at not seeing me as often as they would wish."

James complied, leaving her happily waiting while he approached Simon - who had finished his drawing of the man and was collecting his payment.

Kate continued to apprise the woman who was bouncing up and down in excitement. *She acts as if she doest need the use of a chamber pot!* Mentally chastising herself for her rude thought, she grudgingly conceded that the woman was beautiful, in spite of her childish behavior.

She took note of the perfect oval face and the slight blush to the cheeks. *Obviously the pink is natural.* Her skin looked like a pale pink rose. Kate's eyes swept over the soft brown cape that covered most of the woman's kirtle. She couldn't help but observe that what could be seen of the latter exactly matched the blue of her eyes. The cape had an attached hood that framed the face and was trimmed with white rabbit fur. Golden tendrils peeped out from the sides of a tight fitting wimple. Nervously, the woman fluttered her small white hands.

Her escort beckoned for her to approach and she practically skipped over to where he stood with the artist. Simon invited the lady to sit on the stool that the previous customer had vacated. The woman complied, with much giggling and flirtatiousness.

While Simon busied himself with setting up another sheet of parchment and selecting the tools that he'd need, the woman made a big display of arranging her skirts about her, making sure that the folds fell the way that she felt they should. She threw back the hood of her cape, revealing more of the blond curls that had escaped from the wimple. Tilting her head to one side in a coquettish manner and lowering her chin, she looked up at the artist from under half-closed eyelids. The pose was meant to be seductive.

Simon was unaware of all these arrangements until he'd finished setting up his easel and had selected a piece of charcoal. Finally looking up and noticing the exaggerated pose, the corners of his mouth twitched slightly and his eyes began to twinkle.

Giving a polite cough, he addressed his model. "May I suggest madam that thou raise thy head slightly and look directly at me? If I may say so, from an artist's viewpoint of course, the blue of thine eyes is most striking and needs be shown to full advantage."

His model simpered and blushed, but relaxed so that her body became more natural. Her escort remained silent during this exchange, watching as Simon went to work.

Kate watched with mixed emotions. Although the man's back was now towards her, she was still very conscious of his magnetism. *Verily, but can he not be aware of this strange attraction?*

After a few minutes, he began to shift from one foot to the other – then turned. Hesitating for just a moment, he approached Kate's side. "Pardon my intrusion madam, but it doth seem to me that we hath met, but it is most puzzling to me as to where this could have taken place? This is the first time that my wife and I hath ventured into this part of the city. Hast traveled further afield with thy business wagon, perchance?"

Kate shook her head dumbly, not trusting herself to speak. She feared that her voice would give away her tumultuous feelings. *He must think me an imbecile.* Finally finding her tongue, her voice sounded harsh to her ears but in actuality she barely spoke above a whisper. "I doest not work in the city proper Sir, and I doubt that our paths would have crossed elsewhere."

He shook his head in bewilderment. "Please excuse my seeming boldness in approaching thee." With that, he returned to watch Simon as the artist worked on the portrait of his wife.

She is his wife. His words slowly sank into Kate's consciousness. *What difference doest make thee silly ninny! Why should a man of his obvious station take note of a working girl? A man of such distinction will not be looking twice at a class of person such as thyself, whether he be married or not.* Kate's mind was in a state of utter confusion as she scathingly berated herself.

But he did talk to me, didn't he? This latter thought sent her emotions flying again and she didn't know if she were coming or going! He hadn't remembered the incident on the road from Greenwich Palace- but even so he was aware of having seen her someplace. She was flattered and elated.

This man, who was a knight no less and had a beautiful wife, probably looked upon gorgeous ladies of the king's court whenever he wanted to. Yet, he'd remembered her face.

Twenty minutes later, Simon had completed the drawing. The woman stepped down from the stool and walked over to the easel. After taking a peek she gave a squeal of delight. "See James. Hath he not truly captured my likeness?" James nodded his head in approval and asked Simon his price. All too soon the transaction was completed. The couple left to walk toward a handsome carriage that was parked at a short distance along the road.

Kate stood unmoving as she watched their retreating figures. Reaching the conveyance, she saw the man help his wife inside. But, before entering himself he turned and looked once more in her direction. His glance was much the same as when she'd seen him riding with the king. The next moment the carriage was gone. She continued to stare along the road long after they had left.

Simon's voice broke through her reverie. "Look Kate. See what the fine gentleman hast given me." His voice jolted Kate out of her mindlessness. She looked into the palm that Simon held out. There was a silver shilling lying in his outstretched hand. "T'were generous of the man to give me so much money, doest not think so?"

"Thy talents be t'finest, Simon," she responded loyally, "and the gentleman no doubt thought so too and paid what he thought was thy worth."

Simon tested the silver piece with his teeth to make sure that it wasn't a dud. Smiling with satisfaction, he pocketed his wealth. "Methinks that I shall take my leave Kate, as 'tis getting a chill in t'air. Now I can afford to retire for the rest of this day and take advantage of my warm rooms."

Kate understood. Although it wasn't as cold as it was going to be when the winter was upon them, cool weather always bothered Simon as it made his joints ache. He often said that he wished he'd been born in a hotter climate. She helped him to pack his things, before returning to the task of roasting her chestnuts.

A mother with a young toddler stopped to buy a ha' penny's worth. As her hands automatically filled a bag, her mind dwelled on the gentleman named James. He had stirred emotions that she hadn't known she was capable of feeling.

CHAPTER FOUR

*H*ow long he'd been standing there, she had no idea. She was too busy waiting on customers to notice. People were milling around the wagon, reluctant to leave the warmth of the hot coals after making their purchases.

A sharp nudge from Noll caused her to stop in the act of filling a bag for an elderly man. Kate turned her head ready to give him the length of her tongue, but before she could say anything he gave a meaningful nod towards the church. Turning to look behind her she saw him. He stood at the far end of the steps that led to the church entrance - watching.

It had been over a week since their chance encounter and she'd never thought to see him again. Kate stood glued to the spot.

"Who is he?" Noll's voice was loaded with curiosity. "He hath been staring at thee for the past five minutes." When she didn't answer and continued to ignore a customer, Noll collected the coins from the woman before giving her a bag and bidding her a good day. His puzzled gaze moved between his immobile cousin and the grand looking gent.

Finally, the man moved and headed purposefully towards the wagon. With loping strides James arrived at her side. "Good day to thee mistress. I found myself in this part of the city conducting business and feeling pangs of hunger, remembered that thy chestnut wagon was close by. To appease my appetite I decided to make a purchase from thee."

His words were too ridiculous! Glancing swiftly at her cousin, Kate saw Noll's incredulous expression and his smirking face spoke volumes. Had this man really come back to see her?

James felt like a complete fool. *Why did I feel such a need to see this girl once more? How can I explain my actions, when I doest not understand them myself?* His usual self-confidence had deserted him. He felt awkward and embarrassed. *What folly hath taken possession of me? She must think me an imbecile!*

Without giving any more thought to what he was saying, words started to tumble from his mouth. "Please forgive my boldness in appearing here, but I confess there is something about thy person that puzzles me greatly. My impulse in returning was quite irrational. I beg your pardon and hope that you will excuse my unseemly behavior."

His quandary was obvious to Kate. Yet the fact that this nobleman didn't know how to conduct himself was astonishing and she didn't know how to respond, in spite of the thrill of seeing him again. She wasn't used to having any man seek out her company, never mind such a distinguished gentleman as this.

Kate had no experience in the fine art of conversing with the gentry. Her poor-class associations didn't include gallants and all she could do was to stare dumbly as if she'd taken leave of her senses. The silence lengthened.

I should not hath imposed myself. It was foolhardy for me to come here. James bowed stiffly and turning on his heels, made to leave. Without being consciously aware of what she was doing, Kate impulsively laid a restraining hand on his arm. "Please. Do not leave." Her words sounded unreal to her ears, as if spoken by someone else. Her face turned scarlet. She wanted to die of shame.

In surprise, James looked from the hand on his arm to her face. Kate immediately dropped her hand as if the touch had scalded her. The tension between them was palpable.

"Pardon me Sir, but might I be so bold as to perform the introductions?" Noll's voice broke the strain between them as with his usual aplomb he came to their rescue. "This 'ere girl is Kate. And, would it be too bold of me to inquire as to thy own name?"

She couldn't believe her ears! *He's acting like Lord Muckety Muck!* Noll had outdone even himself this time. His utter nerve was only surpassed by his cocky self-assurance. It was unbelievable that even her brash cousin could act so downright daft! Hysterical laughter threatened to burst from her and she placed a hand over her mouth to stifle the nervous impulse.

While waiting on customers, Noll had been watching the charade with interest. He'd quickly disposed of the last customer, wanting to learn more about this fine looking toff and his connection to Kate.

Yet James didn't seem to be the least put off by Noll's impertinence On the contrary, his body visibly relaxed and he smiled as he held out his hand to shake Noll's grimy paw. "My name is Herewith, my fine fellow – Sir James Herewith. And, may I inquire as to thy own name and relationship to this maiden?"

Dressed in darned hose and a jacket that was missing fastenings, her cousin's flowery introduction was ludicrous. But Kate didn't care. *At least, he kept him from leaving.*

Noll gave another exaggerated bow as he brushed strands of unruly hair away from his eyes, in a fair imitation of a gallant's salutation. "My name is Oliver, Sir James, but me kith and kin call me Noll." With flair, he turned his attention to Kate, acting as if she were royalty. "Kate is me cousin. She was christened Katherine, but for propriety's sake t'was shortened. As she hath no living parents, she abides with my mother, (her aunt from her mother's side) – and myself." Expanding his chest in self-importance, he finished his speech. "We are her guardians, in a manner of speaking."

Kate was stunned. She stared open mouthed from one to the other. *He acts as if he were exchanging banalities with a courtier in the royal palace.* Even droller, this Sir James Herewith seemed to think there was nothing amiss in the situation.

Once again, James turned and addressed his attention to Kate. "May I return and converse with thee Kate? Be assured, my intentions are most honorable and I wish no harm towards thee. Yet, I must confess that the urge to be in thy company is most compelling."

Kate didn't know how to answer. It was as if an unseen force had taken over the control of her will. She longed to grant him his request, but even though he professed honorable intent he was not of her class - and was also wed. This knighted gentleman should not be seeking her out, even though he claimed his innocence.

In spite of the elation at seeing him again, Kate's disciplined upbringing came to her aid. "I feel honored that thou wish to be in my company Sir," she responded, "but as thee can see I hath need to take care of business. I feel it would be unseemly for thee to be seen in these parts conducting conversation with such as myself." It was difficult to rebuff him when her whole being wanted otherwise.

James was duly chastised. Her words had sunk in. "Of course thou art right." He sounded disappointed. "Although I fear it would prove to be more embarrassing for thyself than I, to be seen tarrying with me."

He gave her a little bow, once again making Kate feel as if she were a woman of distinction. "My apologies Kate for being so presumptuous. Please forgive my rash act in coming here today. My only excuse is that I acted on an impulse and did not give thought to thy own feelings." With that he turned and left.

She wanted to cry.

"Well, our Kate. What doest think of that? Seems like thee made an impression on yon gentleman. A knighted dandy, no less! However didst meet such a one as yon fine toff? Hast been sneaking around without my knowledge? What shall Ma say about all this?"

Noll's bombardment brought her back to earth. "He may be a toff but he is no dandy," she replied tartly. "And, I would be obliged if thee did not mention this incident to Bessie. I shall not be seeing him around these parts again, so to worry her unduly over such a trifling matter would not serve any purpose."

He gave a loud guffaw. "Trifling thee do say! Seems to me that yon gentleman was taken with thee strongly enough to travel all the way across t'city just to seek out thy company!" His amused face came close to Kate's. "Thou still hast not told me how did'st meet."

"It's none of thy concern." Kate's eyes flashed sparks and placing her hands on her hips, she threw back her head in defiance. "I mayest tell this much. I was not 'sneaking around' as thou hast accused me of doing. When I first set eyes on him, thou were supposedly taking care of me. That is all I will say about that. If he were not a true gentleman, he would not concern himself with my reputation and might continue to bother me, regardless of my wishes."

"Pon my word, methinks that we art becoming a little high and mighty dear cousin. By the look on thy countenance, I suspect thee to be in a state of bedazzlement over this Sir James Herewith." Noll leaned even closer and spoke in an exaggerated whisper. "Maybe thou be disappointed that thee sent him packing?" He wagged a finger at her. "Might thee be hoping for his return – M.mmm?"

Kate picked up a bag of chestnuts and venting her frustrations, swung them at his head. Fortunately he ducked and the bag sailed over him to land on the dirt, scattering its contents all over the ground.

An urchin saw the nuts flying through the air and rushed to collect them. Stuffing as many as he could into his jacket pockets, he was gone again before anyone could stop him. Not that Noll and Kate were heeding him anyway as they were too busy riling each other.

"Seems to me that thee needs be tending to thy own business and minding thee tongue concerning mine," Kate ranted. "I doest not intend for any man to take advantage of my person, whether he be a pauper or gentleman - or even King Henry himself! So, it would be doing me a service if thee not speak of this matter again, especially to Bessie."

Noll grinned, unperturbed by her outburst. Placing a finger across his lips, he whispered in a conspiratorial manner. "Nary a word shall pass my lips, fair maiden." With false humility he added - "thy honorable reputation is safe with me." He jumped out of her reach, averting the expected blow.

Kate believed she wouldn't hear from him again. She was wrong. Less than a week later, a handsome carriage pulled alongside her wagon. In astonishment, she took in the gold trimmed door with its elaborate coat of arms embossed on its surface.

The driver, dressed in fine livery stepped down from his seat behind the horse and approached. In his hands he carried a big bouquet of red roses, arranged amidst feather- like fern and delicate baby's breath.

Kate gaped as the coachman stood at arm's length, eyeing her as if he were afraid of catching the plague. "Art thou the person who owns this wagon?" The question was asked with an air of someone who was performing a duty below his station.

"That I am." She was staring at the flowers he held.

"I hath been commanded to present this bouquet to thee." He pushed the delicate blossoms towards her so that she was forced to take them from his hand. Their aroma hit her senses with exquisite potency.

With a haughty sniff, the coachman turned and climbed back up to the coach's seat. With a flick of a whip and a curt command, the horse started off at a trot. The carriage rolled along the street, leaving as fast as it had arrived.

Burying her nose in the fragrant bouquet, Kate closed her eyes, savoring the scent and feeling the velvet touch of the petals. Fresh dew still clung damply to them. Finally raising her head and opening her eyes, she saw a folded piece of fine linen parchment attached to a stem. Removing it carefully, so as not to damage a flower, she broke open its seal. Kate spread the paper out to read what was written.

Dear Kate.

Please accept this small gift as a token of my respect, and my further apologies for what must seem to thee to be unmannerly behavior. It was not my intent to force my attentions on thee, and my sincere hope is that thou wilt not think on me with contempt. My only excuse is that I felt compelled to see thee. After visiting the street artist, at my wife's request, I puzzled over the feeling of having met thee previously. Eventually I remembered where this had occurred. You mayest not remember, but it took place this past springtime. Thou were standing at the edge of the crowd that paid homage to our king as the court was departing London. Your presence strongly drew me, as it did so when I saw thee again in St. Paul's Walk. I cannot explain my actions any better than this. The desire to seek thee out once more is unexplainable, even to myself. I sincerely hope that thou believe me when I say that my intentions were not dishonorable.

It was signed with a flourishing letter - *'J'.*

Once more, she lowered her face into the roses.

"By all that is Holy! Where did'st come by such flowers?" She hadn't noticed Noll approaching, being occupied with the unexpected gift. "At this time of the year, no less! Hast someone mistaken thee for dead and sent them to adorn thy grave?"

For once, Kate couldn't retaliate. She merely handed him the note without saying a word.

Noll had difficulty in reading it and peered closely at the words, mumbling to himself as he attempted to sound out the letters. After a few minutes, he'd deciphered the message and looked up in wonder. "I do swear our Kate, methinks that thou hast put a hex on yon fine gentleman!"

He handed the note back to her and watched as she put it inside the front of her bodice, for safekeeping. A chuckle started to slowly arise within him and he couldn't stop himself. He broke into uncontrollable laughter. "By God! I do declare, but the man is besotted! Wiping his eyes, he made an effort to control his mirth. "What say thee cousin? Did thee spit in a frog's mouth, or put some other such spell on him?"

Kate ignored his jibes, but she couldn't deny the feeling of elation that she was trying to hide. In an attempt to cover up the pleasure that she felt, she once again buried her face in the flowers.

"How wilt explain that 'ere posy to Ma?"

The question brought her back to her senses. "I hast not thought on that." This troubling reality brought her down to earth. "I cannot take them home, Noll. I hath no good explanation to give aunt, and she would surely go into a fit of temper if I told her the truth. I shudder to think what she would say. What must I do? "

For once Noll didn't have an answer.

Glancing across the cobble-stoned Walk, she saw Simon sitting contemplating on whatever it was that he was drawing. An idea came to Kate. *I shall give them to Simon for safekeeping.*

He hath an artist's appreciation for beauty. The sobering thought of having to give up her gift deflated her pleasure, but the alternative of facing her aunt's questions was worse. Taking a rosebud from the bouquet, she slipped it into her bodice along with the note. Its heady perfume mingled with her underclothing. *I shall press it between the pages of my Sunday Missal this evening, before retiring.* "I will return shortly."

Puzzled, Noll watched as she made her way towards the artist.

Simon looked up with a smile of greeting as she approached. "Thee doth carry a beautiful nosegay there, Kate. Where did'st come by such a grand posy? They are a rarity to acquire at this time of year."

She answered evasively, "an acquaintance gave them to me Simon, for safe keeping. But I fear that they will die afore I can get them home at the end of the day. I wondered if thee would like to take care of them? Might thee not use them to capture their beauty in thy drawings?"

Simon wasn't fooled by her answer, but kept his council. He hadn't been unaware of the arrival of the smart looking carriage that had stopped at her cart. Whoever owned such a conveyance, had no doubt given her the costly bouquet. *It is not my concern if Kate hath an admirer whose existence she wishes to hide. She is a comely maiden and may good fortune smile upon her.* "I do thank thee most kindly, Kate." Taking the bouquet from her outstretched hands, he looked around to see where he could place them.

The only thing he had was his half-empty flagon of ale that he kept to sip on throughout his day. "This might temporarily serve as a replacement for water." He arranged the flowers in the jug, saying with a smile, "maybe they might enjoy the taste of the ale better than water anyway!"

Kate left him to return to her wagon, feeling somewhat better knowing that through Simon's special gift the flowers' beauty would be kept alive.

CHAPTER FIVE

*F*rom the comfort of the armchair, Cecil watched as his brother paced back and forth. A worried frown continued to crease James' forehead and his stride didn't break as he strode from one end of the parlor's great fireplace to the other. With hands clasped behind his back and head bowed in concentration, James turned once again - back and forth - back and forth.

Cecil sprawled amidst the chair's cushions, saying not a word. Taking a sip of the good mulled wine he looked relaxed - but his appearance hid an alert mindfulness. He could see that his brother was greatly disturbed.

Reaching the far end of the hearth James turned and strode towards Cecil, coming to a standstill in front of his outstretched legs. "I do swear brother my mind is in such a turmoil. What doest think I should do?"

Cecil set down his pewter mug on the small table alongside his chair. Easing himself up from the reclining position, he pensively tapped his pursed lips with a finger. He countered the question with a question. "What doest want to do?'

James turned his head to stare into the blazing fire. "These strange feelings art perplexing to me. I want to rush back to St. Paul's and see her once more, but common sense tells me that this would be most foolish. Besides, she made it quite clear to me that she felt it unwise to meet again. Foresooth she is but a commoner! Even so, I swear that I do not hold my station in life in such high esteem, as to deny that good qualities exist in those born into lesser circumstances. Her manner is equal to any maiden born into gentility – which is why she is conscious of the distinction between our classes. If she were not of such a sensitive nature, she wouldst not mind so. And, I wouldst not be so attracted to her person. For one so young she hath the sensibilities of a dowager."

Cecil looked wonderingly at the sibling who resembled him but slightly. Although James was the oldest by almost a year, Cecil had always felt as if he were the elder. It was not in his nature to be impulsive – like James. In fact, outsiders that didn't know them, assumed that Cecil were the eldest of the two due to his steady and more cautious nature.

In frustration, James' ran a hand through his thick, dark hair. Cecil was reminded of his own thinning crop that made him appear to be older than he was.

Although Cecil was only in his early thirties, his tanned face showed deep creases around the eyes and mouth, caused from spending his days in the outdoors running his sibling's estates in the Sussex countryside. His rugged features were not as smoothly defined as his brother's and as a youth, his nose had been broken. Having carelessly got too close to a distraught cow's hooves during her labor, it was no longer straight but had a decidedly crooked bump to it. Although they were of the same height, James appeared to be taller as Cecil's girth showed his weakness for hearty meals. Also, Cecil preferred to remain at their ancestral home managing the farmlands, while James stayed in his town home and enjoyed the court life of London. Since James' marriage to Clarissa, he'd spent very little time at his Sussex estate, as that good woman disliked the country and refused to live in the inherited Herewith home. Even though Cecil was the younger, he'd taken over the running of the family's land after their father's death.

Cecil only visited James' home whenever it was a necessity to discuss the business of the estates. He had thought this to be the reason for the unexpected message he'd received only two days past. The note had sounded so urgent that Cecil had dropped everything to make haste to London. However, he'd soon realized something other than the estate was on his brother's mind.

Arriving last evening in time for supper, Cecil had no opportunity to talk alone with his brother. Clarissa had monopolized the table conversation with her usual overbearing effervescence. Cecil was quick to note that James hardly spoke a word and he watched thoughtfully as his brother picked at the delicious partridge on his plate, seemingly preoccupied within his own thoughts. *What is disturbing him so?* Clarissa stopped her chatter long enough to prompt her husband into participating in their discourse. Not that his feather-brained sister-in-law cared if anyone else talked. *She enjoys hearing the sound of her own voice too much.*

This morning, Clarissa had announced that she was leaving to make some social calls. "Now I expect my husband to entertain thee Cecil," said she. "I do fear that James hath moped around the house so much of late, that I cannot stand having him underfoot any longer!" After offering her cheek to her husband for the obligatory kiss, she left with the admonishment for him to - "be good now James, and mind your manners." Cecil had felt like a child again in his mother's presence, but his brother seemed oblivious to his wife's condescending manner.

Finally alone with each other, James had revealed an astounding story of meeting with some poor class girl from across the river. "When Clarissa insisted that I take her to see the artist, I was most reluctant to do so," James had confided. "But god's truth, when I first saw Kate, I was absolutely certain that we had met before.

277

The feeling was extremely odd and I puzzled over it all that day." Cecil had listened as James continued with his fantastic tale. "As I was falling asleep that night, it suddenly came to me where I had seen her and why she looked so familiar to me. I became wide-awake, vividly remembering an incident from last spring as I accompanied his Grace and court to Woodstock."

"The king drew my attention to a comely young girl who had caught His Highness' eye. She was standing at the edge of the crowd. It was Kate." James' tone was animated as he talked of the maiden, "I do swear brother that for some inexplicable reason, her eyes held mine as if she had cast a spell on me! Naturally, I brushed the encounter from my mind and soon forgot the incident. That is, until I saw her again in St. Paul's Walk."

Cecil had taken note of the quality of his voice as James spoke of the girl. Who was this wench who could move his implacable brother like this? Granted, his marriage was not a love match but of course this was not unusual among their class.

Their parents had selected Clarissa as the most appropriate match for the continuation of the Herewith's lineage. Even though she had a reputation for being flirtatious with the gallants who were drawn to her beauty, Clarissa had been a virgin. James and she seemed to be compatible enough. His brother was tolerant of his wife's spoiled, empty-headed nature and likewise, James quiet acquiescence to her wishes apparently satisfied her flighty nature.

No doubt it was a disappointment to them both that due to Clarissa's delicate condition, they had not been able to have a child - as yet. During their seven years of marriage, Clarissa had thrice miscarried and the doctor had advised James that it would do well for her to gather her strength, before attempting to conceive again.

Unbeknown to Cecil was the fact that the medics warning had silently relieved his brother. After the first flush of wedded bliss, (if one could call their honeymoon 'blissful') – had worn off, James realized that his wife was more attracted to the social standing provided by being married to a Herewith, than to marital intimacy. In fact, he'd soon learned that his wife was a bore, both inside the bedchamber and out.

James still hadn't answered his question and Cecil repeated it. "So. Once again, I ask. What do thee intend to do about this girl?" Giving a helpless shrug of his shoulders, James rested his hands on the fire's mantel and stared into the leaping flames. "That is the quandary I am struggling with. I do swear, but she hath bewitched me!"

Cecil leaned forward to emphasize what he was about to say. "No matter what thee want, thou must knowest that thy attraction to this girl – what is her name, Kate?" James nodded and Cecil continued, "thee must be aware that this attraction is quite unrealistic. Even if thee were not a wedded man <u>and thou art</u>, this Kate is not marriage material for a Herewith. The only alternative is to take her as a mistress."

James' face visibly blanched. "I could not use her thus. Although I freely admit that I hast thought on this. I would not hesitate to take her should I not hath respect for her person. She may be of a lowly station in life, but she is no trollop!"

"So. What doest plan to do?"

James flopped into a chair, shaking his head mutely.

Cecil leaned even closer, speaking slowly in an attempt to sink advice into his brother's addled brain. He chose his words carefully. "It is obvious that thou hast a strong attraction towards this wench. But thou knowest that it cannot be satisfied in an honest relationship. Therefore, I would urge thee to take control of thyself and dismiss her from thy thoughts." His words were deliberately blunt. "No good may come of any involvement with this person. Most assuredly it cannot bring anything but misery to this girl, as well as thyself." He paused, before continuing. "Hast thou forgotten thy marital duty towards Clarissa?"

James gave him a look that spoke volumes.

279

"Nay. Thou need not look at me in such a way, James. Remember this. Clarissa may not be the ideal loving partner that wouldst wish, but she is still thy legal spouse." His voice took on a note of cynical humor, "thou doest not enjoy the privileges of our king that allows you to cast off wives like old clothing, whenever their bed becomes wearisome!"

The semblance of a smile came to James' face. King Henry's peccadilloes concerning his wives and mistresses were the butt of many jokes. James good humor was beginning to return. "Thy advice is well taken, Cecil. Should thee ever be of a mind to wed, or take a mistress, maybe I can be as persuasive in deterring thee from such a rash act as thou hath been with me this day."

Cecil gave a loud laugh; glad to see that his brother's somber mood seemed to be lifting. "If ever the day cometh that I am thinking to wed dear brother, I would wish to be placed in chains until the madness left me!"

Joining in his brother's laughter James arose and approaching him, placed a hand on his shoulder. "Come. Let us see what my cook hath prepared for our meal." He deliberately changed the subject. "Thou may give me an accounting of our tenants and the crops, while we partake of sustenance. Foresooth, all this heavy talk hath whetted my appetite! "

Cecil didn't need any further bidding. Arising, he draped an arm around his brother's shoulder as they left the parlor. As they followed the appetizing smells of roast pig and dumplings coming from the great hall, he thought of his brother's problem and hoped that James had heeded his words. *He can be headstrong at times and dallying with this maiden, whoever she is, would be most foolish.*

James continued to engage Cecil in talk of the estate's business as they entered the long hall. But, underneath the conversation, his thoughts were elsewhere. *Dare I see her again? Of course not! Cecil is right - - I wonder if the flowers helped to soften her resolve against me…?*

280

A heavy pall as gloomy as the sky lay over her spirit. It had been a fortnight past since Kate had received the roses and in spite of her common sense telling her that she was being foolhardy, she had hoped to see him again. Work helped to keep her mind from dwelling on him. Yet, when trade was slow like today, the hours seemed to drag.

From the far end of the church steps he stood and watched the girl at the wagon. *I must be mad!* He saw her brush a strand of hair behind a delicate ear and noticed how a weak burst of sunlight picked out golden highlights in the abundant tresses. *God's truth, but it is heartening to see her again, even tho' she hath caused me to take leave of my senses.* By everything in his power, he'd tried to control his obsession to see her again. James had buried himself in piddling duties at court and listened with a sense of boredom to the usual gossip and petty intrigue. Speculation, as to whom the king would choose as his next bride, was the current gossip. Cromwell was working night and day searching the European monarchies to find a suitable candidate. The talk and activity only served to make James more aware of his own needs.

Henry's unusual state of an empty bed caused James to dwell on his own loveless marriage. *What a farce*, he'd thought derisively. Then, feeling guilty about his thoughtlessness towards his wife, he'd put forth an effort to make himself available for more social obligations than were deemed necessary. Of course, Clarissa had been puzzled but delighted at his unexpected solicitations.

In desperation he'd made an unexpected appearance at Herewith Hall, on the excuse that he felt a need to be of service to his brother. After two days Cecil had, as kindly as possible, informed him that his presence there was more of a hindrance than help. James had returned to London. This very morning he'd been overly attentive to Clarissa, but her incessant twittering had become so unbearable that he'd felt as if he wanted to suffocate her!

He'd left the house with the intent on walking off his frustrations. That's when he'd determined to see Kate - just one more time.

Noll saw him almost at the same time that she did. Giving her a cheeky grin, he nonchalantly stated, "I shall go and spend time elsewhere. Maybe I can find someone who would like to engage me in a game of cards."

For once Kate was thankful for her cousin's bad habit, but she was also nervous. "Do not stay away for too long a time Noll," she pleaded. "Admittedly, 'tis a pleasure to see him again, but the thought of conversing with him is unsettling."

He patted her arm encouragingly. "Thee hast moped around for this past fortnight and do not think that I hast not known why. Thee must'a known that yon fine gentleman would return."

It was too late to say anything else, as James had arrived at their side. Noll bowed low. "Good day to thee, Sir James. I was just leaving as I hath pressing business that needs my immediate attention. It is good to make thy acquaintance again."

James acknowledged the salutation. "Tis good to meet thee once more, Master Noll." After a few more pleasantries between them, Noll left.

Without being conscious of doing so, they stood soaking up each other's energy. Kate was the first to break the silence. "Thank thee most kindly for thy gift of roses, sir. It was a most thoughtful gesture."

"T'were the least that I could do Kate, considering that I seemed to have offended thee by my presence." She started to speak, but he stopped her with a gesture, "please listen, Kate. If I really do offend thee I will leave immediately, but I had to see thee just one more time and attempt to explain myself. Regardless of whatever decision thou might come to, I must confess that I will not forget thee." He hesitated. "Admittedly I am attracted to thy person more than anyone else I hath ever known but please believe me, my intentions are not to bring distress to thee. Just being in thy company for a short time gives me the greatest of pleasures."

She wasn't used to such gallantry - yet underneath the thrill that his words aroused, there was a nagging unease. It wasn't James himself that produced this feeling. It was a premonition that she couldn't understand or explain. It was like a thundercloud that threatens the summer sun. She felt a need to draw away. Yet at the same time, her whole being wanted to be near this man.

Without intending to sound so blunt, she asked - "doest not thy wife find it odd sir, that thou visit these parts of London?"

His features became shadowed. "My wife prefers her own social duties, Kate. Though verily the word duty should not be applied, as her social activities give her the greatest of pleasures. She doth not question my daily interests, and I do not question hers."

Kate was abashed. Her naive mind had not thought to consider how personal her question had sounded. "Forgive my impertinence, sir. It was not my intent to pry into thy home situation."

James placed a hand on her arm. "Thou hath a right to ask the question Kate and there is no need to apologize. Surely thee might well ask why a married man wants to seek out the company of a maiden?" She remained silent.

"I owe an explanation." She started to intervene once more, but he placed a finger over her lips, "nay, do not speak. I must be honest. Clarissa and I hath a suitable arrangement in our marriage."

So that is her name.

"As long as I perform my social duties as expected and make myself available for her wishes, we have a harmonious home-life. It is an arrangement that suits her well enough and until meeting thee, one that I accepted and lived with unquestionably."

"But since our meeting, I confess that I feel most restless. I realize how much I miss the pleasantries of conversing with someone that I admire, and that also admires myself." He looked as vulnerable as a child as he asked uncertainly, "Doest thou admire me a little, Kate?"

Kate saw the play of emotions pass over his countenance and she heard the loneliness in his voice. She felt moved by his anxious expression as he asked her for assurance of his welcome and her heart went out to him.

His hand still rested lightly on her arm and without thinking, she covered it with her own. "I hast no intention of prying into they personal life, sir…"

James stopped her with a gesture. "If we are to be friends Kate, thou must address me by my given name. Formalities between us seem to be most foolish. The point of being polite strangers hath past, wouldst not agree?"

She nodded her head in compliance and continued, savoring the sound of his name on her lips. "Please understand - - James, I confess that the urge to enjoy thy company is strong, but I am not desireth to bring any distress to thy wife. I doest not wish to take thy company away from her, even for an hour."

James threw back his head and laughed, but there was no mirth in his laughter. Startled by the unexpected response, Kate stepped back.

"Dear Kate. If only thou didst know my wife. Believe me, the only thing that would really distress Clarissa, would be if she found it necessary to spend even an hour in my company. The confession was made in sardonic tones. "Truth be known, if she did not have her so-called, 'social obligations' to attend to and was obliged to spend a whole day in my company, she would be as distraught as if she were a prisoner in yon 'Tower!"

Kate didn't know how to answer this outburst. Having had no experience of matrimonial life, except for vague memories of the infrequent homecomings of her late Uncle Ben, she was at a loss. On the rare occasions when she did think about marriage, she assumed that two people wed because they loved each other and even if they didn't always live happily ever after at least, they took care of each other's needs.

She recalled the situation of the girl, Peggy, who lived along their street. There had been a hasty wedding when Peggy had got herself 'in the family way.' Naturally, her father had made sure that the boy responsible had done right by his daughter. Their marriage hadn't started out ideally, but apparently had been a love match as Peggy now had three toddlers and another one on the way.

James' confession of his marital state sounded as if two strangers existed under the same roof. This not only upset Kate's pre existing ideas of marriage but, was saddening. The underlying loneliness in his cynical admission was obvious.

She looked at him without commenting, but her eyes were clouded with compassion – and something more.

James's sardonic display of humor ceased as abruptly as it had started as he looked into her eyes and saw the emotions mirrored there. He stepped closer. Taking both of her hands into his own, he clasped them firmly. "My dear Kate. I did not mean to affect thee so by telling intimate details of my meaningless marriage. It is not so burdensome that it is unbearable."

"Clarissa runs my home very well and is a popular, amusing hostess at our social gatherings. What more may a husband ask of his spouse?" he concluded, wistfully.

Absorbing the innocent and trusting face so close to his own, he felt a need to hold her close. James noticed how thickly her eyelashes curled. The delicate pink tinges to her cheeks made him want to stroke the skin and feel its softness. His gaze dropped, coming to rest on the lips that looked so soft and inviting.

He bent his head towards her mouth -then realized what he was doing. *What madness hath taken hold of me?* Some inner clarity hit him. With a movement that was almost rough in its abruptness he pulled away, dropping her hands and backing off.

Am I to break my word and act no better than a scoundrel who would take advantage of her goodness?

"I hath taken enough of thy time, Kate. Thy generosity in allowing me to converse with thee is more than I deserve." With great difficulty he squelched the desire that her closeness had aroused in him. "I need take my leave as thy personable company hath kept me longer than I had intended. I thank thee Kate, most humbly." Giving a stiff bow he swung on his heels, leaving before she realized what had taken place.

Trying to gather her wits together, her eyes followed his swift stride that took him back across the steps - to eventually disappear out of sight. Her face was on fire and there was a constriction in her throat that no amount of swallowing seemed to relieve.

As James had pulled her close she'd felt positively faint. For one brief, exquisite moment she'd thought that he was going to kiss her. But, he'd pulled away as if her touch had scorched him. *What wouldst I done should he hath taken such a liberty?* Almost as quickly as she asked herself the question the answer came. *Verilee, I wouldst not hath stopped him.* This latter thought left her shaking with embarrassment.

"So, hast fine gentleman left already?" The sudden appearance of her cousin brought her back to earth. "What, no more fancy flowers, or maybe a honey cake to tempt fair maiden?" Noll backed away chuckling as Kate glared at him, expecting a hand slap or a sharp rebuke from her acid tongue. Neither was forthcoming.

The smile froze on Noll's face as he noticed her flushed face and trembling mouth. "What ails thee Kate? Hast so-called gallant propositioned thee? I swear by thunder I wouldst left thee alone for nothing, hast I known he would act thus with thee!" Noll's voice had risen in anger.

With an effort, Kate composed herself. "Thou art jumping to conclusions my fine friend," she replied sharply. "James is too much of a gentleman to treat me improperly and belittle my person." She hadn't intended to speak so harshly, but she was still shaken.

Noll saw her discomposure and stayed his tongue. *Tis James now, I see.* When he eventually spoke again it was without any of his former banter. "What sayest thou? Has my independent, self-confident cousin become smitten by this gallant?" Receiving no response, he tried to make light as he queried her further. "So. Doest believe he will return again to see thee? More importantly, doth want to see him again?"

Kate said nothing and a potent silence prevailed. Finally answering in such a low voice that it was almost a whisper, she sighed heavily. "I cannot be sure and whether he will return I cannot say. 'Tis a strange feeling that hath taken hold of me Noll, concerning James."

"Doest this Sir James Herewith share these feelings?"

"He is married, Noll."

"Thee hast not answered my question," his voice took on a sharp edge. "Hast our nobleman given any reason to believe that his feelings for thee go beyond friendship?"

"Nay cousin. He hath not." She couldn't reveal how close James had come to kissing her. Noll would not approve and besides, she wasn't really sure what James' intentions had been.

All she knew was that he had reacted in the only way that any gentleman would. The knowledge that he had not succumbed to his desire, only served to enhance her attraction for him. *I admit that this feeling that I harbor for him is stronger than mere friendship. What might Noll think of me if he knew that?*

For the rest of the day, Noll attempted to lighten the melancholia that his cousin seemed to be wallowing in. He went out of his way to help her, actually taking in more money that they normally did because of the manner and charm that he extended towards customers. By the time they were ready to return home, his affability had lifted Kate's spirits and she had pushed the emotional effects of James' presence to the back of her mind. But, she hadn't pushed him from her thoughts.

CHAPTER SIX

*W*hat manner of business is keeping them so late? Bessie was fit to be tied. Once again, they had not yet returned home and the day was rapidly drawing to a close. Standing with her back to the fire, she stared through the window as evening dusk settled. *What is going on with those two?* She was worried and - suspicious.

In the past few weeks her son and niece had consistently returned late from the marketplace. At first she'd not thought anything of it, but after it had become a routine occurrence she began to wonder why? Noll always had a plausible excuse - business had been heavier than normal - a broken wagon wheel - delays while Kate posed for the street artist.

The excuses had become too frequent and too smoothly available on her son's slick tongue. But, her real concern was Kate. Bessie couldn't pinpoint anything in particular, but there was a subtle change in the girl. *She is not as talkative as usual, and doth not ride our Noll anymore. It's almost as if she were mentally deranged!* With an unconscious gesture, she lifted the back of her skirts to warm her buttocks by the fire's heat, as if this physical comfort might warm her chilling thoughts.

A murmur of voices came from outside the door and the next moment it had opened to admit the two young people.

"Where hast been for so long a time?" Her son looked ruffled and Kate's face was full of consternation. "What is t' matter with thee both? Why thee be so late, again?"

Noll looked at his mother's anxious face and hearing the frantic tone of her voice, he brought his own disturbing thoughts under control. Forcing his voice to sound calm, he answered blithely, "our Kate was asked to run an errand for Simon, Ma, and it took longer than we thought it would."

"Why would t'artist be asking such a favor of thyself?" Bessie's suspicious eyes pierced Kate's own. "He must realize that thee be busy minding thy own business, without having to mind his."

Before the girl could answer, Noll spoke again. "A customer offered him a goodly sum for a picture but he needed more parchment. He asked our Kate if she would run to his rooms and fetch more for him."

The woman searched their faces, turning her attention from Kate to her son - then back again. She looked skeptical.

Kate quickly interceded. "That is right, Bessie," her tone was too earnest, "t'were no problem as it was quiet in t'Walk today. Noll said that he could well handle the few customers that we had while I was gone."

Why doest they lie? Bessie continued to stare long and hard, her mouth set in a grim line. She started to say something, but decided not to press the issue. *I suppose they both be old enough to take care of themselves, and god knows I hast tried to teach them to be responsible.* In a voice that couldn't be ignored, she admonished them. "I expect thee both to be home at a decent hour in future, regardless of what manner of excuses thee might make." There was no doubting her meaning.

289

Kate lowered her head, not wanting her aunt to see the shame that she felt. Even Noll had the good grace to look uncomfortable underneath his mother's scrutiny.

Crossing over to the fire-hearth, Noll placed an arm around the woman's shoulders, squeezing her bulky body to his own lean frame. "We hast need to be sorry for worrying thee Bessie. It won't happen again." His eyes met Kate's and she nodded in agreement. "We promise to arrive home at the expected hour in the future, aunt."

Bessie had retired, leaving the young people sitting by the hot embers. The house felt cozy in spite of the crisp, cold air outside. The night sky formed a canopy to the full moon that shone through the kitchen window. It threw an unearthly light into the darkened room. The glow from the fire lit the serious faces of the two young people.

The evening meal had passed without further discussion of their lateness - not withstanding that the usual companionable rapport between them had been missing. In fact, a strained atmosphere had hung heavily over the occupants.

Even the fulfilling taste of the steaming rabbit stew couldn't allay the troubling thoughts that were passing through each of their minds. Bessie had made an excuse to retire earlier than normal. "I hath known an exhausting day," she'd declared, adding caustically, "and worrying about thee both did not help."

Neither had spoken as she arose and went to her room, extinguishing all but one of the tapers as she left. "Do not stay up too long. Seems to me thee both hast been working a long amount of hours of late and need as much rest as possible." There was no missing the sarcasm.

They spoke in whispers, not wanting to disturb the slumbers of the woman in the other room, even though they heard soft snoring coming from behind the closed door of Bessie's bedroom. "Thou must stop meeting with him our Kate. I cannot continue to lie for thee. Even I am running out of ideas as to what excuses to make! Doest not realize how serious this situation hath become?"

Her face showed the strain of the past several weeks of clandestine meetings with James. "I know this and have struggled with my guilt. But I cannot stop myself, Noll. I love him," she admitted, miserably.

Noll didn't know what to say. What was there to say that he hadn't said already? He'd tried every rational argument that he could think of to dissuade his cousin from this foolish infatuation with Sir James Herewith. Love or infatuation, it was all the same to him. The outcome was inevitable, regardless of how real her feelings were for this man.

Sir James was from a different world than his cousin. She was a nobody, and besides, he was married. Noll shrugged his shoulders helplessly. "I cannot continue to cover up for thee, Kate. It is obvious that Ma is suspicious. Thee must work this problem out on thy own." Arising from his seat, he looked down at her feeling a helpless frustration.

Kate's soft hair hid her troubled face as she sat with her head bowed. The hands that lay in her lap, gripped each other tightly. Turning her face up towards Noll, her eyes held his and he saw how reflected moonlight showed the glistening, unshed tears. "I know this and I will not ask thee to lie for me anymore. Whatever happens t'will be on my head, not thine."

Noll stood a few seconds longer, wanting to help her in her turmoil yet not knowing how. Without another word, he turned to climb the ladder to his room.

Kate got up from her stool as if the effort to move was almost too much. Absentmindedly, she banked the embers in the fireplace before readying herself for bed. But sleep wouldn't come. She lay wide-awake, staring at the shadows that the firelight cast on the ceiling. From her cot, she watched the moon through the window as it rose higher in the sky. *Noll is right. Deep in my heart I know this.*

For weeks, she and James had driven in a rented litter to the outskirts of the city. They were conscious of the need to not draw attention in the busy marketplace. Even so, Kate was fully aware that they were not fooling people by meeting this way. Still, she recklessly ignored the curious glances that were directed towards them as James presented himself to her on a regular basis.

Simon had long since stopped showing any surprise at their meetings, even going as far as to give James a courteous nod of recognition. Noll had got into the habit of making sure that he was always with Kate instead of disappearing as he had been want to do. With unspoken acknowledgement, he had taken over the business of selling while Kate went off with James.

Actually, this arrangement proved to be more profitable than expected, as Noll was much more adept at coaxing people to spend their money than Kate. Unfortunately, the hours that the smitten couple spent together had dragged out longer with each successive meeting. It became necessary to conjure up more lies to tell Bessie when they were inevitably late arriving home.

Tossing restlessly, she turned onto her back and stared unseeing at the ceiling. Kate hated deceiving her aunt and even worse, felt heavy with guilt at involving Noll in her deception. She was torn between her absolute need to be with James and the moral code by which she'd been raised. How could she continue with the lies and deception? *It would kill my aunt if she knew and would be my undoing.*

While strolling through the lanes and farmlands of rural London, she felt as if her happiness was complete. As the bond between them grew until they could no longer suppress their longing for each other, it had become more and more difficult to part and return to their separate lives.

Eventually, James approached the subject of having Kate live in his cottage at his country estate. "My brother would be close by to watch over thy welfare Kate, and I could visit regularly. We would no longer have to continue this furtive behavior, causing this constant fear of revealing ourselves."

Kate had been aghast at his suggestion and hurriedly dismissed it. "How woulds't explain to thee wife thy constant coming and going to the estate? More importantly, how could I confront my aunt with such a proposition? No James, it is out of the question. My aunt would not be able to live down the shame of such an act. I would be branded a whore!"

James had visibly flinched at her blunt but honest reply yet had to concede to her rationale. He didn't enlighten her has to Clarissa's reaction, if he took a mistress. There was no doubt in his mind that as long as he was discreet, his wife would be only too happy to have another woman taking care of her 'wifely duties'.

But, he was ashamed to admit that in his zeal to have his love, he had not thought of the problems that it would create for Kate.

Although her social class accepted a young woman's pregnancy out of wedlock as a part of life, it frowned upon the activities of a 'loose woman.' A young miss who was foolish enough to find herself with child either married the father, or fostered the babe out. More often than not, the former took place and the 'premature birth' was ignored. James was all too conscious of this, and wished for the hundredth time that circumstances were different.

In the circles of the gentry a mistress was acceptable, as long as the arrangement was handled with finesse. The king himself was a good example. It was practically unheard of in Kate's world and considered only a short step from being a 'professional tart'. Reluctantly, James had to admit that Kate's thinking was correct. And so, they no longer discussed the subject.

Sleep continued to elude Kate. With eyes wide and staring, she watched moonbeams pick out a small mouse that foraged in the floor rushes, looking for scraps of food that might have been dropped.

Startled into wakefulness by a not so gentle shaking of her shoulder, she sat up in her bed. Noll was bending over her as she groggily tried to focus on her surroundings.

"Come, our Kate. Thou should'st arisen this half-hour past. Doest not always tell me that we need to get to t'marketplace early, to gain a good spot? Yonder sun is high already and thee is still sleeping the sleep of the dead."

She blinked her eyes at winter's weak light shining through the window. She had no idea when she had eventually fallen asleep, but obviously it had been late. The room was icy cold. Wrapping a blanket around herself, she urged Noll to light the fire before Bessie awakened.

They would warm some ale on the fire's hob before venturing into the cold streets. Modestly, she shed her flannel gown underneath the folds of the blanket, and then still holding the covering around her body, she reached for her petticoats and kirtle that hung on a wall peg above her bed.

Seeing that she was stirring herself, Noll left through the back door to refill the scuttle.

The bowl of water on her bedside had formed a thin layer of ice. Shivering, she gave a grimace as she broke it with her fingers before splashing it over her face and neck. It had the desired affect of shocking away the last remnants of sleep from her brain. *Today I will tell him*, she thought dismally.

Before falling asleep she'd made the difficult decision to end her relationship with James. She'd spent hours agonizing over this, but deep down inside she'd known the answer to her dilemma. As heart wrenching as this was, Kate knew that she had to stop seeing him. She had no other choice. Her eyes were red-rimmed from the tears that she'd shed before finally succumbing to exhaustion. Her fitful sleep had brought strange dreams that she couldn't quite grasp, but left her feeling disturbed.

Noll returned, carrying the scuttle full of wood. He took note of his cousin's pallid face with the puffy eyes as he knelt by the hearth to clear out the ashes. He said nothing. Methodically arranging fresh straw and kindling, he put a match to the pile. Flames leapt up as he placed logs around the stacked wood and dried grass.

Kate prepared mugs of ale and sliced bread to eat with a morsel of cheese. Silently, she performed the familiar routine with automatic motions. She knew James would be in St. Paul's Walk at noon.

They would always drive a distance beyond the city boundaries and leave the conveyance behind some hedgerows, hidden from view. Then, they'd walk their favorite path to a small copse that they had come to think of as their own special place.

As she thought on this, she realized that she couldn't be alone with him when she told him of her decision. It went without saying that he would strongly protest and Kate was afraid that she'd weaken her resolve once he held her in his arms. By breaking the news to him in the busy Walk he would not be able to dissuade her either with words of endearment or actions. Of course it was a cowardly act, but she had no choice. Kate was so miserable she wanted to die, and then shook the blasphemous thought from her head, automatically making the sign of the cross over her heart.

The morning hours dragged. She went through the motions of roasting the nuts and bagging them as if she were an inanimate object. Noll chattered to customers, charming the housewives and making the menfolk smile, all the time being aware of Kate's somber mood. He knew instinctively that she'd arrived at some decision that was obviously of a painful nature.

St. Paul's bells began tolling to let worshipers know that the noon service was about to begin. Noll saw the horse-drawn litter coming along the street, guided by a familiar figure.

Kate's body visibly stiffened as James pulled to a stop alongside the stone pavement. He jumped down, eagerly waiting to help Kate into the seat alongside his. The girl walked slowly towards him, making no attempt to take his hand that he held out towards her.

Noll couldn't hear the conversation, but he knew that whatever his cousin was saying to Sir James had shocked the man. The hand that he expectantly held out towards her, dropped to his side as if suddenly lifeless. The delighted expression on his face left to be replaced by an anguished frown.

"May I buy a farthings-worth of the fresh hot ones, please?" Noll looked almost irritated as the polite voice of the elderly lady distracted him, but he quickly recovered. Giving the little woman his most charming smile, he scooped up the hot nuts from the coals, tossing them around to cool somewhat, before placing them in the bag. He threw in an extra one as way of compensation for his initial mindlessness. As the lady proffered the coin Noll took it, giving her benefit of his warmest smile.

What a charming young man. The old woman batted her eyes at him like a young girl, but Noll's attention had already turned back to the couple by the litter. Just in time, he saw Kate abruptly turn her back on Sir James and walk back to the wagon.

James stood as if made of marble. As she reached Noll's side, the lad saw that she was having difficulty in controlling tears that threatened to spill. James still stood in one spot looking as if made of stone.

He finally turned sharply and climbed back into the litter's seat. With a sharp crack of his whip that made his startled horse leap forward, the litter and its passenger hurtled back the way they had come. They were soon gone from sight.

Neither of them saw the woman who stood at the top of the steps of St. Paul's. Hiding behind a pillion, Bessie's glazed eyes continued to stare long after the litter had disappeared. Numb with suppressed anger, she hugged herself to try and stop the uncontrollable shaking of her body. *How dare she do this to me! What hast I done to deserve such deceit and dishonesty from this child that I took to my bosom, as if she were my own!*

Bessie had awakened long before she'd heard the two young people stirring. Lying stiff and quiet in her bed, she'd listened to the faint whispering coming from the kitchen.

Eventually, the opening and closing of the creaky front door and the silence that followed, told her that they had left. How long she had lain there in the silent house, mulling over her dour thoughts, she had no idea. One thought was uppermost in her mind. She intended to go to the marketplace this day, to see for herself what strange business her two children were about. The fact that they were definitely up to something that they didn't want her to know of was most evident.

Bessie had taken her time, methodically tidying the kitchen as well as stoking the fire so as to make sure that it would stay ablaze until she returned. She'd cleaned vegetables in preparation for their evening meal, and made sure that the remains of the ale sat on the hearth, to stay warm.

Under normal circumstances, she would have been making her way to the baker's place to do her cleaning chores, which would have made it impossible to have the time to visit the Walk. As fate would have it, a recent death in the family had sent the baker and his wife to St. Mary's church in attendance of the funeral mass, making it necessary to close the shop for the day. Bessie silently blessed her good fortune that made her plans possible.

After what she considered to be a good time to leave, she'd donned her extra kirtle and placed her worn, but heavy broadcloth cape around her shoulders, fastening it tightly to keep out the cold. Finally, she'd arranged her snug wimple over her head and shoulders, tucking it into the top of her cape for extra protection from the weather. Slamming the heavy door behind her, she'd made her way to St. Paul's.

Bessie had stood at the top of the steps for almost an hour. From this spot, she could clearly look down at the street and observe the goings on at the wagon. The stone pillar hid her from being seen by anyone down below, but still afforded her a clear view. Nothing out of the ordinary seemed to be happening. She was getting fidgety and her body was stiff and cold. *They seem to be minding their business, all right.*

Both Noll and Kate were attending to customers that intermittently came and went. She could see nothing unusual in their behavior. *Maybe I'm being foolish in thinking they be deceiving me.* She was beginning to wish that she hadn't been so rash in deciding to spy on the young folk. Instead of standing in the cold, she could have been relaxing by the warmth of the hearth.

Just as she'd convinced herself that nothing of an ill nature was disturbing the tranquility of her world - the litter arrived.

Unable to believe what she was witnessing, she watched Kate walk purposefully towards the occupant who had alighted. The gallant stood waiting for her to approach.

Even from this distance, she could tell that the man was of a genteel nature. His fine clothing of a rich russet hue with the fancy looking abundance of lace trimmings, stood out like a tropical bird against the dirty gray of London's street. His person most certainly looked grand among the unkempt and poor rags of the peasants that occupied the market place.

What was most astonishing was Kate's demeanor. The girl approached him with such a self -confident manner and seemed to be conversing with him most familiarly. *She seems to be very well acquainted with this grand looking nob.* The next moment, her astonishment turned to disbelief. She gasped in horror as the man took both of Kate's hands and held them in his own! Before the aunt could recover from such an audacious act, he'd placed her hands to his chest as if to have her feel his heart beating!

Bessie's hand went to her mouth. Her throat constricted. She could feel the rapid thumping of her own heart as her chest heaved with emotion. *What manner of scoundrel is this that treats my kin in such a manner?* Then, she realized that Kate was not objecting to this unseemly behavior.

The woman's concern rapidly turned to anger at the girl's immodesty. Instead of pulling away from the man, as any well brought up young lady should have done, Kate seemed to be listening with rapt attention as he bent his head to converse with her. The intimacy of the tableau was undeniable. The stance of his body showed an intensity of purpose, while her niece's manner was quietly submissive.

Bessie felt as if in the midst of a bad dream and her breast continued to heave with emotion. Instinct demanded that she run to her niece and pull her away from the blackguard!

But, it wasn't over yet. In the next instant, she saw Kate's head come up high and her body stiffen. The girl stepped away from the man - - but not before she'd raised a hand to touch his face in an undeniable gesture of tenderness. Bessie covered her mouth to stifle her cry of protest.

Abruptly turning, Kate left him.

The woman standing on the steps turned her gaze towards Noll, noting that he was also taking in this scenario. She sank down onto the cold slab. Bessie's legs would no longer hold her upright and her heart was bounding.

They knew something was amiss. The fire in the hearth was almost out. Only a few red cinders glowed weakly, giving off an occasional weak flicker as if trying to defy extinction. The jug of ale resting on the earth's hob looked flat and uninviting. By this time the dishes and eating utensils were usually set out on the table for a meal but they still reposed on the sideboard.

The table was as empty as the expression on Bessie's face. Folded arms supported the woman's ample bosom as she sat leaning over the tabletop, as if unable to keep herself upright. Her eyes were fixed on the door.

"Ma? What ails thee? Hath something unforeseen happened?" Noll's voice sounded worried. Simultaneously, they moved to either side of the woman.

Kate draped an arm around her aunt's shoulder. "Doest feel unwell, Bessie? Hath received bad news?"

As if awakening from sleep, Bessie straightened her body. She looked at each of them in turn. "No. I am not ill, at least not physically ill. But, something hast happened to disturb me greatly, and methinks that thee may enlighten me as to what is going on."

Noll's eyes caught Kate's over the top of his mother's head. His cousin's held a look of bewilderment, but a gnawing suspicion began to dawn on him. Warily, he questioned his mother, again. "Doest mean to say that it is ourselves that is troubling thee, Ma? See now. We assuredly cannot be late in coming home, and hath made a goodly sum this day." Eager to lighten her mood, he reached into his breeches and drew forth a handful of coins. Dropping them onto the table top in front her, they clinked noisily as they scattered. A halfpenny rolled off the edge, landing in the woman's lap. Her reaction was no more than if the coins had been wooden duds.

"No. Thee hast not arrived late, for a change." Her voice was clipped. "And, no doubt Kate can tell me why?" She looked up at the girl with an icy stare. The eyes held barely suppressed anger. "What doest say, girl? No posing for t'artist today or running errands for folk?"

Kate looked puzzled by her aunt's words and anger. She was beginning to feel a troubling sense of foreboding and felt it best to remain silent.

"What. No glib excuses today? Then again, maybe none be necessary. Maybe t'fancy man sent thee packing, did he?"

The room closed in on its inhabitants. Tension was palpable. In the same heavy tones, Bessie continued, "hast he grown tired of thee? He most certainly left thy side this day as if the devil himself were chasing him!"

300

Kate slowly backed away - afraid of this stranger with such rage in her voice.

"Wait one moment, Ma. Thee doest not know what thee is …" Noll's attempt to intercede was a mistake. The mother turned on him, spitting out words as unleashed fury spilled over. "So. I am also blind as well as a numbskull and doest not know what mine eyes hath seen? Is that what thee be trying to tell me?"

Noll threw up his hands in a helpless gesture. He closed his mouth; waiting in resignation while the inevitable storm took over.

Bessie arose and with hands on hips stood close to the girl, who was staring at her aunt in horrified silence. "Now then, girl. Will thee be telling me that thou hast not been cavorting with this man? I am not as stupid as thee might think!" Her voice rose higher as her control began to break. "What other reason might a man of nobility be making familiar with my kin?"

Faced with Kate's continuing silence, the aunt's fury exploded. "What manner of wench hast I raised that acts no better than a slut? ANSWER ME!"

Kate recoiled! The shock of Bessie's words hit her with the force of a hammer. Her face blanched and tears sprang to her eyes as she looked into the face that was twitching with uncontrollable rage.

Noll jumped in. "Please Ma, calm thyself. Thee will make thyself ill getting so riled up. Kate meant no harm against thee. 'Tis a bad thing to say words to her that thou doest not really mean." Noll laid a restraining hand on his mother's arm, but the woman shook it free. "Do NOT be taking up for her. Thee hast no doubt helped her in this deception, and thy lies are almost as bad as her acts!"

Kate slumped onto her stool by the hearth as a physical ache smote her being. The words hauled at her burned like a branding iron. "I cannot say anything to thee Bessie that will make thee feel more warmly disposed towards me. I can only say that I am sorry to hath caused thee so much anguish." Her voice seemed to echo as if coming from another place and time.

Bessie suddenly felt drained of energy as Kate's words broke through her anger. The woman's wrath began to subside as exhaustion set in. Complete fatigue weighed her down. *What demons hath taken possession of her?* The rapid palpitations of her heart underneath her stomacher, made her conscious of her physical tiredness. *I am getting too old for such excitement.*

The anger had festered all day and she didn't even remember walking home. By the time that her son and niece had arrived, she was almost out of her mind with frustration and worry. Her mind had envisioned all kinds of wild situations that may have happened to her niece.

Is she still a virgin? She looked from her niece to her son. No one uttered another word.

The late afternoon light entering through the window was beginning to fade. It bathed the kitchen in its gloomy rays and shrouded corners in shadow. The kitchen was cloaked as if an undertaker's sheet covered it.

After an eternity, Noll moved and started the business of lighting the tallows to dispel the darkness. The flickering flames did nothing to lessen the grim atmosphere. He took up a small shovel that lay by the fireplace and knelt to clean out the grate's gray ashes, methodically placing them in the empty wood-scuttle. Shovel by shovel-full he worked, until the fireplace was clean. Without a word, he picked up the scuttle and left through the back door to dump its contents and collect more wood from the shed at the bottom of the yard.

The two females remained immobile. Bessie slumped down at the table, completely ignoring the girl sitting on the stool. They were still sitting thus when Noll returned.

"The night air is becoming chill, but t'house will soon be warm once the fire starts burning." He tried to make his voice sound conversationally normal, but his words fell on deaf ears.

He tried again, making his tone more commanding. "Wilt put yon jug of ale closer t'hob Kate, while I light t'fire? Maybe we can find something for supper Ma, if thee tell us what to fix."

Noll was determined to eliminate the tension, addressing the womenfolk in a voice that forced an answer. Bessie finally heeded and turned to stare at her son. He met her gaze without flinching. With a heavy sigh she pushed her body up from the chair, using the table for support. She felt as drained as if she'd climbed the Tower steps from Traitors Gate to its highest battlements.

"There is some left over bread in t'cupboard. I can get some salted cod from yon pantry." As she talked, she made her way to a small door at the back of the house that led to the cellar. It served as their food storage place. "We can wash it down with t'warm ale." Breathing heavily as if she'd been running, Bessie opened the cellar door. "We couldst use some strong nourishment in our bodies, I'm thinking." She spoke to the room in general as she stepped down the steps to the underground pantry.

Slabs of salted meat and fish hung from ceiling hooks. She looked them over, before reaching up to unhook a codfish. As she climbed back up, she took a jar of pickled chutney from a shelf that lined the stairwell's walls. Brined vegetables and wild-berry preserves, prepared during the plentiful summer months were neatly arranged in rows on the shelves. She closed the cellar door tightly behind her to keep out the cold draughts.

Noll had the fire going and the ale in the jug began to simmer. Kate was busying herself with laying out platters, along with knives for slicing the bread. The fire cheered the kitchen so that along with the burning tapers, the atmosphere appeared normal - well, almost. The 'hurricane' that had shattered the lives of these three people had subsided. Even so, the devastation was felt even though it couldn't be seen.

In between mouthfuls of food Noll kept the conversation going, forcing both females to respond in spite of the tension between them. The meal finally came to an end and as usual, they took their seats around the fireside. No one spoke. Bessie picked up her mending from the basket by her chair.

With her head bent in concentration she worked back and forth, darning a hole in Noll's hose. Without lifting her head from her task, she finally broke the silence. "So, miss, doest intend on telling me what manner of relationship thee hast forged with this ne'er-do-well? And, I am curious as to how thee came to meet with a person of such obvious high degree?"

Pausing in her work, she raised her eyes to look squarely at her niece. "Thou doest owe me an explanation and no more lies, mind. I hast received more than my fill of deceit, not to mention lord knows what other kind of sinful behavior."

Shame engulfed Kate as she looked into the distrusting face of her aunt. The woman's fingers continued to work dexterously as she waited for a response.

In a low voice, Kate told a softened version of first seeing James in the King's parade, followed by the accidental meeting in St. Paul's Walk. Talking in monosyllables, she was careful to avoid any mention of his wife.

She tried to hide their deep involvement, but Bessie's sharp ears picked up the tremor in her niece's voice. She observed the girl's eyes, clouded with an aching sadness. *How could she allow herself to become smitten with such a man?* Her earlier anger had not been entirely due to Kate's deceitful acts. She was worried for the girl's welfare. Underneath the hot-tempered disposition was a heart full of love for Kate.

Bessie felt an impotent anger against herself for not having seen this coming. She should have been able to protect the girl from life's pitfalls. *But what could I do that I hast not done already?* Helplessness was new to Bessie's self-sufficient nature. "Doest plan to continue meeting with this so-called 'gentleman'?" She paused in the act of weaving her needle.

Kate shook her head. "I told him this very day that we must not meet anymore, and asked him to cease his visits to me."

So, that was the case when I observed the scene this morn. She nodded her grudging approval. "Well, it consoles me somewhat, knowing thee hast not taken complete leave of thy senses! Doest think that he will honor thy request, and stay away?" Kate nodded her head. "He will not wish any harm towards me, Bessie. He will abide by my wishes. Of this, I am sure."

Noll listened without comment. *Doest my cousin really believe that Sir James will keep his distance? She is a bigger fool than I thought! I know him but little, yet even I can see that he is most taken with her and no man under such circumstances is going to give in that easily. And, I strongly suspect that my cousin hath very little strength against his charms.*

In spite of her words, Kate's own thoughts were following similar lines. She had answered Bessie truthfully, and seemed to have convinced her aunt as well as herself of James' intentions. But the attraction between them was strong. Like a flea tormenting her flesh, the nagging hope for his return itched in the deep recesses of her mind.

Finishing off the neatly darned hole, Bessie bit off the thread between her teeth before folding the hose and laying it on top of her workbasket. "This day hast tired me beyond endurance. I need my bed," she declared. "I believe thee Kate, when t'say that this foolish affair is done with so I expect thee to keep t'word." With a heaviness that wasn't entirely physical, she arose. "No more shall be said of this, but heed my words. Be sure that thou hast learned thy lesson." The stance of her body and her words brooked no nonsense. "Thou must comport thyself in a more seemly manner in the future. Know thy place in life miss, and make certain that yon fine gentleman knows his." With that, she left the room.

The girl didn't move. Noll looked on in quiet contemplation. After a few moments he arose and went to her side. "Thee know Ma is right, our Kate. Sir James is not of our world and 'twain cannot meet in harmony. Even should he not be of such a high station in life he is still a married man, which makes the situation doubly intolerable.

He placed a hand on her shoulder. "Thou didst right to send him packing. Mind thee, be sure that doest not weaken in thy resolve. T'would bring untold wrath upon thy head from Ma if thee went back on t'word."

Kate bowed her head.

Noll hadn't finished. "Thou must know that Bessie loves thee like her own. Doest not realize this and know that her fretting is what caused her anger this night?"

The whispered answer was full of emotion. "I know this Noll. For all the world, I would not knowingly hurt Bessie."

"Think on these things that I hath said, Kate. As much as Ma loves thee, she hast no tolerance for dishonesty," adding with a semblance of his cheeky smile, "besides thee is not as expert as I am at sweet talking t'way out of predicaments!"

"Thou art good to me, our Noll and I thank thee for watching out for my welfare." Her expression remained glum.

Giving her shoulder a consoling pat, he left her side to retire.

She sat staring into the flames. Her head ached - but her heart ached even more.

CHAPTER SEVEN

$\mathcal{T}$he grand carriage turned into St. Paul's Walk and made its approach. Kate held her breath. Her emotions alternated between elation and anxiety. The carriage stopped along side the wagon. As before, the same haughty coachman alighted from his seat. She saw that he held a small rolled parchment in a hand. Before he could give it to her she snatched it from him. Startled by her unexpected rudeness, the servant gave a disapproving click of his tongue but Kate was oblivious.

Such an unmannerly miss! But, what can one expect from a person of such a low class? The snooty coach driver let his gaze sweep over her person as if he smelled a bad odor.

Kate was oblivious, being too busy breaking the seal of the note. Without any further ado, the disdainful manservant remounted his carriage seat and was gone. She was unaware of his departure as she spread out the letter.

Dearest Kate.

This terrible ache in my heart is making life intolerable. I knowest that thou be determined to keep thyself apart from me, yet I beseech thee to take pity on this poor wretch of a man. I can no longer endure this painful separation. If thou hast any pity for the state of misery my lonely soul is in, I implore thee to allow me to be with thee just once more. In the fervent hope that shouldst feel disposed to honor my plea, I will send a hired litter to carry thee to our place in the countryside, where I will be waiting most anxiously for thy arrival. I realize that my presence in St. Paul's Walk is part of the reason for thy anxiety, and it is not my desire to distress thee unduly. Therefore, I shall do everything in my power not to course any undue worries for thee. I shall await, in the hope that thou may be disposed to honor my fervent request. If thou hath any compassion for my miserable state, I beg thee to come to me. My heart is sorely breaking and cannot endure life without seeing thy dear face just once more.

It was signed with the familiar, flourishing letter - *J*

She stared at the note, rereading his entreaties several times until she could have quoted them from heart. *How can I deny him, when my own heart is sorely tried?* She folded the note carefully, until it was small enough to slide into the front of her bodice. *What madness hast taken hold of me? Should Bessie find out that I received this communication from him, she would be enraged beyond imagination. If I break my word to her and meet with him again, I dares't not think of what she might do! She would never forgive me.* She felt as helpless as a fallen leaf being swept by autumn winds. It was as if she had no control over her fate. *I cannot live in such misery. How can I find peace and happiness in such a state of affaires?*

As if in a dream, she mechanically returned to the business of roasting the chestnuts. Turning them so that they would cook evenly, there was no conscious thought of what she was doing.

Verily, I cannot live without him in my life. The only thought in her addled brain was that she must see him again.

An hour later, Noll returned from his own 'business,' whistling cheerfully as he came along the road. He clinked the coins in his breeches' pocket, feeling pleased with himself. Once again, he'd beaten an opponent at a game of dice.

Drawing close to the wagon, he saw Kate's face - and stopped whistling. "So cousin, why hast such a scowling countenance? Thee hast been as listless and as boring as day old vittles these past weeks yet I do swear, now thy face looks positively vapid!"

With a semblance of her old spirit, Kate retorted. "My looks art none of thy concern, so do not be so disparaging." But, the fire left her as quickly as it had arisen.

Seeing the play of emotions cross her face, Noll's suspicions grew. "He hath contacted thee again, I presume?" He really didn't need an answer.

Without a word, Kate withdrew the note from her bodice and handed it to him.

Taking the folded paper from her outstretched hand, he took his time in reading it. His brain stumbled over some of the words, but the gist of the communiqué soon became clear. "And, pray may I ask what thee plan to do about this?"

Without giving a second thought, Kate answered in the only way that she knew how. "I will go to him," she announced flatly.

"I suppose thou hast to do what must." Noll's thoughts were not good. *Where is this disastrous situation going to lead?* He wouldn't allow himself to dwell on his Ma's reaction, should that good woman find out. And, he knew it was no good trying to talk common sense into his cousin.

From the moment they met again they knew without the words being spoken that they would continue to meet no matter what the future held. Even so, their happy reunion was edged with desperation as the insurmountable problems continued to

309

plague them. Whenever he could escape from court functions or home duties – he would come to her. Kate's generous hearted cousin aided in her complicity by minding the wagon - therefore allowing her the freedom to meet with James.

Their clandestine meetings were bittersweet. Whenever they were together nothing else mattered, but apart the dissatisfaction of their separate and alien lives ate at Kate. Her moral upbringing and feelings of disloyalty towards her kin lay like a stone upon her heart.

As for James, he didn't suffer from any pangs of conscience, regarding his wife. Yet, whenever he returned to Clarissa after being with his beloved, he was keenly aware of the contrast between his home-life and the time spent in Kate's presence. His former attitude of bored acceptance turned to frustration. Even the little time that was necessary for him to spend in Clarissa's company, became a loathsome chore to endure.

At first, they were extremely careful. He never came directly to the marketplace anymore. As the bells of the church rang out announcing the noon hour, she would make her way to meet him a short distance from the busy public place. Noll would stay in the Walk. They made sure that she returned in an appropriate amount of time, so she could return home at the expected hour.

Bessie wasn't fooled. It didn't go unnoticed by this shrewd woman that Kate's demeanor had undergone a subtle change. After two or three weeks of apathy, the girl's eyes sparkled again. From the pale-faced uninterested person that spoke only when spoken to, she suddenly returned to her former self.

Not quite, Bessie thought. *She blooms like a summer flower. She is almost fair of face.* The change didn't bring the aunt any peace of mind. On the contrary, her suspicions coursed her to inwardly stew.

In spite of the lovers' good intentions, they unconsciously started to grow careless again. Becoming more and more absorbed in each other they inevitably lost track of time. After the second time of being late in returning home, Bessie was prepared - and waiting.

Noll didn't have a chance to tell his mother the lie that he'd concocted. Apprehensively they entered the house, only to find her standing with arms folded across her bosom. With a face like granite, she confronted Kate. It was useless to try and deny the facts.

Her aunt's words were a death knoll as she made her announcement. "It is very clear that thee hast no respect for my personal concerns, or thy own reputation. Therefore I hath no other choice but to say thee must decide on thy own future. Since thou hast decided to continue this foolhardy dalliance, I must ask thee to leave my house."

The words fell like the swishing of the executioner's axe swinging towards a neck. Noll opened his mouth to protest, but his mother silenced him with an icy glare that brooked no argument.

Neither of them had ever seen Bessie like this. Yes, she had a quick temper and yes, she enforced strict rules, but underneath this indomitable exterior there had always been a heart of gold and a deep affection for them. They were the center of her small world. Never in their lives had they dreamed that this cold stranger existed. Noll especially, could usually bring forth his mother's smile whenever they raised her ire. This stranger stood unmoving and unemotional as she presented Kate with her decision. The room was as silent as a mausoleum.

Rain began to fall and pattered softly against the window. Quickly it changed to a hard pelting and a wind rattled the panes. The door that wasn't completely latched flew open and groaned in protest as a cold blast entered. Noll automatically moved to latch it more securely.

The two females stood staring at each other - unaware of anything, or anybody but themselves. Kate looked at the hard lines of her aunt's unrelenting face, realizing that the older woman was forcing her to change the course of her life.

Straightening her shoulders and throwing back her head in an unconscious gesture, she spoke dispassionately. "I will leave tomorrow Bessie, so as not to course thee anymore vexation. Will thee allow me to stay this night, so that I may make preparations for my departure from thy house?" Bessie nodded her head in agreement. There was no softening of her face.

Noll looked from his cousin to his mother, his brain unable to comprehend such a disaster. The women looked almost like twin statues, cold and impersonal. It wasn't the defining features that were identical but the stance of their proud bodies. For the first time in his life Noll realized how much these two people resembled each other. He felt a heaviness that he'd never felt in his life, knowing that something had taken place this day that had broken the ties between them. Their lives would be changed forever.

Shaking his head sadly, he moved to the ladder that led to his room. Noll slowly climbed the steps. Tonight he wished to be alone.

Silence hung between the two females. Bessie was the first to move. Not uttering a word she left to enter her own room. The door closed behind her with a resounding finality.

Once alone she slumped onto her bed, unable to sustain the weight of her body any longer. Her facial muscles ached from keeping her emotions under control.

Covering her face with her hands, Bessie crumpled and allowed the tears to flow. She had made the right decision, hadn't she? *Of course thee did!* She scolded herself as quickly as the doubt arose in her mind. Under the circumstances, she could not tolerate such behavior from her own flesh and blood. *She is me own daughter, for goodness sake! Well, almost me own. To treat me with such disrespect is not to be forgiven. She hath flaunted her ungodly behavior in my face and hath no repentance in her soul. What kind of heartless blackguard could take her and bewitch her so? He hast turned my Kate into a loose woman. May the devil take his soul!*

Wiping her tear stained face on a corner of the bedcover she lifted it to her nose. From ingrained habit she gave a noisy blow and chastised herself for giving way to her emotions. In all conscience she could not allow Kate to stay under her roof, knowing that she was recklessly cavorting with that fiendish man. Even if he were a rich fancy dandy, he must be one of the devil's own to be acting thus with her niece. *She is just a poor, unworldly girl with no common sense between her ears.* The devastation in her heart was too much for Bessie and she started to weep anew.

Kate left before either Bessie, or Noll were astir. She waited in St. Paul's Walk until noontime. Noll hadn't made an appearance to sell their wares and she wasn't surprised.

Inadvertently, she had turned the family upside down, leaving her feeling heavy of heart. But, she knew that she'd had no choice. It was inevitable that it should come to this impasse. *Even so-, what am I to do now?*

Her worried mind whirled in confusion as she waited until it was time to meet James. A numbing sense of shock from the angry confrontation with her aunt still clung to her. One clear thought remained. She needed to be with James and the security of his love. She would think on what to do, later.

"Let me take thee to my cottage Kate. It is close to the main house so that my brother may heed thy welfare when I cannot be there myself. Thou knowest how deeply I care for thee."

They sat close together in the litter, sharing a thick blanket that covered most of their bodies. She usually looked forward to these times with James amidst the freshness of the fields, instead of the cold dampness of London's dirty streets. But now, the tension of the past weeks that had culminated in Bessie's cold ultimatum, had taken its toll. She felt lost and frightened.

The giant oak sheltered them from a brisk wind, but it never seemed to be as cold in the countryside as it was in the city. A watery sun shone bravely.

James noticed the transparent blue tinges underneath her eyes. The hands that he held underneath the blanket were chill, but they weren't cold from the weather. Regardless, he chafed them to try and find comfort for his own mind, as well as to allay his love's fears.

James had presented her with an option and it didn't seem so shocking anymore. Since their first fateful meeting that seemed so long ago, it seemed inevitable that it would lead to this conclusion. What else could she do? She had no one else to turn to. But even as her desperate mind still dwelled on the situation she'd left behind, there was a light of hope at being taken care of by her lover.

A flush came to her cheeks at the thought of sharing James' bed. Although she knew that marriage was out of the question, she believed that he truly did love her and would take care of her. With her whole being, Kate felt that they were destined to be together no matter what obstacles stood in their path.

And so, it was settled. James tried not to show his elation. He knew that Kate was deeply hurt by the actions of her aunt, yet he couldn't help being secretly glad that fortune had brought his desires to fruition. He made a silent vow. *I will make it up to her for causing the loss of family.* Kate would not regret the sacrifice that she had made.

During the journey to James' family home he regaled her with stories of their childhood, but Kate was apprehensive. *What might his brother think of me as James's mistress?* Thoughts of his brother's reaction continued to trouble her mind. "What if thy brother should feel my presence at the cottage to be an act of disloyalty towards thy wife?"

James chuckled. "Dearest Kate. When wilt understand that my wife hath no interest in what I do? As long as I am discreet

and do not bring any embarrassment to her, she will say naught."
He stopped laughing as he noticed her fearful expression. Taking
her hand he squeezed it reassuringly. "My brother hath never
ventured to advise me about my relationship with Clarissa, except
to caution me to honor her as my wife, at least in public," he
commented, humorlessly. "However, methinks that Cecil cares
naught about Clarissa."

"Although he treats her with the respect she deserves, he is
not enamoured of my wife. In fact, I cannot imagine my brother
being enamoured of any woman! He enjoys his freedom too
much to take them seriously."

Shaking her head, Kate gave him a semblance of a smile.
"Seems to me that yon brother has a strong and sensible mind,
unlike thyself dear heart, who allows himself to become entangled
with a lowly wench with nothing to offer except herself."

He pulled on the horse's reins, bringing the litter to a halt in
the middle of the country road. Turning to face her, he grasped
both her hands. "Do not belittle thyself Kate." His tone was
serious. "Thou hast a genuineness of character and goodness of
heart that is greater than thou realize. Thy honesty and beauty
of spirit, outshines any of the king's finest ladies of the court. I
am a fortunate man to hath won thy affections. My heart is most
honored and humbly grateful for thou having placed me in the
position to care for thy life. I feel unworthy of such devotion.
Most assuredly, I will make every effort to make thee happy."

Kate's emotions overflowed. "Dearest James. Thou hast
already made me happy." His arms encircled her and Kate found
peace in the comfort of his closeness. Thoughts of the sorrow
she'd left behind were brushed aside, even though a small corner
of her heart still ached. She determinedly refused to consider
any thought of the sin she might be committing in the eyes of
her kinfolk and church. Her kin had forsaken her and James was
her savior.

CHAPTER EIGHT

From his study window, Cecil took in the scene below. Even though the cottage was five hundred yards away from the main house, give or take a few feet, his view of its garden was unobstructed. His posture was stiff as he stared at Kate. He saw her stoop to pick a daffodil, adding it to the bunch she already held in the crook of an arm.

The blooms grew in abundance around the edges of the cottage, even spreading beyond the borders of the garden wall. They covered the grassy sides of the driveway that led to Herewith Hall, forming a blanket of bright yellow.

Kate wore a light green bodice and brown kirtle that seemed to blend in with her surroundings. The girl bent to carefully select another flower, absorbed in what she was doing. She wore a mobcap over her hair but strands still escaped to fall around her face, hiding the profile as she bent forward. Sunshine caused golden highlights amidst the brown tendrils and even though he couldn't see her features, Cecil knew that those hazel eyes would be lit with pleasure. Kate was obviously enjoying spring's refreshing air. She straightened her body. He watched as she lifted a small hand, tucking strands of hair behind her delicate ears, still hugging the daffodils to her bosom within the crook of an elbow.

A pulse that beat in Cecil's jaw was the only indication of his feelings, except for the big hands tightly gripped behind his back. He continued to stare as the girl straightened her kirtle, before turning to re-enter the cottage. Kate's head was held in that proud position that he'd come to know so well.

Cecil knew every single nuance of the girl's personality. He knew that the green of the bodice would emphasize the color of her eyes. Without seeing the hands that had held the flowers so lovingly, he knew that they were soft and white, no longer reddened and chapped, as they had been when he'd first met her. It seemed like only yesterday instead of five months that he'd first seen her, sitting alongside James as they rode along the driveway…

Cecil had expected them eventually, as James had kept him well informed of the conflict within Kate's family. On several occasions, James had indicated that he would like to move Kate to the cottage. Taking her as his mistress had apparently become an attractive proposition, as James' initial protestations had eventually been overcome by desire.

"Remember, it was thy own suggestion that I keep Kate as my mistress," he'd reminded Cecil. "Is this not true? Mind thee, I would make her my wife t'were possible but since I cannot, at least I may take care of her and make sure that no harm befalls her. Admittedly, I feel guilt at causing so much unrest amongst her kinfolk. Even so, I am hoping to persuade her to move to the cottage so that I may visit often, without fear of her family intervening." Cecil had long since given up trying to caution his brother, knowing that he was talking to someone who was deaf to logical advice.

He hadn't known what to expect when he saw the litter coming towards the house. His annoyance at his brother's neglect in telling of the arrival was overcome by curiosity. He was about to meet this person who had so entrapped James. Admittedly, Cecil was intrigued.

A shawl covered the person's head, obscuring the face. Yet, even though the features were hidden he knew it wasn't Clarissa. *That lady would not consent to be riding in anything but a closed conveyance during cold weather.* And, certainly not to come visiting here. In fact, Clarissa hadn't made an appearance since attending their parents' funerals, which had closely followed each other. No. This female with James had to be his inamorata.

He stood waiting politely at the entrance to the house, determined at least to show the girl his best manners. His breeding required that he show courtesy, even if he didn't approve of his brother's rash behavior

The litter came to a stop at the bottom of the steps as with much crunching of wheels and snorting from the horse, his brother pulled on the reins. Springing from the driver's bench, James raised a hand to assist his companion in alighting. They approached as he walked down the steps to meet them. The stranger's head was still bowed underneath the folds of the shawl.

"Cecil, my dear brother, I wish for thee to meet Kate." With a wave of his hand, James made the introductions. "Kate my dearest, this is my brother that I hath spoken of so often."

Lowering his head in a mannerly way of greeting, Cecil doubled over in a conventional bow. He didn't see Kate push back the shawl from her face. After a moment he came upright and looked into a face that shook his implacable nature. Kate was looking at him so openly direct that he felt like an oafish yokel. Her expression was defiant, and yet also frightened. She seemed to be challenging him and at the same time beseeching him to accept her.

Without uttering a word, Cecil took one of the work worn hands in his. He raised it to his lips, kissing the fingertips in greeting. Clearing his throat, he found his voice. "It is most pleasurable to make thy acquaintance, Mistress Kate. Welcome to Herewith Hall."

She answered in the common dialect of London's working class, yet the tone was soft and musical. "Thank thee most kindly, Cecil. May I call thee Cecil? James hast told me so much about thyself, that I feel as if I we must be already acquainted." He nodded, still feeling as unsure of himself as he had as a schoolboy when he'd been in the presence of an awesome adult.

"Thee must also call me Kate, as I feel mistress sounds so unfriendly and I do so hope that we mayest be friends." Her expression spoke volumes. "James kindly offered yon cottage to me, as I find myself in the unfortunate position of being without any living arrangements." She looked embarrassed. "I sincerely hope that this will not present any problems by causing inconvenience to thyself. I shall try to be as little trouble as possible, and although James hast assured me that ye brook no objections to my close presence, I would welcome thy own assurance on t'matter."

The speech had tumbled out in a rush of words. Cecil realized that she felt just as unsure of herself with him as he did with her, except with a major difference. He was much older and had the advantage of his position over this vulnerable girl.

Cecil still held her hand. "Thy presence will not be an intrusion, Kate. On the contrary, methinks that having such a comely person as thyself around these parts, will bring much lightness to the dull existence of our tenants. Most assuredly, it will bring pleasure to myself."

James stood looking on, amusement playing over his features. He could see that his brother's normally conservative nature was shaken. *His demeanor is that of someone suffering from the ague!* A smile slowly formed. "I can see brother, that my fair Kate hath already made a goodly impression upon thy person."

Cecil felt his face growing hot under James' gentle jibing and he quickly dropped the hand that still lay politely within his own.

"We hath tarried outside overly long," his voice sounded gruff. "The air smells as if snow is on its way so let us enter and partake of the meal cook hath prepared. I am sure thou both hath need of refreshment after such a long journey. Cook always prepares too much food for one person, so will be happy to know that we hath visitors to help with its disappearance."

"Meanwhile, I shall order that a fire be lit in yon cottage, and a warming pan placed in the bed so that Kate might be comfortable." As he talked, he led the way up the steps and hoped that his lack of composure wasn't too obvious. James trailed behind - still grinning…

The man continued to stare through the window long after Kate had disappeared inside. He could picture her placing the daffodils in a suitable receptacle and setting the table, in preparation for James' arrival later that day. His brother visited regularly, that is whenever duties at court allowed.

Recently his visits had become fewer, owing to all the preparations involved for King Henry's forthcoming marriage to the German woman from the Cleves' Duchy. Sir James Herewith had been selected as one of the many escorts to accompany the bride-to-be on the journey from her homeland to Great Britain.

No doubt the court was curious as to James sudden devotion towards business at the estate. Of course, Cecil was certain that Clarissa already knew of her husband's mistress. Knowing his sister-in-law, he also surmised that she would not be too concerned as long as her husband was discreet. If James stayed available whenever she needed him, his socially conscious sister-in-law would find the situation acceptable.

As for people who were close to the Herewiths, that was a different story. Cecil was well aware of the predilection for gossip among the genteel folk. He could only guess that his brother and the mistress in the country made for some delightful discussions amidst the ladies in their salons and gentlemen at their clubs.

A snuffling whine at his heels brought him out of his reverie. He looked down at the golden retriever, who was looking at him soulfully with her tongue hanging. "Thou too art looking for attention I am thinking, Missy." He bent to give the dog's ears an affectionate scratch, before returning to his desk to take care of the domestic accounts.

Knowing that Kate was at the cottage was both a comfort to Cecil and a sorrow. He'd long since admitted to himself that he'd grown to depend on her company and felt a hopeless fondness for the girl. She wasn't beautiful, but whenever she entered a room, she radiated warmth that drew him like a burning fire on a cold night.

But, apart from the fact that she belonged to his brother who idolized her, he was also aware that Kate had eyes for none but James. To her, Cecil was a good and dependable friend, nothing more and nothing less. Giving a heavy sigh of resignation, he forced himself to focus on the tasks at hand, deliberately pushing thoughts of the two lovers out of his mind.

Kate checked, and rechecked the venison that was cooking in the fireside oven. The appetizing odors of roasting meat, freshly baked bread and fruit pies, filled the kitchen. She gingerly opened the heavy oven door. The sirloin sizzled and spattered in the pan as she poked and turned it around. The meat was forming a deep brown crust on the outsides. Red juices ran out as she pierced it with a long, pointed knife. She carefully closed the oven door again. *By the time that he arrives, it should be cooked just the way he likes it.* Feeling satisfied, she absentmindedly wiped grease from her hands onto her apron. Looking around the room with a critical eye, she rearranged the daffodils one more time, moving them from the center of the table to the window ledge so that the late afternoon light would catch their beauty. She wiped an imaginary speck of dust off the polished dark wood of the sideboard. The pewter dishes shone and were reflected in its surface.

Apart from missing Bessie and Noll, Kate was content. James was a tender and caring lover and very solicitous of her welfare. He came almost every weekend and sometimes during the week, only staying away when an event at court or home required his presence.

Recently, because of court duties his visits were less often, but this only served to make their hours spent together more precious. Kate loved to listen to tales of court life, especially concerning the king and the ongoing preparations for his wedding. Naturally, no matter how many of the king's mistresses produced an offspring they couldn't produce a legitimate heir for England's throne.

Kate was dazzled by descriptions of the ladies' dresses and the many balls that the king loved so much. Sometimes, the king would play his own compositions on his spinet for members of his court, and Kate listened in fascination to James' accounts of King Henry's musical talents. It seemed that there was always some merry activity happening to keep the king and his court amused. She often wished that she could be there too, but having James to herself for even a few hours at a time filled her world completely.

Over her protestations, he showered her with gifts of the finest wool and serge for her to sew into cartels and capes. He brought the softest of linens and laces to make bodices, along with stomachers made by the best seamstresses that London provided. There were presents of fancy ribbons and real leather laces for her stomachers, as well as pretty mules. She had an abundance of over-shoes to wear when she ventured forth into the countryside. Kate squealed with delight when he gave her an exquisite enameled pomander, smelling of lavender.

James enjoyed giving her pleasure and basked in her childlike wonder whenever he presented her with some new bauble or piece of finery. He never dreamed such a love existed as that which he shared with his Kate. During the dark winter months they spent hours sitting by the fire, sharing their thoughts and dreams.

One weekend, when there had been a heavy snowfall during the night, Cecil had joined them outside as they played like children in the snow, throwing snowballs at each other until they lay rolling and gasping with laughter in the white mounds. Afterwards, she had made a good, hot leek soup and they had sat around the cottage fire, dipping hunks of newly baked bread into the rich broth. Feeling merry and carefree, they were as close and as comfortable as three worry-free urchins, needing nothing but their own selves for company.

As the cold weather gave way to the first hint of spring, she and James ventured outside to walk through the fields and woods of the estate. She was astonished at the amount of land that he owned, but even more was her deepening pride at seeing how much the tenant farmers respected him. These simple folk greeted him with affectionate loyalty, and accepted her without question.

Occasionally when James wasn't visiting, Cecil would invite her up to the Hall for a meal and conversation. She was grateful for his friendship and enjoyed his company. They would sit and discuss her favorite subject - James. As Missy lay at her feet Kate would absorb his tales from their childhood.

She soon learned that underneath Cecil's seemingly gruff exterior was a big heart. He would go out of his way to entertain her when James couldn't visit. He'd arrive at the cottage door with the horse and wagon to take her for a ride into the country – or to the local farmer's market in the nearby village. When she'd protest that she was causing him to neglect his overseeing of the estate, he'd answer that he had need to attend business with his farmers, or needed a change for his health.

Kate appreciated his sensitivity to her loneliness when James wasn't around. He never seemed to get tired of her endless questions about his brother and through Cecil she became more familiar with her lover's character. Like everyone else, she began to unconsciously to think of Cecil as being the elder of the two siblings.

Cecil was a good host and Kate was grateful that he accepted her presence without reservation as his brother's paramour. It became a habit for her to spend at least one evening a week dining with him. Her happiness was overflowing. For the first time in her life, Kate felt complete.

A subtle change had come over Kate. Like a butterfly emerging from its cocoon, she had evolved from the pleasant and likeable maiden into a confident young lady who exuded a glow that made her seem beautiful. The self sufficient, yet naive miss had developed into a calmer, self-assured woman. Her girlish impatience had disappeared giving way to a quiet acceptance of life, born not only of the painful estrangement from her relatives but the strengthening knowledge of being loved by James.

She still kept in touch with Noll, with the help of James. She missed her cousin even more than she missed Bessie. But, James made sure to visit St. Paul's Walk regularly, bringing back messages from Noll and news of Bessie's welfare.

Sometimes Noll would send a note, written in his almost illegible scrawl with many misspelled words. Even so, Kate was thrilled to receive the communications. She made sure that she wrote replies as simple as possible so that Noll could read them without too much difficulty.

James would deliver her letters and remain until the lad had read it, tactfully interpreting it whenever necessary and giving him encouraging news of Kate. Always, he would tell Noll that she had asked that her loving thoughts be given to her aunt. Bessie never responded.

Hearing the galloping of hooves, she ran to the door. The welcome sound came from the lane that bordered the cottage. She opened the door just in time to see James' tan colored mare turn into the gates and she ran down the path to meet him. They met in the middle of the garden and clung to each other as if they would never let go.

At the sound of the horse's winnowing, Cecil automatically arose from his chair and moved to the window. He was in time to see the tableau that they made in the garden. With bittersweet thoughts, he watched as the two people entered the cottage with their arms entwined around each other's waists.

CHAPTER NINE

$\mathcal{T}$ he palace was in a state of frenzy. Noblemen and servants alike scurried back and forth between the king's chambers, staterooms - even the kitchens and sculleries.

Naturally, Henry's closest advisor Thomas Cromwell had been closeted with the king for hours, while in the antechambers lesser dignitaries mingled and chattered among each other. Norfolk and Montague talked together in conspiratorial undertones, heads bent close. George Paulet, sitting in a chair next to the old and infirm Boleyn, (father of the late Anne) - leaned forward, conversing in a loud voice so that the deaf old man could hear his words. All over the palace peons as well as courtiers chattered excitedly among themselves, wondering how the king was fairing during his final preparations to meet his prospective bride.

Poor Jane Seymour was hardly in her tomb before Cromwell had urged the king to remarry. Safety for England's sovereignty was of the utmost importance, he'd assured Henry. Because of the unsettling conditions with the royal houses of Italy, France and Spain, they needed an alliance through marriage that would dispel any problems with these countries. Being strongly under the influence of Papist Rome, it would not fare well for England should these countries decide to arm against its king. The royal coffers were already over tasked due to Henry's previous wars with these countries, not to mention his extravagant life style. His monasteries had been depleted of most of their wealth to support Henry's 'necessities' and the palace now had to succumb to the use of pewter dishes, instead of silver.

Apart from these niggling inconveniences, the self-willed king had made enemies of these powerful catholic countries when he'd severed his country from the power of the Pope. A stable marriage would go a long way towards reinstating the monarch's status with the rest of Europe, especially if the queen was from a respected, European country. Of course, of the utmost importance to Henry was another male heir.

Negotiations had been going on for a long time. A list of the most eligible maidens from all the royal families of Europe had been courted with the possibility of becoming England's next Queen.

For a while, everyone thought it would be Christine, Duchess of Milan as Henry had been quite enthusiastic about the portrait that Hans Holbein had painted of her. But alas, that young lady had declined. It was rumored that Christine had made the caustic comment that - "Were I to have two heads, I would gladly give one to Henry." Naturally, this remark was prudently kept from the king's ears.

Finally, Ann, the Duke of Cleves' sister, had accepted his offer. Once again, Holbein had been sent to the Valley of the Rhine to produce a portrait of the damsel. The king was eager to know what manner of person Ann of Cleves was, declaring that - "she must be bed-worthy." Advisors had been hurriedly dispatched to bring back news of her physical attributes.

As the temperamental Henry had informed Cromwell, he didn't need another harangue like Anne Boleyn who had committed the ultimate sin of producing the girl-child, Elizabeth.

Neither did he want a barren old woman like his first wife, (ignoring the fact that Catherine had produced his daughter, Mary.) As for his poor Jane - "Alas," he'd stated as he wiped a tear from his eye with a lace kerchief, "my true love was of too delicate a nature to breed and survive." Even though Jane had given the monarch an heir in the form of Edward, the young prince was a sickly child and may not survive childhood. Henry needed another son to ensure that the Tudor throne would be secure after his death. T'were a pity that his other two children were females and therefore unfit to reign.

With all the ceremonial pageantry befitting England's royalty, Henry was dispatching some of his most trusted subjects to cross the channel in order to escort his intended bride to England. One of those escorts chosen was Sir James Herewith.

There was no question of excusing himself from the duty. His Grace's requests were never ignored, unless one wished to incur his disfavor. *Foresooth, I dares't not disobey unless I desire to find myself languishing in yon Tower.* James' thoughts had been somber when given the news and he'd purposely stalled from telling Kate the news until it was an absolute necessity.

He'd been kept so busy at Greenwich that he hadn't been able to visit the cottage in over two weeks. Although he'd managed to get word to Cecil of his commitments and knew that his brother would pass this information on to Kate, he missed being with her.

She'd been living at the cottage for almost a year and the more time that he spent with her, the more dissatisfied he became with his life in London. Even the small amount of time that he and his wife did spend in each other's company had become close to intolerable.

Being with Kate and her deep understanding of his needs, served only to emphasize the empty farce of his marriage. He might as well have been a part of the household furnishings for all the attention his wife gave to him! Her world revolved around London's elite with her afternoon visitations and tête-à-têtes.

Clarissa's idea of passion was flirting with the gallants at a court ball, knowing that it was safe to do so, seeing as how she was a married woman. James would watch her practiced coquetry with sardonic humor, while the young men responded like bears around a honey pot. His wife's shallowness grated even more than it had before he'd met Kate. Increasingly, he found himself reluctant to be in her company for any length of time. *I give thanks to the good Lord that her activities keep her well occupied.*

The time was fast approaching for his journey to the Rhine Valley and he hated the thought of leaving. After much haggling, he managed to obtain permission to get away long enough to visit Herewith Hall…

Tears of joy welled in Kate's eyes as he held her tight. Locked in each other's embrace, there was no need to speak of all the longing and loneliness that the time apart had brought to them. Kate finally pulled away and taking him by the hand, she led him towards the cottage. Nary a word was spoken as they entered - gently closing the thick oak door behind them.

Cecil started to leave the house to join them, but stopped short at his entrance. He paused and looked thoughtfully at the closed, cottage door. Slowly he retreated to climb the stairs back to his study. He knew that James would join him, all in good time.

Sometime later, he heard the heavy tread of feet climbing the stairs. He arose to go and meet James but before he could reach the door it was flung open. Grinning from ear to ear, James covered the distance between them and grasped Cecil by his shoulders in a grip of affection. Missy jumped around their feet giving loud barks of welcome.

"God's truth, brother! It is good to see thee again. How dids't manage to steal away from thy palace duties?"

James gave a low chuckle as he settled into a chair, the dog immediately taking this as a sign to lie across his feet. "I let it be known that business of the utmost importance needed to be attended to at my estates."

His voice took on a serious note. "Actually, it was a plausible excuse under the circumstances. Others also hath family affairs that need attention, afore departing for the German provinces." He paused before continuing, "I am to leave within the week.

"Henry's impatience to ascertain his prospective bride's comeliness, borders on paranoia!"

"Is Henry pleased with Wrieseley's report of the prospective bride's attributes? What of Cromwell? Doth he seem enamored of this choice?" Cecil was as curious as everyone else regarding this Anne of Cleves. "We all know that Cromwell is hoping to further advance his power through this union."

"Both Henry and Cromwell seem to be satisfied with the secretary's report of Ann, as well as positive words from others that know of her." James gave a heavy sigh. "However, as the time finally draws nigh for his wedding, our Grace becomes most anxious to gain his own confirmation of her fitness as his Queen. There is no doubt that she hath sufficient royal blood running through her veins to be an appropriate match for Henry, but he needs to see for himself that she is fair enough to heat his Tudor blood." James shook his head in tired resignation. "Upon my word Cecil, I can think of more fulfilling ways to spend my time than performing this errand. Apart from the nature of this journey, it doth vex me greatly to be leaving Kate for such a long time."

"Doest know how long thee shalt stay abroad?"

James shook his head. "Our instructions are to stay as long as necessary so that the maiden may prepare well for her journey. It also depends on our good king's whims and fancies."

He leaned forward in his chair with an earnest face. "Dear brother, I must leave Kate in thy care. I know that there is no need for me to explain the extent of my devotion towards her. I trust that thou will protect her in my absence."

Cecil placed a hand on James' knee. "Hath no fear brother. I shall not allow any harm to befall Kate. Rest assured that she is in the most felicitous care."

James visibly relaxed. "Although my heart is heavy, I doth feel better knowing that she is nearby at yon cottage." Arising he made ready to leave, "I must return to London at day break, so will say my farewells now. These last few precious hours with Kate must suffice until my return."

Cecil walked with him to the entrance. Clasping his sibling's shoulders in an embrace, he bade him farewell. "God speed James. I shall attempt to keep Kate from loneliness during thy absence."

Cecil stood at the top of the steps as the figure strode quickly towards the cottage. He saw the door open to reveal Kate waiting to welcome him, once again. Closing his own door, he returned upstairs and sank into his chair.

His mind was on the burden that James had inadvertently placed on him. Of course, his brother didn't realize the extent of his feelings for the girl. *Who else could he ask to care for her? Certainly not her family and she hath no one else. Now fate hath made her my charge, alone. Not withstanding, she is my brother's woman and as such, I must take care of her.* He straightened his back. Cecil was determined to keep his vow to his brother, even though the task of caring for Kate was bitter sweet.

CHAPTER TEN

*T*he ship dropped anchor and came to rest in Calais' port. In spite of the winter rains, the crossing had been uneventful and because of the wind's strength, they'd made good time. In short order the king's entourage disembarked and headed for the Bavarian province belonging to the Cleves' Duchy.

They would return with Ann to the French seaport, back across the channel to Dover and then on to London. It was decided that Fitzwilliam the Earl of Southampton, would stay with the ship until the escort returned with Anne.

In spite of the bitter cold, James found the rugged beauty of the landscape impressive. England was cold, but the intemperate climate in this part of Europe was worse. The cold air stung his face like the prickling of icy needles and it caused the breath to freeze as soon as it left ones mouth. He was glad of the warmth of his horses' flanks next to his thighs as he carefully steered the animal over the hard frozen ground.

The land looked wild. Thick forests bordered the sides of mountains and appeared to be only a slightly darker gray than the sky. Snow glistened stark and white on mountain ridges and treetops, giving the overall impression of a black and white ink sketch.

Eventually after what seemed to be an eternity, they reached the lands of the Duke of Cleves. The turreted and foreboding looking castle came in to view and its granite structure seemed to be a part of the natural landscape. To James surprise, the Duke himself welcomed them with much graciousness. He was a man without the formal pomp that was used by his British counterparts and in no time at all, orderly and efficient servants had shown them to their individual quarters.

James found himself in a moderate sized room, dominated by a huge fire-earth that blazed merrily with a warming fire. Orange flames shot out heat and the scent of sweet smelling pine logs hung in the air. Gratefully, he held out his hands to the fire and forgot about the bleak discomfort of the weather outside. Plopping onto the oversized bed to remove his over boots, James immediately sank into the folds of deep mattresses stuffed with eider down. It was so comfortable after the long journey that he wanted to stretch out and fall asleep. Mentally shaking his head, he forced himself to arise. Rest would have to wait until he'd formerly met with the Duchess.

Within a short amount of time a servant came to help him with his absolutions, before he was led to Ann's private quarters. After a polite knock at the large double doors that led into the waiting rooms, the servant entered and stood back to allow James admittance. Most of the English entourage was already assembled and waiting. James was among the last to arrive. Everyone stood quiet and expectant.

With a swift glance around the room James took in the expansive but austere private chambers. His critical eye noticed the plain adornments that were in glaring contrast to the elaborate and costly furnishings of King Henry's royal homes. Apart from the many colorful tapestries that hung on the walls, the rest of the furnishings were serviceable but boring. The men stood in quiet expectation, taking in their strange surroundings. Everyone was eager to finally meet this person who was to be the new Queen of Great Britain and all her Dominions.

A penny could have been heard dropping. Someone shuffled his feet. Lord Wooton, the king's personal emissary gave a small cough as with delicate fingertips he nervously stroked his moustache. No one spoke as they stood - waiting.

The room smelled fetid. James sniffed the air delicately and wished a window could be opened. Of course, he knew that the walls of thick stone and heavy windowpanes were built to keep out the harsh winter as well as to keep the warmth in. Even so, English homes were built just as solidly but were not as over-heated as this German counterpart. Unfortunately the stuffiness made body odors more noticeable.

The men shifted from one foot to the other.

After an interminable amount of time a door leading off the room opened. A tall, plainly dressed woman entered. Six ladies followed behind, dressed in almost identical gray dresses of an outdated fashion. White wimples that were exaggeratedly winged at either side of their heads completely hid their hair.

James gave the maidens but a perfunctory glance, being too busy taking in the appearance of the woman who preceded them. He scrutinized her as discreetly as possible. *Surely this is not Mistress Ann?* The woman was as tall as Wooton and although that gentleman was not as tall as the king, he was still more than average height. She stood directly in front of the emissary, speaking in her native German. *Is this Ann of Cleves?* James could see that poor Wooton was completely taken aback, as were the rest of the men.

She not only bore little resemblance to Master Holbein's portrait, but apparently she spoke very little English and Wooton spoke limited German. The moment was wrought with an awkward silence.

Suddenly as if swept by a whirlwind, the outer doors flew wide open and a man rushed in. He filled the whole room with his presence as he broke the tense silence. "My most abject apologies for my lateness, distinguished gentlemen." His voice was loud as he addressed the assembled company in guttural English, "I vas to haf presented myself to you on your arrival, but unfortunately something unexpected detained me. I beg most humbly for your pardon." The apology was accompanied by much dramatic waving of the hands and exaggerated bowing. Everyone's undivided attention was focused on him.

The newcomer introduced himself. "I am Herr Braumiester, advisor to our Cleves' Duchy and interpreter for our most illustrious Anna, the Duke's most admired sister." He bowed deeply in the direction of the woman who had spoken to Wooton.

He then turned his attention to Ann and hurriedly began to converse in German. As he talked he nodded his head towards Wooton and the group of men, waving his arms as before in a theatrical manner.

While all this was going on, James took the opportunity to make a more thorough assessment of Mistress Ann. He wasn't overly impressed. As he had first noticed, her dress was a plain and simple style. *The color doth not flatter her complexion.* It was a dark shade of brown, trimmed with bands of orange on the billowing sleeves and neckline. It made her pasty face appear to be even more sallow. He noticed that the cheeks and high sloping forehead had the blemishes of pox marks that were hard to disguise, while her upper lip showed a trace of fine dark hair. The same brown hair could be seen at the edges of her close fitting wimple. *And our King assumed that she would be a handsome, flaxen haired maiden like most German women.* The light eyes were heavily lidded, somewhat protruding and lackluster. As she listened to Braumiester, James saw that her intent face was trying to hide her discomposure.

With a sinking heart he continued to peruse Ann's person. The nose seemed too large for the small pointed face and from what he could ascertain from her dress, the body underneath the clothing appeared shapeless. Above the small bosom, the neckline of her dress showed bony shoulders. *Foresooth how could Holbein have been so blind!* Her eyes darted between her interpreter and Wooton as the former continued to converse in their native language. James shook his head in misgiving, *what will His Graces' reaction be when he meets his bride in the flesh?*

With sardonic humor, he took in the glaring differences in dress and mannerisms between Bruemiester and his mistress. *They are like a peacock with his peahen.*

Whereas her dress and demeanor were quiet and reserved, the interpreter's was most dashing. His brocade breeches were of the finest royal blue borato with black hose that were made of bombazine instead of the common wool.[2]

I do swear his clothing flaunts more lace and furbelows than a woman's undergarments! The hat that he wore was of a red cloth, fitting snugly over his head with a soft brim embroidered in silver and gold brocade trimming. The man's manner and dress demanded attention.

Braumiester finished his brief conversation with Anne and with another theatrical bow, swung around to formally introduce her to Wooton. "Most excellent Herr Vooton – (his German tongue had difficulty getting around English pronunciation) -vit your permission, I am most graciously pleased to present dear Mistress Anna, the beloved sister of our glorious Duke of Cleves."

"It is her vish that I give her many blessings to you, and to convey her felicitations in haffing you as guests in her home and

---

2 Borato: A thin material made of lightweight wool and silk. Bombazine: A fabric made of either silk and wool, or cotton and wool and always black until the end of the 16th century whereas the material was then made in other colors.

country. She also vishes me to convey most clearly that she is honored to haf been chosen by your most illustrious King Henry to be his bride."

"She looks forward to her future role with devotion and humility. It is her greatest vish to serf his most Royal Highness Henry as his queen and loyal companion for the greater glory of our two countries."

With another dramatic gesture he offered Ann's hand to Wooton, whereas that man, having quickly recovered his equilibrium bent to bring the proffered fingertips to his lips.

The fleeting look of disbelief that crossed Wooton's face was not lost on James. He felt a surge of sympathy for the man. Having to convey to Henry the truth of this woman's so-called 'comeliness,' was not to be an easy task.

He barely heard Ann's low, German speaking voice as she continued to instruct her interpreter to relay her welcome to the equerry from England. Meanwhile, her ladies simpered as they cast furtive glances at the men in the room.

After twenty minutes of more pleasantries between Wooton and Ann via the eloquent Bruemiester, a servant was summoned and they were allowed to leave. The ordeal was over. They were led to the Great Hall for a meal. *A quaff of ale will be most welcome after that charade.*

From a long wooden table arose the mouth-watering aromas of various roasted venison and fowl, accompanied by numerous dishes overflowing with hot vegetables, black puddings and gravies. Bowls of fruits and jellies swimming in cream were waiting to be sampled. *It doth seem that the Germans present a noteworthy meal even if their women are less appetizing.* James scanned the table, before making his way to an empty spot at the long bench, next to Thomas of Wickham.

Within minutes the Duke of Cleves accompanied by Wooton,

joined them. The Duke sat at the head of the table above the salt, indicating that Wooton should sit beside him. [3] In faltering, but understandable English he explained to the assembled guests that his sister and her ladies would not be dining with them, so that the men could discuss 'men's affairs' - meaning of course the last minute details of the marriage contract. Ann would join them later.

Shortly thereafter Bruemiester arrived and sat in the vacant space at James' other side. The interpreter wasn't big, but his exuberant manner made him appear to be twice his size. James automatically moved along the bench to give the man more room.

" So, vat is your impression of our good lady, Mistress Anna?" He turned to look closely at James, who took advantage of the fact that he was chewing meat in order to have time to compose a tactful answer. Swallowing the morsel of flavorful pheasant, he turned to answer his companion. "She appears to be of a submissive and demure manner. I am sure she will graciously please King Henry."

Bruemiester chuckled and leaned even closer. "Do not be taken in by her simple and servile manner, Sir James. Mistress Anna may not be as fair as King Henry's former vifes, but she is no fool."

James didn't know what to say. *He appears to be aware of the King's taste in women and how doth he know who I am?* As if reading his mind, Bruemiester continued, "I haf to 'make it my business' as you English say, to know everything I need to know that concerns the welfare of our Duchy. For discretionary purposes, you vil understand. Just as I also felt it expedient to make inquiries concerning your King, ven he showed interest in joining our two countries by wedlock."

"In my position I haf an obligation you understand, to know

---

3 In medieval times, the head of the household sat at the head of the table, followed by his wife and children. Other household members sat along the table in order of their status with the least important sitting at the opposite end. A dish of salt was placed in the center of the table to distinguish between the classes. Hence, the saying that is still used in Europe –"He isn't worth his salt."

the political strategies of other countries. It is most important, and I might add educational to know the vorkings of other minds, regardless of the language that is spoken".

James listened with interest, gaining some insights to this man's character. He remarked curiously - "And may I be so bold to ask where thou acquired such an excellent grasp of our language?"

"But of course you most certainly may ask." Bruemiester paused and waved his hands in the air to emphasize his pleasure at James' compliment, "I should haf explained myself more thoroughly. I did spend two years of my youth at your St. John's College in the shire of Cambridge, whereby I studied the English culture vile I also studied the language. Naturally, I also had the opportunity to study your people. I found both them and your country to be most delightful and your politics most enlightening. As for your gracious King Henry, I found him to be very - -" he paused, "shall I say, entertaining? Is that the correct vord to use?"

A smile played around James mouth and he bowed his head in acknowledgment. Bruemiester's impression of King Henry's personality was equally as tactful as his views on England's political climate. *He would be an asset to England's court – not to mention a calming influence on Henry!* Breumiester was obviously of a shrewd and discreet nature and he'd gained a new respect for this man of the flamboyant persona.

Underneath that flagrantly gaudy exterior was obviously a shrewd and observant mind. *This man would brook no nonsense from anyone, whether he be pauper or king.*

It took them longer to return to Calais as Mistress Ann insisted on having all two hundred of her personal servants with her. The roads were even more difficult to maneuver, due to fresh snow having fallen on the already icy roads, making it treacherous for both horse and man. Along with the rest of the escorts James had to periodically go back and forth along the line of travelers to make sure that no one was encountering any problems.

Not surprisingly, he found that the Germans where unperturbed by the hazardous weather conditions. *They doest fair better than my companions and I, if the truth be known.* He gingerly led his horse up and down the long line of handmaidens, serving men and such who doggedly made their way across the land. Dirty wheel tracks were left in the virgin snow along with occasional steaming, horse droppings. The sun shone from a cloudless sky causing the crisp white landscape to sparkle like a blanket of tiny diamonds. It was bitterly cold. James' breath froze in the air as he blew on his gauntlets to warm his fingers. Once more, he turned his horse to return along the line to look for stragglers. His steed picked its way over the frozen ground, snorting and nervously tossing its head as the snow crunched under his hooves.

Fitzwilliam was waiting for them at Calais with bad news. Because of stormy weather at sea, they were going to be detained in France until the conditions improved. James inwardly groaned, wanting to return to his Kate. *How is she? Doth she miss me as I miss her?* He hadn't allowed himself to think of her while conducting business, but now that this mission was almost over he was becoming impatient.

Fitzwilliam did his best to keep Anne and her retinue amused while that lady, being determined to meet her future husband with some semblance of communication, worked to become proficient in the English language. James admired her tenacity. He saw that she was a smart woman and learned quickly.

James observed the Earl teaching Ann how to play the card games that Henry enjoyed, hearing her squeal with delight when he'd allow her to win a hand. He watched with a mixture of admiration and despair as she tried to learn the English court dances that the accomplished king loved so well. Her rhythm was terrible and her steps clumsy. Her heavy-handed attempts at playing the lute caused the men to cover their ears to try and block out the harsh pinging. Finally after a fortnight of waiting, they were able to set sail for home and James breathed a sigh of relief.

They stopped at Rochester to rest and to everyone's astonishment - found the king and his retinue of lords (including his ever-faithful Cromwell)- waiting. Unable to control his desire any longer the impulsive King Henry had decided not to wait until their arrival at Greenwich. He'd traveled to the royal abode to meet them half way as he wished to see his future bride, now.

The suspense was great. Everyone in the anterooms waited with bated breath as the monarch was admitted to Ann's chambers.

No more than twenty minutes later he reappeared. Henry looked as if he were about to have an apoplexy. Without uttering a word, except to curtly advise Cromwell that he should join him in his quarters, the king strode through the crowd of dignitaries. Before disappearing into his private rooms, James caught a glimpse of the tightly compressed lips and deeply flushed face. Icicles flashed from the small beady eyes.

Cromwell made his way through the people, following his king with anxiety wreathing his countenance. His fingers played nervously with the elaborate chain of office hanging around his shoulders, causing his numerous rings to jingle against the metal. The sound was like that of the ominous jingling of jailor's keys. Cromwell's fluttering hands finally came to rest against his chest in prayerful supplication. Heavy eyelids lowered over the frightened eyes of the man and he wet his lips nervously, muttering a prayer. The slam of the door behind the Chief Secretary echoed loudly.

Even from behind the heavy door, Henry's voice could be heard and the tone raised goose bumps on the flesh of those listening. It was obvious to all who had witnessed his temper in the past that the royal mood was most foul. Occasionally, a few words could be distinguished as the furious voice grew louder and louder. "I WOULDS'T NOT BE DECEIVED SO......!

SHE IS A FLEMISH MARE......! BY GOD AND ALL THAT IS HOLY...!

The silence was deadly. People glanced from one to the other, afraid to utter a word. One by one they surreptitiously made trickling exits. No one wished to be around when Henry reappeared. Everyone trembled for their lives when their king's wrath was high and no person was immune at such times.

James didn't wait to see Cromwell leave the king's presence. It was obvious from the sound of the tirade that the man would no longer be able to wield his power with the king and he felt a deep sorrow for the Chancellor. *I fear for his very existence after this fiasco. But there is nothing I, or anyone else can do to help him. Methinks that anyone foolhardy enough to try and intervene for Cromwell wouldst rue the day that they did.*

He quietly left the almost empty public rooms. *I hath performed my duty and now I must attend to my own affairs.* An air of foreboding seemed to linger in the vast corridors as he walked rapidly towards his own quarters. *One more night and a day of traveling, and we will be in London.*

Dismissing his dire thoughts of Cromwell's fate, James began to dwell on the more pleasant images of Kate. At last his journey was ended. He could be with his love once again.

CHAPTER ELEVEN

She scrubbed at the kitchen table with listless movements, moving the brush back and forth with meaningless strokes. She rinsed it in the pail of water before wiping the table dry with a cloth. Kate's hands automatically went round and around, going over the same spot again and again. *I wonder when he might be allowed to return?* James had been gone for exactly a month and two days, and every day she had asked herself that same question.

After his departure she'd kept her mind and body busy with chores, so as to make the time pass more quickly. She'd checked and rechecked the stone jars of food that she'd preserved during the summer. She made sure that the jams and pickled vegetables were arranged neatly on the cellar's shelves, according to their age.

Cecil had brought rabbits and wild game that his tenants had caught and she busied herself with skinning the animals and plucking the birds, before salting them. Even so, these tasks had eventually been completed.

During the first days of his absence, Kate had deliberately kept herself busy to allay the emptiness of not having his visits to look forward to. But after so much industry, there wasn't anything else that needed her attention.

The long nights were the worst. She'd lie awake in her bed for hours wondering what he was doing in that far away, foreign country. At first, she'd taken long walks in the tingling air that brought color to her cheeks. The autumn sunlight shone through overcast skies, lighting the same fields and lanes that she had walked with James.

Kate would dwell on those times and return to the cottage with tears of loneliness wetting her cheeks. She stopped taking the walks. Apart from her visits to Cecil's house (at his insistence) she didn't leave the cottage. Time lay heavily on her young, energetic shoulders and the waiting gave her hours to think about Bessie and Noll. She missed them. The constant ache was a nagging burden to be endured.

Picking up the bucket, she left the cottage to empty its contents onto the soil of the bleak garden. The only bright spot were the purple Michaelmas daisies growing alongside the cottage wall. The sun was beginning to fade and the early dusk of another dying day was starting to creep across the sky.

From the direction of the lane, the sound of rattling wheels came to her ears. *It must be Cecil returning from London.* She stood by the door to wait for the litter to turn in at the gates. Earlier that day, he had stopped by the cottage to tell her that he had a need to go into the city. Would she like him to deliver greetings to Noll?

Cecil had visited St. Paul's Walk just two weeks past on the pretext of having 'business' in London. Of course, he'd brought back news of her family along with the few paltry items he'd purchased. Kate knew that Cecil hated the grimy city and was fully aware that he was accommodating her, by making these excuses to visit. He was keeping her apprised of Noll and Bessie's welfare, knowing that her pride would cause her to protest if he admitted that this was the reason for his visits. By claiming that his trips to London were a necessity, he could bring back news of her kin without making her feel obligated. *If t'were not for Cecil's solicitude I doest not know what my lot would be.* She waited eagerly for the litter to come into sight.

As the horse trotted through the gates, she saw a passenger sitting on the driver's bench next to Cecil. Puzzled, she pierced the gloom to try and make out who it could be. She gave a gasp of delighted astonishment as the horse stopped at the cottage gate. She couldn't believe her eyes! It was Noll!

Kate ran down the path and threw herself into his arms as he alighted from the litter, almost knocking him off balance. He returned her embrace and held her tightly for a while, before disentangling himself from her arms. Stepping back, he took a long appraising look at her. Tears of happiness swam in Kate's eyes.

She hath bloomed and is fairer of face. "Thee does't appear to be well and happy, our Kate. T'country air must suit thee." He gave a semblance of his familiar smile as he spoke yet she noticed that it didn't reach his eyes. Hungrily the girl searched his face, wanting to soak up Noll's energy that she hadn't felt in such a long while.

He looked older. Shadows clouded the eyes that were usually full of laughter, and the lines at the sides of his mouth were markedly deeper than she remembered. Deep frown lines also knitted the black eyebrows.

He was no longer a boy but a grown man. "What ails thee Noll? Why hast come here without warning?" She looked from her cousin to Cecil, "why hath thee brought him here, Cecil? Not that I am ungrateful for this unexpected pleasure," she hastily added, "tis an uncommonly generous gesture." Regardless, there was a feeling of unease underlying her joy at seeing her cousin.

"May we enter thy cottage Kate?" Cecil spoke in a quiet voice. "Our journey was tiring and the approaching night air is chill."

Kate quickly recovered her manners, apologizing as she led them indoors. "Forgive me, Cecil. This unexpected event hast made me temporarily discourteous"

She closed the door behind the two men, urging them to take seats by the hearth while she moved the jug of ale that reposed on the hob, closer to the fire. Noll pulled a stool near to the blazing Yule logs and held out cold hands towards the heat. The room smelled pleasantly of mingled wood smoke and furniture wax.

Bustling about the kitchen, Kate took pewter mugs from the sideboard's cupboard, trying to rid her mind of the nagging disquiet that she felt. Out of the corner of her eyes she observed Noll's serious profile. Cecil was staring thoughtfully into the flames. Pouring a generous amount of ale into the mugs, Kate handed them to the men before sitting down herself. She sat on the edge of her chair, grasping her own tankard in two hands – before nervously making to rise once more, "thee both must be hungry after thy journey,"she chattered. "I must fetch bread from the pantry. While I fix a meal thee might tell what hast brought Noll to my home."

Cecil stopped her movements with a gesture. "Please sit awhile Kate. There is news that thou must hear."

She sat back down, waiting for one of them to speak.

Noll looked across the space of the fire hearth at Cecil. The older man met his gaze and nodded his head. Noll spoke. "Supper can wait, cousin. I hast something of import to tell thee."

Kate's concern increased. "What is wrong, our Noll?"

He paused, not knowing how to start. Finally he blurted out the words. "Bessie is ill, Kate. She hath asked to see thee. That is why I am here."

The walls closed in around her. Why did she feel so chill?

"How ill is she?" Kate tried to sound calm but her face had paled. There was alarm in her eyes as they met those of her cousin's.

"Gravely ill." Noll was having difficulty in speaking. "The doctor doest not expect her to recover."

Kate slumped. Everything suddenly seemed surreal. Noll began to give an account of Bessie's illness.

Apparently, her aunt had been ailing for some time without

complaining. Of late, Noll had noticed that his mother was pale of face and moved more slowly. She had become quieter and less forthright of nature. When her son showed concern, Bessie brushed his queries to one side, stating that she 'wasn't getting any younger'. Noll assumed that her melancholy was due to her estrangement from Kate. "Ever since thee left, the house hast not been the same," he said.

At first, Noll had tried to pass along the messages of affection that Kate sent Bessie, but after a few futile attempts at trying to share the letters, he'd had to stop. His Ma would either ignore him or change the subject. Eventually she'd turned on him in anger and told him not to ever mention her name again.

Just one week past, he had arisen at his usual time to prepare to go to St. Paul's Walk. On alighting from his loft, he'd been surprised to see that no fire was lit in the kitchen and his Ma wasn't in sight. He'd knocked on Bessie's bedroom door and receiving no answer, had entered.

His mother was sitting on the edge of the bed still in her nightclothes, with her nightcap askew on her head. Her face was ghastly gray and her lips were colored purple. Bessie was grimacing with pain.

Alarmed, he'd assisted her back into bed and Bessie had shown no resistance. Chafing her hands, he asked what was ailing her? She'd managed to whisper, "terrible pain in my chest." He could see his mother's bosom laboring underneath her gown and Noll sprang into action. Propping the woman up onto her pillows and bolsters for comfort and tucking the blankets around her, he'd torn along the street to summon the doctor. Luckily, he didn't have to run far as the physician lived just around the corner.

The doctor answered the loud banging at the door to his surgery.[4] Still wearing his nightcap and gown, he listened to Noll's frantic tale.

---

4 In England the doctor's office used to be attached to his home and the entrance door announced it as "The Surgery"

From Noll's panicked explanation, he'd grasped the situation and told him to return quickly to his house while he packed his bag with things that he deemed necessary. Without bothering to dress, the good man pulled on his breeches over the top of his nightclothes. Throwing a cloak around his shoulders, the doctor mounted his old nag and within minutes was at Bessie's home.

They found Bessie as Noll had left her, but now her eyes were vacant and her breathing came in rasping gasps. The doctor took one look at her state and wasted no time in extracting a vial of foxglove extract from his bag.

"This will steady her heart." The physician ordered him to raise Bessie's shoulders, while he forced the liquid between her lips. Very slowly, the medicine trickled down the woman's throat. Bessie coughed and sputtered weakly, but she gulped and swallowed the liquid.

Making sure that she stayed in an upright position, the doctor began his examination. "Fetch some spirits from yon alehouse," he ordered. "Tell the publican that I hast sent thee. He will understand what I mean." Noll left without further adieu.

By the time that Noll returned holding the spirits in his hand, Bessie's labored breathing had somewhat eased. She had her eyes open and was staring uncomprehendingly at the physician. Taking the tumbler of spirits from Noll's outstretched hand, he gently urged Bessie to drink. She obeyed without resistance.

A few minutes later some of the natural color had returned to her cheeks. Noll breathed a sigh of relief and thanked the doctor profusely, but the good man shook his head and cautioned him not to be too optimistic.

Noll decided to sleep in Kate's old bed in the kitchen, so that he could hear his mother call if she needed him. He barely slept, awakening intermittently to stoke the fire that he kept burning all day and night as he didn't want the house to become chill. The doctor had told him to make certain that Bessie was kept as comfortable as possible.

"She appeared to rally and for almost a week, seemed to be getting better. Even the good doctor's estimation was less dour." Kate sat immobile as Noll talked.

"Two nights hence, I heard her call out. When I entered her room she just stared at me for a moment and then lapsed into an unconscious state." Noll's voice broke. "She hast been in and out of herself for these past two days and when she is awake, she calls out thy name." He leaned towards the girl on the stool. "T'was yon doctor urged me to fetch thee Kate. He fears that she will not last much longer."

Noll stopped talking. Dropping his head to his chest, he sat with his hands clasping and unclasping each other in his lap. Kate said nary a word.

"I should not hath forsaken her." Her voice was barely a whisper but the words seemed to resound with long forgotten 'might-have-beens.'

Cecil had sat listening without comment during Noll's telling of their family's woes, but now he spoke. "Thou coulds't not hath foreseen these events, Kate. The fact is thy aunt did not give any sign that she repented her actions against thee."

Noll raised his head, confirming Cecil's statement. "Cecil is right, cousin. Ma would never allow me to speak thy name in her presence." He tried to console her. "Thou knowest how stubborn Ma can be. Although I knew that she pined for thee, I also realized that she woulds't not recant the decision she made." He paused and his eyes showed his pain. "Now that it is too late, she calls thy name."

"I must go to her immediately." Kate sat rigid as if she were holding on to her own life.

"I hath offered Noll accommodation for this night." Cecil arose and made ready to leave. "Tomorrow I will arise early and send thee on thy way. Now we will leave so as thee might rest. "

As if awakening from a bad dream, Kate protested. "But thou hast need of food and I...." Cecil stopped her with a raised hand. "Do not concern thyself, Kate. My servants are quite capable of providing for Noll and myself. In fact, I woulds't deem that they are aware of our arrival and are already preparing ample nourishment." Peering into her face, he added, "I shall take it upon myself to send warm soup and mulled wine to thee. After such dire news, thou needest replenishment and in no fit condition to prepare a meal."

The girl looked into the kind face of her stalwart friend and her expression spoke her gratitude. Cecil opened the door. "I shall order the litter to be ready to take thee and Noll back to London, as soon as the sun rises."

It was impossible for Kate to sort out the events that had so shaken her world. It was as if the fates had taken complete control of her life. Her aunt's illness was the climax to everything that had changed the course of her destiny, and she felt as if she had come to a dead end.

Bessie lay beneath the coverings with only her head showing. The only indication that she was still alive was the occasional heaving of her breast. The covers rose and fell intermittently, as if 'something' was trying to escape from inside her chest. Her eyelids would occasionally flutter and open to reveal nothing but blankness.

The caring neighbor who had watched over her during Noll's absence, told Kate that she had been thus since Noll's departure. The doctor had looked in on her twice. Dire faced, he'd shaken his head as he examined the still figure.

Kate sat by the bed, unable to believe what she was seeing. She knew this woman as having plump, rosy cheeks and a round jovial face. These gaunt features with the sunken eyes and the nose that seemed to protrude hawk-like - had little resemblance to the Bessie that she knew. Skin at the neck hung like crepe paper as her jowls sagged. The full-lipped mouth hung open as she labored to take in oxygen. The girl found herself holding her own breath, waiting for her aunt to take her next inhalation.

She'd arrived an hour past and had been sitting by the bed ever since, but her aunt had remained unaware of her presence. Kate sat on the stool by the bedside, watching and waiting for some sign of recognition from the woman. Tears began to slowly trickle down her cheeks and chin. With an absentminded gesture, she licked them away. The taste of salt reminded her of bitter vetch.

As she sat watching and waiting for she knew not what, her mind went over the events of her life since meeting James. How the fates had altered her life's course! She relived the terrible images of her aunt's tirade against her person all those many moons past. *How I wish that circumstances could have been different.* Kate loved this woman, dearly. Bessie was the only mother figure that she had ever known. There's had been a bond that should never have severed, but Kate's actions had cut those ties.

Now, she realized how much Bessie must love her. It was finally clear to Kate that her aunt's raging anger had been caused by her very own foolish actions. She had defied the moral standards by which she had been raised.

Her passion for James was not an excuse for discarding God's laws. Kate had become complicit to adultery. Her willfulness had caused tremendous worry for her aunt – and undue grief. She finally realized how greatly she had wronged this person who now lay dying.

The tears poured unheeded down Kate's face. Regardless of her love for James and the fact that she would always love him, she had acted recklessly and selfishly without regard for anyone but herself. She'd deceived and lied to this woman who had nurtured her since birth.

Bessie had always protected Kate and given of herself, without thought for her own well-being. Her aunt had given selflessly so that she could care and provide for the child that she'd taken in as her own. The flaunting of her adulterous behavior and selfish unconcern for this woman, were unforgivable.

And, what of Noll? Her cousin had also lied for her. *Hast I not wronged him too?* Despondency engulfed Kate. Had she not placed him in the position of having to risk the loss of his mother's trust, in his attempts to protect her? Even though it didn't bother Noll's conscience to deceive Bessie as far as his gambling was concerned, it was a more serious deception that Kate had instigated. *I hath taken advantage of Noll's affection and loyalty.*

Her spirit was heavy under the burden of so much guilt. Full of shame, she covered her face with her hands. Images of James swam in front of her closed eyes as she sobbed uncontrollably. *The most terrible sin that I hath committed is that of discarding my moral standards.*

She thought on James's wife, realizing the sin that she'd committed towards Clarissa. She had usurped the affections of that lady's lawful husband. Kate relived the scene in St. Paul's Walk, observing the beautiful woman who had held James' arm. Kate realized that in her desire to have James, she hadn't given any thought to his lawful wife. No matter what the situation was between he and Clarissa, his wife deserved better treatment. *I hast sinned most grievously against my own self. Even worse than this, I aided my lover in his sins.* She didn't know James's wife, so had given no concern for that lady's feelings. Although James and Clarissa seemed to have little affection for each other, Kate had helped to further their estrangement. *He hath wronged his wife, because of me.*

She didn't know how long she had sat by the bed, but was brought abruptly back to the present by a faint whispering of her name. - " Kate."

Startled she raised her head to see Bessie with eyes open,

looking at her. The woman was making an effort to talk but only her lips moved uncomprehendingly. Kate slid from the stool to her knees, and leaned close to her aunt's face.

The weak sound came again. "Is it really thee, Kate?"

Fresh tears made their way down Kate's cheeks as the reddened eyes searched Bessie's own. "Dearest aunt. It is really I, your niece that hath so grievously wronged thee. I beg thee to forgive me."

The frail woman tried to raise her hand towards Kate's face and the girl grasped it between her own. It felt so icy cold and trembled like a tiny bird between her palms. She raised it to her lips, gently kissing the withered flesh.

Once again, Bessie whispered something. Kate leaned an ear close to Bessie's mouth to discern the words. "Thee art my own sweet Kate… Hast given much thought… doest rue the day….. forgive me, Kate… The woman gave a weak cough and gasped for air as the effort of trying to talk tasked her remaining energy. She closed her eyes. The body was still.

Kate waited for her to take another breath but none came. After a few seconds, a rattling sound escaped from the slack mouth - then nothing. Bessie had gone.

Sometime later, Noll entered the room. The girl didn't hear him. He unclasped Kate's fingers from the cold stiffening hand of his mother. Gently raising his cousin to her feet, he led her unresisting body from the room.

CHAPTER TWELVE

*J*ames stared in bafflement at his brother. "What sayest thou? Where hast she gone?"

"Sit, while I explain."

The distraught man obeyed, sinking into the overstuffed chair in Cecil's study. Taking this as an invitation, Missy moved from the hearth where she's been laying and stretched her sleek body across his feet. Absentmindedly, James patted the dog's silky head.

He'd driven his horse unmercifully in his eagerness to reach the cottage. The longing to see Kate again had become a physical ache, increasing in strength with each day that he'd been absent. Escorting the king and his promised bride back to Greenwich had seemed to take an interminable amount of time.

The journey had not been pleasant as His Grace's mood had been most foul. James had escaped from the palace as soon as he was able and managed to avoid the final preparations for the royal wedding. The palace was so crowded with dignitaries that he'd escaped the exhausting ceremonies without being missed. Paying a necessary visit to his home took another week of his precious time away from his love. At last, he was able to announce to

Clarissa that urgent business required his presence at the estate. Naturally they both knew the real reason for his departure, but neither mentioned the cottage and its inhabitant.

He'd been surprised to find the place empty, but assumed that she was visiting with Cecil. The garden looked neglected which puzzled him, as Kate loved tending her flowers and vegetables. Weeds were starting to sprout between budding crocus and snowdrops.

"Tell me, where is Kate? When will she return? Hath something happened to her?" The voice was full of stress. Cecil moved from his stance in front of the fire. Giving a heavy sigh he took a seat, facing his sibling. He began the story of the affliction that had befallen the aunt and Kate's consequent return to London.

James rudely interrupted. "But why hath she not yet returned, now that the aunt is buried? Kate promised to wait for me. Is she still at her aunt's house?" He started to rise, "I must go to her immediately."

"Be still." The tone was sharp. "Kate is not in London," said Cecil.

James was silenced - his alarm growing.

"She hath entered a nunnery."

"WHAT!" James' exploded. The dog jumped, startled out of its comfortable snooze.

Cecil continued as if uninterrupted. "She hath been gone for sometime. Noll received but one communication from her; a short note to say that she is doing God's will."

James was only half conscious of his brother's voice as he explained the story of Kate's departure...

After Bessie's funeral, Kate barely spoke to anyone. Noll voiced his concern to the doctor, fearing for her mental state, but the physician had reassured him that Kate was mentally strong but suffering from a tremendous grief. "Give her time lad. Kate is strong and will recover herself, eventually." Noll had been consoled by the good doctor's words and patiently waited for his cousin to revive.

It had been a little over a fortnight after his Ma's death that she'd announced she needed to take a walk, to gain some fresh air. This announcement had brought Noll some thankfulness after living with her melancholia. His cousin was finally recovering. Two hours later, Kate had returned as silently as she had left. Noll had warm ale brewing and re-heated stew that one of their neighbors had dropped off for them.

Since the wake, the kitchen had been full of food donated by people that Noll and Kate had barely known. The people that considered Bessie a friend surprised them and they realized how well she had been held in good esteem.

The stew smelled appetizing, being steaming hot by the time that Kate returned. She closed the door quietly and took off her cloak, obeying Noll's request to join him in the meal. The only sound in the warm kitchen was Noll's slurping as he dipped thick slabs of bread into the broth and crammed it into his mouth. In between bites he watched Kate move her spoon indifferently around her bowl. Occasionally, she'd take a small bite of the nourishment but seemed unaware of its tastiness.

Noll lifted his dish and licked the sides to get the last remnants of gravy. Satisfied that his dish was clean, he laid it down and wiped his mouth on his sleeve. "Well, our Kate. Dids't yon walk make thee feel less morose?"

"I dids't not walk far Noll, only to St. Mary's rectory." He looked surprised. "Thee do say!"

Her head was lowered into her chin so that he couldn't see her expression. "I needed to speak with the priest. My thoughts of late hast troubled me greatly." Noll waited. It was obvious that she had something on her mind. After a few moments, she continued. "I hath something of import to tell thee Noll - - I hast decided to enter a convent."

His mouth gaped in utter astonishment, but before he could comment she hurriedly continued. "Tis a decision that I hast given much thought to since Bessie's passing. The burden of my many sins lie heavily upon my spirit and the guilt of my feelings for a man that is married to another, cannot find relief."

She lifted her head and looked at him directly. There was an expression on her face that he'd never before seen. It wasn't exactly determination, more like an acceptance of her lot.

"The only solace that I hast found is in prayers to the Lord, and the comfort this brings to me." The voice shook with emotion. "My aunt's death brought home to me many things that hath lain dormant and neglected within my heart."

"Since I was a child learning the scriptures, I hast not thought on these things. Now, I find that I need the peace and solitude that the Lord's teachings provide. I need the security and blessings of a convent life, to repair all that my spirit hath lost." The speech ended. Kate sat with her hands in her lap.

Long after she'd finished talking Noll continued to stare at the person sitting across the table from him. This stranger bore little resemblance to the Kate that he knew. Not so long ago, his Kate would scold him with her sharp tongue and quick temper, or give him a good smack whenever he was vexing. The Kate he knew would toss her hair with pride and give as well as she received. This submissive stranger sitting across from him wasn't the same person.

The next day, Kate had wrapped a few of her belongings into a paper parcel and left for St. Mary's. From there, she had explained, an old Sister would escort her on the journey by wagon to the isolated convent in rural Suffolk.

Noll had tried pleading and cajoling for her to recant her decision. "How will I fair without thee Kate? Whom shalt take care of my needs as thee and Ma used to?"

Pressing his shoulder in affection, she had given him an enigmatic smile. "Thee art more than capable of taking care of thyself, Noll. It is for sure thee doest not need a nursemaid. Thou art almost a full grown man and can well take care of thyself."

Her manner had been impenetrable. Only when he asked who was going to tell Sir James did she show any sign of hesitation. For a brief moment her eyes clouded over and her voice trembled as she answered. "I am hoping that thee will find a way to make contact with his brother, so that Cecil might enlighten him. I cannot wait for his return to tell him of my decision. 'Tis my fear that his persuasions would weaken my resolve."

She placed a hand on his arm. "This may be the last time that I shall take advantage of thee goodness, Noll." Her voice lowered to almost a whisper but nevertheless, sounded resolute. "James hath a wife and his responsibilities lie with her. Likewise, his emotional and spiritual needs lay at Clarissa's hearth."

Noll watched from the doorway as with a deliberate gait she made her way along the street, heading for the church. Only when she had disappeared from sight did he go inside and slowly shut the door.

The next day, he persuaded the greengrocer to lend him his horse and cart for a few hours. The man grudgingly agreed, after Noll had promised payment of thruppence as soon as he found a card game and could acquire the money. Noll's reputation as a lucky gambler still remained firm.

He'd hitched the horse and wagon and headed for Herewith Hall. Although Cecil had been surprised to see the lad, he wasn't surprised by his news.

"It was as if she were but a shell of her former self," Noll had told James' brother.

Long after Noll left to return to London, Cecil remained pondering over the revelations. With a sad feeling, he thought about all the events that had turned Kate's world upside down. If anything, Cecil understood Kate's actions better than anyone.

In the many months that they had lived so close, he had grown to understand the complexities of Kate's sensitive nature. He knew that she loved his brother and he envied James that love. But, he'd also seen a side of her that James had not been privileged to see.

In spite of the joy that James obviously brought into her life, there were the days during his absences when he'd notice her restlessness - and something else that he couldn't quite fathom.

Whenever she thought that she wasn't been observed, he'd catch an expression of somberness on her countenance. The sparkling eyes would darken as if a light had been momentarily eliminated. Her lips would tremble –oh, so imperceptibly.

No one else would have probably noticed, except Cecil. He had memorized every nuance of this girl's personality and knew that she wasn't always comfortable being his brother's mistress.

Kate's actions were hard for her cousin to understand, but Cecil understood. Kate was no longer an innocent girl. She was a grown woman and had experienced more of life since knowing his brother, than many young girls experienced in an entire lifetime.

She had known the blissful heights of loving and being loved, but she had also known the depths of despair. Cecil realized that she was taking back control of her life in the only way that she felt was right.

Who was he or Noll, or even James, to rebuke her desire? If nothing else in coming to know Kate, Cecil had learned that she was a forthright, determined person and had a mind of her own. He had no doubt that she must have given a great amount of thought to her dilemma before coming to this decision. She must have concluded that it was the only decision to make.

Cecil knew that Kate would not take her new life lightly. *She loves my brother far too much to have continued to live as his mistress. And, she hath too much self worth to be able to indefinitely live such a life.* Cecil loved his brother, but understood that he was a selfish man, especially when it came to Kate. *Will he contain his fortitude, and understand that she needed to act thus?*

The fire had burned low. As the late afternoon light streaming through the window diminished, darkness began to creep over the room. Cecil arose to light the tapers and replenish the fire with fresh logs.

James stared fixedly into the firelight. His head felt as if it were full of feathers, stifling his brain so that he couldn't think clearly. Without even being conscious of doing so, he turned to look out the window. If he arose from his chair and stood in front of it, he'd see the cottage at the end of the driveway. *But Kate is no longer there, is she?* His love had gone. That's what Cecil had said. *How could this be true?* Why had his adored Kate not waited for him as she promised?

He turned his gaze away from the window as Cecil poured more wine into his half empty mug. "Drink brother. Thou hast need of its potency"

James raised the wine-mug and took a swallow. "Why hath she done this to me, Cecil? She doth love me truly. I know this. How could Kate forsake me! "

"Stop!"

The dog looked up at his master with questioning eyes. "Must thou only think of thy own feelings? Can thee not imagine how Kate might be feeling? Hath not heeded a word of what I hast said?" James had the good grace to look abashed.

Cecil arose and paced the floor. Missy watched with tongue hanging, panting excitedly. After a few moments he stopped his pacing and sat down again. The dog moved to sit at his feet, looking up at his master in concern. Cecil bent to comfort the animal with a reassuring pat.

"My dear brother, I know that thou love this woman truly. But, thee must try to think rationally and place yourself in her situation. Thou hast not had one rational thought in thy head since meeting Kate."

James squirmed uncomfortably and took another drink. "I knowest this, Cecil. Why remind me?"

Cecil gave an exasperated sigh. "I do remind thee, because even now thou art not thinking clearly. This ending of thy affair with Kate was inevitable. Thou knowest this, even with thy reluctance to do so." He emphasized his next words. "I commend Kate for her decision to end it this way, before more damage couldst be wrought to both of thy lives."

James glared at him fiercely.

"No. Do not raise thy anger against me. Doest not understand the pain that Kate hast suffered as thy mistress?"

His brother's words began to sink into James head.

"The girl hath lived with the guilty knowledge of broken ties with her kinfolk. And, doest know how she really felt, living as a kept woman to a married man?" Cecil's words were blunt. "Kate is not a courtesan."

James flushed and his scowling expression changed to sadness. " Thou knowest that I would marry her if t'were possible and …" Cecil interrupted as if he hadn't spoken. "The death of her aunt was also the end for Kate. Thee hath need to understand this. Her sensitive nature could no longer bear the burden of so much pain and self-recrimination. Even her love for thee could not assuage such an overwhelming grief as that suffered by the death of her aunt. This woman was the only mother she ever knew. Kate made the only choice that she deemed possible in order to find her own, true self again." Cecil ran out of words and stopped.

The room was quiet, except for the snuffling of the snoozing dog and the crackling of the fire.

After a lengthy silence James spoke with despair. "I did'st not realize that she was so lost." His voice cracked. "Thou art right brother. Dearest Kate gave me more than her heart - she also gave me her spirit. God forgive me! I hast not intended to break either. Laying down his empty wine cup he leaned forward, staring with unseeing eyes into the flames…

361

The heat of summer lay over the countryside, causing steam to rise from the marshlands. The soft thud-thud of a trowel digging into soil could be heard above the steady drone of bees as they buzzed among blossoms. The convent's garden was as serene as it looked.

The novice lifted the skirt of her habit, out of the way of the soft earth as she stooped to extract a weed that clung stubbornly to the base of a rosebush. Jabbing the trowel around the roots she gave a tug and it finally gave way.

With a sense of satisfaction, Kate dropped the weed into a bucket by her side before wiping moisture from her face. She straightened up, arching her back to relieve the ache in her muscles.

Shading her eyes from the sun's glare she watched a swallow in graceful flight, singing his song of freedom and joy. The warmth of the sun on her face felt good and she smiled.

The chapel bell began to toll reminding her of mid-morning prayers. Raising herself from her knees, she wiped her hands on the apron that covered her skirt before untying the strings that held it around her waist. She folded it neatly and tucked it underneath her arm as she hurried towards the convent that she called 'home.' She'd just have time to go to her dormitory cell to refresh herself. Mother Superior frowned upon anyone being late for prayers, especially one of the novices.

Kate couldn't say that she was brimming over with the happiness that she had once known, but neither did she feel the terrible agony that had torn at her insides so unmercifully. She was at peace. The daily routine of her life was uneventful, but the sanctuary and her prayers served as a healing balm that anointed her soul. Kate asked for nothing more than this.

WHERE OR WHEN

NEW YORK CITY
2001

HAPPY NEW YEAR! The roar rolled over the city as if a gigantic tidal wave had crashed ashore. Horns honked deafeningly, mingling with screams of joy that floated high above the skyscrapers. Such celebration! Such frenetic gaiety! An aura of orange glowed over Manhattan's rooftops, shimmering and quaking from the noisy blast of energy.

Breaking through skyscrapers the sound arose effortlessly above the city lights to become a part of the serene atmosphere beyond. Gradually it faded into a whisper as it met with the night sky - - eventually dissipating into space.

Folks crushed together yelling hysterically in celebration as the huge ball in Times Square dropped, welcoming in 2001. Gaily colored streamers rained down on peoples' shoulders as New York celebrated another year. Naturally, TV cameras were there to capture the moment for the millions of people to see at home. All over the country people were watching from the comfort of their living rooms.

Should anyone have bothered to look up to the night sky they would have seen the blinking lights of a jetliner traveling miles above them. It seemed to be moving oh - so-o-slowly – hardly distinguishable against its backdrop of stars. From the ground the jet appeared to be almost motionless. It resembled a small wind-up toy, dependent for its motion on some power beyond itself. Rhythmic blinking of the lighted wing tips gave the only indication that it wasn't a natural star.

Nobody noticed. Nobody cared.

Whistles and sirens competed with the sounds of Auld Lang Syne. Even the flamboyant neon signs and giant television screens advertising celebrity shows, seemed to shudder under the noisy onslaught. Oh, how sharply this earthly celebration contrasted with the serene and mindful universe.

Juel laughed and reached up to kiss Les' cheek as he hugged her waist. Turning her attention to Rita crushed against her other side, she yelled above the commotion. "Happy New Year, you two."

"Same to you girl" Les responded, as he blasted a paper horn next to her ear. Juel clamped gloved hands to the sides of her head in mock despair. "Enough already! It's going to take me all night to get my hearing back without you adding to the problem."

The three friends had been celebrating since early evening and she caught Rita's arm as someone bumped into the girl, causing her to stumble. Rita had drunk too much and wasn't too steady on her feet.

"You need some coffee," Juel stated. Still holding the girl by an arm she nodded towards a red blinking neon sign. "Let's see if we can get a table in that coffee-shop over there," indicating a sign a few yards along the sidewalk. The bright neon showed a coffee pot simulating the movements of coffee being poured.

As Les moved through the crowded sidewalk, Juel automatically followed, dragging Rita along by a hand. Reaching the heavy glass door leading into the restaurant, Les held it open to allow the girls to enter. A blast of warm air hit Juel along with the smell of freshly brewed coffee. She scanned the room for a table. The place was packed.

"Over there." Les pointed a finger. "Follow me." Being well over six foot he had the advantage of being able to see the room more clearly than his shorter companions and pushed his way between the close-knit tables. Maneuvering his body around tables, he squeezed between an obese woman and her male companion who were blocking the aisle. "Excuse me." Juel wiggled through the space that Les was creating – still with Rita in tow.

"Thank you." Les dropped smoky grey eyes on the young woman who was pulling her chair closer in to let him pass. The girl gazed up at him giving Les benefit of a smile that promised him anything.

Juel noticed that the girl's attention still lingered on her friend as they passed her table. The appraising eyes slowly wandered down Les' body, coming to rest on his well shaped butt in the snug fitting, Calvin Klein's. *Sorry lady, but you're wasting your time.* Juel smiled to herself in amusement. It wasn't the first time she'd seen this reaction towards her companion.

They reached a booth by a back wall that a couple had just vacated and slid into the seats. A waiter came over and giving the tabletop a perfunctory swipe with a damp cloth, picked up the tray of dirty dishes he'd collected. "I'll be back to get your orders," he promised before departing with the loaded tray. Rita scanned his retreating back with bleary-eyed interest. "You're not going to feel so hot, tomorrow," Juel remarked prophetically.

The waiter returned holding a pot of steaming brew. As he poured coffee into a cup and placed it in front of Rita, she looked into his face invitingly. Her deep-set eyes were a blood-shot brown and in reality she looked as if she were about to fall asleep rather than seductive. No matter. The waiter didn't even give her a passing glance. He was too busy staring at their male companion. As he leaned across Les to pour coffee for Juel, he gave him an appreciative once over before leaning close to fill his cup.

Taking their order for a plate of hot cinnamon rolls, he pointedly asked Les if there was anything else that he desired. The innuendo was blatantly obvious and Juel snickered rudely as the waiter left to fill their order.

"I think this city is full of queers," Rita muttered in disgust.

Choosing to ignore the derogatory remark, Les gave Rita a flashing smile that showed teeth reminiscent of a movie star's false caps. "Let's face it my dear you just don't have what it takes," he drawled, giving an exaggerated wave of dismissal towards her.

Juel choked on her coffee and Les obligingly patted her on the back, grinning from ear to ear.

"He's not that funny - or for that matter he ain't that good looking either." Rita glared at Juel balefully and her tone took on a sorrowful whine. "You just think he's great because you've known him longer than you have me and you like him better." By this time her boozed brain was making her act silly.

Attempting to control herself, Juel leaned across the table and patted her friend's hand consolingly. "You've had too much to drink and you're feeling sorry for yourself," she chastised gently. "Be nice to Les for a change. If it weren't for him we never would have found this vacant table. And, we definitely wouldn't have got service so fast if that waiter hadn't taken a shine to his gorgeous bod!" Warming to her subject she turned her eyes on Les, looking him up and down in mock approval. "Just think of him as being our very own god-like stud, put on this earth just to protect you and me. We're probably the envy of everyone in this place. Especially the male clientele!"

In protest, Les threw up his hands. "Okay. Enough is enough! So far, I'm enjoying myself and I'm not going to have the rest of the night spoiled by you two dissecting my assets. Besides, as much as I like you darlings, neither of you fit my type."

"And neither does our waiter for that matter." He scrutinized the employer who was now waiting on a table a few feet away. "He's much too skinny for my taste. And, he looked at me like a dying cow!"

He gave an exaggerated sigh, holding the back of his hand to his forehead in a fair imitation of a silent movie star. "Woe is me! Being drop dead gorgeous does have its drawbacks. " People sitting close by turned to stare at the booth where the loud laughter was coming from.

Les had been a puny kid but over the years his gangly frame had filled out in proportion to his height, thanks to genetics plus regular visits to a gym. His broad shoulders and mop of curly brown hair, (artificially frosted) - made him a photographer's dream. Consequently, in his job as a model he was always in demand. An aquiline nose and a chiseled jaw, plus a cleft in his chin added the finishing touches to his soap opera good looks. Women were drawn to him wherever he went - young or old, but he had no sexual interest in any of them. Les had long ago accepted his homosexuality and was comfortable in his own skin.

He and the girls had known each other for most of their lives and after they'd finished with school had miraculously found a small apartment in a decent part of the city. By splitting the rent, they were able to afford it. Because Les made the biggest chunk, he paid for the utilities and still had plenty left over to indulge in his favorite past time of gambling on the lottery. Sometimes he went to the horse races and occasionally backed a winner. For the girls, there was the added benefit of using him as an escort to various functions whenever they didn't have a date. The arrangement suited everyone perfectly.

By the time they were ready to leave, the crowds in Times Square had thinned out, somewhat. Revelers were either heading for their homes or going on to other parties.

At the same time that Juel reached to pull open the door to the street, someone entering swung it inwards. Quickly, she stepped out of the way to avoid getting hit.

"Sorry." The culprit apologized - then stopped in his tracks as he caught sight of the girl. Juel recognized the man. He was the firefighter who frequented 'her' cafeteria across the street from where she worked. He smiled in recognition as he held the door, waiting for her to pass through. They both hesitated - staring at each other.

"Come on Mark, I'm cold and hungry."

The moment was gone. Juel's attention was drawn to a tall willowy blond who had moved alongside him. The girl had taken possessive hold of his arm and was dragging him towards a table. But his eyes followed Juel until the door close behind her.

"What took you so long?" Rita was in a peevish mood. "It's getting too cold to stand around in the street." Obviously she wasn't feeling so good now the booze was wearing off. Les put himself between them, linking his arms in theirs. "Come on! Let's head for the subway before this mob gets the same idea."

She hung onto the strap with one hand while the train careened through the maze of tracks and tunnels. It was almost as full as the rush hour surge, but Juel hardly noticed. The loud noise of the rattling coach with its familiar smells of stale perfume and crowded bodies rumbled underneath the city, but Juel's thoughts were on the man, Mark….

Most mornings, she would stop for coffee before going to work and looked forward to seeing the fireman who frequented the place. It seemed like her day always went better after she'd seen him. He always came in with another firefighter and they'd sit in the same place, at the opposite end of the counter from where she sat.

Juel had been transferred to the travel agency's new branch three months past and loved the new location. Situated on the street level of one of the older buildings of downtown Manhattan, her desk was placed so that she had a view through a big, plate glass window of the skyline. With an air of pride, the magnificent towers of the Trade Center dwarfed the other buildings. As she'd sit at her desk looking out she'd think of them as a modern version of Egyptian obelisks that she'd seen pictures of in advertising folders. She'd always wanted to visit Egypt and had promised herself a trip to see the pyramids when she had enough money and time. Those towers always reminded her of that vow.

The little cafeteria was cat-a-corner from her office and Juel had found it convenient to stop and get her 'caffeine fix' before starting work. She'd noticed him that very first morning. He was in his uniform, deep in conversation with another firefighter, but he'd looked up when she'd entered. Juel had been conscious of his eyes following her as she walked towards the counter and perched herself on one of the high vinyl and chrome stools. Five minutes later when she happened to glance his way, she caught him staring again. Hurriedly finishing her coffee she'd left, feeling as flustered as a silly schoolgirl.

Since then she'd see him at least twice a week, and sometimes more. He always sat in the same place and more often than not was accompanied by the same man. He never spoke to her but Juel was well aware of his presence and became familiar with every nuance of his expressive features.

When he was in uniform, he reminded her of the hero in her favorite 'cops and robbers' TV show. His dark hair was combed straight back, but always had one lock that refused to stay away from his forehead. Juel would find herself waiting for his ineffectual efforts to brush it back with his long, sensitive looking fingers. Whenever she'd catch him glancing her way, she'd melt inside. His eyes were the color of golden brandy....

The train gave a squealing lurch as it sped around a corner and she almost lost her balance. Her hand gripped the strap tighter. *Knock it off you silly fool.* She shifted her tired feet to a more comfortable stance as the jerking coach jockeyed her body. In spite of herself, her thoughts drifted back to the firefighter….

She'd got to know when he was working a night shift because then he (and his friend) - would come in the café wearing street clothes. He would usually have a slight growth of blue bristle around his jaw and the hair-lock would refuse to stay back. The waitress apparently knew them well as she always spent a few minutes laughing and joking familiarly with them. From eavesdropping on their conversations, she'd learned their names. Mark and Chuck. Juel barely looked at Chuck, except to notice that he'd be really good looking if he went on a diet. She'd watch the man eat a loaded plate of bacon and eggs with hash browns and toast, realizing why he had a double chin and too much blubber around his waist. Apart from this she never gave him another thought. She was too busy watching the one called Mark….

I wonder if he's living with that girl he was with tonight, or maybe they're married? I've never noticed a wedding band on his finger. Still, that doesn't mean anything.

"What time is it?" Rita broke through her reverie. Half asleep, the girl stood propped up between her two friends.

Juel glanced at her watch. "It's half past two."

"Thank God we don't have to go to work tomorrow." Rita repositioned her legs, leaning further against Les.

"It's already tomorrow and a year older." Les reminded her.

"I don't feel like I'm a year older."

"Wait 'till you wake up later today." Juel eyed the girl's flushed face. "I bet you'll feel more than a year older once that hangover hits you."

The train slowed down and they inched their way to the door.

She felt let down. He wasn't at his usual spot. Juel felt

ridiculous - as if she were a kid who'd expected a treat that didn't materialize. Idly crumbling the croissant on her plate she picked up her mug, draining the last remnants of coffee before laying it back on the counter top. *You're acting like a stupid teenager!* Automatically glancing at her watch, she saw that she'd be late for work if she didn't move.

Throwing a tip on the counter, she headed for the cash register. *You silly idiot, get over it! You don't even know the man. What did you expect to happen, even if he had have been here? Did you think he'd come rushing over and throw himself at your feet? Get real!*

The waitress smiled and rang open the cash register drawer as Juel handed her some money. "Didya have a nice New Year?" Sally was a friendly soul and the waitress now accepted her as one of her 'regulars'.

"I sure did," Juel replied. "How about yourself?" The middle-aged woman reminded Juel of the late actress Shelly Winters that she'd seen in old, late-night movies.

Sally handed her some change. "Me an' the old man stayed home an' watched all the fun on the boob tube. He's not int'a going out on New Years Eve an' running the risk of gittin' hit by drunks. T'was all the same to me as I sooner rest the sore feet after been on 'em all the time." Juel smiled sympathetically and hurriedly left to get to work.

He wasn't there the next day - or the next. On the fourth morning she decided to order her coffee and a roll to go but on entering, she saw the two of them sitting in their usual place at the end of the counter. Changing her mind, Juel walked to her seat at the opposite end, aware that her progress was being watched.

I wish I'd bothered to fix my hair. She brushed a chestnut strand away from her face that had escaped from the casual twisted knot that she'd formed at the nape of her neck. Les had hogged the shower, barely giving her time to apply her make-up. As usual, Rita had taking her time in front of the only well-lighted mirror in the place. She'd had to resort to using the steamy bathroom mirror.

From over the rim of her coffee mug she cast a surreptitious glance at him. He and his companion seemed to be in a deep discussion. Before she could avert her eyes he turned and met her gaze. To her consternation, he arose from his seat and deliberately headed in her direction. *I don't believe it!*

Before she could gather her wits he was standing alongside her stool, leaning an elbow on the counter top. His face was close and she caught a tantalizing whiff of his after-shave.

"Hi. I hope you don't think I'm trying to hit on you or anything but after almost knocking you down on New Years Eve, I feel that I owe you an apology."

The lob sided smile he laid on her gave Juel a warm, fuzzy feeling.

"You already apologized that night."

Her abrupt response brought a flush to his face. She could have gladly bitten off her tongue and mentally kicked herself. *You stupid fool!* Quickly, she tried to make amends. "Sorry. I didn't mean to sound rude. Thanks for the concern but no damage was done. The door didn't hit me."

Juel's brain finally kicked into gear and started functioning on all cylinders. But, the cylinders were obviously rusty because once again - she put her foot in it. "Did you and your girl-friend enjoy the night together?" *My God! Why don't you just come out and ask him if he slept with her!* His eyebrows raised a notch and his eyes held a suspicion of amusement.

She wanted to die. Lowering her face into her mug, she tried to hide her embarrassment.

"Yes, I had a good time and - she isn't my girlfriend. At least, she isn't a girl friend in the sense of being the girl friend, if you know what I mean." Now it was his turn to look uncomfortable. "What I mean is, she's just a good friend. I mean…" He stopped not knowing how to continue. An uncomfortable silence descended.

With a gesture of helplessness, he spread out his hands.

"Look. My name is Mark and I thought that seeing that we seem to occupy the same space in this world for at least half an hour almost every day, we might as well be formally introduced." Once again, he gave her benefit of the smile that turned her into instant mush. "After all, if I'm going to be running into you again in the future, at least you should know who it is that is placing your life in jeopardy!"

Juel laughed and he visibly relaxed. The ice was broken. "My name is Juel and I don't think it's necessary to run me down again in order to get my attention."

"Can I get you anything else?" The waiter was pointedly giving them a message.

"No thanks," Mark replied, not even looking at the man. He was too busy searching the face of the girl sitting across the table from him. *I can't decide what color they are – green - aqua?* He noticed how the delicate winged arch of the eyebrows emphasized the large, expressive eyes. Her thick main of shining dark hair added the finishing touch to the creamy complexion. She wore a sweater the same color as her eyes. *She's beautiful.*

The waiter left. Juel glanced around the restaurant and noticed that most of the other diners were gone. Except for one other couple that occupied a table on the far side of the dining room, the place was empty. "I think he wants us to leave. They're probably getting ready to close."

Mark looked at his watch. He couldn't believe they'd been in the restaurant for most of the evening! They'd been so engrossed in getting to know each other and enjoying the easy rapport that existed between them, that time had become non-existent. Even the delicious pasta had cooled on their plates.

Juel felt the chemistry flowing between them. *Never before have I felt this good in any man's company. I feel as if we've known each other all our lives.*

She'd given up on the hope that he'd ask her for a date. Maybe the blond he'd been with on New Years Eve, really was more than just 'a friend.' Since the morning that he'd first approached her she'd only seen him twice. Even so he'd nodded and said, "Hi." *It was better than nothing.*

Almost two weeks later, she'd been sitting on her stool when he and his friend had come through the door. But he didn't go to his usual seat. Instead, he'd come straight to where she sat.

Once again, she caught a whiff of his after-shave and had to stop herself from leaning closer. "Hello there. I've been wondering. If you're not doing anything Saturday, could I take you out to dinner?" The unexpected invitation came out in a rush and he continued before she had time to respond. "Of course that is, if you haven't already got a date, like with a steady boyfriend… or something." He waited.

Juel stared. She couldn't believe she'd heard correctly!

When she didn't answer, he looked deflated. "Sorry. I understand. You're probably already tied up…"

"I'm not tied up and as it happens, I don't have a date this weekend. Yes. I'd love to have dinner with you."

She practically floated across the street, completely oblivious to the rushing cars as they honked their horns at the mindless jaywalker. Her boss had looked at her very peculiarly when he'd caught her with an idiotic smile on her face, staring blankly out of the window….

Reluctantly, they prepared to leave. Juel had learned quite a lot about him during the evening. Mark and Chuck worked at a fire station within walking distance of the cafeteria. After graduating from High School, he'd gained a football scholarship to college but after attending for a year, he'd realized that his heart wasn't in it so he'd quit. "I've been a firefighter for almost ten years," he said. "For as long as I can remember I wanted to be a fireman, but ma always insisted that I needed to do something less hazardous. She died not too long after I started college, so I just didn't see the sense in not doing what I really felt cut out to do."

Apparently, he and Chuck were life-long friends. "Even as kids our favorite game was playing at firemen." They would usually round up the rest of the neighborhood boys to play around empty abandoned buildings, pretending that their water guns were fire hoses putting out fires. Whatever Mark did it seemed that his friend followed suit.

One time when they'd just learned how to swim, Chuck dived in the deep end and wrenched his ankle. He panicked and couldn't get out. "I went in after him and was struggling to pull him to the side. When the lifeguard saw what was happening, he dived in and helped me to drag Chuck out. He'd sprained his foot pretty badly and was hobbling around for a coup'la weeks." Mark grinned as he related the event. "Now, whenever I need a favor from him I remind him that he owes me his life!"

"Does it work?"

"Every time," he laughingly responded.

After his mother had died of cancer, his father had gone to pieces. Apparently, the poor man had never quite got over the loss. He was twenty years older than his wife and had always taken it for granted that he would go first. "After ma's death, there seemed to be an unspoken agreement between us that I'd stick around until he'd recovered from his loss and after a while, it was easier to just stay."

"He's had severe bronchial problems for as long as I can remember and she always made sure that he took his medication. Dad's a pretty independent old guy, but I know that if I weren't there to make sure that he visits the doc. Regularly he wouldn't bother."

Juel's respect for him grew as she listened to this obvious bond that existed between father and son. *How many men would*

376

bother to stay at home and take care of a parent? She'd shared with him her own life growing up with Les and Rita.

"People think that Rita and I are related as we both have the same coloring and similar features. But, my great-grandparents came from Eastern Europe and Rita's mother is from Palestine. Her Mom and Dad met while he was there on a job. Les was born and raised next door to our house. His mother had to work a lot as his dad was killed in a car crash just before he was born. So, he spent a lot of time at our place."

Mark helped her into her coat and as he walked her outside into the cold air, seemed reluctant to end the date. When he suggested a 'night cap' before taking her home, she readily agreed.

"You sure got home late last night, or was it this morning?" Les' critical eye took in her dishabille as she wandered into the kitchen. She wasn't fully awake and still had the remnants of make-up on her face. Her hair was a mess and the eyes looked puffy with mascara smudges ringing them. She looked like a raccoon.

"It was twenty minutes to three, exactly," Rita announced, as she flipped bacon over in the frying pan. It made a loud spatter as she gave it a vigorous mashing with the spatula. Any other time the aroma of frying bacon would have tempted Juel's appetite, but this morning all she wanted was coffee - in peace and quiet. The coffee smelled promising but as for the rest, she was out of luck. Rita wasn't about to shut up.

"She thought she was being quiet but she forgot that the bedroom door squeaks when it's opened. Besides, she let her shoes thud on the floor when she kicked them off. Even her bed groaned as she plopped into it."

"Hey! What's with the Inquisition?" Any other time Juel would have ignored her but this morning, she didn't have the patience. "Anyone would think you two were my parents." She poured herself a cup of the fresh smelling coffee and slid into a chair across the table from Les. Mark had taken her to a club bar and one nightcap had led to two – and that was one too many for Juel. Her head ached.

Glancing at the ceramic clock hanging on the wall, she was surprised to see that it was almost noon. *No wonder I feel so groggy.* She gratefully took a swig of the hot brew. *Ah! Nectar from the gods!*

Rita laid a plate of crisp bacon and scrambled eggs in front of Les then taking toast out of the toaster, she put it on a plate alongside his breakfast. She stood scrutinizing Juel with hands on hips, not moving. "So. Is this the guy that you've been talking about for so long, the one that you see at the coffee-shop?"

Juel nodded, her face buried in her coffee mug.

"What do you know about him, except that he's a firefighter?" Without bothering to wait for a response she continued, "of course being a fireman doesn't tell me much, anyway." Rita was quiet for a moment, watching as her friend slowly sipped her coffee. "Did he bring you home?"

Juel didn't answer and Rita took this as a 'yes.' She didn't care anyway. She was on a roll now. "Do you think it's safe for him to know where you live?" The voice took on a dramatic tone as Rita's wild imaginings took over. "Don't you know there are all sorts of crazies out there? Did it ever occur to you that he might be a rapist – or even a maniacal killer? Remember the Boston Strangler who disguised himself as a policeman so women would trust him – or was it a fireman?"

"For Pete's sake!" The empty mug rattled as Juel slammed it down. "Just listen to yourself. You're so ridiculous! Anyone would think you were my mother the way you're going on. No one gives you the third degree after you've been out on a date."

"I don't date anyone that I haven't thoroughly checked out first." The retort came back fast.

"Oh? What about that creep that worked in your office building and wouldn't take no for an answer?" Juel's head was really pounding. "Seems to me you'd only known him for five minutes before you agreed to go out with him."

"I had NOT known him for only five minutes!" Rita's voice raised a few notches. "You know perfectly well that I'd worked in the same building with him for six months before I agreed to go out with him. And, he was always polite and seemed harmless." She glared across the table at Juel, "how did I know that he was only interested in jumping my bones as soon as he got me alone!"

"STOP IT!" Les' voice bounced from the walls. He laid down his fork and wiped his mouth with a napkin. "Good lord, you're both over twenty one and neither of you have to answer to anyone but yourselves."

The girls didn't say a word, but the atmosphere could've been cut with a knife. Rita returned to the stove in silence.

My head is splitting. Getting up, Juel moved to the counter to refill her mug. The tick of the clock sounded loud.

"Hey Rita. How about some more toast? Those eggs were great but I'd like to make a sandwich out of my left-over bacon." Les was attempting to relax the tension.

"I thought you were watching your diet," Rita replied gruffly as she placed more bread in the toaster.

Giving a helpless shrug of her shoulders, Juel moved next to the girl who was scraping the greasy frying pan as if her life depended on it. She draped an arm around her shoulder. "Come on Rita. I'm sorry I brought up that date with the obnoxious moron. But, Mark really isn't a rapist. In fact he didn't even kiss me good night and if you want to know the truth, I was disappointed." She gave the stiff shoulder a small squeeze. "I can really take care of myself you know," she finished quietly.

"I sometimes wonder about that." Rita was somewhat mollified by Juel's apology, but still felt a need to assert herself. "I'm only looking out for you, 'cause you're so impulsive and don't always stop to think."

Juel shook her head in resignation and carrying her refill back to the table, sat nursing her mug. Rita was only two months her elder, but she'd always treated Juel as if she were her personal responsibility. It was as if Juel was her younger sister and needed 'baby-sitting'. Even as youngsters they'd often quarreled over this trait and it hadn't changed much as they got older. In truth, it had probably become worse.

Juel had long since learned that silence was golden whenever Rita was in one of her 'mothering moods,' as Les referred to the girl's overly protective attitude. *I should've stayed quiet.* But, after getting to bed so late and still feeling less than human, she'd lost her cool and allowed Rita's nagging to get to her. She finished her coffee and arose. "I'm going to go and take a long shower," she said to the room in general. She hoped to get rid of the headache and maybe by the time she got out, she'd be in a better frame of mind to handle Rita.

"More coffee, Hon'?" Juel nodded her head at the waitress. Sally refilled her mug before turning to refill Chuck's. The waitress smirked knowingly at Mark as he held out his empty mug for a refill. "'Bout time y'all saved me from havin' to walk from one end of counter t'other." The grin on her round face grew wider as Mark raised his mug in a mock salute. The two men were sitting either side of Juel at 'her' end of the counter.

Chuck gave Sally a conspiratorial wink. "Don't ya know that's the only reason we all decided to sit together? You should feel flattered that we're being so considerate of your health."

"You're full of it too!" she guffawed. "So how come your friend 'ere, wasn't so concerned about my health before Juel started coming in of a morning? Seems to me you two clowns have bin comin' in 'ere forever, an' you've only just shown any interest in my welfare."

Juel drained her mug and exchanging a 'we –know –men' kind of smile with the woman, stood up. "I've got to get outta here or I'll be late for work. I'll leave you two in the capable hands of Sally." The laughing waitress moved away to serve another customer.

Mark and his friend had caught up with her, just as she'd been about to enter the cafeteria. Chuck had introduced himself. "Hi there. I'm Chuck," he said unnecessarily, holding out his hand to shake hers. Juel liked his friendly grip, noticing that the warmth of his voice extended to his friendly, blue eyes. Without giving it a second thought they'd all sat together. The place had been as busy as most mornings, but customers had started to dwindle as they left to go to their various places of business. Hence, Sally had the time to pause for conversation and make her pointed comments.

"I'll 'phone you later this evening," Mark called after Juel as she opened the door to leave. She waved her hand in response and entered the busy street. The traffic signal turned green and she floated across the street, grinning like an idiot. *Life is great!* The day was bright and pleasantly warm. She blinked against the blinding sunlight that reflected from the windows of the Twin Towers. It was as if they were saluting her and honoring her up-beat mood.

CHAPTER TWO

*E*xasperated, Mark listened to the phone messages. There were three of them, all from Pat - all basically saying the same thing. "Mark, honey. Where are you? I need to talk to you. I'm getting absolutely desperate! Call me."

His father sat in his chair, sucking on his pipe and giving him the 'look' that spoke volumes. Mark glared at the old man. "Don't say a word." Before Con could answer he added, accusingly, "you're not supposed to be smoking."

Con took the unlit pipe out of his mouth and eyed his son. The twinkling eyes underneath beetling eyebrows resembled shining onyx. They continued to bore into the younger man. "I'm not smoking. I'm just savoring my pipe."

Mark shrugged his shoulders, throwing up his arms in defeat. "When did she leave this last message?"

"Late last night."

"Why didn't you answer it when you knew it was Pat? You could've told her I wasn't here and didn't know where I was."

"Why should I lie? I told you after she called the first time, but you obviously didn't respond. You could've answered that call at the beginning of the week when you weren't working and had plenty of time."

Con picked up a tobacco pouch from his chair-side table. With deliberate movements, he took a generous pinch of tobacco and pushed it firmly into the pipe-bowl. "If you don't want her to keep calling you, tell her so yourself." Carefully, the old man continued to press down the tobacco and just as carefully took matches from his shirt pocket and lit the pipe. Taking a deep, satisfied puff he leaned back in his chair and watched the blue smoke rise from the bowl. The smell of burning tobacco was pleasantly potent. Suddenly, he gave a deep, rasping cough.

"You knew that would happen," said Mark, in triumph. "You're self destructive!"

"Ah! Who's been self-destructive? Seems to me that someone else likes to play with fire and has forgotten how to put one out."

Mark scowled but had the good grace to look uncomfortable. With a frustrated growl, he rubbed his hands through his hair. "I don't know what to say to her that I haven't said already. I've tried telling her that I just want to be her friend, but she doesn't listen. I wish she'd find herself a serious boyfriend so she'd leave me alone."

"If you're leaving with Juel for the weekend, you'd better call her before you go. You don't want me to answer the phone because you know I won't lie." The old man's eyes were full of mischief. "I'd hate for her to show up at the lodge looking for you." Settling back in his chair and putting his feet up on the ottoman, he puffed away at his pipe, choosing to ignore the angry flush that crept over his son's unhappy face.

In resignation, Mark picked up the phone. *Thank heaven she has enough sense not to call me on my cell.* Everyone knew that his cell phone was out of bounds for personal calls as he kept it strictly for job related emergencies. No one used it unless they wanted to bring down his wrath – not even the unquenchable Pat!

She picked up on the second ring. Hearing his voice, she began to lay a guilt trip on him. It was just enough to make him feel remorseful, yet not enough to give him reason to end the conversation. He apologized for not answering her calls and made the excuse that he's been working non-stop.

"Are you free this weekend, sweetie?" Her breathy voice held a note of expectation.

Mark hated it when she called him 'Sweetie'. It made him feel like a little kid. "Sorry Pat, but I'm going to be tied up this weekend…. Silence…. "Maybe we can meet for lunch one day next week?" he suggested. "I'm not working Wednesday." *Hell! Why don't you have the balls to tell her that you're going away for the weekend with Juel?* Out of the corner of his eye he saw the old man shaking his head. He deliberately turned his back to him. *After all I haven't been committed to her in years, so why not tell her that I'm serious about Juel? Why does she always manage to make me feel like she still has me on a leash?*

He knew why of course. He'd always felt an unreasonable sense of responsibility towards Pat, as if it were his job to watch out for her welfare. Underneath that sexy facade, she was just a vulnerable girl who had always relied on him to take care of her needs. Even when she'd been married to that jerk with all the money she'd turned to him for emotional support, especially when she was going through the nasty divorce.

Heaving a sigh of relief, Mark hung up the phone. She'd finally been pacified with his promise to meet for lunch. *I'll tell her about Juel when we meet.*

"I'm going upstairs to pack an overnight bag." He stood unmoving, waiting for his father to say something.

Con didn't respond. He didn't need to. The expression on his face spoke volumes. The pipe had gone out and he sat nonchalantly sucking on it. Mark was reminded of when he was a kid and caught doing something he wasn't supposed to do. "What?" Mark waited for a comment but the old man only smiled, knowingly. "So? Why don't you say what you're thinking – that I'm too damn chicken to tell her I'm spending the weekend with Juel?"

"Why should I when you say it so much better!"

Con's laughter followed his son as Mark climbed the stairs.

She awoke to the sound of birds chirping. Juel lay on her back underneath the sheet, enjoying the feel of Mark's warm body close to her own. Turning her head on the pillow, she looked into the face by her side. An arm draped across her abdomen and his breath gently fanned her cheek. His breathing was slow and rhythmic. As he lay on his side in a deep sleep, she searched his features.

He'd worked eighteen hours straight before getting this three-day break. Juel had shuddered when he'd told her about the horrendous fire that had broken out in an abandoned warehouse full of flammable material. Luckily, apart from one fireman having been overcome by smoke and needing medical help, there were no serious injuries. Nevertheless it brought home to Juel the stark reality of how dangerous Mark's job could be.

How thick his eyelashes are. They cast a faint shadow underneath his closed eyelids. *What a woman wouldn't give to have them.* His tousled hair looked more unruly than it normally did and she curbed the urge to run her fingers through it. Her gaze moved down to the hard chest with its dark mat of hair. *He looks so vulnerable when he's sleeping.* Very carefully, she removed his arm from across her body.

Swinging her legs over the side of the bed, Juel reached for her satin robe that lay draped over the back of a chair. She slipped her arms into the sleeves and tied the sash firmly around her waist. The sleek material clung to her body, outlining the curve of her hips as she walked softly towards the sliding doors that led to the patio. Sunlight streamed into the room through the glass and Juel could hear the distant hum of a lawn mower. Slowly, so as not to disturb the sleeping man, she slid open the patio door. The humming of the mower became more distinct and the air smelled sweetly of cut grass.

Juel stepped outside and inhaled the fresh scents of spring. A warm breeze ruffled her hair as she gazed across the acres of neatly manicured lawns. Meandering pathways held planned and orderly borders of flowers. Yellow daffodils and red tulips mingled and beyond was a wooded copse that separated the lodge's expansive grounds from farm fields. On the far horizon, she could make out the dusky blue of the Atlantic. She lifted her face to the early morning sun.

Mark had been planning this get-a-way for sometime and they'd finally been able to coincide their days off so they could spend three uninterrupted days together. Even though she got along great with his father and enjoyed visiting their home, being completely alone was much better. Last night, knowing that they were alone in their own space, their lovemaking had been exquisitely abandoned, even if their space was only a rented cabin at a lodge.

Her face glowed. She absentmindedly watched the riding mower being steered back and forth across the grass, only half-conscious of her surroundings. Juel thought about the deepening bond that existed between them....

They'd been dating steadily for about three weeks when he'd invited her to his home. Juel had felt a bit nervous at having to meet his father but her concern had been unnecessary. When they'd driven up to the house in Queens, the parent had been sitting on the front porch waiting for them. Juel expected him to be an older version of Mark but there was little resemblance. As she followed Mark up the porch steps, she took stock of the round and swarthy, face. The heavy black eyebrows looked startling against the shock of white hair and emphasized the dark eyes beneath them. As he stood to greet them, she noticed that he was also much shorter than his son.

Even so, the warm smile that he gave Juel was definitely a family trait. Walking forward to greet Juel, he told her that she was the most beautiful girl that he'd seen outside of Greece!

Juel knew that Mark's parents were of Greek origin as he'd told her all about his family. His father had come to America as a young man and when he'd felt the need for a wife, he'd written back home to relatives and asked them to find him a suitable bride. A photo had been sent of a girl from his village and liking what he saw, he'd sent for her. It seemed that they had been perfectly matched and had a happy marriage, until her untimely death.

Mark fixed dinner and Juel was pleasantly surprised to find that he could cook. "After ma died it was a matter of either learning, or starving to death!" he said. "Dad was in no condition to do anything and he'd never had to cook when she was around to see to his every need." Mark confessed that he'd had help from his sister who was eight years older.

Tula was married (pregnant at the time) - and lived about a fifteen minutes drive from their house. After the death of their mother she'd left her understanding husband with their toddler daughter and stayed at the house long enough to help the two men organize their 'bachelor' lives. "She showed me how to use a cookbook, along with a few cooking tricks that ma had taught her."

Over the meal of excellent roast chicken and rice pilaf, his father regaled Juel with family tales. She was fascinated by the stories of his youth spent in his homeland.

Con (short for Constantine)- spoke of Greece with such love.

The old man made her feel completely at ease and they'd hit it off from the moment they met. After dinner she watched him fill an old pipe with meticulous care, then settle back in his chair to enjoy it. After a few puffs he started to cough and seemed to be having difficulty breathing. Immediately, Mark gave him his 'puffer,' grumbling at him for smoking.

Within a few moments he was okay but his son continued to gripe. "You know your doctor warned you not to smoke that thing."

"Stop fussing!" Con snapped. "What does that young whippersnapper know? I was smoking when that doctor and you were still wet behind the ears." He leaned forward and pointed the pipe at his son." I've given up cigarettes but I'm not giving up my pipe. Anyway, at my age why should I care how long I live?"

Mark gave Juel an embarrassed look of resignation and she shook her head in sympathy. To ease the awkwardness, she offered to make some coffee.

After that first day, Juel became a regular visitor to the house as Con invited her, whether Mark was with her or not. "You're better looking than my son and your presence lights up the house. I see him often enough - my daughter too, but I can only take those noisy grand kids in small doses." He was referring to the four offspring that Tula had produced over the years.

Underneath Con's tough exterior, Juel guessed that the man still missed his wife and was lonely for female company. She got into the habit of making the trip out to Queens pretty regularly if Mark couldn't get home.

When Mark had first suggested she stay overnight with him, Juel questioned whether or not Con would approve? "Your dad's from the old country and he may not like our sleeping together under his roof."

"It's my home too and he's never questioned what I do," adding, "if I were living by myself it would be nobodies business and it goes the same way in this house."

Juel had still hesitated but he'd over rode her qualms. "If it makes you feel better, we'll tell him that you're considering staying over for the weekend and see what he says."

For a fleeting moment her mind questioned whether or not she was the first girl that he'd brought to stay overnight? Juel quickly dismissed it as irrelevant. *He's asking me and that's all that counts.* Still, she had to admit that the idea of Mark sharing his bed with another female bothered her. She mentally slapped herself. *Don't be so naïve. He's certainly not celibate. What difference does it make if other women have shared his bed in his father's house? He's inviting me now."* She thought of the first time he'd kissed her. It had made her feel weak at the knees. *No man kisses like that without having had plenty of practice….*

The breeze danced across the patio and played with her hair. Juel idly brushed a tendril away from her face. She recalled how nervous she was when Mark had told Con that she was staying overnight.

After dinner, Mark had casually broken the news. "By the way dad, Juel isn't going home tonight. Seeing as how neither of us has to work this weekend, we might as well spend our time with you. And, there's no reason to make extra work by using the guest room. She'll share my room." Juel literally held her breath.

"Makes sense to me." The old man didn't bat an eyelid. "In fact, I'll have an extra key made for you Juel, so that when you visit without my son I don't have to bother answering the door."

Juel's mouth fell open. Mark gave her a smug look that said 'I told you so' and she wanted to kick him! True to his word the next time she visited, Con handed a key to her, for the front door….

Arms suddenly encircled her body from behind, startling her out of her reverie. He pulled her close in to him. "How long have you been standing out here?"

She turned in the circle of his arms. "Not very long. You were sleeping so soundly I didn't want to disturb you." She kissed him, softly. "You were so tired."

"Not so tired that I want to miss any time with you." The inevitable lock of hair brushed his forehead. Juel reached up to gently move it to one side. His eyes held hers as he took her hand and caressed the palm with his thumb. Lifting it to his mouth, he kissed the palm. "You know something, sweetheart? I believe I've loved you ever since I first saw you."

Juel felt her emotions overflow. "I think I've loved you for longer than that."

Rita rolled the pin towards the outer edges of the dough, before flipping it over with an expert maneuver of her wrists. Shaking more flour onto the rolling pin, she repeated the same process - flattening and shaping the dough to form the flaky piecrust. "So, what time did you say they were supposed to be here?"

Juel gave an audible sigh. "I've already told you. I told them that we would eat around eight o'clock and suggested that they get here between seven and seven thirty for cocktails."

She sat at the kitchen table, watching Rita. Standing in front of the counter, the girl carefully placed the pastry shell into a pie dish, then took the brandied peaches out of a bowl and arranged them inside the shell. Juel had no doubt that the finished result would be delicious.

"I'm still not so sure that this is such a good idea - inviting them for dinner, I mean." Rita paused in the act of rolling out more pastry for the pie's lid. "After all, we don't have a proper dining room. Besides, we only have three water glasses that match." Another pause ensued as she deftly placed the cover over the peaches. "Do you think we've got enough ice for drinks?" Her big brown eyes looked anxiously at Juel.

"Stop worrying. Why are you so nervous? They're just a couple of ordinary guys. We're not inviting the president to dinner, for heaven's sake! You've already met Mark and Chuck is just a nice friendly guy. You'll like him."

"I doubt that if he's anything like your Mark." The tone was full of sarcasm.

"OK. So you don't like him. You've made that obvious on

several occasions." Juel's annoyance was laced with perplexity, "but I still don't understand why?"

Rita crimped the edges of the crust before making slashes in the top with a sharp looking knife. Wielding it deftly, she crisscrossed the pastry as if she were a Samurai warrior wielding his sword. "I don't know." Her voice sounded equally as perplexed as Juel's. "There's just something about him that bothers me," she answered vaguely. Her eyebrows knitted together. "He's too good looking for one thing. No man should be that good looking."

She opened the oven door and almost threw the pie inside. "I bet he's never gone short of having women falling at his feet! I just don't want to see you getting hurt," she finished lamely.

Juel couldn't help but laugh at her friend's illogic. "So, he's good looking. Does that make him a Blue Beard? Les is good looking. Do you think he's always up to no good?"

Rita turned from the oven and faced the girl at the table. "Les is a different story and you know it. We've known him practically all our lives and we know he's really a decent guy, in spite of his sexy looks." She wiped a strand of dark hair away from her flushed face, leaving a smudge of flour across her cheek. "You know as well as I do that underneath that beautiful body, Les is just a pussy-cat and wouldn't harm a fly."

She paused, not really knowing how to express her feelings about Mark. "This guy of yours is different. There's something about him that bothers me…." Rita stopped. The frown on her face deepened. Turning her back on Juel she went over to the sink to wash flour from her hands, as if the act would also cleanse away her disturbing thoughts.

Rita tried to sort out the antagonism that Juel's boyfriend caused her to feel. "I don't know why - - - I just don't trust him."

Juel saw that she was genuinely troubled and her amusement disappeared. Rising, she went over to the sink as Rita wiped and re-wiped her hands on a paper towel. Hugging the girl, she tried to be reassuring. "You worry too much about me. I'm sorry you don't like Mark but believe me, he's very good to me and I know that he wouldn't do anything to hurt me."

Rita wasn't convinced. *How can I explain this dislike I have for him when I can't even explain it to myself?* She hadn't taken to Mark from the first moment that Juel had introduced him, and the feeling hadn't dissipated. Mentally, she nudged away the negative thoughts. *So what? Juel is obviously gone on him so who am I to rain on her parade?* She gave a shrug of resignation. "All right, so you trust him and I guess that's all that counts. At least he's not going to be able to say that I didn't fix a decent meal!"

"From the smell that's coming from the oven, I don't think that either of them will have any complaints about that prime rib or that pie," Juel declared. The awkwardness was eased.

Seeing that Juel was constantly bragging about her boyfriend's cooking expertise, Rita was determined not to be outdone in the kitchen. Consequently, she'd outdone herself in preparing the meal for this evening's guests.

Only the day before, she'd come home from work loaded down with grocery bags. She'd walked through the door just as Les was about to leave. He was on his way to Florida for a photo shoot and seeing her struggling he'd relieved her of the load, in the process taking a fast peak inside one of the sacks. "Good lord girl, are you entertaining only two guys, or all of New York's bachelor population?"

She'd shoved him out of the door with a promise to fix him something good on his return. "I'll hold ya to that," he'd called out as the door closed behind him.

They sat around the tiny living room feeling well fed and relaxed. The dinner had been superb and Rita had felt a sense of satisfaction when Chuck asked for a second helping of everything. She'd even felt some warmth towards Mark after he'd begged for another slice of the pie.

"Boy! I sure haven't eaten like that since I left my mother's house. You two girls really fixed a great meal." Chuck sat nursing a beer at one end of the couch and looking completely at home in his surroundings. From the opposite end, Rita sent him her most engaging smile.

"All the credit goes to Rita" Juel responded, loyally. "All I did was fix the salad dressing and toss the salad." Sitting on the floor at Mark's feet, she reached for the hand that he'd placed on her shoulder.

Leaning forward in the armchair and lightly resting his chin on the top of her head, Mark caught a whiff of her shampoo. He literally had to stop himself from running his fingers through the silky mane, wanting to lift it from the back of her neck and nuzzle the familiar spot behind one of her small ears. Glancing up, he saw Rita scrutinizing him from across the width of the coffee table. In a brief flash he saw the cold, flinty expression in her eyes. *Why does she dislike me so much?* For the hundredth time, Mark puzzled over Rita's barely disguised antipathy towards him.

Hoping to win some points with her, he complimented her cooking. "It sure was an excellent meal, Rita. Thank you for fixing it. Juel has often told me what a great cook you are and she wasn't exaggerating."

Rita nodded in acceptance of the compliment and gave him a polite smile. *I still don't like him but at least, he's got manners,* she admitted to herself. *One thing is for sure I've never seen Juel so crazy about a man. And, I guess he can't be all that bad if Chuck is his friend.* She turned her attention to the big man sitting a couple of feet from her. *He's really nice and he appreciates good food. He has such a kind looking face.*

Juel noticed the easy rapport between her friend and Chuck as they continued an animated conversation. Obviously they were hitting it off. *Thank goodness she at least approves of Chuck. I guess I have to be thankful for small mercies!* Turning her head to look up into Mark's face, she smiled knowingly and gave a slight nod in the direction of the couch. Mark understood and raised his beer can in a silent salute.

CHAPTER THREE

*H*ow *can they stand such activity in this heat?* Juel sat at the picnic table, watching in amusement as the two men demonstrated how high they could jump on the huge trampoline. *They're just a coupla overgrown kids.* Tula's two boys were trying to compete with the men, while their baby sister screamed in excitement from her spot on the sidelines. The three year old jumped up and down on the grass as she imitated the leaps of those on the trampoline. Her sister, standing by her side, looked on with all the scorn of an older sibling.

For the umpteenth time, Juel wondered how the trampoline could hold the combined weight of both Mark and Chuck, never mind the addition of the boys. Lolling in his chair under the shade of an Elm, Tula's husband yelled encouragement to the two clowns.

"They're as bad as the kids, aren't they?"

Juel turned to the woman sitting alongside her on the bench. "They're worse," she rejoined with a laugh.

Tula was a female version of her father. Her eyes were Con's and although the round facial contours were more delicate, the features were the same and she was also short in stature.

"Let's face it" Juel gave an exaggerated sigh, "men are really kids in big bodies,"

The Fourth of July barbecue was an annual event at Tula's home and in full swing. Of course Chuck was always included in the festivities, but this year he'd brought Rita along as his date and of course, Juel was Mark's. Tula hadn't waited for Mark to invite her. She'd telephoned Juel at work to make sure she would be there.

Juel had run into the sister one Saturday at Con's home when they both happened to be visiting. As Juel had climbed the porch steps she'd heard Tula's rambunctious brood long before she'd let herself in.

The two females had hit it off immediately and before she'd left, Tula had invited her to dinner. "Tell that brother of mine that it's about time he brought you to visit me. I'll call him next week and he knows I won't take no for an answer." True to her promise, she'd called. Mark had told Juel that he had been 'ordered' to show up for dinner with her on his next weekend off duty.

Tula's husband had answered the door and Juel was reminded of a big, cuddly bear. Jack hadn't waited to be introduced. He'd welcomed her in a booming voice that matched his expansive body, overwhelming her in a crushing hug. Although he wasn't any taller than Mark he must have weighed at least a hundred pounds more. His shock of light brown hair was turning gray and he looked as if he hadn't visited a barber in months. Covering the lower half of his face was a stubbly growth of beard that was more gray than brown. It matched the thick mat of hair showing on his chest that was only partially covered by a gaudy, Hawaiian-style shirt. Only the bottom two buttons were fastened. To top it off, he wore baggy mustard colored shorts that ended just below his knees, showing the rest of his hairy legs and big feet that were thrust into a pair of yellow flip-flops. The overall effect was that of the Sesame Street bird in drag!

After seeing the amount of food that Tula had prepared that day, Juel was no longer amazed at Jack's size. Over her feeble protestations, her plate had been piled with huge helpings of delicious Greek style food. When she gave pleading excuses for refusing a second piece of the homemade cheesecake, she was playfully accused of eating like a sparrow.

The barbecue grill continued to emit odors of smoking meat but most of the food on the picnic table had been devoured.

Rita's voice drifted over to the picnic table as she called out to Chuck. The man jumped down and slumped into a canvas chair under the shade tree, next to his girlfriend. Rita handed him a paper napkin and he wiped his sweating brow.

Seeing that his friend had given up, Mark followed suit. Stripping off his T- shirt, he used it to mop perspiration from his face and chest before walking over to join the women sitting at the picnic table. *Just looking at him makes me tingle.* Squeezing onto the bench next to Juel, he leaned over to give her a kiss. "Having a good time? She nodded and returned his kiss.

Chuck bent to whisper something into Rita's ear and the girl burst into laughter. *There's a subtle change in her.* Juel looked at the two heads so close together. She couldn't exactly pinpoint what the change was but she silently thanked Chuck for his calming influence on her friend. Her attitude towards Mark wasn't quite as antagonistic and she seemed to have mellowed. Juel suspected that she was still wary of Mark - but at least she'd stopped her sarcastic comments about him. Absentmindedly, she took a bite of the fat Greek olive that Mark held out.

There was an air of lazy congeniality in the suburban garden. Even though the day was hot, the rapport between the inhabitants was relaxed and easy.

Tula absentmindedly wafted a fly away from the remains of a wilted salad and arising, started to gather up dirty dishes. "Will you carry those glasses into the kitchen for me, Mark?"

He dutifully did her bidding and followed his sister across the grass. Juel's eyes followed him, appreciating the sight of his hard rippling back muscles. After disappearing through the back door, she let her idle scanning swing over to where Con was sitting.

The old man sat alone under the shade of the patio table's huge umbrella. Late afternoon shadows were covering the concrete, making it the coolest spot in the yard. Even so, Juel noticed the pallor around his mouth that contrasted sharply with the rest of his olive skin.

Getting up from the bench, she crossed the few yards that separated them. "Hi Con. Are all these festivities getting to be too much for you?"

He patted the seat next to him, indicating that she should sit. The lips that sucked on the stem of his unlit pipe were blue tinged. Removing it, he appraised her admiringly. "You're a sight for these old eyes, Juel. Keeping me company for a while is just what the doctor ordered." He inhaled a gulp of air. "Watching those fools jumping around with the kids has made me breathless." His chest labored with the effort of talking.

"Are you alright Con?" His voice sounded raspy. "Can I get you some lemonade, or a cold beer?"

"Beer sounds good. This heat has made me thirsty."

Juel went over to the cooler to get a beer from its nest of ice. Flipping open the top, she walked back to the table and handed it to him. Con took a long swig then began to cough.

"You know, you really shouldn't smoke that pipe. Where's your inhaler?"

"You're beginning to sound like my son." Fathomless eyes twinkled at her as he reached into his checkered shirt pocket to withdraw the small 'puffer'. Placing the bowl between his lips Con pressed on the stem and inhaled deeply. The man gave another cough, pausing before repeating the dose. It helped.

He gave Juel a wry smile as he returned it to his pocket. "Not as enjoyable as my old pipe but it does the job."

His breathing slowed and Juel was relieved to see normal color gradually return to his face. They sat in comfortable silence.

Not a breath of wind stirred. Rhythmic sounds of swishing water came from the neighbor's lawn sprinkler. The screen door banged. Tula and Mark came out of the house and the woman sat down again at the picnic table. Mark joined the group underneath the tree.

"HI THERE FOLKS! The tranquility ended. "Just stopped by to say hello and happy fourth to y'all." The high-pitched lilting was like a sudden raindrop that promises a summer storm.

Juel turned to see a good-looking blond who'd appeared around the corner of the house. Mark shot out of his chair. The girl in very skimpy denim shorts looked familiar and it took a few seconds for recognition to dawn on Juel. It was the same girl she'd seen with Mark on New Year's Eve.

She watched in fascination. The girl with legs that went on forever, glided towards the shade tree, while Juel's eyes swung between the newcomer and Mark's open-mouthed gawk. The look of astonishment on his face was a picture. Mesmerized, she watched the gorgeously tanned creature as she floated across the grass.

Everything seemed to be moving in slow motion as the blonde's ponytail swayed in synchronization with her hips. Juel's gaze dropped to the bright scarlet toenails in the thong sandals. They exactly matched the color of lipstick on her smiling mouth. Her scrutiny took in the beige colored top that barely covered the pert bouncing boobs. It was obvious that she wasn't wearing a bra. Tantalizing flesh showed between the girl's midriff and shorts. The shorts hardly covered the necessities. *I never would have thought a belly button could be provocative!*

"Well, hello there Pat. What a nice surprise." Jack gave a loud appreciative whistle while Mark stood as if made of stone. An idiotic expression stayed glued to his face as the girl came to a halt in front of him.

Juel absorbed the scene as if viewing a bad movie – then did a double take as the girl threw her arms around Mark' neck. Planting a long lingering kiss on him, she moved her mouth seductively against his.

Juel froze.

"I haven't seen you in so-oo long." The blonde's caressing voice echoed across the yard as she finally came up for air. Very slowly, Mark disentangled himself from the girl's embrace.

Juel felt numb.

Con watched the play of emotions on her face as she stared at the couple. "Mark and Pat have known each other for years," he said, by way of explanation. "She was his high school sweetheart but they both went their separate ways after they left for different colleges."

Juel didn't respond.

"Just a lot of water under the bridge, Juel. They've been friends ever since they were teenagers. Nothing more."

That must have been a hell of a lot of water to warrant such a greeting.

Mark bent his head to say something to Pat and they both turned their heads to look in her direction. Juel tried to gain control over her outraged emotions as he headed for the patio with the blond in tow.

Coming alongside her chair, he bent and kissed her lightly on the cheek. *Sure different than what he just exchanged with her!*

"Juel, I want you to meet a good friend of mine. This is Pat. She and I went to school together. We haven't seen each other for a while."

She detected a sheepish awkwardness in his voice. *He should squirm.*

"We've been friends for a long time," he added.

Obviously! She was seething. Juel managed to smile politely as he continued with the introductions. "Pat, this is Juel. Remember I told you about her when we talked on the phone?" *They keep in touch by phone do they - even if he hasn't seen her for ages? Or has he?* In spite of her good intentions, Juel was getting madder by the minute. Her face ached from trying to keep a smile fixed in place.

 "So you are Juel. Mark positively droo-ooled, when he told me about you!" The blond gave her an ingratiating smile showing small, pearly white teeth.

They look like shark's teeth. The old hit song 'Mack the Knife' leapt into Juel's mind. "It's nice to meet you." *God forgive me for being a hypocrite.*

The siren continued to gush. "I have to admit, you're even more gorgeous than he said you were!" Her ice blue eyes swept appraisingly up and down Juel's body. "My goodness Mark, wherever did you find such a beautiful creature?"

Oh Paleeese! You're overdoing it bitch! I'm not a prize cow!" She wanted to smack the flawlessly made up face.

Pat continued to purr like a cat that had eaten the bird. "I'm so-ooo happy to have finally met you, Juel. Mark has told me all about you. In fact he was literally ga-ga when he told me what a special person you are."

"I'm sorry to say, he hasn't told me a thing about you." She tried not to sound sarcastic but Mark flushed and had the good grace to look embarrassed. Only he seemed to notice the edge to her voice and see the green eyes flashing sparks.

Not quite. Con had noticed. His expression was one of shrewd discernment as he observed the two girls. They were acting as if absolutely overjoyed at meeting each other and his mouth twitched as he turned his attention to his son. Mark looked as if he wished the ground would open up and swallow him.

"Stay and watch the fireworks with us, Pat," said Tula as she and Jack joined them.

"Yeah, why don't you stay, Pat?" her husband interjected. "You'll sure create some of your own fireworks the way you look in that outfit!" The grin on his face disappeared as he caught Mark's eye.

"I'm so-oo sorry." The false eyelashes batted at Jack. "Believe me as much as I would love to stay I do have other plans. In fact, I really must dash or I'll be late for my date with Charlie." She addressed the group in general. "He's such a pet," she oozed, "and he's so-o-oo patient with me when I'm not on time."

The theatrical drawl made Juel gag. *What makes her think she can get away with sounding like a southern belle with that dialect? Who does she think she is- Scarlet O'Hara of Queens?* Juel hated to admit it, but the broad had the males' attention regardless of her phony come-hither voice. Inwardly seething, she listened as Pat continued to spout her dejection at having to leave such manly company.

"Y'all know don't you that I just had to come by and see you? I miss the fun times that we all used to have together on these special days. I really do!" She gave Jack the benefit of her sexy smile, before turning it full blast on Mark. The intimate, caressing look she gave him under half closed lids caused Juel's blood to boil anew!

Pat turned her attention back to Juel once more. "It was absolutely fabulous meeting you, Juel. We must get together sometime and exchange tid-bits about our favorite man, here." Once again, she laid an intimate, knowing 'look' on Mark. Giving another seductive laugh she blew a kiss towards Con, then to Chuck and Rita who remained sitting under the tree. She waved to the children still playing, before kissing Mark on the cheek. Turning to leave, she patted his butt. Everyone watched the swaying derriere until Pat disappeared from sight around the side of the house.

"Who wants ice-cream?" Tula broke the silence. The children all screamed at once and Jack asked for caramel syrup topping. Chuck called across the yard. "We'll take some, Tula."

Juel's legs couldn't hold her up any longer. Gratefully, she sank back down at the patio table, but Mark moved to sit next to her. Abruptly she shot out of the chair. "I'll come and help you Tula." Without waiting for a response she hurried across the yard, following the woman through the back door.

Obediently she took dishes from a cupboard that Tula indicated, spreading them out on the counter top while the woman rummaged in the freezer for a couple of cartons of ice-cream. "There's caramel and chocolate syrups in that cupboard over there Juel, if you want to get them."

She opened the cupboard that Tula indicated, reaching for the jars that were on a shelf. Although she moved like a robot, her mind whirled in confused anger. *How dare that broad patronize me! And, why didn't he tell me that he was still seeing his old girlfriend? Well, I'm not sure that he's still dating her - but I bet he is if they've been telephoning each other. Especially after the way the oversexed bitch acted with him! And, what makes him think he can discuss me with her as if he'd won me in the lottery?"*

"Can you open those jars of syrup, please?" Tula had placed the dishes on a big serving tray and was busy loading the last dish with ice cream, "that way, everyone can help themselves to whatever topping they want. Oh! Forgot the sprinkles. Can you grab them? They should be on the same shelf as the syrup."

Trancelike, Juel did as she was told. Tula kicked the screen door open with a foot, while balancing the tray with her hands. Juel automatically followed the woman outside. Why was everyone acting as if it was still a perfect day?

That is, every one except Mark. He was half-heartedly tossing a Frisbee to little Bella and turned anxious eyes on Juel as she alighted from the house. She felt his eyes following as she walked over to the picnic table to lay down plastic spoons and napkins,

Talking animatedly to Jack between mouthfuls of ice cream, she refused to look in his direction. The globs of ice cream stuck in her throat and she had to force herself to swallow. Pat's presence lingered like a bad dream.

The suggestive voice refused to leave and the sound of the girl's laughter resonated inside her head like the clanging of a bell. She piled empty dessert dishes onto the tray and headed back to the kitchen.

"Are you okay?" Mark appeared at her side as she walked towards the house

"Of course I am. Why shouldn't I be?" she answered, too brightly.

"Uncle Mark! Get the Frisbee!" Bella's voice was demanding as the toy rolled across the ground, landing in front of their feet.

"Another female seems to want your attention. Get her the Frisbee." She let the screen door slam behind her.

"I TOLD you not to trust him!" Rita felt a helpless rage against the man who had hurt her friend. She stared angrily at the miserable face across the kitchen table from her. "I could kill that no good bastard!"

The apartment door opened to admit Les. He looked fit and bronzed from having spent the weekend with friends at Cape Cod. "Hey guys! I'm back." Dropping his overnight bag on the floor, he walked into the kitchen and stopped. Straight away he knew something was wrong. Juel's glum expression could have soured milk, while Rita's dour face looked as if she'd smelled something bad. "Wow! Who died?"

They ignored him as Rita continued as if uninterrupted, "…. So? What explanation did the jerk give you for that bitch's sudden appearance?"

Juel shook her head. "None really. What could he say?"

"HELLO.o.o! Is somebody going to tell me when the funeral's taking place?"

The girls turned their heads as if only just conscious of his presence. "There's coffee made if you want some," said Rita.

Les moved to the counter and took a mug from the cupboard. Pouring coffee slowly and deliberately, he eyed the two girls. He carried it to the table and sat down next to Juel. "What's wrong, kid?"

There was no answer as he dumped three spoons of sugar into his coffee. He waited –slowly stirring the liquid with the sugar bowl's spoon.

"How many times do I have to tell you not to use the sugar spoon to stir your coffee?"

Ignoring Rita's acid tongue, Les once again spoke to Juel without any trace of his former banter. "What's the matter? You look like you just lost a million bucks."

"I'll tell you what's the matter!" Rita opened her mouth before the other girl could answer. Les listened in silence as she began to enlighten him as to the events of the party at Tula's house, adding her own embellishments. "You should have seen her rubbing her navel against him. She looked as if she was about to rape him right there on the spot!"

"That's enough Rita." Juel's voice trembled.

Les laid a hand over the clutching fists that rested on the table. "Who is this girl, Juel?" he asked gently.

She cleared her throat, "Mark says she's just a good friend. Apparently, he hadn't expected her to show up to the barbecue. I believe he's telling the truth about that, because he acted genuinely surprised." The voice cracked, "but I'm not so sure that she's just a 'friend' as he claims.

Rita made a rude sound. "Friend my ass! The way she came on to him was more than friendly. I was closer to them than you were when she laid that kiss on him. That tongue of hers was working

404

overtime and, if she'd pressed her body any closer he'd have ignited from spontaneous combustion!"

Les looked from one to the other. "Now let's calm down here. It sounds as if you're both over reacting. It was probably something quite innocent." Rita rolled her eyes, repeating the noise that resembled a pig with a bad case of sinusitis.

Juel's eyes glistened. "No Les. Rita is right. I could see the way she was coming on to him - even from the distance of the patio. And, she made no pretence of the fact that she considered me to be a rival. Syrup practically dripped from her mouth when Mark introduced us and she made a point of letting me know that he called her - regularly."

"So? Did you talk to Mark concerning this relationship? Did you ask him exactly what he means by 'a good friend'? " Les made quotation signs with his fingers.

"Of course she did," once again Rita chimed in. "Naturally, that smooth talking S.O.B. had a good explanation. I knew all along I was right about him!"

"Be quiet!" Les' tone meant business. "You're not helping the situation here. Can't you see she's upset enough without making her feel worse?"

"Excuse me for living!" Folding her arms, Rita clamped her mouth like a vice.

Les repeated his question. "Did you discuss the situation with him, Juel? Did you ask him if he was still involved with this girl?"

"Of course I did and he denied it. He claims that he hasn't been interested in her in years, especially since knowing me. He explained that they had been sweethearts as teenagers, but it had been over a long time ago."

Juel continued. "Seems she met someone else while at college. The guy happened to come from a very rich family, so she broke up with Mark and married him. But it only lasted for a short time. Mark admits that when they split, he was pretty miserable.

But every time she had a marital problem she sought him out to cry on his shoulder. After her divorce, she wanted to pick up where they'd left off but he says he doesn't feel anything for her anymore. Still- they've stayed friends."

"And you believe him?" Les asked.

Juel didn't say anything. A heavy pall hung over the kitchen as they waited for her to answer. Straightening her shoulders, she looked first at Les, and then at Rita.

"Yes, I believe him. I have to. Mark says he loves me and I don't know what I'd do if he didn't."

Rita gave a resigned shrug. "Then I guess the subject is closed."

Les said nothing, but his thoughts weren't good. *I have to admit I'm as suspicious as Rita is of this girl.* Attempting to lighten the atmosphere he changed the subject. "Hey! I won some money this weekend! Let's go out and celebrate. My treat."

Juel shook her head negatively, but Rita gave him a look of skepticism. "Where are you going to take us to? Macdonald's?"

"That's right. Go ahead and be your usual, pessimistic self. No. I wasn't thinking of fast food." He turned his attention on Juel, "how about a big, juicy steak? I won't take no for an answer, so go and put on some lipstick. If I'm going to waste my money taking you two out for dinner instead of some appreciative male, at least you can thank me by looking better than you do at the moment."

CHAPTER FOUR

*T*he computer screen went blank. The last of the cruise registrations had been taken care of. Juel heaved a sigh of relief that the day was over. It had been long and hectic with people calling either to confirm reservations, or to request last minute bookings. Everyone wanted to get away from the city's stifling humidity.

It was cool in the air-conditioned office, even though the late afternoon sun was still beating through the window. Juel glanced outside and saw heat practically bouncing in waves off the sidewalk. *New York is no place to be in August.* Sighing, she picked up her pocketbook, preparing to enter the furnace outside.

The phone shrilled. Her clock on the desk said that it was already ten minutes past closing time. She hesitated. It continued to ring. In resignation, she picked it up before the recorder could kick in.

"Juel? Thank goodness I caught you before you'd left!" It was Mark. "I tried your cell phone but you must have it turned off." He sounded out of breath.

"What's wrong?"

407

"I can't make it this evening. I'm supposed to be out of the door right now. We've got a big emergency." She heard a commotion in the background. "Gotta go. I'll call you as soon as I get a chance." The phone went dead.

Juel stared out the window – the receiver still in her hand. People rushed along the streets, jostling each other as if they had some place of importance to go. A mother dragged a little boy behind her, irritably pulling on his arm.

Is he really going on an emergency call? As quickly as it entered, she forced the thought out of her mind. *Don't be such a suspicious fool He's a firefighter, isn't he?*

The phone was giving rapid bleeping sounds to alert her to disconnect. Slowly, Juel hung it up and let herself out of the front door. A blast of hot air hit her and she automatically reached inside her purse for sunglasses. Being the last person to leave, she locked the door. The boss had to leave early and the other employees had left at their usual times, but she'd been detained with a last minute reservation.

Mark's voice rang in her ears as she walked to the subway. Before the Fourth of July fiasco she wouldn't have given a second thought to his breaking a date. "A fireman is always on duty, even when he isn't on duty," he'd once told her apologetically after he'd had to cancel their plans. She understood that didn't she? *Of course I do.* Juel refused to listen to the taunting voice in her head that whispered the name - - Pat.

After the initial confrontation, they hadn't talked about his ex-girlfriend anymore. He'd apologized profusely for the awkward situation that Pat had created by being 'so demonstrative,' as he'd put it. "How do I convince you that I love you, for heavens sake! It was over between Pat and I years ago. I haven't a clue why she showed up like that and acted the way she did….. Of course I had talked about you. Why shouldn't I? …. She always calls me when she's in between boyfriends. That's just the way she is…. I'd told her that I'd met someone who is very special to me, but she still calls whenever she's broken up with her latest conquest. It doesn't mean a thing. Pat thinks of me as an old friend. And, that is all I think of her."

Juel hadn't been completely convinced. Her female instincts screamed otherwise. She was certain that Pat thought of Mark as more than just a friendly shoulder to cry on. Yet, she didn't want to come across as being the jealous possessive type, so she kept her peace. By mutual agreement they had dropped the subject and it wasn't discussed again.

That July night, he'd made love to her like he never had before. He'd been tender yet passionate and had gone out of his way to give her pleasure. He'd made her feel as if she were the only woman in existence for him. She'd fallen asleep in his arms without any further doubts of his love.

In the weeks since, they'd continued their relationship as if nothing had happened, basking in the newness of their love and enjoying every moment of being together.

Even so, something had changed for Juel. It was so subtle that Mark seemed oblivious to it. She couldn't really put it into words, but her feelings for him were no longer so naïve. She loved him but he wasn't a 'Knight in Shining Armor' anymore.

She used her key to let herself into the apartment. Juel was usually the first one to arrive at the end of the day unless Les wasn't on an assignment - but Rita was already home.

"I managed to get away early and beat the rush hour traffic. 'Want a cold soda?"

"No thanks." Juel slipped out of her high heels, wiggling her toes in appreciation. "I'm going to take a long cool shower then see about fixing myself a salad of some sort, and maybe iced tea. It's too hot for anything else."

Rita's eyes followed her as she headed for the bathroom. "Weren't you supposed to be going out for dinner with Mark, tonight?"

"It's off. He called just as I was about to the leave the office. He had to go on an emergency call."

It was a good thing Juel didn't see the look on Rita's face. By the time she came out of the shower feeling refreshed, Les had arrived home.

"Hey. 'You getting beautiful for the boyfriend tonight?" He didn't wait for an answer, "you'd better wear something cool. It's still boiling hot out there."

"No, she's not going anywhere with him." As usual, Rita opened her mouth before Juel could answer. "He had an <u>emergency call</u> at the last minute." There was no mistaking the sarcasm.

Juel didn't say a word. *Why does she have to make it sound as if he's lying?* An uncomfortable silence descended.

"Well, I guess that's what happens when you date one of the city's finest." Les smoothed over the awkwardness. "Be thankful that he's not a cop, Juel. At least he's only fighting fires and not bad guys." As usual, Les had eased the tension.

Juel didn't say anything as she made her way into the kitchen to fix a cool drink. Rita's double-edged remark had only served to raise the nagging doubts in her own mind that refused to go away. She slumped onto a chair, nursing her iced tea as she stared at the clock on the wall. "*Is he really at work - - or is he meeting her?*" She couldn't stop the thought from entering her head and deliberately tried to think of something pleasant.

"I know he's your best buddy, but Juel is also my best friend and I don't want her heart broken." Chuck shook his head in exasperation and dropped the arm that was draped across the back of the couch and resting on Rita's shoulder. He took a long, slow pull from his beer.

They were supposed to be spending a peaceful evening at his place. *Peaceful?* All she'd talked about for the past half hour was the incident at Tula's barbecue - and now, last night's broken date.

Chuck's usual affability had disappeared. He had a long weekend off and had planned to take Rita on a surprise trip the coast. *If I ever get a chance to tell her about it!* He'd managed to convince her that every available man had been called out last night, but she still wouldn't believe that Mark wasn't still seeing Pat.

"Why would he be so stupid as to invite her to the fourth celebration, when he'd also invited Juel?" he said tiredly. They'd rehashed the blasted barbecue over and over again!

Rita grudgingly admitted to his logic, but still wasn't satisfied. "Whether he invited her or not is beside the point. The way that broad came on to him was not the actions of a platonic friend. He's two-timing Juel. I just know it!"

He carefully laid down the beer can. Holding her shoulders and turning her to face him, he spoke slowly and deliberately. "Listen to me. You've got to stop this obsessing about your friend's life. You have to mind your own business and leave them alone. I was hoping that we could spend a pleasant evening together. Besides which, I have made plans for the two of us for the weekend."

Rita opened her mouth, ready to say something further but he stopped her with a gesture. "No. Listen to me. I think a hell of a lot of you and you're putting a strain on our relationship. For heavens sake, you're not Juel's keeper! Whatever is going on between them is none - of - your - business. If you value her friendship, you'll leave her alone and let her sort things out for herself. For the last time, I am telling you that Pat is no longer an item with Mark. Whatever their present relationship is it has nothing to do with his feelings for Juel. I know him well enough to know that he cares for her a great deal. Mark wouldn't deliberately hurt her so let's drop the subject."

Rita had the grace to look uncomfortable as Chuck continued. "I didn't ask you to come over to discuss my best friend's relationship with your best friend." He placed a hand under her chin and forced her to look at him. "Remember me? I'm the guy that you say you enjoy being with more than anyone else you know."

She heard the edginess in his voice. In her concern for Juel, she'd dismissed the fact that Mark was Chuck's best buddy. *I've never given a thought to his feelings.*

Looking into his face, she realized why she cared about him. He was one of the most considerate people that she'd ever known. His loyalty for his friend made her ashamed of her own thoughtlessness. "I'm sorry Chuck. I won't mention Mark and Juel again, no matter what I feel. You're right. It's their affair and it's nobody else's business."

He smiled in relief and placing an arm back around her shoulder, he drew her close. Rita completely eliminated everything else from her mind as he told her of his plans for the weekend. Giving a delighted squeal, she threw her arms around his neck.

CHAPTER FIVE

*L*aughter coming from the swimming pool was followed by sounds of splashing. Subtle smells of chlorine drifted towards her as she lay soaking up the sun. The book she'd intended to read lay untouched beside her canvas recliner.

Juel felt far too lazy to read. She repositioned her body and stretched out. Behind the mirrored sunglasses she squinted up at the tangerine ball overhead, enjoying the feel of its warm rays on her body.

Turning her head towards the man lying on the chaise lounge beside her, she watched his slow even breathing that told her he was dozing. She didn't disturb him. From behind the sunglasses, she could see that his skin was tanned to a deeper color than its normal olive. Mark lay with his head turned away from her with an arm dangling over the side of his chair while the other arm cushioned his head. She noticed that beads of perspiration glistened on the muscles of his back and broad shoulders and dark hairs lay flat and moist on the back of his legs. The effect he had on her libido never ceased to be amazing. *He's definitely one sexy hunk.* And yet, sometimes when he seemed to be as vulnerable as a little boy, she was drawn even more to him.

413

Juel's appraisal of him ended and she let her gaze sweep idly beyond the aqua pool to the cabins of the lodge, picking out 'their' cabin. She loved the calm and solitude of this place – and the privacy.

For the past few months, whenever they could find an opportunity to leave the city behind, they'd 'head for the hills' as Mark would say. Since their first visit in the spring, they'd come as regularly as his schedule allowed. Juel still hadn't grown tired of the place. Here, they could be completely alone in their own little world. *And, I don't have to feel any qualms about sleeping with him under Con's roof.*

She'd grown very fond of Mark's father, but she still felt somewhat uncomfortable at sharing Mark's bed in the parent's house. She was well aware that Con's generation had different moral standards regarding sex without marriage. She wondered what the old man really thought about their relationship, especially having come from a country that was strictly of an orthodox, catholic faith. Her gut instincts told her that had Mark's mother still been alive, that lady would not have approved.

The sun was moving. Shadows were gathering over the pool area. Juel leaned over to pick up the bottle of suntan lotion from the little table by her side and screwed the top back on tightly. Placing it in her beach bag, she did the same with her book. It was getting late. Time to return to the city.

Back to jangling telephones and honking traffic. There was no telephone in their cabin to disturb them and they had deliberately turned off their cell-phones. The only way they could be reached for an emergency was through the lodge's office phone. And, the only people that knew where they had gone were Con, and her two friends. *What a relief not to have to listen to Rita's criticism of him.* Not that Rita said too much anymore, but her body language sometimes spoke louder than words.

414

She'd invited Mark less and less to the apartment because Rita's coolness towards him bordered on rudeness. She was thankful that the same didn't hold true for Les' attitude.

"What time is it?" Mark rolled over onto his back, shading his eyes from the sun's glare. His voice was husky from sleep.

Juel picked up her watch from the table and put it back on her wrist. "It's three thirty. We'll have to be heading back pretty soon."

Stretching an arm across the tiny space between them, he grasped her hand. "I wish we didn't have to go back. We need to be alone like this more often."

She smiled, gently squeezing his fingers before pulling her hand free. Before the incident with Pat she'd have leaned towards him to exchange a kiss. Without even being conscious of doing so, Juel had raised boundaries around her 'space'.

Dusk was falling as they reached the house in Queens. It was Juel's favorite time of the day and stepping out of the car, she looked up at the twilight sky. The first evening star twinkled like a sequin on a misty blue dress.

"The porch light isn't on yet. Dad usually turns it on at the same time he draws the drapes." Mark's comment drew her attention to the dark porch. Walking up the steps, they noticed that the living-room drapes were still open and there was no light in the room.

Juel waited for Mark to unlock the door. As they entered, he called out to his father. There was no answer. The house was oddly still. Juel stood in the hallway, by the old coat rack with its yellow stained mirror. Con didn't make an appearance.

"Maybe he's outside in the yard," said Mark. He moved towards the living room.

She shivered for some inexplicable reason. Normally, the elderly man would emerge from one of the rooms to greet them. The place was too quiet.

"I wonder if Tula came by and took him over to her place?" Mark's voice held a note of uncertainty. He stood in the entrance of the living room and reached for the light switch. The room was suddenly flooded in a soft light. Following behind, Juel saw the top of Con's head peeking over the back of his chair. His pipe was clutched in a hand as it rested on the winged arm.

"Dad?" There was no response.

Juel suddenly felt cold. Mark approached the chair and bending over his father, drew back sharply. His hand reached out to feel underneath the jaw-line – then slowly he straightened up. Mark's face was drained of color as he turned towards Juel. "He's dead."

The words didn't register. Without knowing how she got there, she reached Mark's side and looked into Con's face. The eyes were fixed and staring. An enigmatic, half smile showed on purple lips - as if he knew the punch line to a joke.

"I have to call Tula." The voice came through to Juel as if from a distance. Unconscious of what she was doing, she pried the pipe out of the fingers. They were icy cold. She sat down facing the body. Vaguely aware of Mark's low tones as he talked on the phone, she tried to take in the reality of the old man's death. *He looks like he always does when he sits talking to me.* Except for the blank, unseeing eyes and bloodless face, he could have been telling her one of his stories of his youth spent in Greece.

CHAPTER SIX

*T*he pungent incense hit her senses with a disturbing familiarity. Strange sensations swept over Juel as she entered the church and followed Mark through the doors of the vestibule. The feeling was that of coming home after a long absence. It was as if she were returning to something that she already knew and loved, but was having a hard time remembering what that 'something' was.

Unexpected emotions welled up that had nothing to do with Con's passing. Tears clouded Juel's vision. *Of course I miss him, very much.* Yet these inexplicable emotions weren't for Con's death. She couldn't fathom this intensity of feeling. Overwhelming warmth encompassed her like an old familiar blanket. *What is happening?* Never in her entire life had she known such peace - yet paradoxically, it was a peace that felt disturbingly familiar. The girl struggled with long forgotten memories that were trying to surface yet her brain refused to grasp. Mentally shaking her head, Juel followed Mark along the aisle to the front pew.

From the outside, the church looked much like many other churches that she'd seen. The huge red brick building with its domed roof and elaborate Greek cross was stately. Regardless, to Juel it was just another church albeit one of a catholic denomination.

Apart from attending Sunday school as a child, Juel's religious education had been perfunctory by parents who rarely attended their 'local' Episcopal Church. Easter and Christmas were the only times that the family went to services. She remembered attending a wedding ceremony of a cousin, once. That was when she was an adolescent and apart from that her church attendances were spasmodic. She'd never been inside a Catholic church before this.

The carpeted aisle muffled their steps. The singing voices of an unseen choir mingled with a heavy musk emitted by censers. Juel walked reverentially as if among old friends and slid into the front pew alongside Mark.

A tear escaped and trickled down her face and dabbing at her eyes with a tissue, she cast a discreet look around the church. Greek orthodox religious Icons decorated the walls and also the screens that covered the entrance to the altar. All was serenely beautiful.

A white robed priest was already chanting prayers at the altar steps, while the voices of three deacons replied with words of praise. Juel felt an inexplicable urge to chant the responses – yet didn't know the words. *This is crazy!* Raising her head, she looked up at the high vaulted ceiling. For a split second she expected to see open sky with the sun shining down. Instead she saw a glorious golden chandelier suspended above the priest's head. It's multiple white and red lights cast a brilliant glow over the whole church.

People came to the altar to place lighted candles among the many that were already there, before approaching the open casket that held Con's body. Pausing, they kissed the cross that lay on the chest of the deceased. From her seat, Juel had a clear view of the person in the grand looking coffin. *It doesn't look like Con.* Somehow, the body lying so stiff was disengaged from the person that she'd shared so many cozy hours with and had come to regard with so much affection.

Mark's face was expressionless. He sat staring straight ahead and only the tight grip of his hand in hers gave away his feelings. She saw tears glistening in his eyes and her heart went out to him. Gently squeezing his hand, he returned the pressure while continuing to stare at nothing.

Tula sat at Mark's other side, openly weeping. Stuffed into a black suit that looked out of place on his bulky body, Jack sat alongside his wife. He looked uncomfortable. Juel had never seen him wearing a tie before this. Their two boys were miraculously behaving themselves but she noticed that their eldest daughter was having a hard time trying to stop young Bella from fidgeting.

The church was almost full. Many people who were strangers to Juel (but obviously not to Con's family) - had come to pay their respects. Imperceptibly, she glanced around at the congregation and saw Chuck sitting in a pew across the aisle. He nodded and she gave him a little smile.

As her gaze idly wandered along the rows, they came to rest on a figure sitting at the end of an aisle, halfway down the church. She stiffened.

There was no mistaking that blond hair, pulled back into a demure chignon with a black lace handkerchief covering the crown of gold. Wearing a black mini-skirt with a matching jacket, the perfectly made-up face was set in angelic felicity.

Pat caught her gaze and wriggled the fingers of a hand in a delicate wave. Juel nodded and abruptly turned back to face the altar.

"Blessed are those whose way is blameless. Alleluia."

The congregation made the sign of the cross as the priests and deacons followed the order of the Liturgy.

"My soul has always longed for Your judgements. Alleluia."

Juel tried to concentrate on the ritual funeral mass. She felt numb, yet very much aware of the female sitting a few rows behind. The service seemed to go on forever.

She gave an inward sigh of relief when Pat left after the brief, graveside prayers. Thoughts of having to make small talk with the girl, for the rest of the day, caused knots in her stomach.

Pausing to give Mark a peck on the cheek, Pat apologized for having to leave so soon. "I would just love to stay longer," she said in that sickening drawl. "Seems like I don't get to see y'all often enough anymore. But, I really do have to leave for the city or I'll be late for an important engagement." Placing perfectly manicured fingers on Mark's upper arm, she squeezed the bicep affectionately. Her voice continued to ooze sugary platitudes. "You know don't you sweetie, how much I would love to stay longer and pay my respects to the rest of the family?"

Mark nodded, accepting the excuse and thanking her for coming. Juel suffered in silence.

"I'll talk to you soon, honey." After giving Mark's arm another squeeze, she dropped her hand and turned her attention to Juel. After claiming that she was - "too delighted to have met Juel again" - she turned on her stiletto heels and was gone.

She'd taken a couple of days off from work to be with Mark and after the last of the guests had left Tula's house, they went back to Con's home. The place seemed empty and strange without the old man. Mark was awake for ages, but he was sleeping when she heard the hallway clock strike three. Finally Juel also fell asleep, holding him in her arms like a baby. Her last thoughts before drifting off were of Pat sitting in the church – looking as innocent as one of the saintly pictures.

The day after the funeral, she helped him sort out his father's things. The house was unearthly quiet yet the man's presence still lingered. The living room still smelled of his pipe tobacco. Even his slippers left by his chair, appeared to be waiting for him. When Juel picked them up to place in a box she could have sworn that they still felt warm, as if he'd just taken them off. She could hardly wait to leave and head back to the city.

It had been almost a week since the funeral. Juel had been with Mark as often as possible, but they had avoided spending more than a couple of hours at a time in the house. Somehow, she couldn't bring herself to stay overnight and had been relieved that Mark didn't suggest it. In a strange way she felt even more uncomfortable about sleeping in his bed than she had when the father had been alive. Mark seemed to sense her reluctance and didn't push it.

Juel sat in the kitchen, thinking of all the changes that had taken place in her life since the beginning of the year. Meeting Mark – Con - his sister and her family and his best friend, Chuck. She was fond of them all but she'd really had a soft spot for Con. Now the old man was gone. *I miss him.*

Glancing at the kitchen clock she saw that it was only seven thirty. For some unknown reason she had awakened just as it was getting light outside. She'd tossed and turned for half an hour before finally giving up on returning to sleep. Lying in her bed, she'd watched the sun through her window as it crept over the buildings and changed the sky from a soft pink to a pale blue. She never drew the curtains when alone, as she liked to be able to see the sky, especially at night when the glow of lights from the city rose to meet the blackness beyond. Even a few stars were sometimes visible through the haze. Rita always grumbled about this quirk of hers, complaining that any Peeping Tom could look into their window. Juel had laughingly ignored her illogical objections. The apartment was on the highest floor, and the building itself towered over most of the others on the street. Only Spiderman could have scaled the wall to peek into their bedroom!

She'd lain for a few minutes enjoying the piece and quiet of the early morning. Not having to rush around getting ready for work and fighting for the bathroom was a luxury. Les was in Connecticut for the weekend and Rita was spending it at her folk's place, helping to celebrate her father's birthday. Juel had the whole place to herself.

Finishing her coffee she got up to take a long, luxurious shower. It was good being able to take her time and not have to worry about one of the other two yelling for her to hurry and get out.

A brain wave suddenly hit. *I'll catch the train to Flushing.* Mark didn't have to go on duty until the afternoon. She'd surprise him and spend the morning with him. *I'll stop at the deli on the way and pick up something for our lunch.* He loved Rueben sandwiches and had taken her to a great kosher deli that was close to his house. It would be good to spend a coupl'a hours with him before he had to leave for work. *He's been so withdrawn since his father's death.*

Within no time, she was ready to leave. *At least I can be there for him. He doesn't need to be in that house all by himself.* As Juel rode the elevator to the street level, she dwelled on the recent events that had changed Mark's world. The somber thoughts caused her emotions to well up and she couldn't wait to hold him.

On her way to the subway, she stopped at the corner fruit stand and looked over the fresh looking fruits and vegetables. She settled on some fat, purple grapes.

The streets of Flushing were hot and even dustier than the city. Longingly, she thought about the lodge and wished that they could have escaped to it this weekend. One last respite before the end of the summer would do them both good. *Maybe next weekend, if he can get the time off.* Climbing the porch steps she let herself in with her key, calling out as she entered. "Mark?"

Juel caught sight of her reflection in the coat rack's mirror. It made her features look mottled and distorted and the warped glass turned her skin yellow. She called out again. "It's me."

A door banged at the back of the house. She heard footsteps in the kitchen and the next moment, he came through the doorway from behind the stairs. Astonishment spread across his face at sight of her standing in the hallway. "Juel! What're you doing here?" It was obvious from his wet tousled hair and unshaven jaw that he hadn't been out of bed very long. His chest was bare above his old jogging pants.

Covering the few yards that separated them, Juel wrapped her arms around his neck and kissed him. Teasing him lightly, she pulled back. "Boy. Do you need a shave! It's almost eleven already, and you look like you're still half asleep. You're supposed to be at work in a coupl'a hours," adding laughingly – "are you lazy! I thought you might like to have some company even for a short time, so I decided to surprise you and fix lunch. That is, with the help of the deli." She pointed to the plastic bags that she'd laid on the hallway rack stand.

His smile looked as if it were glued to his face. It didn't match the frown between his eyebrows.

Juel's own smile disappeared. "Mark? What is it?" Something was wrong. "Aren't you glad to see me?"

He pulled her back into his arms, gripping her tightly. "Of course I am. I just wasn't expecting you."

She relaxed. Enjoying the feel of his body close to hers she didn't hear the bathroom door opening upstairs.

"Mark, sweetie?" A familiar voice carried down the stairs.

Juel stiffened.

"I need a towel for my hair. I'm dripping water all over the place."

Juel's heart did a sickening somersault. Jerking free - she backed away from him. She watched the figure begin to descend the stairs –one-slow-step-at-a-time. Pat wore an old bathrobe wrapped loosely around her body. She recognized it as belonging to Mark. The blond hair hung in wet wisps around her shoulders. As the girl moved slowly down the stairs her golden legs escaped the wrap to expose smooth, naked thighs.

In a stupor, she stared…. everything seemed surreal and moved in slow motion.

423

Pat reached a spot on the stairs where she could peer over the rail and saw the two figures standing below. Coming to a halt, a smile slowly spread across her face, showing those small even teeth. "Juel!" Her voice tinkled with delight. "How absolutely marvelous to see you again!"

Juel backed towards the front door. Unconscious of anything except the need to escape, her shocked eyes stayed focused on the half-naked girl. Pat stood still halfway down the stairs –those blue eyes locked with Juel's. With an effort, Juel turned away from the girl's triumphant smile - to look at Mark. Guilt spread across his face as he met her horrified stare.

She needed air. She couldn't breath.

Mark started to speak, "Juel. I'll explain…."

Without waiting to hear him finish she turned towards the door, frantically fumbling with the knob. *Damn!* Why wouldn't it open? *Thank god!* It finally flew open and she managed to make it outside. She almost fell down the porch steps in an attempt to escape.

Suddenly Mark was at her side, grasping her arm and halting her flight. "Juel. Stop! Listen to me!"

Desperately, she shook herself free and ran along the street with his voice ringing in her ears….

Thumpity – thump thumpity thump. Oblivious to anything as the rocking train sped through the underground, her mind tumbled over the scene at the house. *Pat and Mark- Pat and Mark* – Again and again, it repeated like an old stuck movie reel, whirling around and around, keeping time with the rumbling train. A shadowy face reflected back at her from the train window. It wasn't her face. Pat's smiling image stared back from the dirty glass - mockingly self-satisfied.

The train seemed to take forever, but when it finally reached her station she almost missed it. At the last minute Juel realized where she was and squeezed frantically through the doors before they closed. Pat clung like a specter from Hell.

She let herself into the empty apartment and headed for the bedroom. Her legs felt like jelly and she gratefully sank onto her bed. Finally Juel let go of the painful, gut wrenching sobs that wracked her body. Doubled over in a fetal position, she rocked back and forth.

Rita was exhausted. She'd spent almost two days listening to not so subtle hints from relatives that it was about time she 'settled down' and got married. Her mother, (bless her tactless tongue) - must have gabbed about her relationship with Chuck, because she had to suffer the third degree from her uncle. He wanted to know who this man was - what his religious affiliations were - did he have good prospects? Most important - was he a suitable match for his niece? In desperation, she'd signaled to her dad with pleading eyes. Her father had rescued her under the pretext of showing her his garden. Rita couldn't wait to leave her parents' house and get back to her own place. Finally making a lame excuse to leave early, she'd fled the pressure.

Opening the apartment door she was surprised to find the place in darkness. She reached for the light switch and turning it on, saw that the place was empty. *I wonder if she went out with Mark?* She shook her head, remembering that his leave of absence was over. He and Chuck were working this evening.

Rita sniffed the air. She could smell burnt coffee. Heading for the kitchen and turning on the light, she saw that the coffeepot's switch glowed red. The bottom of the glass container was crusted in burnt, brown sediment. Exasperated, she turned it off and unplugged it from the wall socket. She placed the pot in the sink and eyed it balefully. *It will take me forever to get it clean.*

Les wouldn't be back until tomorrow morning, but she knew that Juel hadn't planned on going anywhere. *I wonder where she is? She's going to get a piece of my mind for leaving that pot turned on.*

Honestly! What was she thinking of to leave without making sure that it was turned off? She could have burned the place down. It's a good thing I arrived back tonight instead of waiting until tomorrow.

She headed for the bedroom to dump her bag and get into something comfortable. *Maybe Mark didn't have to work the whole weekend after all and they went out to dinner.* The door to the bedroom was slightly ajar and pushing it open all the way, was met by complete darkness. Rita hesitated. *That's odd. She usually leaves the curtains open when I'm not here to close them.* Reaching for the light switch, she flipped it.

Blinking to allow her eyes to adjust to the sudden light, her gaze swept over the room – and came to a jolting stop. Juel lay on her back on top of her bedcovers, staring blankly at the ceiling. Rita's heart skipped a beat. For one wild moment she thought the girl might be dead. Alarmed, she moved closer to the bed and saw the swollen and reddened eyes blinking against the sudden glare. The face was colorless.

"Good god Juel! You gave me a fright. What's wrong?" She sat down on the side of the bed and shook the girl's shoulder, trying to get some kind of a response. "Are you ill?"

Juel turned her head and looked into the frightened face of her friend. Fresh tears welled up and rolled unbidden down her cheeks. She gave a trembling sigh that bordered on a wail.

Rita stood up. "I'll be right back." Heading straight for the cabinet in the living room where liquor was kept, she searched among the bottles. Finding what she was looking for she withdrew a bottle of scotch that hadn't been opened. In the kitchen the frightened girl fished around in a drawer and found a bottle opener; cursing the tight top as she fumbled to get it unscrewed. *Shit!* It finally came open. Rita poured a generous amount into a plastic tumbler and hurried back to the bedroom.

"Sit up" she ordered, helping the girl into an upright position. Juel sank listlessly against Rita's supporting arm that encircled her shoulders. "Drink this."

Juel shook her head, pushing ineffectually at the tumbler that Rita held to her mouth.

"Drink!" Rita meant business. She held the rim to Juel's lips.

The girl took a sip and choked. Rita waited until she'd stopped coughing before plying the fiery liquid once more. "You need this," she stated.

Juel obediently took another sip. This time she didn't choke, but she refused to drink the rest when Rita offered it again. "You know I hate whiskey," she said weakly. "No more." Rita waited for the liquor to take effect.

After a few minutes color returned to Juel's cheeks. *Thank god!* Her friend appeared to be sufficiently recovered for Rita to be able to ask questions. Haltingly, Juel related the events of the morning at Mark's house. As the story unfolded Rita's face turned dark with fury, but she managed to keep silent as Juel talked.

"Hi guys." Les was home. "How was your weekend without my delightful company?" Sunlight streamed into the apartment and fell onto the girls sitting on the couch. They were still in their pajamas even though it was mid-afternoon. Not unusual in itself, as none of them bothered to dress in a hurry when they didn't have to go to work. Still, he knew something was wrong. They radiated energy as appealing as old newspapers. Walking towards them, Les looked enquiringly into their faces. Rita's held an expression as ominous as a boxer about to k.o. an opponent. As for Juel…. *she looks like she's been run over by a semi-truck!* He'd never seen her looking so unkempt and her face was as blotchy as if she had a bad case of hives.

Les scratched his head and stared quizzically from one to the other. "Well ladies. You both look like you've had a good time without me. That is, if you enjoy spending it in a mausoleum!" Getting no response, he tried again. "You look positively ghastly Juel." He peered exaggeratedly close to Rita's face. "And you don't look much better."

"We're in no mood for your smart ass remarks," she snapped.

Without another word, he headed for his room to deposit his luggage – returning a few minutes later. "Okay. Which one of you is going to tell me what's going on?" He slumped into the big recliner facing the girls, waiting.

Juel didn't say a word and after a few seconds Rita apologized. "Sorry I bit your head off, but I'm so furious I could kill somebody!"

You look like you already have. Les stifled his tongue.

Rita hesitated, waiting for Juel to say something but the girl remained unheeding, so she let go of her pent-up anger. "She caught that no good son-of-a-bitch in bed with his blond whore!"

Juel's face blanched. Biting her lower lip, she stifled the tears that threatened to start again. All traces of Les' good humor left and his voice turned somber as he leaned forward. "What happened, Juel?"

Slowly and with difficulty, she repeated her story of finding Pat at Mark's house. A heavy silence fell as she concluded. Les was deep in thought. *There has to be a logical explanation.* "Even if she was there and had obviously taken a shower, that doesn't mean that she'd been in his bed," he said.

"Are you crazy -or what?" Rita's voice rose. "You want us to believe that she'd just popped in to sample his <u>shampoo</u>? Is his <u>shower</u> so irresistible that she travels from her place to his just to try it out? Give me a break!" The tone was loaded with sarcasm. "That over-sexed broad was looking for more than a 'shower' and obviously got it!" Rita's voice grew even louder as she continued to vent her anger. "That bitch has been trying to screw him ever since she realized Juel was competition!"

"Cut it out!" Les' voice crackled. "It seems to me, Juel needs to talk to Mark and hear from his own mouth as to what took place."

428

"What for? So that two-timing Casanova can tell her more of his glib lies? He's such a smooth talking bastard he'd put a politician to shame!"

"Quit it! You don't know what happened and the only way to find out is for Juel to give him an opportunity to explain."

Rita started to speak again, but was cut off by Juel's quaking voice. "That's enough. Both of you stop." Her voice trembled with emotion but there was still a semblance of her old strength in her words. "I know you mean well Les, but I don't plan to talk to Mark. Period. I don't ever want to see him again. End of subject. Any explanation he might have would be a waste of words… I just don't trust him anymore."

Les stared at the girl from across the width of the coffee table. Although she looked a wreck, there was a determined expression in the pain filled eyes. Unconsciously, she straightened her body and her lips compressed into a tight grim line. Rita's face was just as grim. He knew that it would be useless to try and talk rationally to either of them anymore.

Shrugging his shoulders, he arose. "I'm going to make some coffee. I think we all need some. Whatever you have to do Juel - you have to do. You know that we're both here for you, don't you?" She gave him a tremulous smile, unable to trust herself to speak.

"Let's not discuss this anymore." He directed a meaningful stare at Rita who still looked ready for blood. "This is Juel's life and her decision to make. We need to be supportive <u>but we're not going to interfere, are we?</u>"

Rita got the message. Easing herself out of the cushions she joined him as he headed for the kitchen. "I'll fix something to eat. Neither of us has eaten anything yet. I suppose you're hungry too?" she grudgingly enquired.

Les knew that this was Rita's way of conceding. He gave her arm a squeeze as she passed him. "You know I'm always ready to enjoy your cooking."

Mark stared into his half empty mug. The place was busy this morning. Hungry workers were grabbing a quick bite or a coffee to go before rushing away to their various locations. He and Chuck had another half-hour before having to go on duty.

The door to the coffee shop opened to admit another customer and he found his head automatically turning in that direction. Of course it wasn't her. He'd become so used to seeing her entering of a morning that it was hard to break the habit. Mark's mood hit rock bottom again when a stranger entered instead of her familiar figure. From force of habit, he found himself looking at his wristwatch. *By this time she's already at work.* Besides, she hadn't been near the place since that 'doomsday' at his house.

Inwardly, he continued to flinch at the memory of her face staring at him, horror written all over it. He could have gladly choked Pat with his bare hands! After Juel left, his ex-girlfriend had the sense to also leave as soon as she possibly could. They hadn't spoken a word on the five minutes drive to the train station. When he'd dropped her off, she'd leaned over to kiss him goodbye but Mark had turned away with a shake of his head. The finality of the action spoke louder than words. They hadn't spoken since.

"D'ya want a refill?" Like a pistol, Sally held the coffee pot suspended over his mug. He raised it without saying a word. Chuck pushed his mug forward. "I'll take more, Sal." Her normally cheerful face was unsmiling as she re-filled the mugs.

Sally eyed Mark balefully, "all I can say is, ya must've done something pretty bad to have chased her away from 'ere." Neither man made any comment. "When is one of ya goin' tell me what happened?"

Chuck gave her a look of warning. "Drop it, Sally."

The waitress stared back with icicles in her baby blues. Looking as if she were about to retort, she apparently changing her mind. "Men!" She almost spat the word and clamped her pouting lips together as she moved away to wait on another customer.

"I guess I shouldn't have spoken to her like that."

Chuck's comment broke through Mark's dark thoughts. "She'll get over it," he growled. "Besides my problem with Juel isn't anybody's business but mine."

Chuck stayed quiet for a few seconds before asking, "have you tried to talk to her recently?"

Mark shook his head. "I've given up trying. She won't return my messages I've left on her cell, and the last time I tried to reach her at home Rita answered the phone." He gave a caustic laugh. "You know what Rita thinks of me. She practically dripped venom and told me to quit calling."

Chuck's face turned dark. *I wish she would stop interfering.* His girlfriend could be so sweet when they were alone together, but when it came to Mark she was irrational in her dislike of him.

Granted, his friend had been stupid to let Pat stay at his house, even if it was as innocent as he said it was. Chuck believed him when he'd said they'd not had sex, in spite of her expert seductive powers. Still, he had no illusions about the ex-girlfriend. He'd known Pat for as long as Mark had and knew that she could be very manipulative whenever she wanted to get her own way. *Which is most of the time.* It was obvious that she still wanted Mark. *He's so damn blind. He's oblivious to her tactics at trying to get her claws hooked into him again.* Still, Rita was fanatical about her dislike of Mark and equally as fanatical about protecting Juel. *She acts like a mother hen!*

The episode at the house had only served to make Rita more adamant in her contempt for Mark. By mutual agreement, they no longer discussed the subject, as it had to be avoided if they wanted to keep their own relationship undamaged.

"We'd better get outta here." Mark arose from his stool and throwing some bills on the counter top, started to leave. Chuck drained the dregs from his own mug before following suit.

Mark glanced along the street towards the building that Juel worked in, knowing that if he tried to go in and see her she'd become upset. He'd attempted to, the day after she'd ran

from his house. As Schwarzenegger would say, "Big Mistake."
On seeing him coming through the door, her face had turned
white and she'd glared at him in hatred. Abruptly leaving her
desk, she'd hurried to the back of the room and entered a door
marked "Private" – but not before he'd caught a glimpse of those
sea-green eyes fill with pools of pain.

The supervisor had approached him, politely asking if he
could be of any help? Embarrassed and upset, he'd mumbled
some excuse and retreated as quickly as his impulse had taken
him inside. He didn't invade her privacy again.

The two men walked along the street in companionable
silence. It was still warm but there was a slight breeze. The
morning smelled of the approaching fall. Already the trees in the
many tiny parks around lower Manhattan, showed leaves that
were beginning to turn gold.

He'd told Chuck the whole story and apart from telling him
off for being such a damned fool, as always he'd supported him.
Underneath his breath Mark gave a self-depreciating groan, *I
must've been sick in the head.* For the thousandth time, he mentally
lashed himself for having created the god-awful situation. Things
had got out of hand with Pat all because of his over inflated
ego. Hence, he'd inadvertently caused the break with Juel - and
ruined both their lives. For as long as he lived he'd regret that
fatal day.

Somehow, mentally scourging himself was a sub-conscious
form of doing penance for being so stupid. Inwardly, he still
cringed at the memory of that night with Pat. It was seared into
his brain as if branded there by a hot iron….

At last he was able to go through his father's personal affects,
emptying Con's closets and dresser drawers. In a bottom drawer
among various mementos, he came across a small, well-worn
photograph album. Settling down on his parents' old brass bed
he began to idly flip through the pages.

Faded sepia pictures of people from another time stared back at him. Foreign looking strangers stood, or sat in self-conscious poses. Some were studio portraits, but others were snapshots with scalloped edges like they used to have in European countries. From the background scenery and style of clothing, he knew the locations to be somewhere in Greece.

Turning over the stiff pages, he saw the face of a smiling man standing behind the chair of a seated young girl. An unexpected lump arose in Mark's throat as he recognized the younger version of his parents. In the left hand corner of the picture in gold print, was written the name of the New York studio that had taken the portrait. The studio no longer existed. *They were a good-looking young couple.* Mark's thoughts turned nostalgic as he recalled bygone years of growing up with his parents and sister. He missed those carefree, happy times.

He'd no idea how long he'd been sitting thumbing through the photographs when he heard the ringing of the front door bell. Putting down the album he got up and left the room, wondering who on earth it could be? *It can't be Tula. She said they were going out of town this weekend.* Before he could reach the bottom of the stairs, the bell gave another insistent ring. "I'm coming," he called out in exasperation. He leapt over the bottom step and hurried to cross the entrance hall to the door. *It hadn't better be a salesman or he'll be sorry!* He was in no mood for interruptions.

Feeling irritated, he opened the door and stepped back in surprise. "Pat! What are you doing here?"

"Hi there! I thought I'd bring something over for you to eat." The girl stood holding a bucket of fried chicken, along with a bulging paper sack. With her blond tresses piled on top of her head and tied up with a pink chiffon scarf, she looked a picture of child-like innocence.

"Hey! It's good of you to think of me, but you shouldn't have bothered."

She'd called earlier and learning that he was spending time sorting out Con's things, she'd offered to come over and help. Mark had thanked her but declined, explaining that Juel had done most of the major stuff. They hadn't talked long as he'd cut the conversation short, wanting to get back to his task.

Trying not to show his annoyance, he forced a smile. "I thought I'd told you I'd be doing stuff that could only be taken care of by myself." The last thing he'd expected was for Pat to show up on his doorstep. He stood blocking the entrance.

"I know you did honey, but even you have to take a break to eat sometime." Pursing her lips prettily, she blithely continued, "I just couldn't stand the thought of you being all alone here. It's not good for you," she cooed. "So, I thought the least I could do was to save you the trouble of fixing yourself a meal."

The girl continued to stare at him beguilingly. "Well, aren't you going to invite me in after I've gone to soo-o-o much trouble? This chicken is better eaten hot and fresh." She took a step towards the threshold, looking at him expectantly. "Besides, the biscuits and gravy are going to get cold if we wait too much longer to eat them. Don't know about you, but I'm starving!"

Having no choice, Mark reluctantly moved to one side to admit her, besides which the smell of the chicken made him realize that he'd not eaten all day. Feeling bad at having acted so churlish, he tried to make amends. "This is really great of you Pat and I certainly could use a break."

Taking the grocery sack from her, he followed as she passed through the door and headed for the kitchen. Pat deposited the bucket of chicken on the table and turned to relieve him of the grocery sack. As she leaned in close to take it from him, she lightly brushed his mouth with soft lips. Mark caught a whiff of the familiar perfume she always used.

Not really knowing what to do, he stood and watched as she chattered and rummaged around in the cupboards and drawers. In no time at all, she'd set the table and taking salad fixings from the sack, moved to the sink to wash lettuce. Helpless frustration engulfed him. As hungry as he was he didn't like having his self-imposed isolation invaded, even though he knew she was just being thoughtful.

Mark continued to watch while the girl chattered gaily and tossed a salad in a bowl. His annoyance began to dissipate at sight of the food preparations. *I guess taking a break to eat is okay.* Pat took a six-pack of beer from the bag and after leaving a couple of cans on the table, placed the rest in the refrigerator. *I've got to eat sometime. What's wrong with letting her feed me if she wants to?*

He was only half listening to Pat's conversation as she stretched up, trying to get glasses from the top shelf of a cupboard. Her pink knitted top writhed up to show off a tanned mid-riff above the skintight jeans. The skimpy top stretched across her full breasts leaving little to the imagination.

"Let me help you." He removed the glasses and handed them to her, once again smelling her exotic perfume. It had always reminded him of sunny beaches and tropical flowers.

Holding the glasses in one hand, she cupped the other around his neck to once again give him a kiss. "Thank you, sweetie." Her boobs brushed against him.

Pat's presence in the kitchen reminded him of their high school days. How many times had she come over to share a meal with his family? A warm feeling crept over him, along with an aching sadness. It was not only the raw ache for Con's passing, but also from the memories of his mother bustling around this same kitchen - much the same as Pat was now doing. *I know she means well. Underneath that sexy image she likes to put out, she's really a sweet person. It's good of her to be so concerned about me. No doubt she could be out on a date this evening instead of taking care of me.*

Mark washed the grime from his hands in the kitchen sink and before he could reach for the dishtowel hanging on its rail, she'd handed him a paper towel. "Don't you dare wipe your hands on that dish-towel! Your mother would have a fit if she were here."

All at once he heard his mother's voice from the past. *For sure she'd have given me hell for using her kitchen sink to clean up in, instead of the bathroom.* A pang of loneliness hit him.

They ate in intimate silence and the tension that had built up inside Mark was somewhat relieved. How many times in the past had they sat together like this? Sitting at this same kitchen table with the familiar repetition, was a comforting balm to the ache inside. He hadn't realized just how hungry he was – or how uptight. An hour later he leaned back in satisfaction, wiping his mouth on a paper napkin. All that remained of the chicken were bones and a few wings.

An easy rapport continued between them throughout the evening as they lounged in the living room. They made short work of the six-pack that Pat had brought and at her suggestion, they finished off the beers that had already been sitting in the refrigerator.

Reminiscing about the past, they shared memories of their times together with school friends, families - reliving happier times. For the first time since Con's death, Mark felt like a load was being lifted from his shoulders.

As the beer and a full stomach combined to ease the burden of his father's passing, he realized that he hadn't felt this good since finding Con's body. There was no doubt that Pat's company was helping to alleviate his gloom.

Mark completely forgot about time until the hall clock chiming twelve brought him back to the present. Not believing his ears, he glanced at his watch and was surprised to see that it really was that late. "Good Lord! Is it really mid-night? "

Pat smiled. "It's the witching hour- isn't it?"' She snuggled deeper into Con's chair with her long legs tucked underneath her buttocks. "It's really amazing how time flies when you're in the company of someone you're so close to." She looked at him with eyes as wide and as innocent as a Barbie doll.

An uncomfortable twinge of guilt passed through him as a fleeting thought of Juel came into his head. He hadn't thought about her all evening. He had to be honest with himself. Pat's meal and solicitous attention had satiated more than just his hunger. The old intimacy between them had resurfaced. *She doesn't knock me off my feet like she used to.* But Mark had to admit to himself, she still knew how to build up his self-esteem and make him feel good.

Pat had also brought out his old feelings of protectiveness towards her. Even though Mark didn't want to acknowledge it, her obvious need for him fed his male vanity. Mentally squirming, his thoughts turned back to Juel. He loved Juel as he'd never loved Pat and was deeply committed. But, the shock of his father's sudden death and the stress of its aftermath had sent him reeling. He'd needed this day of solitude to work through his grief.

Needless to say, Pat's unexpected appearance had interrupted his chosen solitude. Even so the years of friendship between them and her warm personality was a solace to his raw and vulnerable emotions. After a few hours of yielding to a pleasant inertia with this very attractive woman, Mark felt lighter of spirit that he had since the funeral.

Of course all that beer sure helped. He felt a pleasant buzz and with some reluctance, decided it was time to call it a day. "I guess I'd better drive you to the subway to catch a train back to your own place."

 Pat had inherited a beautiful colonial style house from her divorce settlement, way out on Long Island. She always said that it was well worth the long ride into the city to be able to enjoy the house and its perfect view overlooking the ocean. Mark had always thought that she kept the expensive home to impress people. The place was nice but inconvenient to get to.

He looked at the girl expectantly, waiting for a response – but wasn't ready for the one he got.

"Too late, sweetie. The last train going out that far left ten minutes ago. I guess I'm going to have to stay the night."

He didn't know what to say. *Why didn't I keep track of the time?* How was he going to handle this? Having his old girlfriend staying over definitely was not a good idea. Yet, what other choice was there? He was stuck. Trying not to show concern, he responded with what he hoped was nonchalance. "That's okay. Of course you can stay the night." His answer sounded strained even to his own ears. "The bed in the guest room is made up and it's comfortable. I'll drive you to the station tomorrow morning before I go to work."

Not wanting to come across as an ungrateful slob, he continued in the same vein. "It was great of you to feed me, Pat, and I sure am sorry for causing you to miss the last train out of here." He gave a small laugh, "my only excuse is that you're such great company I didn't notice how fast the time was flying. God! I have to admit, I haven't felt this good in ages."

Like a cat stretching itself, Pat slowly uncurled her body and arose from her chair. Before he knew what was happening, she'd approached his seat and was straddling him. Her legs hugged his like she was ready to ride a horse and the warmth of the tightly gripping thighs radiated through Mark's jeans. A muscle twitched in his jaw.

Twining her arms around his neck she scooted her body closer, until her face was in his. "Why bother with the guest room?" The voice was husky as her breath fanned his cheek. Her lips brushed against an ear and he felt the flick of her tongue. Heat started to rise in Mark's gut. In the same husky whisper, she reminded him that- "it wouldn't be the first time that I've shared your bed."

A line of perspiration formed on his upper lip as she moved seductively against him. Pat drew back slightly and peering at him from underneath her lashes, slowly unbuttoned her top. Of course, she wasn't wearing a bra.

Trancelike, his gaze riveted on the golden swell of the breasts so close to his face. *She must have been sunbathing in the nude.* The trivial thought flashed through his brain, immediately followed by memories of the times that this girl had shared his bed. Mark knew exactly just how soft and responsive her flesh felt underneath his hands.

Insanity took over. He took Pat's face between his hands and searched the mouth that was slightly parted and waiting. The taste of her aroused old, familiar sensations and his mind exploded.

Pat's mouth was demanding as she twined her fingers into his hair, before sliding them down his back. Her hands kneaded the knotted muscles around his shoulders and along his spine. Just when he thought he would die from the fire she'd kindled - she pulled back. With a slow, sensual movement of a finger she traced the outline of his mouth. A shiver ran though him.

"Let's go," Without a word, she stood up and took a hand to pull his unresisting body from the chair. Mark stood as if he were a lump of putty ready to be molded by this beautiful creature's will. Any lingering resistance had gone by-by.

As he reached for her again, Pat stopped him and backed away slightly. Crooking a beckoning finger, she took his hand and moved towards the hallway. "Let's finish this upstairs in the comfort of your bed."

Like an obedient child he followed as she led him from the room and slowly climbed the stairs. Mark watched the swaying buttocks in the skin-tight jeans as she climbed in front of him. Like a maneuvering puppeteer, Pat was in control.

Before he knew it they were in his room and she was pulling him down onto the bed. With quick expert fingers, Pat undid the belt of his Levi's while he discarded her top and rapidly worked at her jeans. Her devastating tongue continued to flick teasingly over a pulse in his neck - nibbling lightly at his mouth.

439

They hadn't bothered to turn on the light as a full moon shone through the window. It cast an eerie glow over the entwined bodies on the bed.

What was that? Mark stopped in the act of throwing his jeans to the floor. A flash of light coming from the nightstand had his attention. He did a double take. *Jesus!* Moonlight reflected off a silver-framed photo of Juel.

His eyes glued to the flashing frame. From behind the illuminated glass Juel's face stared back at him, full of trust and love.

If he'd been dowsed in ice water, Mark couldn't have felt more glacial. Abruptly pulling away from Pat's embrace, he sat back on his heels. His eyes continued to stare at the photograph.

"Mark? Are you okay? What's wrong, sweetie?"

Pat's voice came through to his consciousness like a phone call with a bad connection. Mark's head cleared. The effects of the alcohol were miraculously gone.

Stone, cold sober – he spoke. "I can't do this." Slowly and deliberately he untangled himself from her body and stood up. Retrieving his jeans, he looked down at the girl lying across his bed.

Golden hair tumbled around her flushed face and moonlight emphasized the tanned perfection of her naked body. He noticed droplets of moisture shining between her breasts and the mouth looked temptingly moist and inviting. Her startled blue eyes were staring up at him - questioningly.

An overwhelming revulsion hit Mark. It wasn't revulsion for this gorgeous creature that was offering what he'd been ready to take. It wasn't revulsion for the girl that he'd known so well and once adored. It was revulsion for himself.

Disgust swept through him. *I shouldn't have let this go so far.* "This is no good." The statement came out flat and unemotional.

"What?" Pat watched as he stepped into his jeans and went through the motions of fastening the zipper and cinching the belt.

"I must be out of my mind. I can't do this to Juel. I love her."

Pat searched his face. Truth finally dawned and a hard shell transformed her features. The searching eyes turned to cold, blue agates. Without a word she sat up and swung her legs over the side of the bed. Reaching for the top that lay on the floor, she put it on - slowly and methodically fastening the buttons. Next, she picked up her panties and jeans and placed first one shapely leg into them and then the other. Giving the jeans a precise hitch, she zipped them up and snapped the fastener. The fastener made a sharp click in the deadly silence.

Mark stood watching, feeling like a heel. Guiltily, he made an attempt to explain, "I'm sorry Pat. It has nothing to do with you. It's not your fault. It's all mine." *I'm such a bastard.* "You're a beautiful and desirable woman, and I should never have allowed things to get so out of hand. *What the hell was I thinking of?* "I really love Juel, very much. I would never do anything to hurt her." His rush of words sounded awkward, "but I never meant to hurt you either. I feel like a real jerk for allowing this to happen. You know that I'm very fond….."

Pat cut him short. "Don't! Explanations are not necessary." Tossing back her hair from her face, she smiled but the smile didn't reach her eyes. Her expression had returned to its usual, self-assured composure but there was a hard set to her mouth. "You sound like a kid, sweetie who's trying to make excuses for being caught with his hand in the cookie jar."

Once again he opened his mouth to speak but again, she interrupted him with a raised hand and a piercing stare. "Don't be so melodramatic you silly idiot. I only thought that a good lay would relax all that tension you've got built up inside you. I was trying to do you a favor!"

"My mistake, sweetie. I'll just take myself off to your guestroom and let you get some rest." Her eyes wandered with critical and exaggerated deliberation up and down his body. "You really look as if you need it." Without another word she turned and strolled from the room, closing the door firmly behind her.

Mark stared at the closed door. *I need a swift kick in the ass!* He knew that underneath that gay exterior, Pat was humiliated and he hated himself for being the cause. Their friendship went back a long way. But what else could he have done under the circumstances? *Not let it get started in the first place, you damn fool.* He shed his pants again and in disgust, threw them on top of the shirt lying on the floor. Exhausted, he climbed underneath the crumpled bedcovers. He didn't think he'd sleep but oblivion eventually eased his self-recriminating thoughts.

Sunshine poured through the window. Coming out of a deep sleep, Mark blinked his eyes against the harsh glare. As he sat up, he reached for his watch and squinted at the dial. It was almost ten thirty. Normally he never slept so late, unless he'd worked longer than usual. He was groggy and his head didn't feel so good. His brain didn't want to function either.

Climbing out of bed, he grabbed his old jogging pants from the door hook and slid into them. He ran his tongue over his dry lips and grimaced. His mouth tasted like it was full of river sludge. *I shouldn't have drunk so much last night.* Clarity finally hit him. Memories of the previous evening started to kick in.

Groaning, he left his room and headed for the bathroom. The door was closed and he could hear the shower running. With a ruthful sigh he started downstairs, running his hands through his disheveled hair. Even his scalp hurt! *I need a shower.* Guilt embroiled him as he thought of the girl in the bathroom and he wondered if a shower would make him feel less 'dirty'. He shook his head in self-depreciation. *A cold shower would probably have done more good.*

Tentatively rubbing a hand across his bristly jaw, he made his way to the small washroom off the back porch. Letting the cold-water faucet run full blast, he splashed his face vigorously -then decided it would be better to dunk his head underneath the tap. The cold deluge helped.

Mark didn't hear the voice calling out to him from the front of the house. Eventually coming up for air, he rubbed at his face and head with a towel, enjoying the feel of its roughness against his bristly jaw. Feeling slightly more human he re-entered the kitchen, letting the porch door slam behind him. Mark walked into the hallway – and stopped dead. Juel stood there. As she caught sight of him a delighted expression came over her face.

The next few minutes were a blur of painful images. Pat walking down the stairs … Juel's face… grabbing her arm and having her recoil from him as if he had leprosy….

Chuck was still talking as they neared the fire station. Turning his head, Mark stared at him blankly. Seeing the somber expression, Chuck shook his head in pity. "You haven't been listening to a word I've said, have you?"

"Sorry. My mind was elsewhere. What were you saying?"

The man slapped his shoulder in sympathy. "It wasn't important, but you'd better get your brain in gear. I have a feeling we're going to be pretty busy today."

Chuck raised his eyes to the patches of yellow sky showing between the towering skyscrapers. "Seems like this past summer has made everything dryer than a tinderbox. It's weather like this that makes people complacent, and careless. They don't use common sense when it's still hot like this."

CHAPTER SEVEN

𝓕or the umpteenth time, Juel plumped up the couch's cushions and swiped a cloth at imaginary dust on the furniture. Wandering listlessly around the apartment, she looked for something else to do. The kitchen was spotless. She'd even tidied up Les' room so that its usual clutter was gone and it looked immaculate - for a change.

On an impulse she'd decided not to go into work today and had called in sick. Apart from taking vacation time off for Con's funeral, she never took advantage of the 'sick days' that she was allowed. Working at the agency was something Juel enjoyed and conscientiously felt she was indispensable.

But, for some reason this morning she felt a need for solitude. The apartment was empty and the peace and quiet suited her restless mood. Rita had left for work already and Les was out of state on a modeling job. She was alone, which was a rarity.

The silence of the place was a balm to the nagging ache inside her gut that she'd almost grown attached to. It sat like a dormant stomach ulcer that gives occasional twinges to let one know that it's still around.

It had been two weeks, two days and god knows how many hours since that day from hell when she'd found Mark and Pat together. *But who's counting?* Juel took a deep breath as she felt the familiar knot tightening her stomach, knowing that pain would sweep over her in overwhelming waves if she didn't keep her emotions under control. If she allowed herself the 'pleasure' she could vividly relive the scene of that half naked broad walking down the stairs. Pat's mocking smile haunted her dreams.

It felt like years since she'd seen him. Life had taken on an ethereal vacancy, as if she had one foot in this world and the other someplace else.

Making her way into the kitchen to wash the few coffee mugs left in the sink, she found it empty. The mugs hung on their stand. She remembered. *I already washed them.*

The days dragged. As if on automatic pilot, Juel went through the daily motions of her routine – going to work and coming home. Watching TV all evening was something to do while waiting to seek oblivion in sleep. If she went to bed too early, she'd awaken in the middle of the night and toss and turn until the alarm clock told her that it was time to get out of bed. She'd begun to think of discarding the alarm altogether, as most mornings she was already awake and waiting to hear its loud buzzing. How she envied Rita who could probably sleep through an earthquake!

Les and Rita had attempted to get her out of the house and 'have some fun,' as they called it. But, they'd eventually given up. The coupl'a times that they'd managed to coax her into eating out she'd gone through the motions as if the food was made of sawdust. One night, they'd talked her into going to a hot, new nightclub. She'd left after an hour and caught the train back home. The hysterical noise and gyrating bodies had made her feel lonelier than if she were in solitary confinement. Making excuses to her friends, she'd rode home feeling utterly depressed.

Of course, they were just trying to help and surprisingly, Rita hadn't said another word about Mark. *I suspect that Chuck has something to do with that* she thought, feeling gratitude towards the big man.

Leaving the kitchen Juel sat in a chair, facing the living room window. Idly she gazed out at the sun that blazed in a clear sky. Not a cloud marred the perfect early morning. The muted sound of traffic in the street below was somehow, soothing. Juel loved this time of the year. The humid heat of the summer was over and September seemed to carry an expectant hush, as if Mother Nature was gently preparing the world for the harsh winter ahead. Relaxing in her chair, Juel mindlessly watched sunbeams play lightly over the room as they streamed through the glass.

A piercing whine suddenly broke through the peace and quiet. It sounded like a jet's roar. Curious as to why it was so loud, she arose and went to peer out the window. In the direction of the Hudson River, Juel saw a screaming jetliner speeding as if a giant catapult had hurtled it through the sky. Metal glistened blindingly as the sun hit its sides and reflected off its portal windows. The plane looked as if it were barely skimming above the river. *That pilot's flying awfully low.* Juel watched for a few seconds until it disappeared from sight, but she could still hear the thundering echo of its jets as it made its way downstream.

She turned her back on the window as the loud noise faded to a rumble. She went back to the kitchen to make some fresh coffee. *I'm drinking too much caffeine just lately.* The coffeepot still had dregs left over from what Rita had made earlier. Rinsing it out, she followed the mechanics of filling the glass container with fresh water and placing another filter in the holder.

Her stomach rumbled. She hadn't eaten dinner last evening and opening the refrigerator door, looked for something to snack on.

BRRR-I-NG! She jumped. The loud ring of the telephone broke the silence. She stopped in the midst of cramming a piece of cheese into her mouth, half-hoping that it was Mark. At the same time she hesitated, reluctant to answer in case it was. *Don't be a fool. He doesn't know that you're not at work so it can't be him. Anyway, he's quit calling, hasn't he?* The phone continued to ring insistently. *Maybe Les forgot something.* It wasn't uncommon for him to call when he was away, usually to beg the girls to do something that he'd forgotten to do before leaving. Gulping down the cheese, she grabbed the receiver from the wall before it could ring again.

"Juel! What took you so long?" Rita sounded excited.

"What's up? I was…"

Rudely interrupting, Rita yelled over the phone, "turn the TV on- NOW! A plane has just hit the Trade Center!" The 'phone clicked and went dead. Rita had hung up.

In bewilderment, she replaced the receiver and went into the living room to turn on the TV set. For some reason the usual station wouldn't come in. She tried switching channels but got nothing except static. Finally, she got reception from a station that they rarely watched.

An unbelievable picture emerged. Juel stared, unable to comprehend what she was seeing. Two familiar buildings jumped out at her from the screen but instead of standing tall and proud alongside its twin, one of them had a thick billowing cloud of smoke coming from a huge hole in its upper floors.

Flames leapt snake-like amidst the dense cloud. A TV reporter was yelling something that was barely distinguishable and lower Manhattan was infested with people who stood in clusters, as if in protection. With their necks craned upwards, everyone was staring at those famous skyscrapers that made the rest of Manhattan look like flatlands. Juel couldn't believe what she was seeing. In a stupor, she plopped into a chair. A reporter was telling what he knew of the accident.

Apparently a passenger jetliner had come out of no-where and crashed into the top floors of the North Tower. Nobody seemed to know where it had come from, or what had caused it to fly into the building. *That must have been the 'plane that I saw flying so low.*

In horror Juel viewed the carnage being played out that would be re- played over and over again in weeks to come. As TV cameras captured the catastrophe for posterity, Juel sat transfixed. She was locked to the screen in front of her – just as millions of others around the planet were glued to this tragic sight.

Ordinary people were instinctively gathering in packs, like wild animals seeking safety in each other's closeness. As everyone stared up at the burning building, it seemed as if they were looking towards the heavens for answers. All the faces gazing at the affected floors held the same expression of powerlessness as a wall of flames devoured the steel monolith. The same sense of helplessness washed over Juel.

"Oh my God! Jesus Christ! Holy shit!" The expletives came through the screen as if people were standing on the brink of Dante's Inferno. Office furniture… airplane parts… disintegrated computer equipment …hurtled from the gaping wound in the side of the Tower. Like Juel, folks in the streets were in shock as they stood covering their mouths in gestures of despair – eyes full of fear and desperation. A sense of impotency radiated from the TV screen.

A sense of doom swept over Juel as she watched the devastation. Tiny figures were clambering desperately, one on top of the other at the too narrow office windows, trying to get oxygen to their suffocating lungs. Folks were hanging on to steel girders and - - *Oh. No!*

People began to deliberately catapult from the flaming building in virtual free falls! Rather than die by incineration, they were choosing to plunge a quarter of a mile straight down to the concrete plaza below. The bodies resembled black crows as with arms flailing like flapping wings, people fell to their death.

Amidst all the death and destruction, Juel saw tattered office paper raining onto the streets below. As if in mockery to man's inflated, egotistical sense of his own worth, bits of computer paper fluttered down like snow.

How many times had Juel sat at her own office window looking out at those magnificent structures? *More times than I can count.* Tears began to trickle down her cheeks. To Juel, they represented all that New York stood for. Even more than the Statue of Liberty, those towers seemed to be a modern day symbol of America's strength. They seemed to be representative of the country's indomitable spirit. Those steel and concrete structures were a reminder to the world that America was a powerful nation. And, like Egypt's pyramids – Juel thought of them as indestructible.

Her body tensed. The screen suddenly showed another plane coming into view, flying straight towards the second tower. *God, it can't be!*

The incomprehensible happened again. Before anyone had time to recover from the shock of the first tragedy, it crashed into the second tower. With a tremendous roar, it burst into a huge ball of fire as steel met steel. Once again a massive, blistering boil erupted. Juel saw the jetliner's nose slowly protrude like a grotesque monster from out of the opposite side of the building. Oily black smoke and flames shot out of the wound as terrified screams came from the crowds in the streets.

Juel wiped a hand across her wet face, covering her mouth in shock. *This is no accident.* She felt a numbing sense of disassociation.

The sound of sirens came from the television, followed by a louder wail that came from the street below. From outside of her apartment building, the urgent wailing blasted loud and clear. Reality hit. - - MARK! Her man would be among those fighting the blaze. Juel's heart skipped a beat, before starting to pound against her ribs as if trying to jump out.

Earlier, the TV had flashed on to a group of firemen entering the first tower and even then the thought of Mark hadn't entered her mind. Now it had.

Juel gripped the arms of her chair – staring rigidly. She struggled to keep her rising fear from turning into panic. Is he all right? GOD, LET HIM BE ALL RIGHT!

How long she sat there she had no idea but the nightmare wasn't over yet. The first tower began to crumble and cave in, just as if made of papier-mâché instead of steel and concrete. Her breath came in gasps. *He must be in the thick of it.* It was only a matter of minutes before this immutable powerhouse had buckled and collapsed. Juel watched its demise as if she were a robot.

My god! Where is he?

Within minutes nothing was left except a mountain of rubble and a horrendous, thick cloud of smoke and debris spreading upwards and rolling outwards.

I know he's okay. He just has to be safe!

The gray/black smoke looked as if St. Helen's, the Washington volcano had erupted again. The thick black cloud increased in size and momentum has it hurtled along streets. Juel sat paralyzed. *I refuse to think the worst.*

People yelled and screamed in panic as they raced helter skelter in an attempt to get away from the deluge. "Oh SHIT! Oh shit…!" The curses were carried from person to person like dominoes falling over each other.

Dear God! Where is he? She felt suffocated.

The mountainous ball seemed to be chasing people as it swept through buildings and streets, covering everything in its path. It looked like a science-fiction horror movie, except that this was no fiction. It was terribly real.

Please god! Don't let him be dead! Her gut hurt.

Less than thirty minutes later, the remaining tower's topmost floors began to sway and crumble. The fate of the first tower was repeated. One minute her two familiar friends were there and the next they were gone without a trace, except for the acres of twisted rubble. The spot resembled a gigantic cremation pyre. It was the death of an era.

He isn't dead. I refuse to think such a thing.

Juel's fists gripped the arms of the chair, her nails sinking into the soft upholstery. A fingernail broke. She didn't notice.

He knows how to take care of himself – doesn't he? Of course he does.

The TV cameras panned to an image of a few firefighters sitting among the debris looking dazed and shaken, hunched over as if incapable of bearing such a tremendous burden. Juel found herself silently praying, as she had never done in her entire life.

Dear God. I'll do anything if only you'll make sure he's safe. I'm so terribly sorry for being so angry with him. I don't care what he's done, even if he really does love Pat and not me. It's not important anymore. Just don't let him be dead! Please God make him be safe. Send him back to me. Juel's mind raced as wild thoughts tumbled over each other.

She sat watching as horrific pictures of what could only be described as the machinations of the devil were projected from the TV. She felt as if evil itself had reached through the screen and was squeezing her heart in a vice.

The sudden ring of the telephone blasted through her thoughts. Like a jack-in-the-box, she came out of the chair. With legs made of rubber she made her way into the kitchen. "Hello?"

"Juel! Thank God you're alright!" It was Les. "I tried to call you at the agency, but there was no answer and I can't get through on your cell phone, either." He sounded upset. "I also can't get through to Rita. Seems like all the phone lines are either jammed or not working. It's a miracle that I got through on this one. I was afraid that you might have been caught in all that chaos downtown and was going to leave you a message. I didn't expect you to be home - are you ok?" His voice sounded anxious.

"I'm fine, Les. I didn't go into work today, which is probably the luckiest thing that has happened to me in ages. I'm sure the rest of the folks at the agency are too busy with what is happening around them to have time to answer the phones, even if they are still in working order."

"I think our building is too far away from the towers to have sustained any damage from the blast." She paused for a second before continuing, trying to keep her voice from shaking, "Les, I'm so worried. Some firefighters went into that first building before it collapsed." There was a potent silence from the other end. "Les? Are you still there?"

"Yes, I'm still here." Another silence. Juel choked back a sob.

"Take it easy, Juel. There's no sense in worrying until you know everything that's happened. Nobody seems to know too much of anything right now, so just stay calm and….." his voice started to break up, "my phone is going out of range…Got to go… Don't worry….Call you la…"

The line went dead. Even so, Les' call had helped. His calming voice had allayed the panic that threatened to overcome her common sense. She hugged herself and gave a shuddering sigh. Juel had never been so thankful to hear from Les. She'd felt as if she were caught in some terrible nightmare that she couldn't get out of and his 'wake-up' call was a blessing. *They say that no news is good news, isn't it?* She tried to control her shaking nerves. Walking back into the living room, she turned off the TV. She couldn't stand to watch anymore. All she could think of was seeing those firemen walking into that building before it collapsed. A chill seeped through her bones.

Pacing the floor, she thought of calling his fire station but realized that all the men would be at the site of the disaster. *Besides that, even if someone did answer, what could they tell me?* In desperation, Juel tried his cell phone. No answer. It didn't surprise her. Either it was turned off or out of order. She refused to think of any other possibility. Exhausted, she sank into the couch.

Inevitably, Juel began to relive all the events of that morning at Con's house and the painful aftermath. In the past two weeks she'd gone through all the gamut of emotions, from shock and disbelief to a smoldering anger – to a grieving that was as bad as mourning for a dead loved-one.

At first she'd felt sorry for herself, but that had rapidly turned into to an impotent rage against Pat. And even worse, there was the pain of loss. It was as if she'd been on a mediaeval torture rack. The worst torturing pain was the overwhelming sense of betrayal.

Now all she could think of was that Mark might have been killed. *I refuse to think such a thought.* Juel was terrified. Straightening her shoulders, she returned to the living room. She stood and stared out of the window.

Dense black smoke was drifting over the sun, turning it from a bright orange to an ominous blood red. It looked more like pictures she'd seen of the planet Mars. Juel remembered reading somewhere, that some people considered Mars to be the planet that represented conflict and war. She shuddered as if someone had walked over her grave. The sight of the deep crimson orb seemed to portend more death and destruction. *Stop it! You don't know what has happened yet.*

The day dragged on. Intermittently, she turned on the TV - only to turn it back off again. Watching the repeated bad news was worse than thinking about it. People were desperately working to try and rescue survivors as they sifted through the debris. Even worse was seeing a stranger in a firefighter's uniform and wondering about Mark. The only effect accomplished by watching, was to heighten her fear for his safety.

Throughout that interminable day, Juel considered her life without the one most important person in her world. She relived all the times they had been together - two souls in perfect harmony. Would she never see his warm crooked grin again, or those eyes that crinkled at the corners when he looked at her with love in their depths? The idea was inconceivable. What if she could never again breath in his special male scent -taste the

453

sweetness of his mouth against hers? She relived every nuance of his personality, terrified that those broken, disemboweled towers may have claimed his life.

The chasm created between them on that day of their own, personal 'disaster' seemed to be so stupid in comparison to this day's fatal catastrophe. The wall of pride and outraged ego crumbled in Juel's mind as quickly as those proud, staunch structures had disintegrated.

To Juel, the whole scenario in lower Manhattan was symbolic. This national tragedy had not only opened her eyes to the follies of human hatred and fear en-masse, but had also brought home the truth of her own insecurities and anger. Juel realized that her own human fears and her egotistical jealousy had contributed to the disastrous rift between her and Mark. Even more significant, this shocking day had opened her awareness to a new reality. This terrible destruction had brought home to her the finality of - death.

How could she have allowed Pat to come between them? She knew the girl was a manipulator. The ex-girlfriend had made no secret of the fact that she wanted Mark. Hadn't she seen that for herself at Tula's house? The performance she'd put on that day had been so blatantly obvious. Mark had been openly embarrassed by the display. *She deliberately set out to course trouble between us and I played right into her hands.*

Granted, he should have had more will power, but Juel could tell that Pat was used to getting what she wanted, especially with Mark. *Let's face it. Most men are pushovers in the hands of a woman who wants something from them.* A little bit of flattery and a boost to their ego went a long way. *She wanted me out of the way and I allowed her to shove me right out of the door!*

Today's tragedy had shocked her into thinking rationally, without anger or self-pity. Juel's own personal 'tragedy' seemed so insignificant in comparison to this national tragedy. It had taken this life-altering disaster to show her the amount of destruction that fear and hatred could accomplish.

She couldn't believe that Mark would have instigated the whole nasty affair at his house. *Even if he is a typical, gullible male with over active testosterone!* Juel shook her head at her own stupidity. *I should have fought for him instead of crumbling like a cookie.* Blinded by jealousy and rage, she now realized that she'd allowed herself to dismiss all the love and tenderness that Mark had shown towards her. *He loves me.* Juel knew this. She felt it in every pore of her being, in spite of his having succumbed to Pat's clever seduction.

It had taken today's deadly results of mass hatred to open her eyes. She'd become acutely aware of the fragility of life. This diabolical act of terrorism had smacked her in the face and shocked her into wakefulness. Nothing else could have brought her to the stark reality of having to face life without Mark.

What if it's too late? What if he was one of death's victims? Staring out of the window at the smoke blackened sky, she felt as if the world had gone completely insane. It was as if the universe was reaping its wrath on earth's foolish inhabitants. *Why would human beings self-destruct through hatred and fear under the guise of religion and politics? - -* Why had she allowed her own hatred and fear to destroy her own life?

Con's face suddenly appeared in her mind's eye with his enigmatic smile and twinkling eyes. Juel vividly recalled the look of amusement on his face as he'd observed the dynamics between Pat and herself at that July barbecue. Their mutual animosity had crackled louder than the Fourth of July fireworks. Con's attitude had annoyed her then. Now, she understood his amusement.

The old man had lived long enough to know what a futile waste of living it was to create hatred out of fear. She shook her head miserably, remembering Mark's face that day. He'd looked so bad at being in the middle of two females sparring over him. *Please God. I'll do anything you ask of me, if you only bring him back alive. I'll never distrust him again.*

He'd never been so utterly worn out in his entire life. It wasn't just physical exhaustion. It was a spiritual tiredness. Mark felt as if he'd been battling the smoldering fires and digging through stinking remains for eternity, instead of only twenty-four hours. He swiped a hand ineffectually across his sweaty face as if the act would wipe away the god-forsaken images indelibly printed on his psyche. As long as he lived, he'd never forget what he'd witnessed. Never!

Along with the rest of the crew, he was finally taking a break before having to return to that hellhole again and continue the search for hot spots - and bodies.

What Mark had already seen was nauseating beyond description. The sight of charred and bloodied bodies strewn amidst twisted steel and rubble was a living nightmare. How he'd stopped himself from throwing up, he had no idea.

He lay on a cot too strung out to even think of sleep. His eyes were stinging and the stench of charred remains seemed to have seeped into his own skin. *If I live to be a hundred, I don't think I'll ever get rid of that smell.* Every muscle in his body ached - but he couldn't relax. His heart ached even worse. Closing his eyes just made the hellish scenes even more vivid.

"I finally got through to Rita." Chuck appeared at the side of his cot. Red-rimmed eyes looked down at him out of a dirt-blackened face. Chuck's usual affable expression was somber and his face looked gaunt. Sweat plastered down the firefighter's hair and he smelled like a skunk. Mark grimaced, knowing that he smelled just as bad. He could only guess at what he also must look like.

"She says that Juel didn't go in to work yesterday. The travel agency has closed its doors until things are back to normal."

Normal? Will we ever be normal again? Chuck's words slowly sank through to his tired brain. What had he said? Juel was safe at home? Christ! She was all right!

456

After all his worrying, she'd been nowhere near the disaster yesterday. Even as he'd worked at his grim job, thoughts of her had been constantly in the back of his mind. He knew the agency's building hadn't been affected thank god, but he'd agonized over her having to walk out of lower Manhattan safely.

The subways weren't running and thousands had crammed the bridges and other routes out of the city as people trudged away from the carnage, trying to get to the safety of their homes.

Chuck still stood by his cot. "Why don't you call her? Rita says she's been out of her mind worrying about you. She's been up all night, refusing to go to bed."

Mark nodded and without a word sat up on the cot, rubbing at his burning eyes. The knowledge that she cared enough to be so worried about him, helped to lighten his load of guilt. He reached in his pocket for his cell phone, hoping it was still working. *She still might not want to talk to me. I can't blame her if she doesn't.* Regardless, he could at least let her know that she didn't need to be concerned for his safety. Of course, Rita would have given her news but let's face it, he wanted to hear her voice. *At least if she's worried about me, she mustn't completely hate me.* Nervously he dialed her number, hoping that he could get through.

Les had just returned home. There was a sandwich on a plate, covered in aluminum foil along with a note welcoming him back home. Rita had fixed it for him before leaving for work. Munching on a potato chip, his thoughts were on the volatile girl. She seemed to have softened of late. *Maybe she's finally got it through her head that Juel can take care of herself.*

He picked up the phone on the second ring, recognizing the voice at the other end. "Hey, man! How're doing? Are you okay? - - Pause - - Hold on." He called out to Juel. Rubbing a towel through her hair as she emerged from the bathroom, she headed towards the kitchen. Looking enquiringly at Les, she wrapped the towel around her head. He held the phone out towards her. "It's for you."

She took it from his outstretched hand. "Hello?" Her heart skipped a beat. "Mark! Are you all right?" A torrent of words began to pour from her mouth, "I was so afraid that you'd got hurt in that mess. Thank God you weren't one of those men who went into that building! I don't know what I'd have ..." she stopped, unable to continue. Uncontrollable sobs of relief shook her as she fought to gain control. Feeling like a person who'd been deprived of food and drink she listened to the sound of his voice, soaking in his energy.

"I'm fine Juel. It's like being in Hell around here, but I'm okay. I was never so relieved when Chuck told me that you didn't go into work yesterday." He stopped talking as a trembling sigh came through the phone. "Juel? Are you okay?" No answer. "I need to see you sweetheart." Worry laced his words, "I have so much explaining to do and forgiveness to ask. I've been ..."

"Hush Mark." The small, shaky voice interrupted him. "You don't have to explain anything. I love you and I know that you love me. That's all that counts – except that you're alive."

EPILOGUE

SEPTEMBER 2002

*T*hey stood behind the barriers amidst thousands of close-knit people. Everyone was of the same mind; sharing a common need to pay homage to the almost three thousand victims of that unforgettable day. The healing process had begun. *Has it really been a year since it happened?* Juel was having a hard time acknowledging this fact. Time seemed to have escalated since 911. What was it that Mayor Guliano had said in answer to the question as to how many people had died? She would never forget his words. "Too many for any of us to bear." She grasped Mark's hand as if afraid that he too would disappear like those other ill-fated firefighters. The warm familiar pressure of his fingers entwined in hers felt reassuringly alive.

Candles held by the people illuminated the night sky. Their light seemed so delicate as they flickered with gentle warmth, yet paradoxically the flames glowed strong and steadfast against the backdrop of powerful electricity pouring from the windows of surrounding skyscrapers. The candlelight shone on a multitude of glossy photographs held high in the hands of loved ones. Each one showed an image of those who had died that fateful day. Arms stretched upwards to display them in a commonality of faith - in memorial to lost lives.

Some of the photographs showed mature men and women, but most were very young – too young to die. Many of the smiling faces were police and fire personnel. *Thank you god for not taking my man.* How many times had Juel uttered those words over the past twelve months? She shuddered involuntarily. *But for the Grace of God, Mark could have been one of those victims.* This memorial service meant more to Juel than honoring the people who had perished in those towers. It meant honoring and thanking a god who had kept Mark alive. She was here not only to mourn death but also to celebrate life.

Juel had always thought of those towers as being guardians of Manhattan Island. Yet like this changed landscape, she had changed. For that matter everyone in America had changed. But, the consciousness of New York had been awakened even more so than the rest of the country.

People no longer felt insulated from the outside world. America had not been attacked on its own shores in two hundred years and now, its citizens were suddenly aware of their own vulnerability. New Yorkers in particular were no longer as self-absorbed. They were tragically conscious of the fact that the world didn't end at the Battery.

Juel was no exception. Within the space of a year she'd seen death's power over life, personally via Con's passing and nationally through the death of the people in those ill-fated towers. She was oh, so aware of how lucky she was! Death had not taken her loved one as it had taken so many others. Juel would never take life for granted again. And, she would never again take Mark for granted. She would honor love as she honored life.

Turning her head, she looked at Chuck and Rita who stood alongside Mark before giving her attention to Les standing by her other side. She saw the same expression of determination on the faces of her friends, as the rest of the crowd. A spiritual strength shone like a halo from the combined energy of this mass of humanity. Everyone was soaking up a new kind of faith in this place.

In this bustling seemingly impersonal metropolis with its incessant honking of horns, sirens and other ear splitting noises, these thirteen acres of land bore an omnipotent silence. Somehow, this spot in Manhattan had evolved into a spiritual center. It had the same effect on Juel as that of the church used for Con's funeral. It seemed as if all the souls of those who had died here were actually bringing solace to these people and a tremendous love seemed to blanket the area. This loving energy seemed to be giving these people the needed courage to go on with their lives.

Like the mythological Phoenix that arose out of the ashes of destruction, the energy that arose from this gathering was climbing from the ashes of 'dooms-day.' This energy soared far beyond the city skyscrapers – far beyond the night's magnitude. And so, the stars in the heavens welcomed and accepted the offering.

For Juel and Mark, the negativity in Man that had destroyed so many lives had served to bring them together again. No matter what personal disasters they may encounter in the future, they both knew that their love for each other would survive. The enormity of this tragic loss had given these two young people a new respect for Life - and for Death.

Finally these two souls had returned and completed their cosmic plan. Even though the world would continue to reap the effects of 911 for years to come, these two people had completed their own karmic lesson. Through what had come to be known as the tragedy of 911, two people had finally learned the meaning of Unconditional Love.

It seems we stood and talked like this before
We looked at each other in the same way then.
But I can't remember where or when.
Some things that happen for the first time
Seem to be happening again
And so it seems that we have met before,
And laughed before, and loved before,
But who knows where or when

Music by Richard Rodgers. Lyrics by RogerHart.
@ 1957 by Chappell & Co. Inc. NY